Unforgettable Novels of the West by
Jack Ballas

Few writers capture the true spirit of the West as well as Jack Ballas. With startling authenticity and hard-as-nails prose, Ballas's tales are a panorama of the raw beauty and savage glory that is the old West of a young America.

GRANGER'S CLAIM: Colt Granger defends justice and his Montana claim against the murderous outlaws who are terrorizing settlers in the West—and have their own personal vendetta for Colt. . . .

BANDIDO CABALLERO: Once a Confederate spy, Tom Fallon has found a new career stealing gold from the French and giving it to Mexican rebels. He's becoming a legend on both sides of the border as the mysterious gunslinger Bandido Caballero. . . .

THE HARD LAND: Though Jess Sanford left Simon Bauman for dead, the man is still alive. And there's one thing more relentless than the law: a shamed son with all the wealth of the Bauman family behind him. . . .

THE RUGGED TRAIL: Ex–Confederate soldier Hawken McClure watched as the carpetbaggers took away everything he fought for—and now the ex-soldier for the South is ready to give them a whole new war. . . .

TRAIL BROTHERS: Cattleman Quint Cantrell is about as tough as they come. He's settled down to a solid job and a beautiful wife—but when his adopted family is in trouble, he's ready to risk it all to help them. . . .

WEST
OF THE
RIVER

JACK BALLAS

BERKLEY BOOKS, NEW YORK

This is a work of fiction. Names, characters, places, and incidents are either the product of the author's imagination or are used fictitiously, and any resemblance to actual persons, living or dead, business establishments, events, or locales is entirely coincidental.

WEST OF THE RIVER

A Berkley Book / published by arrangement with the author

PRINTING HISTORY
Berkley edition / January 2001

All rights reserved.
Copyright © 2001 by Jack Ballas

This book, or parts thereof, may not be reproduced in any form without permission.
For information address: The Berkley Publishing Group,
a division of Penguin Putnam Inc.,
375 Hudson Street, New York, New York 10014.

The Penguin Putnam Inc. World Wide Web site address is
http://www.penguinputnam.com

ISBN: 0-425-17812-9

BERKLEY®
Berkley Books are published by The Berkley Publishing Group,
a division of Penguin Putnam Inc.,
375 Hudson Street, New York, New York 10014.
BERKLEY and the "B" design
are trademarks belonging to Penguin Putnam Inc.

PRINTED IN THE UNITED STATES OF AMERICA

10 9 8 7 6 5 4 3 2 1

1

ROAN MALLOY, UNITED States marshal, folded his cards, half his mind on the two remaining players and the other half on his latest assignment, which he'd gotten before leaving Saint Louis.

Somewhere west of San Antonio, women, young women, were disappearing. It was his job to find out what was happening to them—those orders came directly from the president himself.

He studied the two remaining players in the hand. Through the night, even though his thoughts were not entirely on the game, his pile of chips had grown from the takeout of five thousand dollars to almost twice that.

Across the table from him sat the Ice Lady, so called by all who played poker on the Mississippi riverboats. Her never changing expression indicated that she never let her guard down. Her eyes, as deep blue as the sea, her ash blond hair, her patrician features, and her figure, that of a Greek goddess, made her the most beautiful woman Malloy had ever met.

Despite her gambling, bucking a man's world, to Roan's knowledge no one had ever gotten close to Megan Dolan. She always won, but Malloy had never seen her deal a crooked hand. And he would know. There was nothing he couldn't do with a deck of cards, and he would know if anyone tried the things he knew so well—but never used. The Ice Lady won because she was one helluva poker player.

She again looked at her cards, reached to her pile of chips, counted out ten thousand dollars, and pushed them to the center of the table. Malloy threw his folded hand into the discards.

Clint Burston, the player to Malloy's left, fingered his small pile of chips, studied the Ice Lady for a moment, again ran his fingers down his chips, reached inside his coat, and pulled a sheet of legal-looking paper from its pocket. "Ma'am, this's the deed to my saloon in Laredo, Texas. It's worth much more than that pot. If you'll trust me as to its worth, I'll call your bet."

Megan turned her look on the players. "Any here who can vouch for him having a saloon?"

The two who'd earlier thrown in their hands shook their heads. Malloy nodded. "Yes'm, I've been in his place. It's worth every cent of what he says, if that paper he's offering is any good."

She nodded slightly, her face cold as a winter wind.

Malloy caught a glimpse of Burston's cards. He had four deuces. The Ice Lady had better have a helluva good hand.

Megan turned her cards faceup—aces full of treys. Malloy felt a twinge of regret. She would lose this hand. Then, with a faint smile, Burston folded his hand and tossed it into the pile in the middle of the table. Still smiling, but now seemingly a forced smile, he said, "Reckon you own a saloon in Laredo, ma'am."

While the Ice Lady dragged the pot, Roan lighted a

cigar and studied the two of them through a cloud of smoke. Why had Clint Burston folded the winning hand? Why had he put up his saloon in order to call the entire bet when he could have bet the chips he had left and been in for the pot? He asked himself a dozen more questions to which he had no answers, and shrugged.

Malloy cashed in his chips. "Reckon I'll hit the hay for tonight." He looked at Megan. "You gonna play again the night before we get to New Orleans?" At her nod he smiled and said, "Save me a seat." He tucked the sheaf of bills into his coat pocket alongside his United States marshal's badge.

When he stood to leave, Megan ran her eyes over his tall frame dressed in a dove gray swallow-tailed coat with black piping, tight-fitting trousers of the same color, snow white shirt, and black necktie. Although it would violate the rules she'd set for herself, she wished she could know him better. She played only two more hands before heading for her stateroom.

After dressing for bed, she sat at the small table in her room and looked at the deed to the saloon she'd won. What was she going to do with a saloon? She'd always thought of herself as a lady. Gambling on a riverboat was a separate part of her, a part she never let touch her private life. There were no men in her world—she'd never seen a man she wanted to let know the real Megan Dolan.

Saloon owner. That somehow didn't fit her plans. It would be much more difficult to keep people, especially men, at a distance in that environment, especially when that environment was in Laredo, Texas, one of the roughest towns west of the Mississippi.

She sat staring at the bulkhead but not seeing it. She sipped the last drop of thick Louisiana coffee, and again thought about "her" saloon. Should she go out there and see what she'd won? She could go, see it, sell it, and come back whenever she wished. Cards had been good to her through the years. She had more money than she'd ever need. Yes, she would go, then come back to New Orleans at her convenience.

The next night the game lasted until daylight. After cashing in, Malloy brought his luggage from his room and stood at the boat's railing. He lighted a cigar, inhaled the rich aroma, and waited for the big stern-wheeler to draw abreast of the dock. Megan Dolan stood a few feet from him, her bags sitting at her feet.

"Miss Dolan, if you'll permit, I'd be happy to help you with your bags."

"Thank you, Mr. Malloy, but my driver is meeting me. He'll take care of them." Her voice, although not cold, held a tone that invited no further conversation. Roan nodded, tipped his hat, and moved a few feet farther along the boat's railing.

An hour later, he stowed his bags in the small cottage he'd bought soon after the War Between the States. He stayed only long enough to tell Josh he'd be back in time to dress for dinner. "Lordy, Mistuh Roan, you don't no more'n come in the doah 'fore you go back out it—'most 'fore you git it closed comin' in."

Malloy chuckled. "Can't seem to stop anywhere for long, Josh, but I promise I'll be around for a few days yet."

"Yes, suh, shore do get all happy when you say such. Ah miss you all the time havin' somethin' foah me to do."

From his cottage Malloy went directly to the bank and added to his account the winnings from his trip up and down the river. He looked at the high six figures the banker showed him as the result of this latest deposit. "Whew! If I keep this up I'll soon be a millionaire."

The tall, gray-haired man nodded. "Why don't you quit and enjoy the spoils of your wayward ways, Roan? Hell, you're gonna get yourself killed one of these days. You already have more than the most able men'll earn in four lifetimes."

Malloy stared at the man who had watched him grow from a lanky twelve-year-old into manhood. He shook his head. "Raul, I'd die from boredom a lot sooner than from a bullet if I did as you suggest. No. I'll keep chasing the government's bad boys 'til I tire of it, then maybe I'll take your advice."

Raul Menard shook his head. "Damn if I don't think you and Jean Lafitte would've made good partners. You be careful now, you heah?"

Malloy shoved the thousand dollars he'd kept from his winnings into his wallet and left, knowing it might be six months or more before he saw his friend again.

As soon as he entered the door, the rich, spicy aroma of Cajun cooking told him that Josh had prepared his favorite meal. The darky, about Roan's age, hovered over him as if afraid his friend and employer would disappear in a puff of smoke if he let him out of his sight. "Can tell, Mistuh Roan, you gonna do like you always does. You gonna hang 'round heah 'bout a week reading yore books, not goin' out at all, then you gonna git gone fer a long time agin."

Malloy cocked an eyebrow at his friend. "You're gettin' to know me too well, Josh. Gonna have to get rid of you one of these days and find me someone who's not so damned nosy."

Josh laughed. "No, suh, you ain't gonna do that, 'cause

they ain't nobody you'd trust like you do me." He shuffled from one foot to the other. "Too, they ain't nobody gonna put up with you." He chuckled deep in his throat. "Reckon I feel like I got a job foah life."

Roan sighed. "Reckon you're right, old friend. One of these days, though, when you tell me you're ready, I'm gonna buy you a nice cottage and let you do for yourself all these things you do for me."

The next morning, the musty, ever present odor of the swamp which surrounded the town, mixed with the not altogether unpleasant smells of the private stables where he kept his horses, caused Malloy to breathe deeply, then smile at the thought that in only a few days he'd be in the desert country west of San Antonio.

A big line-backed dun trotted over, stretched his neck across the stall's door to nuzzle him. Malloy held a couple cubes of sugar in the palm of his hand while the horse lipped it into his mouth. He patted the horse's neck and left.

On this day he wore faded jeans, a chambray shirt, runover at the heels western boots, a floppy-brimmed, flat-crowned black hat, and a day's growth of beard. Few would recognize him as the same debonair man who occasionally visited the "gentlemen's clubs" of the town or gambled on the riverboats. With another week's growth of beard, and dressed as he was, he doubted even his closest friend would know him.

He walked from the stable, pleased at the condition of his horses. They'd have a long trail to plod if Megan Dolan left town to take a look at the saloon she'd won. Roan thought to follow her wherever she went. Clint Burston deliberately losing that poker hand to her had a reason Malloy had not yet figured out, but he kept homing in on the fact that if he wanted someone out of town, he'd dan-

gle enough bait to cause them to leave. Too, what better
bait than having acquired a piece of valuable property elsewhere? And he had no doubt that Burston already had a
plan for getting the deed back.

All that week he shadowed the Ice Lady. Finding where
she lived had been no problem. She owned a townhouse
bought from a planter who could no longer afford it after
the war. And when she visited the stage station, a couple of
silver dollars loosened the agent's tongue enough for him
to tell Roan she'd bought a ticket to Laredo. She'd done as
he thought. She was going out to see the saloon, see if
she'd been rooked. And she was leaving two days from
now—a Saturday morning.

Malloy spent those two days cleaning and oiling his 1873
Winchester .44-40, his Colt .44 revolver, and honing his
Bowie knife. He also checked the double-barreled derringer
he kept in a boot holster. Then he made a list of all he wanted to take on his westward journey and started packing.

The morning of Megan's scheduled departure, Malloy
saddled the big dun gelding, checked the cinches on the bay
horse carrying the loaded packsaddle, and toed the stirrup.

Across the cobblestone street from the stage station,
Malloy sat slouched indolently in his saddle. Megan arrived
in a surrey driven by an old darky who pulled enough luggage from the backseat to make Malloy wonder if the Ice
Lady might be planning to stay in the desert country.

The rattle of trace chains and sound of shod hooves on
cobblestones drew Malloy's attention to the stage pulled
by an eight-horse team. He smiled to himself. The stage
was a large, luxurious Concord—a far cry from what
Megan would be riding the other side of Houston, and the
clammy, moisture-laden air here in the bayou country
would soon give way to dry, skin-cracking heat.

When the stage drew to a stop in front of the station, the old darky held her elbow to help her aboard. At the same time, a group of five giggling young women, led by Clint Burston, walked to the side of the stage. Despite their obviously loose lifestyle, Burston helped each of them aboard. That little courtesy raised him a notch in Malloy's opinion.

The skin on Malloy's neck tingled. Burston again, and this time with five attractive young women. Did these women's exodus from New Orleans have anything to do with his assignment?

He lighted a cigar, even though he preferred his pipe, inhaled, blew out a cloud of smoke, and squinted to peer through its haze to see if all the women boarded the stage. They did, as did Burston. He'd like to know what, if anything, Burston had to do with those ladies heading west. He nodded. Somewhere between here and San Antonio he'd try to get acquainted with one of them and learn what lured her out of New Orleans.

He smiled to himself. Thinking like a lawman came as second nature. He shrugged. Thinking in such a manner had led to his being one of the most successful marshals in the West, and it had kept him alive more than once. The reason he lived in the swamp city? It was closer to his headquarters—and the Ice Lady.

2

MALLOY STAYED BEHIND the stagecoach to Houston, and on toward San Antonio. He didn't look for trouble until they reached the other side of San Antonio, but it didn't hurt to be careful.

The vegetation gradually changed, and for several days now the predominant tree growth had been live oaks bordering the trail in hilly, dry country. Roan felt as though he'd returned home. Someday, when he turned in his badge, he might go on farther west and establish a ranch, but for now he liked what he did best—hunt men.

He urged his horse a little faster, and pulled him into the square in front of the Alamo, wanting to see what Burston did with the five girls he'd brought out of New Orleans.

The stage stopped in front of the Minger Hotel. Megan Dolan stepped down, helped by the doorman. She apparently watched every valise unloaded, then spoke to the doorman. Then the Ice Lady preceded her luggage through the doorway.

Burston stayed on the stage with the ladies and soon settled them into a clean, comfortable hotel not as grand as
the Minger. Then Burston left the girls and headed back to
the Minger.

Malloy sighed, imagining the feel of warm, sudsy water
washing trail dust from his tired body—but it would not be
seemly for a tired, dirty, out-of-work cowhand to stay in
the best hotel in town. Besides, he wanted to make the
acquaintance of the women Burston had accompanied
from New Orleans.

He stabled his horses, with orders for them to be watered
and grain-fed, then went to the same hotel where the five
women were staying. He bathed but remained unshaven.
His beard, now long and scraggly, altered his looks enough
to fool anyone. He put on clean clothes, went to the saloon,
had a drink, and went into the lobby. He read the front page
of a paper he found in one of the chairs, and had just turned
to page two when the girls came down the stairs as one body.

He stood, pulled his floppy-brimmed old hat from his
head, and said, "Howdy, ma'ams. Seen y'all check in here.
You gonna be stayin' a while?"

As one, five noses tilted toward the ceiling, as though
smelling something bad. "Oh, my golly, ladies, I didn't
mean to offend y'all. Jest wanted to be friendly." He
replaced his hat and turned toward the door.

A pretty little blonde stepped away from the group.
"Mister, I ain't snobbish. No, sir, we ain't stayin' here only
long 'nough to get rested an' sleep comfortable a couple o'
days, then we goin' on to Laredo, Texas." She giggled.
"Don't rightly know where that town is. Fact is, I never
heard about it 'til we all got a job there." She clasped her
hands together at her waist. "The job sounds exciting.
We're gonna serve drinks, an' even dance with the customers. Course they gotta pay for us to dance with 'em."

Malloy smiled at her. He'd gotten more information in only a few moments than he'd hoped to get while staying here. "Well, ma'am, that's the same place I'm headin'. We might meet up down yonder some day." He tipped his hat and went back into the saloon.

Drink in hand, he sat at a table from which he could see into the hotel lobby and the street in front. He wanted to find a way to ride the stage with them. He studied on that a while, then cast the thought aside. With two magnificent animals to ride, he could hardly justify tying them to the back of the stage and riding inside. Nope, he'd have to trail them as he'd done thus far. Besides, if anything happened, he wanted to be out where he could take a hand.

His thoughts shifted to the language he'd used with the girl. He spoke, read, and wrote Spanish, French, and English fluently, but he counted Texan as a fourth language. He felt comfortable talking Texan, more friendly.

As soon as he left New Orleans, he'd strapped on his gun belt, and felt better for it. Not tied in with his being a marshal was a name he'd gotten along the way—The Gunfighter. He didn't give a happy damn what they called him so long as he got his job done. He'd never deliberately picked a fight with anyone, but he'd never dodged one either.

He stood at the bar, took a swallow of beer occasionally, and studied the people, both those inside and those who passed along the street. There were men he'd know, either from posters or those he'd crossed trails with in the past. If any were here, it might give him an edge as to what to expect, or when trouble might strike along the trail.

He finished his beer, pushed away from the mahogany bar, and walked outside. Never one to idle away time, he walked around the square, then decided to stop in and see if he knew the Ranger assigned to these parts. He'd met a number of them while on different assignments in the state.

He pushed through the door of the Ranger station, and before his eyes adjusted to the darkened room, a tall man gripped his hand. "Roan Malloy! Figured I'd be seein' you soon. Bet they sent you down here to see what wuz happenin' to all them women."

Malloy took a step back and gazed into the eyes of his old friend Stan Turnbull. Everyone called him Bull. He grinned. "Damn, man, didn't expect to see you here. Fort Worth was the last place we met, wasn't it?"

Turnbull nodded. "Yep. Things got a little tame up yonder. Didn't have much to do, so I asked for this town. Ain't been bored a ounce since I got here." He shook his head. "Now that you're here, I know I made the right move."

He pulled Malloy toward a chair across from his desk. "Sit. I'll pour us some coffee."

Moments later, Roan put his coffee cup on Bull's desk and leaned forward. "These women disappearin' got the attention of Ranger headquarters yet?"

Turnbull nodded. "Just barely. For quite a spell they ignored it, thinkin' maybe it was like so many o' these women do, wander from town to town." He shook his head. "I finally got their attention. Several o' them women who got lost wuzn't saloon girls. In fact, a couple of 'em wuz married to ranchers down in the valley."

"You got any idea what's happenin' to them?"

Bull nodded. "Got a idear, but nothin' solid to put to my figurin'. If we went the other side o' the Rio Grande far enough, maybe Monterrey, I figure we'd find they been sold to them bordellos down yonder."

Malloy nodded. "Yeah, an' maybe quite a few o' them didn't get any farther than Nuevo Laredo right across the river."

"You may be right." Turnbull took a swallow of his coffee. "A lot o' them women are blondes or redheads. I figure they gonna send them farther into Mexico."

Malloy studied the grounds in the bottom of his cup a moment, then pinned Turnbull with a swordlike gaze. "Gonna tell you for a fact, Bull, you know, an' I know, my badge ain't no good across the river, but if I have to, I'm gonna go as far into Mexico as I have to." He stood, twisted his chair around, and straddled the seat. "You figure this thing's bein' run from the States or from Mexico?"

The Ranger shook his head. "It ain't bein' run by no run-o'-the-mill bunch of Mexican *bandidos*. I figure the boss o' this bunch is either in New Orleans, Laredo, or right here in SanTone."

Malloy grimaced. "Damn, that's gonna spread me out pretty thin." He looked at the Ranger, and cast him a sly grin. "You gonna give me a hand if I ask for it?"

Bull laughed. "Thought you'd never ask. Hell, yes, I'll help. Fact is, far as I'm concerned, we'll forget what badge we're wearin' an' help each other."

Malloy slipped his hand into his vest pocket. "You know that as a U.S. marshal I have the authority to hire as many deputies as I figure I need to do the job." He grinned. "I know of one who hired as many as a hundred—believe he was workin' outta Fort Smith at the time. Anyway, here's a deputy U.S. marshal's badge. Use it when you figure it's the right time. Now hold up your hand while I swear you in."

"Hell, Malloy, I cain't do that. I already got a badge."

Malloy nodded. "Yes, you can. There isn't a damned thing that says a man can't take pay from two law enforcement agencies. Now hold up your hand." In only seconds, Bull lawfully carried a deputy U.S. marshal's badge. "Now, Bull, you can wear it, or leave it in your pocket like

I'm gonna do. I don't figure to let anyone know I'm a marshal until it's necessary."

"You don't do that, I reckon you gonna go back to bein' The Gunfighter."

Malloy nodded, then grinned. "Tell you for a fact, Bull, having the name of a feared man actually keeps me outta more trouble than it gets me into." He stood. "I'm gonna follow a hunch I have. It'll take me from here to Laredo. I need anything outta you, I'll holler."

Malloy turned and left. He whiled away a couple of hours wandering about the square; went in a few stores, bought an extra canteen, another box of .44 cartridges, a slab of bacon, a couple cans of peaches, coffee, and beans; went to the stable and stashed his purchases with his gear.

About to step toward the door of the livery, a whisper sounded at his back. "Do not turn around, *señor*. I 'ave a *pistola* pointed between yore shoulder blades."

The voice, although trying to give the impression the speaker was Mexican, didn't set right with Malloy. "Cut the phony accent, *amigo*. I got you figgered to be as American as I am."

A long sigh sounded behind him, followed by a young-sounding voice. "You're right, Mr. Gunfighter. But I got a heap o' trouble, an' I always heard you're as honest as they come. I need help."

Taking the chance the youngster wouldn't shoot, Malloy turned toward the speaker. He was right. The speaker was barely out of his teens, and he'd already lowered his handgun to his side. "Son, tell me what kind o' trouble you figger you got."

"Sir, I ain't got no money, but I'll pay you with bein' yore handyman forever if you'll help me." The youngster looked at the ground, toed a fresh horse apple, then looked into Malloy's eyes. "Sir, my sister's done disappeared from right outta SanTone. She ain't one to leave without sayin' nothin'."

Malloy's scalp tightened, his shoulder muscles knotted. "When this happen, son?"

"Well, sir, she wuz s'posed to meet me for supper yestiddy evenin' after she got through shoppin'." His face crinkled as though he were about to break into tears. "Sir, she never showed up. Please tell me you'll help."

Malloy, perhaps six inches taller than the youth, stepped closer, put one hand on the boy's shoulder, then took his chin in the other hand and turned the young man's face up to peer into his eyes. "Son, you got no reason to sell yoreself to me as a servant. What's your name?"

"Sam Cahill, sir."

"Well, Sam, where's your folks?"

"Me an' Maggie got no folks. Comanche got 'em two years ago—killed 'em. Maggie an' me, we took over Pa's place, 'bout four hunnerd acres, an' been raisin' vegetables on it to sell to the market here in town. We run a few head o' cows, too."

Malloy studied what the boy told him. He pulled his pipe from his pocket, packed and lighted it, then asked. "What's your sister look like? I want to know about her, right down to her shoe size."

"You gonna help me, mister?"

"I sure as hell am. Now tell me about your sister."

"You mind me buyin' you a beer while I talk, mister?"

Malloy smiled. "Nope. Was just about to ask you the same question. Let's go."

A few moments later, sitting at a table against the back wall of the closest saloon, and having ordered a couple of beers, the lawman looked at the boy. "Okay, let's hear it."

Sam talked for quite a spell, and every word indicated how much he loved his sister. "Now, sir, I done told you how stubborn she is, but you need to know she's 'bout the prettiest girl in these parts: honey-gold hair, blue eyes, slim—but jest now beginnin' to show she's a woman." He blushed. "She's only sixteen." His jaw jutted in defiance. "But she's gonna be the most woman you ever seen when she gets a year or two more behind her."

Malloy placed his hand on Sam's shoulder. "Son, I'm sure she's gonna be just as much woman as you say." He took a swallow of his beer. "Now, I'm gonna ask you to do the hardest thing you've ever had to do."

Sam slanted him a look that said "Let's hear it." Malloy puffed on his pipe, took a swallow of beer, then, knowing he was going to get an argument from the boy, said, "Son, I want you to go home, work your garden, and wait for me to bring Maggie to you."

Sam's head wagged from side to side before Malloy finished his sentence. "No, sir. Ain't gonna do nothin' but go with you."

"No, you ain't, son. You want Maggie to come home to a burnt-up garden, cows stolen, maybe squatters taken over your home? Nope. You asked for help, an' you gonna get it, but we're gonna do it my way."

For a moment Sam looked as though he would argue further. His shoulders sagged, then he eyed Malloy. "Sir, you wuz flat-out right when you said what you wuz gonna ask me to do wuz hard, but if that's the only way I'm gonna get yore help, I reckon I gotta do it yore way."

Roan thumbed his hat to the back of his head and nodded. "Believe me, son, it's the only way I can figure. If I had you with me, you might get us both killed. If I'm alone, I won't have to worry 'bout you. I can fight my own fight." Then, trying to make the youngster feel better, he said, "Believe me when I say if I fight my own fight, I'm pretty good at it."

"Oh, I believe you, sir, it's jest that I'm gonna sit back here worryin' 'bout what you doin', might' nigh makin' myself sick for fear you ain't gonna find Maggie."

With more confidence than he felt, Malloy gripped Sam's shoulder and said, "Now, now. You jest take care of things at home, so when Maggie an' I ride up to your house, she'll feel right proud she has a brother like you who can run a ranch all alone."

Cahill looked Roan straight in the eye. "Gonna tell you, Mister Gunfighter, you ain't spoofin' me an ounce. I know you gonna have a hard time findin' her, but I don't see no other way out." He nodded. "I'm gonna do like you said."

Malloy nodded. "Okay, kid. I'll see if I can pick up anything here in town. Right now I'm startin' to look for her."

He pulled his hat down over his eyes and stepped from the saloon. He went straight to the Ranger's office.

"What brings you back here so quick, Malloy?"

Roan went to the coffee pot, poured them each a cup, and straddled the same chair he'd left only a short while before. "Bull, you know a couple o' Cahill kids?"

Turnbull's eyes narrowed. "Yeah. Good youngsters. Run that small ranch all by themselves. Why?"

"Maggie's missin'."

The Ranger set his cup down on his desk—hard. "The hell you say! I jest seen 'er last night in the store across the street."

Malloy nodded. "From shoppin' she never met her brother. I figure whoever took her headed straight for the border. He'll skirt Laredo and ford the river one side or the other. I figure upstream." He studied the spur-scarred old desk a moment, then looked at Turnbull. "I'm followin' a hunch, or I'd take out after 'em. You reckon you could try to beat them to the river?"

The Ranger's only answer was to stand, pull a

Winchester from the gun rack, draw his six-shooter, open the loading gate, check for loads, then turn to Malloy. "Get me some trail provisions and a box of .44 shells. Bring the stuff to the livery. I'm gonna saddle up."

3

TURNBULL SADDLED HIS horse, put a packsaddle on another, and put lead ropes on two more. He was standing to the side of them when Malloy showed up. Malloy grinned. "See you figure to catch 'im 'fore he has a chance to get to the Rio Grande."

"Damned straight. If these horses cain't do it, I'll climb down and catch 'im afoot." Bull reached for the gunnysack of supplies Malloy held out to him. "Feels like more'n I asked you to pick up."

"Yeah. I figure when you get the girl back, she's gonna need to eat, too." He eyed the Ranger. "Bought a couple extra boxes o' .44 shells. You might need 'em."

Bull toed the stirrup, settled himself in the saddle, and cast Malloy what he knew was a cold smile. "Looks like I made the right move, leavin' Foat Wuth to come down here."

Malloy gave him a jerky nod. "You lookin' for trouble, you did." Then the Ranger felt the full force of Malloy's look. "Tellin' you straight, Bull, you run into a pack o' those varmints who have Maggie, leave 'em alone 'til you can get help."

Turnbull chuckled. "Old friend, you know better'n that. You done heard the sayin' 'You got a peck o' trouble, get one Ranger, you got several pecks o' trouble, get one Ranger.'" He sobered. "Tell you the truth, I get that girl in my sights, I ain't turnin' loose 'til I get her safely home." He held up a hand, nodded, and reined his horse toward the door, his hand gripping the lead ropes of three horses.

The sun beat down, pulling sweat from every pore in his body. Holding to a fast pace into a freshening wind, Bull soon pulled his bandanna up over his nose. With the wind came dust. He had no tracks to follow, so he didn't worry about the wind drifting them over.

His thinking said whoever snatched Maggie would head straight for the border, stopping only long enough during the night to rest the horses. But if he had the *bandido*, or *bandidos*, figured right, they wouldn't have spare horses. Every two hours he stopped long enough to switch his saddle to a fresh horse, then resumed the pace that would wear a ridden horse to a frazzle.

Come sundown, he continued the chase. By now the bandits would be forced to slow their horses and make camp soon after dark. Turnbull had no such notion. He figured to make up any time lost before the sun broke the eastern horizon, and be in their camp while they slept.

About nine o'clock he thought to stop and brew a pot of coffee, then cast the idea aside. His mind had worked steadily with the time and distance. If he figured right, he'd catch them by midnight.

He stopped twice to swab out his horses' nostrils, at the same time he cleaned the dust from his own. If there was any chance of catching smoke smell, he wanted that chance, although he thought it a slim one. The wind blew from behind him now.

When the stars told him it was close to eleven-thirty, and still banking on the idea he had time and distance figured right, he turned at right angles to the direction he'd held all day and began a slow circle, hoping to catch a whiff of smoke from their campfire.

He'd completed one circle and was halfway through the second one when not smoke but the faint glow of dying embers drew his eyes for a better look.

He reined his horse in, stepped from the saddle, looped the lead ropes over his saddle horn, and sucked in a deep breath, hoping to loosen his knotted nerves. He pulled his Winchester from its saddle scabbard, then shoved it back in; this would be close work, handgun work.

He breathed deeply again. It still didn't work. His back muscles ached with fatigue. He took a spare handgun from a saddlebag, tucked it behind his belt, and stepped silently toward the ember glow. Inch-deep dust under his boots muffled any sound.

With his horses ground-reined downwind from the camp, the bandit's horses would have no reason to give him away. But the Ranger almost gave himself away. He came within two feet of a sleeping man, huddled in his blankets against the cold desert air. Turnbull froze.

He swept the area for more lumps that would signal sleeping men. He studied every inch of ground from where he stood to the dying fire, then with painful slowness examined the ground surrounding the embers.

After what seemed hours, he nodded to himself. He'd found four forms huddled in blankets. He frowned into the darkness. How the hell could he tell which blanket held the girl?

The gallant notion of giving the enemy warning before

opening fire was a bunch of hogwash; he observed that
nicety only in a stand-up gunfight. The Ranger's full
intent, once he knew which blankets held the bandits, was
to blow them into the middle of hell. But first he had to
know he was in fact dealing with the bandits he hunted,
and if he was, then he had to make certain the girl was not
in the line of fire.

He moved his eyes from the sleeping forms to the
fringes of the camp. The top spines of a dead yucca came
under his gaze. He nodded to himself, and stepped silently
toward the plant.

Reaching it, he stooped, swept the spines into his hands,
tossed them on the embers, and drew his holstered handgun and the spare from behind his belt. The yucca spikes
burst into flames. Bull fired one shot into the ground next
to the nearest blanket. Figures jerked erect. The golden
hair of the girl showed above the farthest blanket. The
Ranger didn't hesitate. His handguns spat a steady stream
of lead at the three blankets nearest him. Something tugged
at his shirt, another pulled at his pant leg. One bandit fell
to the side, a hole in his throat gushing a red fountain. The
gunman in the blanket closest to the girl still groped for his
gun hidden under the blanket when Turnbull's next shot
took him in the gut.

A fiery streak burned Bull's side before he could turn
both guns on the remaining bandit. He flinched. Bull's
guns went silent. Maggie, on hands and knees, held the gun
of the second bandit in both hands and triggered another
shot into the last of the three. For safety's sake, the Ranger
put another shot into the one he'd gut-shot, then turned a
tired look on the girl. "Ready to go home, Maggie?"

A scared smile broke the corners of her mouth. "Mr.
Turnbull, seems like I been waitin' a year to hear them
words."

While Maggie spoke, Bull went to each bandit, toed him onto his back, and studied him with a look that said he'd not forget his face until he could check his wanted posters. They were all Anglos. That knowledge would help both him and Malloy.

"They're all dead, Maggie. Gonna get my horses, be only a few seconds. While I'm gone, collect their weapons. I'll check their pockets when I get back, then we'll ride off a ways, make camp, fix some breakfast, an' let you rest a while."

"Don't need no rest, Mr. Ranger Man, but you look as how you do. Reckon you been in the saddle without stoppin'."

"You're right, pretty lady." He stepped from the dying glow of the fast-burning yucca spikes to get the horses.

When he came back, Maggie had the bandits' guns stacked in a pile by the fire, onto which she'd thrown a couple of sticks of scrub oak. Turnbull went through the bandits' pockets and money belts. Each bandit yielded over a hundred dollars. He pointed to the small pile, mostly gold coin, and looked at the girl. "You take that. Know you and your brother can use it."

"Mr. Turnbull, you're right 'bout that, but don't know as how I can take it. It might make trouble for you."

Bull shook his head. "You let me worry 'bout that, little one."

Maggie glanced at the sprawled forms of the three outlaws. "You gonna bury 'em, Mr. Ranger Man?"

Turnbull looked from Maggie to the dead men, then shook his head. "Nope. Come daylight, I figger the coyotes an' other scavengers'll have 'em gnawed down to bones. No need to waste our time."

While he talked, Maggie saddled one of the bandit's horses and put the others on lead ropes. "Let's go find a place to cook that there breakfast you promised me. Then I reckon you better catch a wink or two of sleep. Your eyes, red as they are, tell me you rode after me without stoppin'. I'll stand watch 'til you wake up, then we can head for home."

Three hours later, the ranger and the girl had eaten breakfast, Bull had had a couple hours' sleep, and they were headed back to San Antonio. Maggie looked across her shoulder at Turnbull. "Hope my brother's not taken it in his head to try to catch them bandits. I know he sets right smart store by me, an' he's likely to try some fool thing to get me back."

"Now don't you worry 'bout that, Maggie. Sam's been sent back to your ranch to keep things runnin' smooth out there. He figured to hire The Gunfighter to go after you."

"Hire The Gunfighter? Mr. Turnbull, I don't reckon Sam has enough money to buy pipe tobacco for that man."

Turnbull chuckled. "He wuz gonna practicaly make himself a slave to the man if he'd take on the job, but The Gunfighter made 'im promise to go to your ranch and stay there while folks who know how to catch outlaws took on the job."

Maggie laughed. "I'll bet my brother's antsy enough to chew nails. He ain't one to set still while things need doin'."

The Ranger nodded. "I wuz fearful he'd up an' head out on his own, but The Gunfighter told 'im if he did such, that him, or the law, wouldn't be able to do their jobs. I reckon he made a believer outta the kid. He'll be at the ranch when we get you there."

Riding hard, the Ranger and Maggie made it to the ranch by sundown. Sam looked up from a stack of firewood he'd been working on, dropped the ax, and ran toward them. Maggie launched herself from the saddle into his arms. Turnbull had never seen two kids so happy to see each other. Finally, Sam stood back, looked from Maggie to the Ranger, frowned, and said, "I gotta find The Gunfighter, tell 'im you done found my sister."

Bull shook his head. "I'll tell 'im. You look through those weapons we collected from the bandits, take the best ones for you and Maggie, an' I'll take what's left on into town." He smiled. "Too, Maggie has a little surprise for you. The outlaws made a contribution toward your and your sister's bankroll. Make life a little easier for the two of you."

After going through the captured weapons, Sam and Maggie invited Bull to come on in and have supper. He declined, saying he better get into town and tell his friend that Maggie was safe with her brother. What he really wanted was to get with Malloy and go through the wanted posters, to see if they could come up with a lead toward identifying where the gang was operating from—or whether this kidnapping of Maggie was a random one that had no tie-in with the gang grabbing young women in the area.

Malloy stood leaning against a post outside the saloon across the street from the Ranger office when Turnbull rode into town. He straightened, stepped into the street, and took the reins of the Ranger's horse. "Step down, Bull. I'll take the horses to the livery. Go in and get us a beer. I'll be there in a minute." When the Ranger just stood in the street's dust, Malloy grinned. "Don't need to ask if you got the girl. Know you'd of not stopped this side of hell if you hadn't."

Bull nodded. "Got 'er. She's back home with Sam right now." Bull pushed his hat to the back of his head, and looked toward the saloon. "Malloy, I'm dry as a west Texas wind in August. You gonna keep me out here in the middle o' this dusty street, or you gonna buy me a beer?"

Malloy took his friend by the shoulder, twisted him to

face the batwings, and steered him toward the watering hole. "Soon's we get you beered down, we need to sit down and trade information. I'll probably be leavin' here tomorrow or the next day—soon's that stage for Laredo leaves, I'll be trailin' it."

"Somebody ridin' it you think might be tied in with them we're after?"

Malloy frowned. "Don't know yet, but I'm here to tell you there's a whole covey of pretty women ridin' that stage. If I ever figured there was prime bait for the gang doin' all the mischief, that stage'll be haulin' more'n you or I could ever hope for."

They stepped up to the bar and ordered their beers. Bull about drained his glass before Malloy could find the handle on his mug. He banged it onto the polished surface to get the bartender's attention, signaled for two more, and looked at the U.S. marshal. "You want me to go with you? If they's that many good-lookin' women aboard that stage, you know damned well they might be a whole passel o' them skunks out to take them to Mexico."

Malloy shook his head. "Won't be anything I can't handle, Bull. Don't want people to begin to associate me with the law. There's a lot o' people figure I'm straddlin' the line 'tween outlaw an' good citizen. Don't want to give any of 'em reason to change their mind. Besides, there's a gent ridin' that stage with the women who I still have some questions about. Soon's I make up my mind about him, I might have part of the puzzle solved. *Then* I'm gonna need all the help I can get."

Bull drained his second beer about as fast as he did the first one, wiped his mouth with the back of his hand, and started to order another. Malloy slid his second one in front of the Ranger. He grinned. "Drink this one. I already had two 'fore you rode into town."

Finished with the beers, they went to Bull's office. Bull pulled two drawers of his desk open, pulled stacks of Wanted notices out, and placed them on his desk. "I'll go through these, and as I go through, I'll slide 'em across to you. First, I'm lookin' fer them three I found with the girl. Next, I wanta pull out those who got the habit of harmin' women. Want you to do the same."

Malloy shook his head. "There's not a thing in that stack o' paper that won't wait'll morning. It's late, you're tired, I'm hungry. We'll tackle these notices in the morning."

Bull smiled tiredly. "Reckon you're right. That woman I'm boardin' with'll be holdin' my supper warm. I better git on over there an' take care of what she saved, or she won't be savin' me any again."

Malloy stood, shoved back his chair, and stepped toward the door. "See you here 'bout seven in the mornin'?"

"Seven it is." Bull unbuckled his gun belt and hung it on the peg behind his desk. "I gotta take care of my horse and bring in them guns I collected out on the trail."

"No. You get on down to your boardinghouse. I'll go to the livery and take care of your horses and gear." Malloy stepped to the peg Turnbull had hung his gun belt on, took the holster in hand and handed it back to Bull. "Better start wearin' this everywhere except to bed. I have a hunch we're gonna be makin' some powerful enemies. Fact is, you probably opened the ball when you brought Maggie back."

"You think they're watchin' us that close already?"

Malloy nodded. "This's a big operation. My opinion is, they won't be takin' chances with anyone messin' up their game. Go on an' eat supper." He slapped his friend on the shoulder and headed for the livery.

When he stepped through the big double doors, two men stood by the horses Bull had brought in. Malloy walked around them and began to strip the gear from them.

"What right you got to take tack off'n them horses? You ain't the Ranger what brought 'em in, an' even if you wuz, you ain't got no right to them three horses standin' there. They b'long to saddle pards o' ours."

Loosening the cinches on the last of the three double-cinched Texas rigs, and not looking up, Malloy finished what he was doing, sucked in a deep breath, and looked over his shoulder at them. "Reckon the Ranger had a reason for bringin' these horses in, saddles empty. Too, I'm doin' him a favor. He helped me outta a scrape once. Anyway, you got no claim to what's in them saddlebags. I'm takin' them to his office. You got a claim on them, make your grab for 'em with him."

The taller of the two, rail thin, shook his head. "Naw, don't reckon it's gonna work that way. We're tellin' you we want them guns, saddles, an' bedrolls."

Malloy slowly, so as not to cause them alarm, straightened his legs, flicked the thong off his Colt, and turned to face them. "You just made your second mistake. You should have taken me while my back was turned. Your first was tellin' me how this gear was gonna be yours."

The shorter of the two, as thin as his friend, raked Malloy's lean body with a glance from head to toe. He smiled a slit of his lips. "Heered 'bout you. They call you The Gunfighter. Well, I'm here to tell you, Mr. Gunfighter, I never seen nobody who said they wuz scared o' you. Figure me an' Hank here gonna be arguin' 'bout which one o' us put lead in you first."

From the first, Malloy had figured this was a situation from which he'd have to shoot his way clear. His neck muscles tightened, and sweat ran down his back. He sucked in a deep breath and let it out. It didn't help. His nerves were stretched tight as piano wire. Two men, regardless how fast their opponent, were never to be taken lightly, and he wouldn't take *one* man as a cinch. These two exuded confidence, as though knowing either of them could beat him to the draw.

He breathed deeply again, grinned to throw them off, and drew. His first bullet knocked out two front teeth on the way through the head of the shorter man. By then, Hank apparently knew he had more trouble than he'd figured on. He made a stab for his handgun. Fast—very fast. Malloy thumbed off two shots, the sharp crack of the second overlapping the first.

His first shot took Hank about an inch below his belt buckle; his second put a black hole about a hand's width above the first. The black rimming the two holes now spread a red stain across Hank's jeans and shirt. His eyes widened, then a frown creased his forehead, his eyes squinted, and he strained to squeeze off a shot. It cut through Malloy's jeans at his boot top. Hank's knees buckled, then folded, and he toppled onto his face.

Malloy walked to the side of the dying gunman, who twisted his face off the manure-covered floor to stare at the marshal. "Y—you never give us a chance, Gunfighter. Damn you!"

"You're right, Hank, I never gave you a chance. That's why I'm still alive to see you buried." He toed the gunman's six-shooter out of his reach, and shook his head. Against one man, he would observe the gunfighter's code—but not against two men. He snorted the stench of cordite from his nostrils and cocked his head to listen to the pound of running feet outside the stable doors.

Turnbull, followed by several men, one of whom was the town marshal, barged through the door. They pulled up short when Malloy turned to face them. "Bull, they figured that gear and horses you collected were theirs to take since they recognized the horses you brought in. I didn't figure it that way." He pushed his hat to the back of his head. "Just to set the record straight, I didn't give 'em a chance. I drew first and didn't miss. You, or the town marshal there, got any problem with that—say so. You don't, I'm goin' to the café an' eat supper."

Bull glanced at the .44 still hanging from Malloy's hand. "You done messed up my supper. One o' us might's well get 'is gut full. Go ahead. I'll take this stuff o' theirs to the office."

Several doors down the street, Clint Burston ran his finger around the rim of his glass, head cocked for the sound of more shots—not an unusual sound in his hometown of Laredo, but here in San Antonio, the source of mild surprise that tightened his nerves. He looked at the bartender. "What you reckon that was all about?"

The bartender, owner, and sometimes waiter shrugged. "We don't have much o' that kind o' thing around here anymore, not since we got Shug Bentley for town marshal. Then along come Ranger Turnbull. 'Tween the two, this towns danged near tame."

He went down the bar, served a couple of beers, and returned. "But this shootin' we just heard don't surprise me none. I seen The Gunfighter headed down that way a few minutes ago."

Burston frowned. "The Gunfighter. That the only name you know 'im by?"

Barkley the bartender nodded. "Don't know as anybody 'round here ever heard his name." He grinned. "An' I'll tell you for damn sure—I ain't gonna ask him what it is."

"Same situation down my way," Burton said. "He drifts into Laredo every few months, has a few drinks, don't never bother nobody so long's they leave 'im alone, then he disappears for a while." He sipped his whisky, put the glass back on the bar, and frowned. "What I can't figure is, what's he do for a livin'? Man who owned a ranch next to mine, maybe fifty miles away, hired him once for a few months. Says he's a top hand with gun, rope, or saddle work."

"You got a ranch around Laredo?"

Burston nodded. "Yeah. Had a saloon, too, until recently, but got shed of it."

Barkley tilted his head toward the door. "Speak of the devil."

Burston stared into the mirror behind the bar. The Gunfighter walked to stand beside him, motioned to one of the bottles, and waited for his drink.

Barkley introduced the two men. Burston nodded. "We've met. The Gunfighter's been in my place in Laredo several times." He looked into Malloy's eyes. "Don't reckon you remember me. The Silver Buckle, 'til a few days ago, was mine. I lost it to a pretty lady."

Malloy gave a slight nod. "I remember you. You ran a clean saloon and dance hall."

"That's the only way I'd have it, sir. Reckon over the years I've imported as many as fifty girls to dance and serve drinks. Those two things only." His face softened, then he grinned. "Fact is, I'm beginnin' to think I ran a marriage bureau. They's a many a rancher an' cowpoke down my way has married one of my girls." He sipped his drink. "I made this trip to replenish my number of women, hired 'em, then lost my saloon."

Malloy tossed out some bait. "You reckon the new owner'll run a clean business, too?"

Burston's nod was emphatic. "Not a doubt in this world. The new owner's a woman, a beautiful woman, and all lady." He nodded. "Yeah, she'll run a clean place."

Malloy knocked back his drink, held the glass out for a

refill, and motioned Barkley to fill Burston's glass. A glance in the mirror showed Turnbull pushing through the batwings. "Pour another, Barkley, Bull's gonna want one, too."

Turnbull walked to stand on the other side of Malloy. He nodded. "Howdy, Burston. Another trip to New Orleans?"

Burston smiled. "Yeah. Reckon this time I hired the new owner of my saloon a bevy o' girls to dance and serve drinks."

"Didn't know you sold out."

"Didn't. I lost the Silver Buckle in a poker game." He shrugged. "Was 'bout ready to get outta that business anyway. Still got my ranch, though, an' I wanta spend more time with it and my men."

Turnbull nodded. "Never did figure why you stayed in the saloon business." Bull tossed his drink down and motioned for another round. "If I remember correctly, you got the Silver Buckle the same way you lost it."

A slight smile broke the corners of Burston's lips. "You remember it right." He twisted to look at Malloy. "You workin' for the law now?"

Malloy shook his head. "Not so's you'd notice." He pulled his pipe out, packed and lit it. "Fact is, Bull there might tell you he'd arrest me if he could ever make up his mind I rode the wrong side of the law." He grinned. "All he's been able to get on me is that I don't walk around trouble. That ain't no crime."

Bull, following Malloy's explanation, grunted. "There'll come a day, Gunfighter. You'll slip. I wanta be there when you do."

The U.S. marshal put his glass on the bar, tossed a couple of silver dollars alongside, and looked at Turnbull a moment. "Don't bet on it, Mr. Lawman. Now I'm gonna go surround a steak 'bout the size o' this town."

He left before either of the two could offer to join him. He wanted to sit alone and study what little he knew of Burston. The man seemed a decent sort, but why had he deliberately lost the Silver Buckle to Megan Dolan?

4

THE NEXT DAY Malloy checked the stage station, found out the coach would arrive about sundown and would head out again the next morning. At his hotel the girls scurried about more than usual. He asked Jeannie, the girl who had befriended him, if they were leaving soon. She verified that they'd be on the stage.

A trip to the general store satisfied his provisioning requirements. He figured to stay far enough behind the stage to not be detected but close enough to enter any fight aimed at taking the girls from the stagecoach.

As soon as he felt certain he'd not overlooked any item he might need on the trail, Malloy went to the livery, checked his horses, stashed the provisions near his pack-saddle, and gave the hostler an extra cartwheel to watch them until he came for them.

Then he went to his room, packed his saddlebags, cleaned and oiled his guns, honed his Bowie knife, and went to bed.

He set his mind to waken at four, and when he opened his eyes and checked his watch, it showed two minutes until four. He rolled out, dressed, went to the livery, and loaded his packsaddle. Then he saddled his horse, put lead ropes on his other horses, and went to the café. There, as he'd expected, he found Bull already eating. He pulled out a chair across the table from the Ranger, and ordered.

"Stage's leaving in a couple o' hours, Bull. I figure if there's gonna be trouble—any attempt to grab those girls—it'll be between here and Laredo, and I wanta be where I can join in."

The Ranger finished chewing a huge bite of ham, swallowed, and pinned Malloy with a look. "Sounds like you think whoever's been snatching women out here will make a try for them girls."

Malloy nodded. "Can you think of any better bait? Five good-lookin' young girls, and the most beautiful woman I've ever run across. Megan Dolan alone would be a prize for that gang. If there's any way to keep them safe, I figure to be there to do it."

Turnbull took a sip of coffee, blew through pursed lips, and said, "Damn, that's hot." He took another sip. "Malloy, soon's you figure you got a hot trail, send word. I'll be there. Don't be fool enough to tackle that bunch alone."

Roan grinned. "Hey, Ranger Man, why you think I gave you that badge you got tucked away somewhere? When I say I'll send for you, I ain't just whistlin' Dixie." He sat back, packed and lighted his pipe.

Turnbull put his knife and fork on his now empty plate. "Malloy, far as I know, there's not a man west of the Mississippi who don't wonder why you ain't in jail, or dead. Don't none o' 'em figure you for a lawman. You ought to be able to get information that I'd not be able to get in ten years."

Malloy stood. "That's what I'm bankin' on, Bull. If I'm lucky, I might get invited into the kidnappers' bunch."

Turnbull shook his head. "Naw, ain't nobody gonna make that mistake. You got the name of a gunfighter. A fair, square gunfighter. Reckon you better figure on havin' to dig out any information you come by the hard way."

Out on the street, the pound of horses' hooves and the yelling, cursing voice of the coach driver announced the coach pulling up to the station. Malloy grinned. "Sounds like Rawhide's ready to load passengers. Reckon I better get my gear and get ready to follow." He held up his hand in farewell. "See yuh."

Burston helped Megan Dolan into the stage, and handed each of the girls he'd hired up into the hot, dusty vehicle. His voice came to Malloy, who stood at the corner of the hotel, "This stage ain't what you got accustomed to 'tween here an' New Orleans, but it'll get us to Laredo." When he'd helped the last of the women into the stage, he pulled his Winchester from the straps on his valise and took it aboard with him.

Malloy frowned when Burston took the rifle aboard with him; his frown deepened when the former saloon owner jacked a shell into the chamber—a sure sign he expected trouble. Roan brushed the walnut handles of his Colt with his fingertips. He wondered who Burston would be firing at if the stage was attacked—the bandits, the stage driver, or him.

The stage pulled from the station. Malloy waited a few moments, collected his horses, and set out only a quarter-mile or so behind the coach, off the trail a few yards into the chaparral.

Dust churned up behind the stage and its six-horse team. Malloy thought a goodly part of the nostril-clogging alkali settled on him. After only a few miles, his own mother would not have recognized him.

At the first stage stop, he watched from the brush,

chewed a strip of jerky, and wished he could join them for a hot meal. While the passengers went into the stage stop to eat, the wrangler hitched a fresh team. Thus far, Roan had switched horses twice. Old Rawhide Phillips set a fast pace.

After a short rest, the passengers straggled back to the stage and tiredly climbed aboard. All of them, except the Ice Lady, wiped perspiration from their necks and faces. She looked as cool as though she sat in the drawing room of her home.

An hour from the stage stop, the trail took a sharp bend to the south. Malloy urged his horse to close the distance between him and the yelling, cursing driver. Before his horse settled into the faster gait, the sharp crack of a rifle split the hot afternoon air. Roan put spurs to the gelding.

Dust boiled around the stopped vehicle. Shots, close together, shattered the air. Malloy held his Winchester ready to fire. The first thing he saw was Rawhide lying across the driver's seat, alive and firing a sawed-off scattergun. Five men, all crouched close to the ground, fired toward the stage. Burston hung out the window on one side, firing toward the outlaws. Malloy pulled his Colt and urged his horse into the middle of the renegades, thumbing off shots as he rode.

The first man at whom he aimed his handgun went down, the side of his head spread across his shoulder. Malloy shifted his aim slightly to another of the bandits. Before he could fire, that outlaw went down, clutching his chest. Another of the renegades went down under what had to be Rawhide's scattergun, because his chest became one large mass of raw flesh.

A bandit stood to get a better shot at Burston. Malloy reined his gelding to ride the man down. The horse's shoulder hit the bandit and knocked him down; Roan fired into his face when he rode past. Two shots, one the deep roar of a shotgun, the other the sharp crack of a rifle, sounded as one—then deep quiet. A pall of gun smoke hung over the small area. It hung like a blanket over the gory scene.

Malloy reined his gelding to the side of the stage. "Anybody hit in there?"

Burston pushed the stage door open and stepped to the ground. "Nope. Seemed like that bunch was mighty careful to avoid shootin' into the passenger compartment." His eyes raked Malloy. "You take any lead?"

Roan shook his head. "Nope, but I figure Rawhide took some. Get back in the stage. I'll check 'im, see what I can do for 'im. Then I'll get my horses. I'll drive."

Clint Burston studied him a moment. "Gunfighter, that was one of the dumbest tricks I ever seen a knowin' man pull." He shook his head. "Ridin' right into the middle of a shoot-out. Hell, man, with what you know 'bout fights, you shoulda known you could get killed that way. Fact is, I mighta shot you myself."

Malloy pinned Burston with a look that was both questioning and thankful. "I reckon you mighta, if you'd been on the wrong side. I had to gamble on that."

"What you mean, 'on the wrong side'?"

Roan shrugged. "You mighta been one o' them." He glanced toward Rawhide to see if he'd stirred. The old man sat stiffly on the seat, reloading his scattergun. "Where you hit, Rawhide?"

"Ain't took no lead, but figger my leg's broke. Caught my boot heel under the mail chest when I twisted to face them what wuz firin'."

Malloy climbed to the boot, ran his Bowie knife up the driver's leg, and probed along the bone with his fingers. He shook his head. "Don't figure it's broke, but you done twisted hell outta it. We'll stuff you in there with the womenfolk. I'll drive. Burston can ride up here with me." He glanced at Burston, then Rawhide. "Reload your weapons. We might not be through with this bunch yet."

"You think there might be more of 'em farther along the trail?" Burston asked the question while punching shells into the magazine of his rifle.

Roan pulled his pipe from his pocket, packed and lighted it. "Don't figure they is, but it shore don't hurt to be ready." He glanced in the passenger compartment. The five girls sat huddled together, obviously scared. Megan Dolan sat alone, hands folded in her lap. She appeared as cool as an early spring day. Malloy went to get his horses.

After tying them to the rear of the stage, he climbed to the driver's seat, took the reins in hand, and looked at Burston, already seated in the space next to him. "If you ain't never rode shotgun 'fore, you 'bout to get indoctrinated." At his use of the word, Burston's head snapped toward him. Roan thought to try to cover up his mistake, but decided to let it ride. He might make the former saloon owner even more suspicious.

Malloy whipped the team into a trot, then told Burston to keep his eye peeled for any small dust clouds—or smells; to watch the chaparral on each side of the road for movement or any burst of bird-flight from the brush. In the middle of his instructions, Burston looked at him, an amused smile crinkling the corners of his lips and eyes. "Gunfighter, long before I owned that saloon, I was a cowboy, drover, hostler, rode shotgun on stages, even a town marshal." He nodded. "Yeah, I'll keep my eyes busy."

Malloy's face heated with the surge of blood. "Sorry. I didn't mean to try teachin' you somethin' most o' us already know."

Burston's smile broadened. "No offense, Mr. Gunfighter. I'd a probably done the same. Don't pay to reckon a man knows more'n what he does."

Malloy felt Burston's eyes studying him. Finally, after several moments, Burston said, "Don't mean no offense, but don't it bother you when people call you Gunfighter or Mr. Gunfighter?"

"Burston, I reckon one name's as good as another out here. Nope, it don't bother me, long's they say it the same way they'd call me mister anything. If they make it sound like something dirty, I reckon it'd bother me some, but I ain't had much cause to get bothered."

They rode through the sweltering heat in silence for perhaps an hour before Burston broke the silence. "Gunfighter, you find a place where them women can have a small bit of privacy, it would be well to give them a chance to relieve themselves."

"Been thinkin' 'bout that, but didn't know how to tell 'em that's what we stopped for." He looked at Burston. "You reckon you could tell 'em why we stopped, bein' you're used to dealin' with women?"

Clint Burston laughed, choked, and laughed again. "Gunfighter, for a man as hard-shelled as you're s'posed to be, damned if you're not like a schoolboy underneath them whiskers you use to hide your face from the world."

A surge of cautious but angry blood rose past Malloy's neck. "You gonna tell them women why we stopped?" He clipped off his words.

"Yeah, I'll tell 'em. Find us a place."

Roan kept the stage moving at a steady pace, but far slower than Rawhide had pushed it. About a half-hour later he came to a place with a slight land swell off the side of the trail. He pulled the team to a stop, put the brake on, and tied the reins to the handle. He looked at Burston. "While you tell 'em why we stopped, I'll check for rattlers." He climbed from his perch on the driver's seat.

He'd gone only a few feet into the brush, and barely crested the slight rise, when he saw what he'd really come out here to find, and was hoping he wouldn't: moccasin tracks, fresh as though made only a whiff of time before he pushed into the brush. Why hadn't they attacked?

He froze where he stood, studied the ground, and raised his gaze, trying to penetrate the thick brush. One set of tracks. No pony sign, but Indian smell still permeated the motionless air. The only way he could figure it was that the one warrior had been out ahead of the others, leaving his horse with them. Then, when the stage came into view, he'd gone back to tell the main party. Malloy didn't wait. He spun about and raced for the coach.

The women had just reached the ground when he burst past the huge prickly pear cactus into the trail. "Get back in the stage—now!"

One of the women opened her mouth as though to argue. "Do as I say, right now. Indians." His words were sent at them in little above a whisper, but apparently they all heard. They scrambled to get back through the door they'd come through only seconds before. "Get inside with the women, Burston. You and Rawhide can protect them better from there. I'll do the best I can from on top." He climbed to the boot while he talked. A glance showed him when all were again in the vehicle. This time he didn't spare the whip. It cracked above the team's back like a pistol shot. The horses lurched into an all-out run.

Malloy's abrupt move to get the team into an all-out run put him ahead of the seven yelling savages. They came onto the trail only fifty yards or so ahead of where he'd stopped the stage. That put them fifty yards behind him now. His whip cracked again. The horses strained harder. Rifles cracked from inside the bouncing, jolting vehicle.

Malloy pulled his Colt, but knew there was little chance he'd hit anything while trying to keep control of the team. He shoved his six-gun back into the holster and glanced over his shoulder.

One warrior outdistanced the others. He pulled even with the coach. Malloy reined the team slightly to the right. The stage skidded in that direction. The Indian's horse tried to veer away from the wheel, but it caught him along the shoulder. The horse went down, throwing the warrior off, under the wheel.

Malloy glanced again to the rear. There were only three Indians left. They pulled their horses down to a walk, then halted them. While he watched, one of the three, knocked backward by a rifle slug, dropped to the ground. Two left. They made no attempt to follow.

Malloy kept the horses running for at least another quarter-mile, then reined them down to a walk. When he was sure they were safe again, he looked for a place for the ladies to relieve themselves, found one, and stopped.

While waiting for all to get ready to travel again, Malloy looked in on Rawhide. "How far you figure 'til the next stage station?"

The old man struggled to sit, groaned, looked out, scanned the trail both fore and aft, frowned, and said, "Reckon two more hours, the way you drive. 'Course, I ain't gonna gripe none 'bout goin' slow. Reckon every bump in the trail throws pure-dee hell through my laig." He shook his head. "Now, you jest take it easy. We'll be there soon 'nough."

Rawhide's estimate turned out to be accurate almost to the minute. Roan pulled the horses in, jumped to the ground in time to help a couple of the girls and the Ice Lady down, then helped Burston get Rawhide into the station.

Burston asked the station keeper to set out a few pans of

water in the kitchen for the ladies to freshen up with, then to stay the hell outta there.

While the women took care of their needs, Malloy, Burston, and Rawhide told the station keeper what had happened. The man, called Slim, looked at Malloy. "You of a mind to drive that team on into Laredo? I ain't got no other driver."

Roan nodded. "Had it figured that way. I'd just as soon take Rawhide with us. A doctor'll know how to get 'im back on his feet pretty fast." He glanced toward the counter. "You got anything like beer or whisky here?"

Slim grinned. "Jest gonna ask y'all to have a snort with me. Figure one'll make Rawhide feel a little better." He went to the counter and poured them all a drink. "It's done got a mite late, but if'n you folks wantta spend a little more time with me, I'll fix up somethin' to eat."

Malloy nodded, then looked at the other two men. "Figure that'd be a good idea. We'll eat, unharness the team like we're gonna stay the night, tary 'til after dark, then harness a fresh team an' get outta here. I figure if they's any more Comanche hangin' 'round, they'll give it up if they think we're gonna stay."

Burston and Rawhide agreed. Roan glanced at the bottle Slim had left sitting on the counter. He'd drunk better whisky, but like sailors said, "any old port in a storm." He wanted another drink but, seeing the bottle almost empty, wouldn't ask for another.

Slim apparently saw Malloy's glance, and his reluctance to ask for another drink. He smiled. "Aw, hell, I got another jug stashed under my bunk. 'Sides that, havin' company for the next few hours is worth seein' my supply go down."

While they ate the rabbit stew Slim had prepared, Malloy felt Megan's eyes on him. He tried to keep his face away from her in case she might remember something about him that would trigger her memory as to who he really was.

"Mr. Gunfighter, since you've been so helpful to all of us, it would seem proper that we call you by your name. You do have a name, do you not?"

Malloy swallowed the bite of food he'd been chewing. "Yes'm, but it's been long since I used it. I don't take it as an offense to be called Gunfighter, so reckon that name'll have to do 'til a better one comes along."

Megan stiffened visibly. "Very well, sir, I'll call you whatever you wish. I wonder what your thoughts are as to why we were attacked by those bandits. I've not been made aware of a shipment of money on this stage."

Roan stared into his bowl. "Well, ma'am, they ain't no gold nor nothin' like that aboard, but they's somethin' much more valuable to the likes o' them who attacked us."

"Well for heaven's sake I'd like to know what that could be."

Malloy locked his eyes on hers. "Ma'am, you an' them girls we got on that stage'll bring more money in the brothels below the border than all the gold we could carry." He shifted his gaze to Burston. "You hear anything 'bout a band o' bandits stealin' women up here an' carryin' 'em to Mexico?" Roan studied Burston's expression when he asked the question, hoping for some suggestion that the man knew what was going on. He was disappointed.

Burston returned his steady, penetrating look. "Gunfighter, I know they's a whole bunch o' women disappearin' around here. Don't know where they been goin', but figured they wuz jest gettin' tired o' what they wuz doin' and drifted on, hopin' to find somethin' better."

Malloy wasn't satisfied with the answer.

Megan, obviously not scared by his words, stared at

him. "Mr. Gunfighter, do you always use your gun like the white knight?"

Malloy smiled to himself. The white knight—how would a dumb cowpoke, or gunfighter, for that matter, — know to what she referred? King Arthur's knights would not be part of his reading. "Ma'am, don't know who this here white knight is, but if he kept his gun on the side o' the law, I fit the bill."

They finished eating and settled back to wait for the coming night. Megan studied her traveling companions. Of course she knew Burston, and despite his having lost his saloon to her, he was most attentive and always a gentleman. If he regretted her winning, he never gave the slightest hint. She liked the man.

She shifted her gaze to Malloy. She wondered what might be in his past that kept him from revealing his name. There must be something he didn't want to follow him. Rough around the edges, hard as granite, dressed in clothes that had seen better days, The Gunfighter seemed to accept whatever hand fate dealt him. Her eyes swept his tall, powerful frame sitting slouched against the wall. Abruptly, he stood, his movement slow, graceful, fluid. In that one instant she knew he could be a most dangerous antagonist.

Megan compared that slow, indolent movement with the man she'd seen ride hell-bent into the middle of the bandits. Separately they didn't tell her much, but when taken together they spelled a man who was what he had to be, depending on the occasion. She continued to study him as he went to Slim's bottle and helped himself. She drew her brows together, puzzled that so many of his mannerisms brought a much different picture to her mind. She searched his face, wishing her eyes could penetrate that forest of a beard. She wondered if the beard hid a scarred, ugly face or a handsome one. Then, aware she'd been staring at the man beyond what polite behavior would allow, she shifted her gaze to the window. The westering sun sent tendrils of light through the ever present dust.

   She hoped The Gunfighter would stay with them.

5

MALLOY HAD FELT Megan's eyes studying him for quite a while. When he stood to get a drink of Slim's whisky, it had been more a matter of trying to break the Ice Lady's concentration than of his wanting a drink. If she continued to study him, he knew she might find him doing something that would jog her memory. He wasn't ready for that.

Before going out to harness the team, Slim warmed the stew and insisted they eat again before heading out. He did it more for the company than for any other reason. In addition to wanting the company, he felt a whole lot safer with a man like The Gunfighter under his roof. As soon as the stage left, he'd pull down the shutters, bar them and the door, stand his Winchester by his bunk, and turn in. So far the Comanche had left him alone, but they were a notional people, and there was no telling when they'd decide to eliminate him from their land.

Malloy went to the door, scanned the sky, walked a short way from the stage station where it was quiet, and cocked his head to listen. The act was more for his comfort than anything else. If the Comanche were standing next to him, they'd not be heard unless they wanted to be. Too, he wanted to think on what to do next.

He went back inside when he heard Slim head back after harnessing the team. Inside, he pinned all in the room with a gaze. "Tell you folks how it is. Don't know if them Indians gave up gettin' us this afternoon, but if none o' you minds, I figure to ride out ahead and do the scoutin'. Ain't no sense in all o' us losin' our hair, an' if they try to take me, I figure to raise enough hell, it'll warn y'all enough so's you can ready yoreselves for an attack."

"Do you think to fight them all by yourself, Mr. Gunfighter?"

Malloy looked at Megan. She stood in the middle of the dirt floor, rigid, still the Ice Lady but a hint of fear in her eyes. He hoped the fear was for him. "Ma'am, don't reckon I got much choice. I figure to leave as many men with guns on the stage as possible." He let a slight smile break the corners of his lips. "And, ma'am, if I run into that there white knight out yonder, I figure to get 'im to join up with me."

For the first time since he'd known her, Malloy saw emotion break her icy reserve. The blue of her eyes darkened almost to obsidian. Her eyes closed to slits. "Mr. Gunfighter, are you not even a little frightened? You don't impress me as being dim-witted."

He let silence settle between them for a long moment. "Yes'm, reckon I have to admit to being scared, but there comes a time when it seems a man don't have no choice. This here's one o' them times." He smiled. "As for bein' dim-witted, ain't nobody ever said I had an overabundance of brains." As soon as he used the term "overabundance," he knew he'd made another error. Megan's eyes widened, then she shielded them behind her icy facade.

"Mr. Gunfighter, I'm one who would never make that mistake. I, for some reason, think there is much more to you than you let the world see."

Malloy thumbed his hat to the back of his head and grinned. "Shore hope you're right, ma'am. I might even make somethin' of myself someday if that's the case." He nodded, pushed his hat forward over his brow, picked up his rifle, and slipped into the darkness.

Rawhide Phillips was checking the harness when Malloy walked up with his packhorse on a lead rope. "Old-timer, I'm gonna be out ahead scoutin'. Mind if I tie my packhorse to your stage?"

Rawhide spit a stream of tobacco juice off to the side. "Gunfighter, if'n you gonna help us, you kin tie ever' danged thing you own to this here stage." He let another stream fly off to the side. "Wuz wantin' to ask you to stay with us, but don't never figger to git no man to ante up fer that kind o' trouble." He nodded. "Yes sir, I'm right happy to know you gonna be out yonder ahead o' us. But you be mighty careful, you heah?"

Malloy left his packhorse with Rawhide, toed the stirrup, and rode silently into the night.

As soon as the chaparral closed off the station from sight, Malloy's gut muscles tightened and his hair seemed to stand out from his head; but along with it, all his senses sharpened. His eyes, now accustomed to the dark, could see farther; his hearing sharpened; and in the dusty earth, he heard night animals moving about. The sense he depended on most was his sense of smell. If there were Comanche out here, the odor of the rancid bear grease they covered themselves with should warn him long before they became aware of him—if the wind was in the right direction.

He'd told Rawhide to wait about ten minutes before leaving, and to hold the team to a slow pace to keep down the noise. With every leather creak his saddle made, his nerves tightened. He'd not told those on the stage, but he had a hunch the savages hadn't given up their quest to take all on the stage. Their most coveted prize would be the horses. They would most likely enslave the women and kill the men.

He'd ridden a little over a half-hour when a look behind showed a red glow along the skyline. His jaw muscles tightened. Slim wouldn't be making any more rabbit stew. But now there was no doubt the Comanche were on their trail.

He reined the dun around and ran him all-out back to the stage. As soon as he rode alongside, Rawhide pulled the stage to a halt, Malloy tied his horse to the rear, and climbed up beside the driver. "I figure Slim's harnessed his last team, old timer." He flipped his thumb toward the rear. "Looks like them red devils done 'im in."

Rawhide glanced in the direction of the marshal's thumb. "Damn, an' they ain't nowhere to fort up. No rocks, no nothin'."

Malloy glanced behind, saw no indication of pursuit, but knew it was only a matter of time until the Comanche took after them. "Get this stage rollin'. There might be a dry wash somewhere up ahead. If there is, we'll have the ladies lie in it while we do the fightin'."

Rawhide slapped the reins against the horses' backs, turned his head to the side, and spat. "Figger they's what we're lookin' fur up the road a short piece. Maybe a half-mile."

"Get to it, then. I don't figure we got much time to get ready." Before Malloy finished his sentence, Rawhide's whip cracked over the team's backs. Malloy swung over the side and through the window. He dropped into the seat next to Megan. "Sorry, ma'am, to barge in this here way, but we got trouble."

He looked across the space separating the seats to Burston. "There's a dry wash up ahead. Gonna set the stage an' horses down in it. Want the ladies under the stage. You, Rawhide, an' me are gonna stay just below the bank. Don't want no firin' 'til I say so. Don't know how many o' them devils we gonna be facin', but we gotta be ready."

Abruptly a jolt, a hard bounce, and Rawhide's curse announced they had left the trail. Then the vehicle tilted as though to turn over, righted itself, and stopped. "This here's fur as this stage's gonna go right now, folks," he called. "Climb down an' do like I reckon The Gunfighter's done told y'all to do." While talking, the old stagedriver reeled out a length of rope from a coil lying on the roof. "Gunfighter, give me a hand hobblin' these here cantankerous horses. Hate fer them red devils to git 'em. Reckon we'd be the next ones they'd try to take. We wouldn't stand a chance afoot."

Burston made as though to help with the horses, but Malloy told him to take station at the top of the bank, then told the women to get under the stage.

"Mr. Gunfighter, I can shoot as well as most men. If there's a spare rifle, give it to me."

Malloy looked at Megan a moment, then shook his head. "Ma'am, I don't figure to let one hair on yore pretty head get harmed. Now get under the stage with the rest of the women." She made as though to argue, then clamped her mouth shut and did as he'd said. He turned his attention to the rest of them. "Don't want no noise outta any o' you. We get lucky, they might pass us by." He hadn't the slightest hope his words were true.

He checked the horses, looked to see that the women

were where he'd told them to be, then motioned for Rawhide to join him at the top of the bank.

Malloy lay next to Burston, his ears separating the night sounds: the wind rustling the yucca, small nocturnal animals scurrying about, wind swishing over the wings of night hunting birds of prey—then the quiet deepened, the noises he expected to hear ceased. He touched Burston's arm, put his finger to his lips to signal quiet, and slipped down the bank.

He'd not smelled them or heard them, but they were there. He would've bet his favorite handgun on it. At the bottom of the wash, he worked his way to the other bank, changed his mind, and moved toward the horses. Every nerve tight as a lariat holding a two thousand-pound bull, he pulled out his Bowie knife, hoping if he found an Indian that the surprise would at least be mutual. He got lucky.

The faint stink of rancid bear grease crossed his nostrils. He froze. The wind gently caressed his right cheek. Now a sudden move could get him killed. He turned, slow enough that he wondered if he'd ever face the direction he wanted. Finally, he felt the wind full against his face. At the same time the stench strengthened. Again, as slowly as before, he let himself to his knees. It worked.

No sooner than he'd turned his face upward to try to silhouette all above him against the starlit sky, he saw the Comanche within only a few, maybe three, feet of him.

He sprang like a coiled rattler toward the warrior, and swung his Bowie at the same time. The Indian, perhaps sensing danger, sprang backward, the glint of steel in his right hand. Malloy went in under the Comanche's swing. From the feel of it, his knife cut deep across the Indian's chest and arm.

Malloy's spring carried him past the Indian. A burning across his shoulder told him the warrior had scored, too. He twisted to face the Comanche, and caught another slice down his side. He thrust his big knife straight out, and felt it slide through flesh until it hit something hard. Bone. Malloy hoped it was the Indian's backbone, hoped his blade had gone all the way through. Again he felt the Indian's knife. This time it only tugged at his shirt, then the dead weight of the Comanche hung against his knife hand. His knife had the warrior spitted through his chest up to the handle.

Neither Malloy nor the warrior had uttered a sound during the fight. The marshal eased his knife from the Indian's chest, wiped it through the stiff, coarse hair atop the Comanche's head, and turned his attention to the horses. They blew, stomped, and moved about. Something, or somebody, moved in their midst. Malloy moved toward them, making no more noise than the wind playing through the yucca spikes.

He'd not reached the horses when two rifles spoke almost as one at the top of the ravine's bank. The Indian among the horses hurried his movements. That told Malloy his whereabouts.

He moved in on the spot he figured the Comanche occupied. He shifted his knife to his left hand and drew his handgun. Now the warm flow of blood down his back told him he better get rid of this Indian soon—before he became so weakened as to be unable to fight. He had no choice.

Out of the darkness the warrior's squat form materialized as though from a puff of smoke. Malloy thumbed back the hammer of his Colt, let it drop, then did it again. The Comanche slumped to the ground. The marshal stepped toward him. The Indian sprang from the ground, then fell with a solid thump. Malloy stood over him. The warrior must have used the last breath, strength, and bit of life he'd had to make that last effort to kill him.

The rifles on the bank spoke twice more—then silence, a silence so thick, Malloy thought he could cut it with his knife. He swayed. He must have lost more blood than he thought. He tried to make his way to the top of the bank. He needed to check on Burston and Rawhide. His knees felt as though they were made of wet rags. He pushed his feet against the bank. They slipped from under him. He reached to pull himself up. His hand failed to grasp and hold anything. Strange. All the stars seemed to fade to darkness at once, and he felt that he was falling into a deep black hole. Why hadn't he seen the hole when they first entered the ravine? The hole swallowed him. His eyes closed, his body limp, he slid to the bottom of the dry wash.

When the abrupt silence engulfed them, Megan's hand tightened around the handle of the .25 caliber revolver she'd taken from her reticule when she crawled under the stage. Had the Indians won? Would they be crawling in and around the stage in a moment? Where were the three men? Were they dead? Then a voice—Burston's, from somewhere along the bank: "You ladies safe? I figure we got no more Comanche to worry 'bout tonight."

"Mr. Burston, the question is, are all you men all right?" Megan couldn't keep the tremor from her voice, and was ashamed for letting her emotions show.

Burston walked to the stage, Rawhide beside him. "Come on out, ladies. Rawhide'll harness the horses." His head swung from side to side. "Where's The Gunfighter? He came down into the wash to protect the horses."

Megan scooted from her place of safety and ran toward

where she'd heard The Gunfighter and Rawhide hobbling the team. For some reason she cared a lot whether the man called Gunfighter was all right. He was the most fearless man she'd ever met. Too, the man was vaguely familiar. She stumbled over a yielding shape—a body, and it didn't smell like an Indian. She stooped and found what she feared most.

6

MEGAN'S HANDS FIRST encountered hair, not the thick, coarse hair she'd expect to find on a Comanche, but clean, soft hair. Her hand traveled from the top of the head to the face. A heavy matting of beard told her she'd found The Gunfighter. She twisted her head toward the coach. "Mr. Burston, I think I've found The Gunfighter. Come help me, please." Now her voice was firm, controlled, belying the quivering, jellylike thing that was her stomach.

Burston arrived at her side. He dug in his shirt pocket, came up with a lucifer, dragged it across his pant leg, and held it close to the man's face. Malloy lay prone in the soft dust, his face turned to the side. Burston glanced at Megan. "It's him all right. From the blood on his back, and probably more on his front, he put up a helluva fight 'fore them savages killed him."

"Mr. Burston, you haven't checked him for a pulse or heartbeat. I refuse to believe he's dead." Megan knelt. "Please help me turn him over."

Burston bent and flipped Malloy to his back, effortlessly and with a great gentleness.

Megan slipped her hand under Malloy's shirt and felt for a heartbeat. Faint—but there was a beat against her hand. "He's alive. Tell the girls to find some clothing and tear it into strips. And I'll need something to clean these cuts with. Build a fire and collect the canteens. I want the water hot. Infection is what we have to fear. He's lost a lot of blood, but an infection will kill him just as quickly."

"Ma'am, I build a fire, it might bring more savages down on us."

"Mr. Burston, I don't give a damn if it does. This man gave all he had to keep us alive. We can do no less for him." Her voice brooked no argument. Burston went to the stage to tell them what to do. Then he gathered scraps of wood from the desert floor and soon had a fire going. Megan noticed he was careful to keep the flames as low as possible and still be able to heat water in the canteens.

Megan peeled Malloy's vest off first, and as she was doing so, his pipe fell to the ground. She picked it up and slipped it back into its pocket. Her hand encountered a smooth metal object. She fought back an impulse to pull it from its resting place and examine it. The Gunfighter's business was his own—but she could have sworn the metallic thing was a badge of some sort. She placed the vest at Malloy's side and opened his shirt. Burston reached for the vest.

"No. That vest, what's in it, or in the rest of his clothing, is his business. We'll not pry." Her voice was firm.

Burston squinted at her through half-closed lids. "Miss Dolan, I had no intention to pry, as you put it. Reckon I only wanted to give you more room to work on 'im."

"I'm sorry, Mr. Burston. I guess I'm still on edge after

what's happened. But I do think we should leave his things alone."

When the water heated to her satisfaction, Megan cleaned each knife cut of all debris and put a heavy bandage on it to slow the bleeding. As a child she'd done much the same thing for wounded Confederate soldiers during the War Between the States.

Finally, she stood. "Gently, you and Rawhide put him in the stage. You better ride up top with the driver. I'll keep the girls huddled close so we'll have room to stretch him out on a seat."

Burston studied her a moment. "Ma'am, you're some sort o' woman. Any man ever gets you, he's gonna be 'bout the luckiest son of a gun on the face of this here earth."

"Sir, I've never considered any man 'getting me.' " She picked up Malloy's vest and headed for the stage. She held the vest carefully, so that nothing would fall from its pockets. She got the girls into the coach and instructed them where to sit; by then Burston and Rawhide had Malloy settled on the hard seat across from them.

When the team settled into their traces, Megan felt the coach sway, signaling that the two men had climbed to the seat above. When the stage jolted, bumped, and swayed getting to the trail from the ravine, Malloy groaned, then settled quietly onto the seat. The Ice Lady, not feeling at all like ice when she looked upon Malloy's bearded face, watched for any sign of pain.

Aside from the one moan, he lay quietly, but toward morning, about four o'clock, he began to mumble. Megan felt his forehead. Fever. She took a canteen, wet a cloth, and washed his face and neck. She wished she had whisky, or anything, to disinfect the wounds on his back and side. His delirious mumbling became clearer. The Ice Lady glanced at the girls to see how much attention they paid to what he said—not so much what he said as to how he said it. The girls, now her girls, seemed to pay no attention other than to look at him with sympathy.

His words were clear; his grammar, excellent. His ramblings—some in English, some in French, and a bit in Spanish—were of his horses, some business dealings, and a goodly bit to some friend named Josh. He didn't utter one word that would lead one to believe he was a Texan. Her brow puckered. This man was not at all what he pretended to be. She finally decided that with the mixture of different languages, he must be from New Orleans. Along with that decision, she was getting the feeling that she had met him before.

She sat there, much of the time trying to penetrate the bushy beard to determine his facial contours. She wondered if he was handsome, ugly, had a disfigured face— what? Finally, tired to the bone, she let her weariness take over. She laid her head back and slept.

Sitting atop the coach, Burston and Rawhide talked. The old driver held the stage to a slow pace, dodged holes and rocks in the trail, and cursed when he couldn't miss a chuckhole. He slanted a look across his shoulder at Burston. "You reckon The Gunfighter's a outlaw what reformed, one what don't want to take up his old habits?" Then, without waiting for an answer, he spit to the side. "Know what I think? I figure if the law knowed who he wuz, he'd soon be wearin' a noose fer a necktie."

Burston shook his head. "Don't b'lieve so, old-timer. I've known about The Gunfighter for some time, even knowed a few men who said they knew him 'fore he growed that beard. Not a one o' them could say they knew of anything he ever done outside the law." He chuckled. "Not a one of 'em could, or would, say what he looked like back then neither."

Rawhide grunted, and spit again. "Cain't say as how I give a hoot whether he's a outlaw or not. He's done took a likin' to us, an' fer as I'm concerned, that's enough." They lapsed into silence. Half his thoughts on driving, and the other half on the fight, Rawhide wondered if he and Burston had killed any Indians. They'd found plenty of blood, but no bodies. The only dead Comanche they'd found had been the two The Gunfighter had killed. That brought a chill running up and down his spine. He said out of the corner of his mouth, "You reckon we seen the last o' them varmints what attacked us?"

Burston nodded. "Reckon so. What they wanted wuz the horses. When the two they sent to get 'em failed, an' our meetin' 'em head-on like we done caused some o' 'em to take lead, I figger they had enough."

"How many you figger they wuz in that there war party?"

Burston squinted toward a curve in the trail. " 'Bout eight. Reckon I'm right 'cause I counted the spots where some heavy bleedin' wuz done. Then I counted heel marks where some o' them we hit got drug off." He nodded. "Yep, I reckon 'bout eight would be right."

Rawhide didn't know how much Burston knew about Indians, but mentally gave him credit for knowing what he was talking about. He knew Burston had run the saloon only because he'd won it, but was considered one of the best cattlemen around Laredo.

Burston broke into Rawhide's thoughts. "When you reckon we gonna reach Laredo?"

The old man shook his head. "Don't know, but figger as slow as we're goin', it'll most likely be day after tomorrow, an' I'll garan-damn-tee you I ain't gonna drive no faster. Ain't gonna cause that man down yonder any more hurt than I have to."

Burston sighed.

• • •

Rawhide had been off on his estimate by a full day. When they pulled into the stage station at Laredo, Burston and Rawhide told the station agent what had happened, and that he'd better see about getting another keeper for Slim's station. They took Malloy to the doctor.

Megan wouldn't leave his side. She asked Burston to take the girls to the Silver Buckle and get them settled in. She smiled. "That'll give you a chance to tell all your help about the new owner. Tell them not to expect any drastic changes. I'll be over as soon as I make certain The Gunfighter's going to have good care."

A frown creased Burston's brow when she said that. She wondered if Burston had something against the most feared man in Texas. It never entered her mind that he could be a little jealous of the attention she was showing the hurt man.

Carrying Malloy's vest, she followed the men who volunteered to carry him to the doctor's office.

When the men had deposited him on the table, they left. After a glance at Megan, the doctor carefully removed the bandages and probed Malloy's wounds. "Who bandaged these cuts, miss?"

"I did."

The doctor grunted, then picked up a jar of some sort of salve. "You did a good job, miss. Is he a friend of yours?"

Without thinking, Megan gave a quick look at the hurt man. "Yes, doctor, I'd say he's the best friend I have in this world. He saved my life."

The doctor cleaned the wounds, applied some of the salve, rebandaged them, and then touched several scars. "These wounds aren't the only ones he's had in his lifetime."

Megan nodded. "Yes, I noticed them when I had his shirt off. I'm afraid he's led a violent life."

"Yes, he's led a violent life, and from the looks of some of those scars, he's been hurt badly several times. But if this salve works like I think it will, he'll be up and around in a couple of days."

"I hope so, doctor. From what I've seen of the West so far, men like him are sorely needed." She smiled. "And anything that smells as foul as that salve you used will have to work. It smells like rotten eggs."

"So it does, young lady."

Megan left to go to her new business, the Silver Buckle. She hoped there were living quarters for her within the establishment.

Megan had been gone only a few minutes when Malloy opened his eyes. He'd become aware of his surroundings before she announced that he was her best friend. Hearing that, he shamelessly pretended to be unconscious. He wanted to hear more, but was disappointed when no more was said on the subject.

Malloy lay there, wishing the doctor would come back. He had a couple of questions for him. He had only a few minutes to wait. The doctor, Barry Ellis, came to Malloy's side, looked down at him, and grinned. "Gunfighter, if there were a couple more people in this town like you, I'd have to find another sawbones to help me."

Malloy let out a fake groan. "Aw, hell, doc, you ain't never give me no sympathy. You gonna let me stay here 'til I can move about a little? Soon's I can, I'll get a room at the hotel."

Ellis smiled. "You can stay on that hard table long's you want." He chuckled. "Reckon by sundown you're gonna get up to hunt a softer bed."

The door opened and shut while he was talking. Megan Dolan stood only a foot inside the room. "I heard what you said, doctor. I have quarters at the Silver Buckle. We can take him there as soon as you think he's able to be moved."

Malloy stared at her a moment. He could think of nothing he'd like better than to be that close to her. He could watch over her as well as get to know her better, but he couldn't imagine her having much privacy with him lying there. "Ma'am, there ain't much I'd like better'n to be took care of by you, but it's no dice. I'd be in the way. You'd have no privacy, an' the worst thing of all, it'd give you a bad name. You don't want that, an' neither do I. You're a lady, an' I want this whole town to know you are."

Megan stared at him a moment, then shook her head. "Mr. Gunfighter, I thank you for your opinion of me. You and I know I'm a lady. That's good enough for me. We'll move you to my quarters as soon as the doctor says we can."

"There's nothin' preventin' him being moved now, only big as he is, I don't reckon there's any two men in town able to carry 'im."

Malloy looked at the doctor and grimaced. "Ellis, you been wantin' to get me helpless an' under yore thumb a while. Well, I'm here to tell you, you ain't keepin' me here. I'm gettin' up right now."

Ellis grinned, then nodded. "All right. Get up."

Megan made as if to go to the table and help him stand. Ellis shook his head, his smile widened. "No, let the bull-headed son of a gun go ahead an' try."

Malloy made an effort to move his legs to the side of the table and swing them to the floor. They moved only slightly—sort of twitched.

"Well, Gunfighter, come on and get up—or you can wait there like a good little boy until we find someone to move you."

Malloy felt like a spanked child, but even more ashamed that Megan had seen him in such a weakened state.

"Ma'am, if you'd put yourself out enough to go to the hotel an' rent me a room, I'd surely be beholden to you. An' maybe a couple o' them big bouncers you got at the Silver Buckle would come haul me over to the hotel."

She nodded. "I'll see that you are placed in a comfortable bed, sir." She nodded to the doctor and left.

She'd no sooner left than Ellis walked to the side of the table on which Malloy lay. "How did such a quality lady get to own the Silver Buckle? She doesn't belong in a place like that."

"You're right, Doc, but I got a idea she can handle it and still be known as a lady by all who meet her."

"You know how she got the saloon away from Burston? I can't imagine her buyin' it."

Malloy nodded, and said in a weakened voice, "Yeah, I know how she got it, an' no, she didn't buy it." He grinned. "An' I ain't gonna tell you a damn thing about it. Let you stew a while."

Ellis shook his head, grunted, and went to his desk. Malloy watched him, knew he'd give his front seat in hades to know the story, but he'd not ask again. The U.S. marshal had played enough poker with Doc Ellis to know him for a good man, one who wouldn't pry once it had been indicated that the problem was none of his business.

He lay there until long after dark. Doc Ellis went about his business as though Malloy were in the next county. Then, about midnight, by Malloy's reckoning, two huge men he recognized as bouncers from Megan's saloon came and, without a word, picked him up and carried him through the dark, into a building he didn't recognize as the hotel, up a flight of stairs and into a well-furnished room—a man's room, he judged by the gun rack on the wall, leather upholstered chairs, and a deer head and a javalina head mounted and hung on the wall.

He looked around the room and then centered his gaze on the men who'd brought him there. "Where the hell am I? This ain't no hotel I ever been in."

The bigger of the two, although each would top out above two hundred thirty pounds, glanced at Malloy. "Ain't no hotel. It's Mr. Burston's rooms. He always kept 'em for when he wuz in town, times when he didn't want to ride back out to the ranch."

"I figured Miss Dolan would be stayin' here."

The smaller of the two nodded. "She is. She's right over yonder." He flicked a thumb toward a door leading into another room.

Malloy swung his eyes in that direction. Megan stood there, cool as ice. "Mr. Gunfighter, you'll be my guest until you're able to shift for yourself." If possible, her expression became even more inscrutable. "I'll hear no argument from you. This is the way it's going to be."

He'd seen her play poker hands with more expression on her face, and even then she was unreadable. He nodded. "You say so, ma'am. But you know what the townfolks gonna say. I shore hate to be a party to that."

"Sir, I believe I've told you, as long as I know I'm innocent of any wrongdoing, I'll do as I please. And right now it pleases me to take care of a sorely wounded man who saved the lives of six women and two men out there on the trail."

Again he felt like a spanked child. "Yes'm, I'll git outta yore way soon's I can stand—an' I figure that's gonna be tomorrow."

"Sir, I'll decide when you're healthy enough to leave." She looked at the two who'd brought him there. "Put him in the spare bedroom, get his clothes off, cover him. Then I'll take over."

While they did as Megan directed, Malloy reenacted the

scene, and knew the bouncers would spread the story of how The Gunfighter had been bullied into doing what the new owner of the Silver Buckle dictated. It might make him a laughingstock, but it would be good for business. He'd bet his bottom dollar every man in town would flock to the saloon to see the new owner, not only because she'd bested him in a battle of wills but also because the story would be accompanied by a description of her beauty.

When the bouncers had finished, they turned the wick on the lamp down to barely burning and left the room. They'd not been gone long when Megan came in. She stood at his bedside a moment, staring at him. Finally she said, "Now that you're here, and we're in the privacy of what I'll call home for a while, you can start using proper grammar like you used while you were delirious. I don't know who you are, or what game you're playing, but based on your actions thus far, I'm betting you're honest, and would be considered a gentleman anywhere you desired that opinion of you."

Malloy tried to turn onto his back, remembered that was where he'd suffered his worst wound, and stayed on his side. He wondered what he'd said while feverish, and decided if he'd let it be known he was a U.S. marshal, or if she'd recognized him as the man she played poker with on the river, she'd tell him. He settled his shoulder against the pillow and nodded. "Ma'am, reckon I can talk better'n I do most o' the time, but the fact is, I'm right comfortable talkin' Texan. 'Nother thing, the way I talk or the way I dress has nothin' to do with my bein' a gentleman."

Her icy calm almost broke with his words. She blushed and, apparently in an effort to cover her embarrassment, straightened the covers around his shoulders. Then she looked him in the eye. "Mr. Gunfighter, there's something about you that stirs memories in me. I haven't determined who you might be, but I know we've met before." Now that she'd obviously collected herself again, her look sharpened. "Sooner or later, I'll solve that little puzzle." She reached for the lamp to snuff the flame.

Before she could extinguish it, Malloy touched her arm. "Ma'am, I'm going to ask a favor of you. When you do determine who I am, I ask that you keep it to yourself. I've done nothing wrong—that is, nothing outside the law. I'll not tell you where, but yes, ma'am, we've met. Now please let it go. When the time comes, I'll tell you who I am."

She made no effort to shrug his hand from her arm. Instead, she stood very still, stared into his eyes, and after a long moment nodded. "Sir, I believe I can trust you. All right, until something happens to prove I have misplaced my trust, we'll do it your way. Now, good night. I'll bring you breakfast in the morning."

For a long while after she left the room, the delicate scent of her perfume lingered. If the pain from his wounds had not been enough to keep him awake, the scent of her perfume would have been.

Megan stepped into the hallway outside of Malloy's room, placed her back against the wall, and sucked in a tremulous breath. The Gunfighter was everything she thought she disliked. The only thing she knew about him was that he dressed like a range bum, spoke in poor grammar because he liked it, had the most unkempt beard she'd ever seen— and yet had the most magnetic personality she'd ever encountered.

Despite her promise to herself never to get too interested in any man, she found herself drawn to The Gunfighter. She'd spent a large part of her adulthood gambling because the only other option for a woman to make a lot of money was unthinkable. She was wealthy by any standard, and thought she was content with that. Now she knew differently. She'd best be careful.

The next morning, Megan put on an apron, went to the kitchen, and rummaged around for the makings to prepare breakfast. Burston's cook, Wing Sung, tried to help, but she shooed him aside. "Some other morning, Wing. I want to prepare this meal myself." Then, seeing his look of disgust, she said, "I'm not taking your job. This once is something I want to do."

He settled into a corner of the kitchen while she went about frying bacon and eggs, baking biscuits, cooking grits, and brewing a pot of coffee that would have done justice to the strong brew of New Orleans.

When all was ready, Wing brought her a tray, and she took it to Malloy. He was sitting up in bed when she entered. "Well, Mr. Gunfighter, if you're going to get well soon, you've got to eat. I thought this would help."

Malloy looked at the tray, then looked at her. "Ma'am, looks like you're tryin' to get me well in a hurry. I didn't know they wuz this much food in all of Laredo." He took a sip of coffee, then looked her in the eye. "Didn't reckon as how you knew how to cook, but I'm here to tell you, everything's just the way I like it: soft yolks in the eggs, crisp bacon, grits to mix it all up in, an' them biscuits're so fluffy my ma could've cooked 'em."

She flushed under his praise. "Thank you, sir. You'd be surprised at the many things I can do."

He shook his head. "No, ma'am, don't reckon I'd be surprised. I figure you for a woman to ride the trail with." Her face turned a brighter red.

Malloy tried to get up after breakfast, but almost fell on his face. Megan watched, with only a hint of a smile at the corners of her lips. She then told him he'd stay in bed for three days, long enough to get strong enough for his legs to support him. Then he could work his way back to full recovery. It worked that way.

The morning of the third day, he slipped his trousers on while still covered in bed, then she helped him stand. From that point, it took him another four days before he strapped on his Colt and Bowie knife, and announced he would find a room at the hotel—he'd encroached on her hospitality long enough. " 'Sides that, ma'am, I figure if I don't take a bath soon, you'll have to fumigate this room."

"Mr. Gunfighter, I'd be happy to do that. You've been a very good guest." She smiled. "But judging by what the doctor said, I certainly understand. He said you were the first cowboy he'd ministered to that he didn't have to cut through a layer of dirt to get to your wound. He said you obviously bathed every day."

"Well, ma'am, when there's water to be had, bathing is a habit I've long been used to."

Anxious to get back into what he was here for, Malloy, after getting settled in the hotel, went directly to the marshal's office to renew acquaintances. He'd known Miguel Provo for several years. Provo did not know he was a U.S. marshal, but did know he stood with the law.

As soon as he pushed the door open, Provo put a cup of coffee on the desk in front of him. "Wondered if you'd come see me when you got through loafin' in that beautiful lady's room."

Malloy's eyes hardened, his face stiffened. "Provo, that there woman's as fine a lady as you're ever likely to meet. We met when the stage got attacked. I got hurt. She figured she owed me, so she took care to see I got well."

The marshal's face flushed under his swarthy complexion. "Aw, hell, Gunfighter, I didn't mean no harm. I been in the Silver Buckle since she took over. She's runnin' it as clean as Burston did 'fore he lost it to her."

Malloy's nod was stiff. "Apology accepted. Just remember, if you hear anybody talk against her, she ain't the run-o'-the-mill woman." He sat, picked up his coffee cup, took a swallow, and pinned Provo with a hard look. "Anything much happening down this way?"

Provo shook his head, stopped, and grimaced. "Yeah. I figure somethin' is happenin'. Course most around town don't see nothin' out of the ordinary."

"What you think is goin' on, amigo?"

Provo poured himself a cup of coffee, then settled back in his chair. "Don't know. I ain't been over on the Mexican side in a few weeks. Ain't got no business over there. But I hear from them what goes over there to the brothels that they got a whole bunch o' new women, young American women, workin' the cribs. Some o' these men say them women don't act like they're there by choice."

Malloy frowned. "Why you figure they're there, then? Ain't nobody tied a anchor to their butts. Why don't they just come back to our side o' the river?"

Provo shook his head. "Don't know, 'less they're bein' watched pretty close, an' are afraid to make a break."

Malloy finished his coffee, stood, hitched his holster to a more comfortable position, and looked at the marshal. "Gonna tell you somethin'. I don't like any woman bein' mistreated. Figure to take a little ride over there. I'll let you know what I think when I get back."

Provo's face hardened. "*If* you get back, amigo. From what I hear, ain't nobody gonna welcome a curious Americano, much less an American *pistolero*." He stood and held out his hand. "Use much care, my friend."

Malloy smiled. "You've known me a long time. You ever know me to be careless?"

"Not so's you could notice, but still, be careful."

Before pushing through the marshal's doorway, Malloy checked his Colt, shoved a cartridge into the empty chamber he usually let the hammer rest on, settled the six-shooter gently in its holster, and left. He thought to get his line-backed dun and ride across, then decided to leave him in the livery. Getting his horse stolen was a worry he didn't need.

He stopped at the first cantina he came upon, pushed through the batwing doors, and circled toward the bar. There he put his back to the wall and scanned the room. About half the men there were American, most of them, he judged, cowboys in town for their usual payday drunk. They'd drink more whisky than they could handle, have a woman, throw up, stagger to their horses, go back to their home ranch, work another month, then do it all over again. Malloy shrugged mentally. To each his own.

He swept the room again with a more careful look. A number of hard cases, both Mexican and American, came under his gaze. There were always some of this stripe, but today there seemed to be more than usual. The familiar feeling pushed into his awareness. Something was in the making, something that boded ill for those across the border. These were the kind of men who backed off from nothing as long as it meant an easy buck or two. He decided to visit some of the cribs and see if he could run across any information there.

He knocked back the drink he'd ordered at the bar, turned to head for the door, and came up against the chest of a swarthy, smelly man about his own size. "You been lookin' us over pretty hard, hombre. Why you so interested in us?"

Malloy thought to try to avoid trouble, apologize, and move on—but his temper got in the way. "Anytime I'm interested in a bunch o' hog swill, I figure it's my own damned business. Get outta my way, or they'll carry you out."

The hard case didn't wait for more. He swung from the waist. Malloy stepped back, chopped a short left to the man's chin, pulled his Colt, and swung it in a roundhouse right to the side of the man's head. He went down without a murmur. Several in the room, already on their feet and apparently anticipating a longer fight, pushed toward Malloy. The feel of the wall against his back was comforting. It gave him a small sense of safety from that direction.

He swung his handgun to cover them. "Any y'all figure I'm gonna be as good to you as I wuz to him's all wrong. I'm gonna blow the first man what steps toward me to hell. Any takers?"

Every one of them stopped in his tracks. Malloy inched around the wall to the batwings. He pushed through, and instead of heading toward the river, he ran the opposite way. At the corner of the building, he cut along its side, circled to the back, and entered the back door of the cantina he'd left only seconds before.

He edged along the back wall, selected a seat in the darkest corner, and watched.

7

MALLOY SAT IN the semidark corner for several minutes before a girl serving drinks came to his table. She took his order, gasped, leaned closer. "Señor, they look for you. They weel keel you eef they see you here."

Malloy put a cartwheel on the table where she could see it. "You gonna tell 'em I'm here, señorita?"

She looked at the silver dollar, looked at him, and shook her head. "I weel not tell that cow dung anything, amigo. Put your money away."

Malloy dug in his pocket for another silver, put it beside the one on the table, and smiled. "Señorita, bring me a cold *cerveza, por favor*, and keep both of these." His glance swept the room again. "Do you ever sit at the tables with the customers?"

"Si. Eef I like them."

"You like me enough to sit with me a little while?"

"Si."

"All right. Sit and keep me company for a spell."

She scooped up the money, went to the bar, and brought

back a cold beer, which she put in front of Malloy. She
brought with her a drink of some sort for which Malloy
insisted on paying another cartwheel. "Señor, I 'ave done
nothing to earn so much *dinero*. What ees eet you want?"

Carmelita, her name was. By skillful questions he found
out that most of the Americanos in the cantina usually
came to town during the night, brought with them anywhere from one to five or six white women, mostly blonde,
then sat around drinking and raising hell for two or three
days. Then they'd disappear for a month or more. The
women they brought never showed up in any of the brothels or cantinas. They were never seen in Nuevo Laredo
again. Carmelita said she thought another bunch of men
took them farther into Mexico.

Malloy had found out more than he expected, but the big
question was who was running the show. He figured to find
the answer to that question if he had to hunt for the rest of
his life. Carmelita, after about thirty minutes, said she had
better get back to work, and returned to the bar.

Malloy drank another beer. His eyes, now accustomed
to the dark room, saw all in it clearly. It was obvious that
he was the topic of conversation at several of the tables. He
sat there a few moments more, stood, then went out the
back door. A last glance at the room showed no one interested enough in his movements to follow. Now he had to
find a place where he could stay out of sight until darkness
covered his movements. But where?

He decided that the other side of the river would be his
best bet, but getting there might pose a problem. He
worked his way along the backs of shops and other places
of business. Garbage and human waste littered the area.
The stench threatened to make him vomit. Breathing only
enough to keep from passing out, he made it to the bridge.
Federales lined each side of the rickety contraption.

Malloy stopped at the corner of the last store, and studied them. They only glanced at the Mexicans, but carefully studied each American headed for Laredo. *They looked for him.*

Whoever in this town was on the wrong side of the law also had the Federales under their thumb. Coming to that conclusion had not been hard. The Federales, most of them, could be bought for little or nothing, only a couple of pieces of silver; and in this instance fear would keep them loyal, even if they were offered more money. He shook his head. He'd not try to buy them off. He walked back along the line of shops until he was a couple of hundred yards into the town, stopped, and looked over the area.

Finally the desert, only a few yards from where he stood, offered the only solution he could think of. He sprinted into the chaparral, hunkered in the shade of an old yucca, looked at the sun sitting at about three o'clock, sighed, and settled back against the dried spikes along the bottom. This country had to be the front door to hell. Heat like a man should never have to withstand beat down on him. His barely healed wounds itched, sweat ran in rivulets down his back and sides. He wished every second or two that he had a canteen—and pure heaven would have been one of those cold *cervezas* Carmelita had brought him. He pushed those thoughts from his mind. Night had to come soon; then he'd check out the cribs.

By the time the sun slipped below the horizon, every stitch of clothing Malloy wore was soaked and crusty with sweat salt. The night brought only small respite. The desert didn't give up its heat as it often did. Oppressive was the only word he could think of. Nights like this usually brought big, booming thunderstorms. A glance toward the northwest verified what he'd already decided was about to happen.

A constant flicker of lightning lit the low-hanging

clouds, still too far away for the sound of thunder to reach him. He'd better get to crib row, see what he could see, and head for the bridge. He didn't want to be on it if a wall of water swept down the Rio Grande. That bridge had washed away several times. One of those times he'd been on it only seconds before. He figured a lifetime without experiencing that again would be long enough.

He walked back into the town, and bought himself a sombrero and a serape: he'd decided to cross the bridge as a Mexican. He then slanted his course to the closest line of brothels and walked along the row of cribs, most of them only a lean-to made of desert brush, boxes, tin sheets, anything to keep out most of the weather. And a poor job they did of it.

Lamplight glowed in a small arc beyond the edges of the cribs. Malloy, his cowboy hat tucked under the serape, and wearing the sombrero low on his forehead, slouched along only a little out of the light. He studied the women, mostly young, Mexican, and very poor. Their customers were mostly vaqueros in from the dangerous, boring life of thirst, cattle, storms, and bandits.

It didn't take long for Malloy to decide the women being brought across the border were being taken much farther south. Those who carried them across the river, probably Americans, turned them over to Mexican *bandidos* in, or close to, Nuevo Laredo, who then took them deep into the desert country. The lightning came closer, and the boom of thunder rattled the cribs. It was time he tried to cross the river.

Although he wanted to jog to the bridge, Malloy forced himself to continue a shuffling slouch in that direction. A couple of hundred yards before he reached the first Federales, a few large raindrops spattered the inches-deep dust of the street—then came the downpour, in sheets.

The rain was a godsend. The Federales tucked their necks down into their serapes, pulled their hats down—and gave those wishing to cross the bridge only a cursory glance.

Malloy glanced upriver several times. The rain falling here didn't worry him, but that which had fallen upstream did. That was where the wall of water would come from.

He heard the roar before he saw the approaching wave, at least ten feet high, rushing toward the bridge. His time for acting the vaquero ended. He pulled the serape around his shoulders and sprinted toward the American side. Others had seen the danger, too. They pushed, bumped, shoved, and cursed as they sought to pass those in front. Some slipped and fell; others, pushed against the railing, fell into the roiling waters below.

Malloy pulled his Colt and used it as a club. He swung right, left, and to the front. It was now him or them, and he figured to make it them. He was twenty yards from the end of the rickety contraption when the first force of the surging river hit the bridge uprights. The bridge shuddered, heaved, and moved downstream, but remained in one piece.

Malloy pushed and shoved harder, now slugging anything in front of him. The boards began to buckle under his feet, and the entire bridge began a slow rotating motion to flow down the river, end first. The broken end, now only a few feet in front of him, slowly revolved away from the muddy bank. A few seconds more, and there would be nothing but the raging river to jump to. With every muscle in his body bunched for the effort to save his life, Malloy leaped for the bank.

Only a few seconds passed, but they seemed like forever. His feet, with only a cushion of nothing beneath them, continued to churn the air. Malloy hit the bank feet first. They grasped only muddy slime. He slid toward the watery hell below. He went to his knees. Frantic, he dug at the bank with hands seeming too small and too weak to gather enough mud to stop his slide. He not only slid toward the water, but it rose toward him.

As though in a dream—a nightmare—Malloy kicked down with the pointed toes of his boots and grasped at the earth with fingers now raw from digging at the slick bank. His toes dug into the bank far enough to hit solid earth. He pushed upward, gained a few inches, and did it again, all the time clawing for a handhold.

Once he was started toward the top of the bank, the climbing became easier. Now, every few feet, he slid back only inches toward the death below. With the knowledge that he could defeat the mud, he clawed harder.

Finally, breathing as though he'd never get enough sweet air into his lungs, Malloy pulled himself over the top of the bank and lay there, panting, his eyes on the black death only a few feet below his boots. He forced himself to stand.

He stood gazing at the muddy track his body had made up the bank, now being washed away by the heavy rain. A man's struggle for life showed only a few moments, and then melted into the raging waters of the Rio Grande. He marveled that it was so. He compared it with the totality of life. Our struggles, to us a lifetime, only lasted a flicker in the whole of eternity.

Then guilt and shame washed over him. His insane, cowardly flight from the bridge, shoving, killing so that he could survive, and then the fear-crazed struggle to climb the riverbank. He shook his head. A man learned much about himself in times of travail. He would think less of himself from now on.

Malloy held his raw, torn hands out for the rain to wash away the mud and blood, stood there a moment, then turned toward the main street of Laredo.

As he went through the hotel lobby, he ordered hot water for a bath, then went to his room. There he cleaned the mud from his Colt, oiled it, then cleaned his Bowie knife, holster, belt, and boots. By the time he had that chore done, his bathwater arrived. After his bath, he went to the closest café to eat, then to the Silver Buckle.

Megan sat at a table off to the side, looking as cool and fresh as ever. Malloy walked to her table, took off his poncho, and asked if he might sit with her. Burston, at the table, cast Malloy a sulky look when he sat. Malloy ordered drinks for the three of them.

When he tried to pick up his drink, he winced and left it on the table. Megan fixed her gaze on his hands. "What happened to your hands?"

Malloy told them about getting caught on the Mexican side when the deluge came, leaving out his frantic rush to safety and his cowardly actions during his escape.

"Can't imagine a man goin' to Nuevo Laredo 'less'n he wuz lookin' for a woman." Burston's words were obviously meant to put Malloy in a bad light.

Malloy's face turned hot. His look, meant to fry the rancher, failed. Burston smiled, and said, "Course it ain't none o' my business what you went over there for."

Anger pushing hot blood to his temples, Malloy held the rancher's gaze. "I'd say you're right, rancher man; it ain't none o' your damned business. But so the lady'll know, I'll say I got friends over yonder. I've spent a lot o' time down here, an' find some o' them Mexicans are mighty nice people." This time it was Burston's turn to flush.

Megan looked from one to the other. "Here, now. You two have shared much adversity together. Don't argue. And yes, I'd say it is Mr. Gunfighter's privilege to choose his friends wherever he so desires."

Malloy carefully picked up his glass and knocked his

drink back, then ordered another. As he was drinking it, his
mind half on Megan and half studying the customers, he
decided that if there were any women in Texas worth stealing, Megan Dolan would top the list. He made up his mind
to stay right close to her. His decision was not in the best
interests of finding out who headed up the bandits—but it
might keep her safe. His interest in keeping her safe stood
in the way of his solving the case he was working on, and
he knew it, but he couldn't abandon her to the chance that
she stood in danger's way.

Stan Turnbull sat across his desk from Shug Bentley. Shug
put his coffee cup back on the desk, and looked at Bull.
"You an' The Gunfighter seemed mighty close when you
brung Maggie Cahill back from bein' stole, sort o' like you
trusted him."

Turnbull, on the verge of telling Bentley how he'd gotten involved in bringing Maggie back home, clamped his
mouth closed. Yeah, Bentley ran a tight town, didn't put
up with anything from anybody, but Turnbull's relation-
ship with Malloy was his own. Besides, many of the town
marshals in the West rode one side of the law, then the
other, whichever served their purpose at the moment. And
Malloy being a U.S. marshal was none of anybody's business but his own. This case of missing women, and who
might be the head of the gang stealing them, was too sen-
sitive to let anyone know the suspicions as to where the
gang was headquartered, or when he and Malloy came up
with a person to pin it on. The less anyone knew, the better.

He looked at Bentley a moment. "Gonna tell you
somthin', Bentley. I don't trust, or distrust, nobody 'til they
give me reason. The Gunfighter never give me reason nei-

ther way. That Cahill kid went to The Gunfighter to get 'im
to find his sister 'cause he's got a reputation with that gun
o' his. I told The Gunfighter that findin' the kid's sister was
my business, an' to stay outta it. He did."

"You reckon her gettin' stole's got anythin' to do with
the rest o' these missin' women I hear about?"

Turnbull went quiet inside. How did Bentley know there
were women considered missing by the law? Town marshals were not notified of such matters. Was Bentley trying
to find out if the Rangers were interested in their disappear-
ance, or if the Rangers considered it something to work on?

Turnbull frowned. "Yeah I heard somethin' 'bout some
women not showin' up where they wuz 'sposed to, but the
Rangers ain't told me to look into it, so I won't. I got
enough work to do, an' things to worry 'bout, without
lookin' for more." While Bull talked, he studied Bentley's
face. Did he see a sign of relief, a less intense look—or
was it the lawman in him always looking for a culprit?

Bentley took another swallow of coffee. He looked at
Turnbull over the rim and, talking into the cup, said,
"Soon's I heard 'bout them women, The Gunfighter not
bein' around, an' when he did show up, another woman
gettin' snatched, makes me wonder has he got somethin' to
do with 'em gettin' took."

Blood surged to Bull's face. He squelched his anger.
"Far's I ever figgered, The Gunfighter's honest. He's had
gunfights, but if you check into it, every time he had to pull
iron on a man, it was a man the law was damned glad to
see took outta circulation—permanently."

Bentley nodded. "Yeah, he's done me that kinda favor a
couple o' times." He stood. "I better make a round of the
saloons. Usually it's right quiet this time o' day, but you
never know 'til you look." He stepped toward the door.

"You hear anything 'bout them women, let me know. I might be able to help you find 'em."

After Bentley closed the door, Bull stared at it. He didn't like Bentley, but tried not to let his feelings interfere with doing his job. Maybe the man had heard about the women through rumor repeated over a drink. Maybe the town's citizens had heard enough to become concerned; they might even have heard more than the Rangers. Perhaps the Rangers should have gotten interested long before now— or perhaps he should take a closer look at Bentley. He stood, put on his hat, buckled his gun belt, and headed for the telegraph office.

An uncomfortable truce settled between Malloy and Burston as they sat at the table with Megan. Megan ignored it although she was glowing inside with the unspoken compliment the men paid her. She thought each, in his own way, had decided to watch over her, keep her safe, and, as far as possible, keep her from the cheapening effect of running a saloon. The obvious truculence of the two toward each other probably stemmed from that. She looked at Burston. "After we close tonight, I want to talk with the entire staff." She smiled. "You know, you've not officially turned the Silver Buckle over to me. I know they've all been told that I'm the new owner, but I want you to make it official."

Burston nodded. "I'll pass the word." He looked at Malloy. "Don't see any need for The Gunfighter to be here, 'less'n you want him to be."

Megan nodded. "We've all been partner to some pretty rough times. I'd like to think we can stay partners." Burston, obviously disagreeing, shrugged and walked from the table. He stopped at each of the girls, then the gaming tables. Without turning her glance from Burston,

Megan said, "I think he's a nice man, Mr. Gunfighter. I wish the two of you liked each other better."

Malloy pushed his wet hat to the back of his head. "Ma'am, I don't reckon I like or dislike him. I ain't made up my mind 'bout 'im yet."

"What do you mean?"

Malloy shrugged. "Don't know, ma'am. It's been my habit to figure a man out, then decide whether I like 'im or not. I ain't reached that point yet."

Megan turned her gaze to Malloy. "You're very careful to whom you give your trust, aren't you?"

"Ma'am, bein' that way has kept me alive." He smiled. "Probably longer'n many would like."

She frowned. "Do you really have that many who dislike you?" Then, not waiting for an answer, she said, "I've never seen you do anything that would draw enemies."

He shook his head. "Miss Megan, in my business others often choose my enemies for me." He ran his finger around the edge of his glass, then rolled the glass around on its bottom and studied the wet ring it made. He looked up. "You see, ma'am, I reckon I come by the name Gunfighter honestly. I don't like it, but that's what I'm branded with. Reckon I gotta live with it."

With emotion he'd never seen her show before, she placed her hand over his. "What a shame. I sense there's much more to you than that big six-gun you wear."

The touch of her hand sent a shock up his arm that, much like an arrow, pierced the depths of his being. "Miss Megan"—he forced a smile—"you know, you may be right about that. Someday you'll know whether your trust in me is justified."

Her face sober, she said, "I do believe you forgot to use your Texas talk."

He nodded. "Reckon I gotta be more careful 'bout that."

Burston returned to the table, breaking up a conversation Malloy was happy to end. He pulled out a chair and sat. "All set, Miss Dolan." He pulled his watch from his vest pocket, glanced at it, and looked at her. " 'Bout time to serve the last round. Soon's we get rid of all the customers, we can use this room to talk in."

Thirty minutes later, they held their meeting. After Burston told the employees Megan was the new owner and turned the floor over to her, she told them she would not have a crooked card dealt in her establishment, nor would she have a girl work for her who had ideas of getting business for herself after the bar closed. "You girls will serve drinks and dance with the customers—nothing else. If you meet a nice man who wants to take you out for a meal or a buggy ride, bring him to me. I want to meet him and pass judgment as to whether he has honorable intentions." She smiled. "If I sound like your mother, so be it. That's what I intend to be as long as you work here. If you can't accept that, say so now."

She waited a moment, and then a tiny, pretty girl stepped forward. "Miss Megan, I reckon I like what you said. Keeps me from havin' to tell those men I ain't gonna do nothin' with 'em." She stepped back while the others nodded. Megan then turned to the dealers. "You all heard what I said about straight deals, and I'm telling you right now, I'll be able to tell a crooked deal when I see one. You deal bottoms, seconds, or crooked shuffle, and out the door you go. You won't stay long enough to gather your effects, and I'll make certain the name 'crooked gambler' follows you wherever you go."

Burston swept them all with a look. "The lady means what she says, folks. And I'm here to tell you she can do exactly what she said. The best thing about it all is that you won't have to change a thing you been doin' all the time I've had the place. Good luck." He turned to Megan. "Reckon we could have a drink of your good whiskey even though the bar is closed?"

Megan nodded. "You know where it is better than I do. Pour us all a drink."

While Burston went for the drinks, Megan's eyes followed him. "You know, Mr. Gunfighter, I think you're both nice men."

When the rancher came back to the table, he took a drink before sitting, then said, "While I had the place, I had several small cottages built over on the edge of town. Two girls shared a cottage. I let them pick who they wanted to live with. You gonna change that?"

Megan shook her head. "I intend to run it just as you have. If I decide to stay here, I'll have fewer things to change."

Burston's face froze into the mask he wore while playing poker. "Shore hope you don't decide to leave. But if you do, reckon you might let me buy the Silver Buckle back from you?"

"Yes, I think that would be a good idea. There would be at least one first-class saloon in town. You can have it back any time you wish, at the price of what I covered in the pot in which I won it from you."

Malloy sat and listened even though the saloon was of no concern to him. But if Burston wanted it back, why had he deliberately thrown in the winning hand that night on the Mississippi? He wanted to like the man. He seemed a gentleman. But that one poker hand stood in the way of giving him his trust.

He went back to his room at the hotel, and after he'd turned the lamp down, Malloy pondered who might be taking the women. Had he ever met the person or persons

heading up the gang? Were they perhaps people he knew?
He thought over those he knew in New Orleans, people
with whom he'd gambled, men he'd had to track down in
the past. After hours of staring at the ceiling, he gave it
up. He had nothing to go on. One thing, however,
emerged from his toying with the problem. Those girls
living in the cottages were without any protection. He
decided to patrol the cottage area after the saloon closed
each night.

8

BURSTON DECIDED TO stay in town due to the late hour. He went to the hotel and signed for a room. In bed, he did much the same thing Malloy had done. As he lay there, his thoughts centered on Megan Dolan. He'd never seen a woman he wanted so badly. He'd known many women, beautiful women, but Miss Dolan stood above them all. Yeah, he'd deliberately lost the Silver Buckle to her—he could think of no other way to stay close to her. Business took him to New Orleans, but not often enough. He'd not worked his nerve up to where he would ask her to dinner, so he'd settled on getting her out here close to his ranch. Losing the Silver Buckle seemed a cheap price to pay, even if he could look at her only occasionally. Then The Gunfighter pushed into his thoughts.

Why the hell had he come to Laredo? Burston frowned. The man had shown himself to be a hero and was there when needed, and Megan seemed to like him despite his rough clothes and reputation. Reluctantly, Burston admitted to himself that The Gunfighter was a helluva figure of a man: well above six feet tall, wide shoulders, slim waist, wavy black hair, and green eyes, and he would probably be handsome without that bushy beard. He had no reason to dislike the man. Fact was, they'd probably be friends—if it wasn't for Megan.

The third night of scouting the girls' cottage area, moving from shadow to shadow, Malloy made a couple of circles around the several small cottages and again marveled that Burston had been thoughtful enough to build them. Everything he'd seen the rancher do said he was a good, law-abiding man, not a man given to mistreating women, not a man who would steal women. But why had he lured Megan Dolan to this far outpost of civilization?

On his third round, Malloy chose a dark alley from which he could see all of the grounds about the cottages. He sank to his knees, rifle cradled in his arms. He saw movement. At first he thought it might be a stray dog or cat. He fixed his gaze on the spot, then, as careful as he himself had been, a man's form emerged from the dark. The movements, stealthy, were in his direction. The skulker would pass within a few feet of him.

Malloy tensed his muscles. He wanted the man alive. He'd question him, and might find another piece of the puzzle. The shadowy form drew nearer, staying in the shadows as much as possible. Then, when Malloy was ready to step out and club the man on the side of his head, he changed direction. Malloy didn't wait.

"You make a move for that handgun, I'll break your back with a .44 slug." The skulker's hands shot to shoulder level. He turned to face Malloy. Burston!

"What the hell you doin' sneakin' around here?" Malloy's gun didn't waver.

Burston, his voice rough, no give in it, said, "I'll ask you the same question, Gunfighter. What the hell you doin' out here in the dark? I'm tryin' to keep them women in them cabins safe."

"What makes you think they need to be kept safe? Ain't heard o' nobody wantin' to harm 'em."

"Well, Gunfighter, you said it yoreself after the stage got hit. Whoever attacked the stage prob'ly wanted the women. Them same women are livin' in them cabins."

Some of the tension left Malloy's muscles. "All right, Burston. I got to thinkin' along them same lines. No point in both o' us losin' sleep. You go on back to your room. I'll take it the rest o' the night. You take it tomorrow."

Burston hesitated a moment. "Gunfighter, we cain't keep this up forever. I could ride out to the ranch an' get some o' my men to take over."

Malloy shook his head. "I figure a couple or three nights, an' them same *bandidos* gonna make another try. We ain't gonna have to spend but them few nights out here."

"That bein' the case, I figure two of us out here can do them more damage than one while the other sleeps."

Malloy nodded. "Right. We'll both stay. If nothin' happens soon, we'll call it off an' figure both of us was jumpin' at shadows."

They kept watch for a week. The only thing that caused their nerves to tense was the movement of stray dogs and cats. The morning of the eighth day, Malloy walked around the end of the last cabin to meet Burston. "Buy you a drink, cowboy, then I'm gonna go eat breakfast. We ain't doin' nobody no good losin' all this sleep."

"You buy the drinks. I'll buy breakfast. I got a idea I want to try on you." Burston fell in at Malloy's side as they headed for the only saloon that stayed open all night.

Standing at the bar, Malloy cast the rancher a chagrined

look. "Always wondered what kind o' damned fool would
have a drink soon after daylight—now I know." He
knocked back his drink while Burston did the same. Then,
staring over the edge of his glass, he said, "Gonna tell me
yore idea now, or wait 'til we get our stomachs full?"

"Gonna wait'll we get some ham, eggs, potatoes, an'
coffee in front of us. I might have to argue you into it."

They had eaten almost all their breakfast when Burston
put his knife on the edge of his plate and pinned Malloy
with a look that would pierce steel. "You ever had a room-
mate?"

Malloy grinned. "Not so's you could tell it. And don't
want one, neither."

Still holding Malloy with his eyes, Burston shook his
head. "Don't say no 'til you done heard what I got to say.
First off, I got a good foreman out at the ranch who can
look after things out there. Second, one o' them cabins I
had built for the girls is empty. We could see Miss Megan,
an' ask her to rent it to us. That way we can be right close
to them girls if somethin' happens."

Malloy stared into his coffee cup. Burston wasn't giving
him any additional reasons to suspect him of being part of
the *bandidos*. But, Malloy admitted to himself, he was
trapped. He had to find the brains behind the outlaw band,
and he could think of no better way than by staying close
to the women.

Malloy looked at Burston. "Okay. We'll see Miss
Megan. Cain't think o' no reason why she wouldn't let us
rent it." He squinted at Burston. "You know we gonna have
to tell 'er why we want it. That's gonna upset her. Hate to
do that."

"Gunfighter, don't you reckon she already knows the
danger them girls're in, what with them livin' on the edge
o' town like they are? After the stagecoach bein' attacked,

an' her havin' run the Buckle a couple weeks now, I reck-on she's done heard all the gossip goin' 'round 'bout women bein' stole." He shook his head. "No, I don't think it'll upset 'er. I figure she's gonna feel better 'bout her girls bein' out here with us to watch 'em."

Malloy nodded. "Okay. Let's see what she says. Reckon it just flat makes good sense to stay close where we can help."

Burston cleared his throat, stared at Malloy a moment, then said, "Don't mean to hurt yore feelin's, Gunfighter, but if you ain't got the money for yore part o' the rent, I kin handle it."

Malloy let a thin smile break his lips. "Cowboy, I don't like sayin' it, but gunfightin's been good to me far as money's concerned." He deliberately put on a hard expression, his eyelids squinted. "But you better believe it, cow-boy, I always choose who I fight for, an' am real careful to make sure I believe in what I fight for."

Before he finished, Burston was shaking his head. "Aw, now, I didn't mean to rile yuh. Fact is, I didn't mean noth-in' but good by what I said. I jest didn't want to rope you into anything that maybe you couldn't afford."

Malloy nodded.

They finished breakfast, drank several cups of coffee, then decided Megan must be awake and have had her break-fast. When they found her and approached her with the idea, she sighed. "Oh, I'm so glad the two of you will be out there to take care of them. From all I hear, no young, pretty woman is safe around here. I'll hear no offer to pay for that empty cabin. The sooner you both move in, the better.

Malloy nodded. "Figgered you'd see it that way." He smiled. "It ain't gonna take me but a few minutes to gath-er my gear. Don't reckon it'll take Burston much longer. We'll be there 'fore they quit work tonight."

Burston stepped toward the door. "Let's get after it, Gunfighter. Don't figure them what steals women'll be watchin' them cabins durin' daylight."

Later, sitting on the edge of one of the two beds in the farthest cabin, Malloy stripped his weapons down, cleaned and oiled them, then honed his Bowie knife.

Burston looked at him, a thin smile crinkling the corners of his eyes. "Looks like you gonna be ready when trouble hits."

Malloy glanced toward the other bed. Burston was busy doing the same thing. "Notice you said '*when* trouble hits.' When you figure that'll be?"

"Don't know, but I got a feelin' in my bones we ain't gonna have much longer to wait."

Shug Bentley opened the door to his office, pushed it wide, and propped it open with an old horseshoe. Maybe he could let a little of the slight breeze cool down the close, hot space. He went to his desk, sat, put his feet up, pushed his hat back, wiped his brow, and studied his problem. This job kept him tied down. He had no freedom to leave town, no freedom to do anything but keep the peace.

He thought about quitting, then shook his head. He couldn't do that. He needed this job to keep his finger on what was happening farther west. His boss would keep him aware of things between San Antonio and New Orleans. And he didn't think Grafton Sotello or his boss would stand still for him quitting—his badge was too good a cover for his other activities. Then the idea hit him. If he had help, he'd be free to move around without questions being asked. He'd go to the city fathers and ask for funds to hire a deputy. He swung his feet to the floor, stood, and headed for Clausen's General Mercantile store. Clausen wielded a heavy hand over the City Council.

He walked the two blocks in dust that came over his boot soles. Clausen's store sat only a hundred yards from the banks of the San Antonio River. Giant cottonwoods and live oaks bordered the river. In the loading yard outside the back door of the store, Bentley wove his way around buckboards, hitched horses, stray dogs, and even a few Mexicans dozing in the shade. One dog, little more than a puppy, stood between the town marshal and the door. Bentley kicked at the scrawny pup. It jumped to the side and yelped.

Inside the store it was dark and cool. Bentley squinted, tried to focus his eyes, then stepped to the side of the door and waited until his eyes adjusted to the dim light.

He swept the room with a glance. Clausen wasn't in evidence. He headed for the office.

The store's owner sat at his desk, thumbing through a stack of papers. He looked up. "Bentley, what can I do for you?"

The marshal didn't like Clausen, didn't like his patronizing attitude, didn't like his obvious affluence. In fact, he didn't like anything about him. But he had to deal with him. "Figgered to ask a favor. You run the City Council with a hard fist. I'm askin' you to get 'em to set money aside for me to hire a deputy."

Clausen frowned. "You're not having any problems keeping the peace. Why do you need a deputy?"

Bentley pushed down the hot blood that threatened to choke him. "I need a deputy 'cause I'm workin' seven days a week, never a day off, an' I figger that once in a while I need a day to lay back, have a few drinks, an' fergit this town." He noticed the muscles knotting around Clausen's jaws. He was going to get an argument.

"Ah, but marshal, the town is so quiet I imagine you could take any day you wish, and do the things you feel you need to do."

Bentley shook his head. "Mr. Clausen, I been keepin' the peace here for fifteen months now. Ain't never took a day off. I got the need to go outta town fer a spell. Take maybe a week."

Clausen's head wagged back and forth before Bentley finished his sentence. "Impossible. I've not taken that much time off in the seven years I've owned this store. The Council will not agree to such."

"You sayin' you ain't gonna ask 'em for me?"

Clausen nodded. "That's exactly what I'm saying."

Bentley stared into the store owner's eyes a moment. "All right. I'll ask 'em myself at the next meetin'."

Clausen's smile would have frozen hell a mile. "You do that, Bentley. But I'm here to tell you, you won't get it approved. Like you say, I wield a heavy hand with the governing body." He nodded. "Good day, *Marshal* Bentley."

Bentley spun and stomped from the office. Any other town, any other time, he'd have pulled iron and shot the smug bastard—but things being the way they were, he needed this job. If he quit, he'd get cut out of the take—and the take was a whole lot of money. Heavy-footed, he made his way back to his office, where he sat and fumed.

In his office down the street, Turnbull read the replies to his telegrams. None of them could identify Bentley as having ever been in trouble with the law. None of them admitted to ever hearing of the man. Bull slammed the sheaf of papers to his desk. "Damn! I never heard of a man that good with a gun who hasn't left a trail behind him. He's gotta be usin' a name what ain't his." Abruptly realizing he was yelling, he sat back, tightened his lips, and settled down. He'd find out who Bentley was if it took him the rest of the year—but he didn't have a year. A cool beer might settle him down. He stood and headed for the saloon next door.

The bartender slid a mug with at least an inch of foam riding the top of the brew down the bar to him. He'd taken only a swallow when Clausen pushed up to his side. Without preamble, the storekeeper asked, "How you feel about shouldering an extra load for a while, maybe a week?"

Turnbull slanted him a sour look. "Don't figger to shoulder nothin' but the job I got. What you talkin' 'bout?"

Clausen ordered a drink and eyed Bull. "Bentley figures he needs some time off, wants me to get money from the Council for a deputy. I don't see as how I'll ask them to spend money like that. I thought perhaps you could handle his job for a week and let him have a little vacation."

Turnbull didn't like the smug, sanctimonious townsman, but tried to keep a civil attitude toward him. "Mr. Clausen, you got a quiet town here. Ain't been but two gunfights in the last week. Your marshal is the one who keeps it quiet. I figure you don't git a deputy for him, he'll quit—or try makin' money on the side. Don't figure you want neither o' them things to happen." He pushed his hat to the back of his head. "To answer your question, I ain't takin' on no town marshal's job. I'm a Texas Ranger, an' I figure to stay one long's they'll have me."

Clausen's face hardened. "I might have something to say as to whether the Rangers'll continue to have you in their fold."

Bull twisted to face the storekeeper full on. "Clausen, I don't take kindly to threats, so don't you never do it. I might take a notion to knock the pure cow dung outta your flabby-butted body."

The storekeeper's eyes turned muddy, mean. "Turnbull, you might take some of your own advice. You might find it harder to kick the cow dung, as you call it, out of me than you think." The bartender brought him his drink. After picking it up, he eyed Bull. "I intend to write to your head-quarters as soon as I get back to the store."

"You do that. You'll find my outfit cottons to real men." He took a swallow of his beer. Instead of this trip to the saloon settling him down, raw, angry bile boiled deep in his throat. "You or me's gonna move down the bar. The stink got a helluva lot worse when you walked up." Then his anger got the best of him. He tossed the rest of his beer in the storekeeper's face, followed it with a right to the gut, swung a left hook to the face, then another right to the gut. Clausen folded in the middle like a soggy blanket. But he didn't stay down.

Turnbull, surprised the bastard got to his feet, stood back. Then Clausen brought a right up from about his knees. His fist grazed the Ranger's jaw. Bull stepped in close, pumped a right, then a left, to the storekeeper's stomach, then did it again. Clausen, knocked to his back-side, bounced, then tried to get to his knees—they wouldn't hold him. He fell flat on his face.

Hot blood pumped through Turnbull's head, clouded his vision, turned him into what he'd always disliked about himself. He was ready to kill—but Clausen didn't move. Bull turned to the bartender. "Draw me another beer."

While filling another mug, the man behind the bar stared at the storekeeper's limp body. "What the hell was that all about?"

"He tried to make me do a job he wanted done. I refused. Then he threatened to take my job." Turnbull thumbed his hat to the back of his head. "Reckon you could say I don't like threats. If you make 'em, you better back 'em up."

The bartender, still staring at Clausen, nodded. "Yeah, reckon you could say that." He grinned. "Know one thing, I ain't never gonna threaten you." He took a bucket of water from under the counter, poured some into an empty mug, and threw it into the storekeeper's face.

Clausen sputtered, put the palms of his hands flat on the floor, and pushed himself to a sitting position. Mouth hung open, eyes glazed, he swung his head from side to side. Then he looked toward Turnbull. His mouth worked a few moments, then he said, "Your office will hear about this."

Bull nodded. "Damn right they will. I'm gonna write 'em 'bout it soon's I get back to my office." He tilted his beer, drained it, and walked out.

Back in his office, he sat at his desk, his brow wrinkled. Hitting the storekeeper wasn't the smartest thing he'd ever done. The Rangers didn't like their men fighting respectable townsfolk, and any way he looked at it, Clausen was an honest, respected man, although many in town didn't like him. Turnbull put that fact down as being because the man was tightfisted with a dollar, and used his wealth to hammer others to his way of thinking. He shrugged, pulled out a sheet of paper, and began to write.

In the saloon, Clausen mopped the water from his face, stood, went to the bar, and ordered a whisky. He knocked it back, ordered another, did the same, then another. After the third drink, he tossed a coin on the bar, turned, and walked out. He went directly to his store, entered his office, and slammed the door.

While he cleaned the cut over his eye that Turnbull's left hook had opened, he fumed. The thing that made him even angrier was that he didn't dare create a stink about the fight. He didn't want to cause the Rangers to take a close look at his past, and certainly he wanted no one probing into his present. He had his fingers into every pie available in this godforsaken town. Rustling, bank and stagecoach robberies, and, being an officer of the bank, embezzling. He didn't dare carry out his threat against the Ranger. That brought more hot blood to his head.

There were ways to get even besides getting a man fired. A bullet from a dark alley, or fired into his office during the night hours; or a sliced throat, an art in which one of his Mexican friends was so adept.

9

MALLOY AND BURSTON, now settled into their cabin, went to the Buckle each night about an hour before time for the last drink, 2 A.M. Then one of them would go back to the cabins ahead of the girls while the other would shadow them from behind, until they saw the last of them close and shut the door to their cabin.

After a week of this, they heard of a young rancher's wife disappearing, then two days later, another young woman came up missing. Malloy looked across the room at Burston. "Whoever's doing this ain't just got eyes for these girls we been protectin'. Wish to hell we could watch over 'em all."

Burston pulled his foot out of a boot, dropped it on the floor beside his bed, and tugged on the other. "Gunfighter, we cain't do no more'n we're doin'." He sighed. "Reckon I been wishin' the same, but we just ain't enough to cover the territory." He unbuttoned his trousers and pulled them down over his long johns, then slanted Malloy a look. "I been wonderin', what the danged jumped-up hell you gonna get outta catchin' them varmints?"

Malloy had wondered when Burston would ask him that very question. He didn't know how to answer. He frowned at the empty cup in his hand. Burston had done nothing to indicate he had anything to do with the *bandidos*. He'd shown only genuine concern for the girls, and it seemed he'd let everything at his ranch go until they could find an answer. He had begun to trust the rancher, but the knowledge that Burston had given his saloon away still nibbled at the back of his mind. What would make a man do such?" He pondered that question, as he'd done deep into the long hours of the night, ever since setting out to find the answer to the most horrible crime he'd undertaken to solve. He still had no answer. He looked at the rancher. "Tell you how it is, cowboy. I don't really know why I'm doin' this. I done asked myself the same question. Only answer I come up with is I ain't never done much for nobody, so maybe I can even the debt a little by helpin' these here girls."

That answer seemed to satisfy Burston. Then Malloy said, "Gonna ask you the same question. What you figure to get outta all this?"

For a few seconds the rancher studied the pants he still held in his hand, then he looked at Malloy. "Gunfighter, I brung these here girls out here with the promise of a good safe job." He shrugged. "Don't see as how I can do any less. If one of 'em gets hurt, I don't reckon I can ever forgive myself."

Malloy wanted to ask why he'd brought Megan along with the title to the Silver Buckle, but bit back the words. He'd save that 'til later.

Two nights later, the thing he had feared yet hoped for happened. He'd hoped for it so he'd have something to get his teeth into. A scream came from a cabin down the line. He was into his jeans, shirt, boots, and gun belt as soon as Burston. They hit the door running. Each held a six-shooter.

Now screams came from every cabin, accompanied by shouted commands in rough, uneducated English. Horses milled outside each cabin. Other voices tried to quiet the horses. Then the screams stopped, as though hands had been clamped over the women's mouths.

Malloy ran into the middle of several men. Not figuring they were there to help, he fired two shots. Two men dropped. Close by his side another handgun opened up. Burston had entered the fight. Then struggling figures emerged from the cabins. Malloy lowered his weapon and at the same time yelled for Burston to hold his fire. "You might hit one o' them girls."

Not firing, but using his handgun as a club, he hit one man alongside the head, felt his skull give, and knew he'd killed him. A glance to the side showed Burston swinging a blade so large it could only have been a Bowie.

Apparently not having figured on any opposition, the men holding the horses panicked. They toed the stirrups and, dragging the led horses with them, bolted. Those trying to wrestle the girls toward the horses uttered a string of curses, turned the women loose, and ran for the horses. "Cut 'em down!" yelled Burston. His six-gun rolled out a volley of shots.

Malloy fired as fast as his thumb could slip the hammer. Four men dropped. Two ran for the darkness of an alley. Malloy threw a couple of shots toward them with little hope of hitting anything. Then only the sobbing and terrified mewlings of the women broke the silence. Malloy glanced through a thick fog of gun smoke, then snorted to clear his nose of the acrid odor. Burston stood at his shoulder.

"Better see can we calm them girls down a little, Burston. They've had more'n most could take an' retain their sanity."

"Yeah. Wantta see did that trash get away with any of the women. They did, an' I'll follow 'em to hell."

Malloy walked to one of the downed gunmen, flipped him on his back with his boot toe, and marked him off as dead. He had a hole above his left eye. He did the same to the others—all dead. Then he collected their guns and knives, piled them outside the nearest cabin, and headed for the alley to which he'd seen the two men run. He thought both would be long gone by now, but he'd look. He lucked out.

One gunman lay groaning. There was no sign of the other. Malloy took the man's weapons, caught him by the collar, and dragged him to the circle of light shed by a lantern Burston had had one of the girls fetch. He stooped at the man's side, turned him over, and saw a gaping hole about an inch below his belt. The outlaw writhed in agony, moaned, cursed, and sobbed. "You done broke my hip bone. Cain't walk, cain't do nothin'. Git a doctor. I'm gonna bleed to death."

A closer look showed Malloy that a huge sliver of wood, probably knocked from one of the buildings at the side of the alley, protruded from the man's abdomen. A doctor could not help the man. But the lawman wanted answers before it was too late.

He went to his knees at the outlaw's side. "A doc ain't gonna do you no good, you done bought the farm. 'Fore you die, tell me who sent you. Where'd y'all git together?"

The bandit shook his head. "Ain't tellin' you nothin'."

Angry bile boiled into Malloy's throat, hot blood pushed at his temples. "Gonna tell you somethin'. If that big sliver o' wood stuck through you don't kill you, I'm gonna.

'Sides that, you don't owe nobody you rode with nothin'. They ran off an' left you. Tell me who called the shots on this raid."

The outlaw moaned again, clamped his teeth, and tried to pull his legs up to his stomach, but the piece of wood stopped him. He turned pain-filled eyes up to Malloy. "You right. Th-they run off an' left me. Don't usually ride with quitters. They said a man named Sotello ordered this raid."

Sotello. Hell, there must be a hundred Sotellos scattered around. Malloy bent closer, ignoring the man's stinking breath. "Where you meet this Sotello? Is he from around here?"

Feebly, the outlaw shook his head. "Ain't never met 'im. The one who hired me didn't know 'im neither."

The bandit's eyes widened. Fear blossomed in them, then resignation. "You got a drink o' whiskey on you, cowboy? I shore could use one 'bout now."

Malloy turned his head to the side and yelled to Burston, "If you've accounted for all the women, get a bottle outta my gear. Gonna give this man a drink."

"All the women are here," Burston yelled, then turned and ran toward the cabin he and Malloy shared. Inside, he stuck his hand into the marshal's saddlebag, moved it back and forth, felt something smooth, pulled it out, and stared at it. A U.S. marshal's badge. He dropped it back where he'd found it, and looked in the other bag. There he found a quart jar of clear liquid. He unscrewed the lid, sniffed, and grinned. "This here's the real stuff," he grunted. He screwed the lid back on and headed back to Malloy.

On the way, he mulled over his discovery. The Gunfighter was a government lawman. It didn't surprise him. The man always had money, never had a job anywhere, and was always on the scene when order needed serving. If The Gunfighter wanted it kept secret, so be it. He would tell no one.

After handing the bottle to The Gunfighter, he gathered the dead men's weapons and took them to their cabin.

While Malloy stayed with the dying outlaw, Burston gathered the girls into one cabin. They had calmed down to no more than a sniffle now and then. "Gonna tell y'all right now, girls, I didn't figger on nothin' like this happenin' when I hired you. Any o' you want to quit, I'll buy you a ticket back to New Orleans. Cain't blame none o' you if you go."

A dark-haired beauty looked at the rest of the women, then shook her head. "Mr. Burston, I came out here with you to make some money. I still think to do that, sir. Bad things happen everywhere, especially to women like us who have no menfolks. I'll stick."

A redheaded girl, barely out of her teens, looked at the others. "I feel the same way, sir, if we can count on you and Mr. Gunfighter to be close by."

Burston nodded, then smiled. "I'll be here, an' I figger I can speak for Mr. Gunfighter, too. He'll be here."

From the doorway, Malloy spoke up. "He's right. I'll be here. We ain't gonna let nothin' happen to you—if we can help it." He looked at Burston. "Gonna go see if Miss Megan's all right. Don't figure this bunch had it in mind to try to take her, bein' she's right in the middle o' town, but from now on, we gonna make sure she ain't one o' them we cain't protect."

A surge of jealousy pushed through Burston's chest. He choked it back. "Good idea. We gotta think o' some way to keep 'em all together after the Buckle shuts down for the night." He looked at the women. "Y'all stay here. I'll stay with you." He turned his attention back to Malloy. "You go ahead. I'll think on some way we can watch all o' them. You think on it, too."

Malloy smiled. "Sorta had that in mind, cowboy. We'll talk 'bout it later." He turned his steps toward the saloon.

Outside the cabin in which Burston had taken the women, a small crowd had gathered. Malloy smiled to himself. They'd made damned certain the gunfire had stopped before they left the safety of their homes. He sighed. But then that was always the way townsmen acted. There would be a place for men like him at all times and all places.

He stopped long enough to tell a couple of men to gather the dead and take them to the undertaker. "See if they got anythin' in their pockets says where they're from, an' if they got enough money to pay for plantin' 'em. I'll tell the town marshal you're takin' care o' things."

A few moments later, he stood outside the saloon. The place was locked up. Malloy picked up a handful of small pebbles and tossed them, one at a time, against Megan's window. After perhaps the fifth one, the window opened a crack, and Megan's voice came to him. "What is it you want? We're closed."

"Miss Megan, it's me, The Gunfighter. We had some trouble down at the cabins. I wanted to make sure you're all right."

The window opened wider. "Yes, I'm all right. I hope no harm has come to the girls."

Malloy nodded in appreciation. She thought of the girls first. He liked that. "Ma'am, yore folks down yonder didn't get nothin' but a good scare. May I come up?"

"I'll come down and unlock the door. Just a moment."

The window shut, and in what seemed only a few seconds the inside lock rattled. Megan, holding a lantern in one hand and her robe together with the other, pulled the door wide and stepped aside. "Tell me about it, sir."

After going to her sitting room, Malloy told her what had happened, then studied her to see if his words alarmed her. She sat there cool as ice. "I knew if you were there, they'd be safe."

Malloy shook his head. "Ma'am, you're puttin' too much trust in me. Mr. Burston was there, too. Neither one o' us was 'bout to let any harm come to them. We figured, you bein' here in the middle o' town, they wasn't gonna do you no harm." He hesitated. "But ma'am, we gonna make more sure after this."

A slight smile touched her lips. "And how do you propose to accomplish that, Mr. Gunfighter?"

Malloy wished he could read her mind at that moment. He was sure she was imagining all sorts of ways that he and Burston would come up with. He shook his head. "Don't rightly know, Miss Megan, but I'm here to tell you. We ain't leavin' you alone 'til we get this woman-stealin' thing cleared up."

"Don't I have anything to say about it, sir?"

Malloy groped for his pipe, then shoved it back in his pocket.

"Go ahead, Mr. Gunfighter, a pipe doesn't bother me."

While filling his pipe, ways to protect her raced through his mind, most of them discarded as soon as he thought them. He lit his pipe; then, through a cloud of smoke, said, "Ma'am, would you consider sharing a cabin with one of the girls for a while? Mr. Burston and I'll make it as short a stay as possible."

She studied him a moment. "Why are you taking such an interest in what happens to the girls and me? I can understand why Mr. Burston does; he brought the girls out here, and is responsible for me being here. But why you?"

Malloy, using his pipe stem, pushed his hat to the back of his head and grinned. "Well, ma'am, I could lie an' tell you that I jest flat don't like nobody breakin' the law, but I ain't gonna lie." His face sobered. "Gonna tell you the truth. I like you, like bein' around you, like the way you play what cards are dealt you whether good or bad. So 'til you tell me to get lost an' leave you alone, reckon I'm gonna be right close whenever you need me."

Megan felt her face flush. She was tempted to put on her icy facade, then decided not to. She had already admitted to herself a strange attraction to this rugged, hard man, and now he admitted to feeling something more than friendship for her. Maybe it was no more than a man would feel for his sister, or perhaps what any strong man felt for a strong woman. She decided to let the cards fall as they would. "Mr. Gunfighter, I do believe that I've met you before, although I can't for the life of me determine where." She shook her head. "Don't wait for me to, as you say, 'tell you to get lost.' I won't do that. I feel so very secure when I know you're near." She stood. "All right. You and Mr. Burston decide how you're to protect the girls *and* me, and I'll do what you think best."

Malloy pushed his hat forward on his brow and nodded. "Reckon you gonna be safe here the rest o' the night since we done took care o' them what was meant to hurt you. Tomorrow we'll let you know what we come up with." He tipped his hat. " 'Night, ma'am. Get a good night's sleep."

Megan followed him to the front door, closed and shot the bolt when he was clear. She smiled into the darkness when she heard him stop outside until he heard the door lock go into place. He was a gentleman and a protector, something she'd wished for in a man since the day her father got killed. She shook her head. He wasn't *the* man for her. Her mind refused to place him in a closed-in, civilized environment. He was like the wind—but this wind always blew toward trouble. She couldn't imagine herself in places that seldom knew peace.

She walked back to her room, slipped her robe off, lay down determined to go back to sleep, but sleep eluded her far into the night.

Malloy faced Burston across the crude table in the middle of the room. Each had a tumbler full of Megan's best whisky in front of him.

"I figure to move Miss Megan down here with the girls, where we can watch 'em all at the same time," Malloy said. "Miss Megan's done agreed to that if you an' me think it's best. She puts a lot o' faith in what you an' me come up with together." He knocked his drink back and poured another, then one for Burston, who had also swallowed his in one gulp.

Before Malloy could take a swallow of his fresh drink, Burston pinned him with a look that had hope, but also much doubt, in it. "Gunfighter, gonna ask you somethin' straight out. I know you got other things to take care of. Don't know what they might be. You ain't no drifter, so what's yore interest in Miss Megan?"

Malloy locked eyes with him. "Gonna answer you the same way—straight out. She don't know it, but I been admirin' her for a pretty good spell now. The whole time I reckon I been figurin' her to be the most beautiful woman I ever seen, but never figured in my line o' work I'd stand a chance with her." He knocked back his second drink, stared at the empty glass, reached for the bottle, shook his head, and withdrew his hand. Two drinks was enough. "But, cowboy, like I said, I'm gonna answer you honest. I done changed my mind. Even if I gotta change my line o' work, I'm gonna try to get her interested in me."

Burston's face paled. A knot showed at each side of his

jaw, small beads of sweat popped out on his forehead. He shifted in his chair to bring the grips of his Colt close to hand. Still holding Burston's gaze, Malloy nodded. "Yep, that's the way I got it all figured." He lowered his eyelids to a squint. "Now, I'm gonna ask you the same question: What's yore interest in her?"

Burston lowered his gaze to stare at the rough tabletop. Then, so low Malloy had trouble hearing him, he said, "Gunfighter, I been in love with Miss Megan for a considerable while. Fact is, I done a dumb thing. I caused 'er to come out here. She don't know it, but I'm the reason for her bein' here." He raised his eyes to look at Malloy straight on. He then told Malloy about the poker game on the riverboat, about deliberately throwing in the winning hand so Megan would win and have a reason to come to Laredo. He thought that, being close to her, he might have a chance to court her, win her love, and marry her.

The longer Burston talked, the more sense the past happenings made. Most of it Malloy already knew, but the mystery of why Burston threw in his hand did two things: it solidified and justified his growing trust in the man, and it put them solidly against each other in their pursuit of Megan's affections. He thought to tell the rancher about witnessing the poker hand, but decided against it. To tell him that would expose him as being the gambler on the riverboat. He wasn't ready to let that be known.

He leaned across the table. "Gonna tell you somethin'. What you done told me, I believe. But it also puts us against each other. I ain't gonna give up on gettin' her interested in me, but I give you my word I'll play my hand out where you can see it. I ain't no sneak." He poured them each another drink. "I'm gonna ask you to play your cards the same way—and hope we can end up friends, regardless who wins." He picked up his drink. "I'd like us to drink to it workin' out that way."

Burston picked up his glass. "If we can. We're both pretty damned good men. I'll drink to that."

They knocked back their drinks, then, on impulse, Malloy reached in his pocket and fingered his badge. "Gonna tell you somethin' else, an' I'm askin' you to not say a word about it 'til I say you can." He pulled his hand from his pocket and placed the badge between them.

Burston glanced at the badge, then looked at Malloy. "That don't surprise me none. You always seemed to be just where you was needed, when you was needed." He nodded. "Yep, I'll agree to keep yore secret, but reckon that calls for another drink." This time he poured, and cast a sloppy grin at Malloy. "Reckon I'm gittin' a little drunk, but what the hell, it ain't every day a man makes a friend, an' at the same time agrees not to fight dirty for the woman he loves." They both laughed, knocked back their drinks, and went to their beds.

10

MALLOY WOKE WITH a head that felt like the borders of Texas were too close together to hold the pounding, throbbing bundle of pain. He rolled over, groaned, looked across the room at the snoring Burston, then stood. He had work to do. He had to see if there was anything in the dead men's pockets that would indicate where they were before they came here.

At the town marshal's office, he asked Provo if he could look at the stuff the men had in their pockets. The lawman squinted at him. "What the hell for? You ain't no law officer."

Malloy's temples pounded harder with the fresh supply of angry blood. He squelched his anger. "Gonna tell you why. Them men got killed by me an' my partner while we wuz doin' yore job. I wantta see if they's anybody I need to write 'bout how they died."

The lawman leaned over, pulled out the top right-hand desk drawer, and set it on the desktop. "It's all in there, 'cept for a few dollars they wuz carryin'. He'p yoreself."

He stood. "I'm gonna go in the front cell and lie down fer a spell. Had a hard night." Without waiting for Malloy's reply, he pulled open the barred door and stepped into the cell.

Malloy picked through the pocket knives, balls of twine, small change, plugs of tobacco, and one set of keys tied together with a leather thong. He tossed the keys onto the pile, turned his eyes to the next object, then swung his gaze back. Keys? Not many cowboys, or outlaws, had use for keys. He picked them up. Turned each of them from side to side. All looked to be of the ordinary variety except for one. It had a name with which Malloy was familiar: the Jean Lafitte House. That rooming house, clean but inexpensive, stood at the end of Canal Street in New Orleans. Was it possible that another town had a place of the same name? Possible—but not very probable. He untied the thong, removed the key, and put it in his pocket. He stepped to the barred door, told the marshal he'd put the drawer back in place, then left.

He went to his hotel, told the clerk to send a sheet of paper, a pen, and an inkwell to his room.

He wrote to Turnbull, told him of the happenings in Laredo, explained about the key, said he wanted the Ranger to go to New Orleans and inspect everything in the room, to confiscate anything that might be of interest or have a bearing on the case, and to take it back to San Antonio. He also told him his deputy U.S. marshal's badge would keep him out of trouble after crossing into Louisiana. He finished the letter, wrapped the key in a strip torn from a well worn shirt, packaged it, and went to the post office. Every step made him wish he dared leave Laredo to attend to the search of the room in New Orleans himself, but a team of horses could not have dragged him from looking after Megan and the girls. He'd find the man—or men—heading up the outlaw gang after making certain he'd tied up loose ends in this part of the state.

On the way back to his hotel, under the hot sun, his head ached worse. A cool beer might ease his pain. He altered his course to the nearest saloon.

He'd been at the bar only a few moments when a man— young, and a gambler by his dress—stood and walked to face him across the curve of the bar. "You The Gunfighter?"

Malloy, not used to having a hangover, and wanting no conversation with anyone at that moment, nodded. "Some call me that."

The man raked him from head to foot with an insolent look. "Well, I've never seen a so-called gunfighter who stank of overnight drinking, stood bleary-eyed at a bar, and swilled another drink. Seems to me you ain't earned the name. I figure to see if you can earn it."

Malloy's neck muscles tightened. His heart pounded a bit harder. The man standing before him was too young to have to kill. But he obviously fancied himself a bad man. Malloy didn't want trouble, but damned if he'd walk around it. "Sonny, I don't want trouble with you. Ain't done nothin' to you." Then, before he could get a leash on it, his temper came to a boil. "Sit, and put a lock on yore mouth 'fore I close it fer good."

The young gambler took a hesitant step back, and Malloy followed. He tossed his beer in the boy's face, dropped his glass, swung his right at the same time, then followed it with a left hook and another right to the jaw. The man's face took on an oddly lopsided look. His jaw hung limply off to the side—broken. Malloy grabbed the gambler's shirt up close to his neck, twisted it, and pulled him close. "Pack your things, tinhorn. You're leaving town. You ain't a good gambler, you ain't a gunfighter, you ain't no kind o' fighter. Go back east where men won't kill you so easily." He pushed and turned loose of the man's shirt. The boy stumbled and fell into the filthy, spit-laden sawdust.

He rolled to his back, placed his hands flat on the floor and pushed to sit. Malloy drew his .44. "Don't put them hands nowhere close to yore vest." When the gambler focused on him enough to know he was looking down the barrel of a handgun, Malloy walked behind him, holstered his Colt, reached under each of the gambler's arms and drew a snub-nosed Colt from a shoulder holster under the left arm. He emptied the shells from the cylinder and tossed the gun in front of the would-be bad man. "Now go home, tell yore mama what you done, an' maybe she'll let you off without a spankin'."

The gambler's eyes squinted, blood pushed up behind his eyes, painting his face red. "Mister, when I tell my brother, Max Braden, what you done to me, without even givin' me a chance, he'll kill you right where you stand." He talked like his tongue was wrapped around his teeth, and with each word pain pushed up behind his eyes.

Malloy's head pounded even worse. "No, you two-bit tinhorn, if he's got any sense, he'll thank me for not killin' you—that is, if you shut yore damned mouth right now an' don't get me any madder. You keep jawin' at me, an' I'm gonna give 'im a funeral to attend."

Slightly behind and to Malloy's side, a voice said, "You won't be around long enough to make good on that threat, Gunfighter. I'm the kid's brother."

Most losers in situations like this were those who needed to talk before opening the ball. Malloy wasn't one of them. His hand dived to his side while he twisted and threw himself to the floor. His .44 belched flame and lead while he fell. The voice that had threatened him belonged to a well-dressed man about his own age. But the two holes in his chest—one through each shirt pocket—put a stop to his getting any older.

Malloy rolled to his feet, smoke curling from the barrel of his six-shooter. The bartender came around the end of the bar. "I heard you was a right sudden gent, Gunfighter. Now I seen it with my own eyes." He walked to the corpse, bent, and felt for a pulse. "Dead. You don't need to worry none. He already had his gun out when he said them words to you."

Miguel Provo, the town marshal, came through the batwings. "I heard what you just said, bartender." He looked at Malloy. "Don't know how you do it, Gunfighter, but you always seem to be able to claim self-defense."

Malloy stared at the marshal. His face felt like old, dried leather, stiff and hard. "Marshal, anytime a man threatens me from behind, I ain't gonna wait 'til I know he's got a gun on me. I'm gonna start shootin' soon's I can get my handgun clear o' leather."

He walked to the man's side, knelt, went through his pockets, left all on the floor beside him except a key he palmed from among the pockets' contents. He nodded toward the now white-faced gambler. "That sorry excuse for a man is this man's brother. His mouth's as big as his guts are small. Better get 'im away from me or you gonna have another one to bury."

Provo stared at Malloy a moment, his eyes hard as blued steel. "Seen you palm something from his pockets." He snapped a thumb toward the corpse. "Gonna give it to me, or I gotta take it?"

Malloy let a thin, cold smile crack the corners of his mouth. "Far's takin' it from me, Provo, you might find you done saddled a bronc you cain't ride." He nodded toward the batwings. "Let's go to yore office, I got somethin' I reckon I better show you." Without waiting for Provo to follow, he moved toward the door.

He'd been in several gunfights in this town, and in every one Provo had given him the benefit of the doubt. He'd long ago made up his mind that Miguel Provo, Laredo town marshal, was an honest law officer. Now he would do what he seldom did with anyone.

A few moments later, he stood across from Provo's scarred wooden desk. "You gonna invite me to sit, an' maybe have a cup o' that thick mud brewin' there while I tell you about what's goin' on?"

The marshal's eyes crinkled at the corners. "If I don't, I got it figured you gonna pour you a cup an' sit anyhow."

Malloy nodded and did exactly as Provo predicted, then he leaned across the desk, blew on the hot liquid, sipped, and reached in his pocket. "Gonna ask you to keep what I'm gonna show an' tell you between us." He pulled his U.S. marshal's badge out and dropped it on the desk.

Provo looked at the badge, then at Malloy. "Don't know why that don't surprise me, but it don't. Now show me what you took outta Braden's pocket—an' tell me why."

Malloy took the key out and studied it a moment. It was from the same place as the key he mailed to Turnbull. He put the key on the desk between him and Provo. Then he told the marshal the story of the missing women—and about finding a key like the one he showed the marshal on one of last night's *bandidos*. "I'd like to keep this key and send it to one of my men. I want the room searched. It don't figure as a coincidence that two men this far from New Orleans just happen to have keys from the same rooming house. I wantta know what these men have in common—an' who they're workin' for."

Provo nodded. "You got it." He glanced toward the door,

then said, as though he could see the Rio Grande beyond it, "Most o' them what breaks the law here cross that muddy stream, an' know they're beyond any law we got here. How you figure to tackle that problem?"

Malloy smiled. "River? Border? Hell, Provo, I ain't gonna be able to see no river or border if I get a chance to get them what's been takin' them girls." He leaned across the desk. "Marshal, them I been gettin' acquainted with ain't Mexican. They're trash from our side o' the border. I ain't lettin' no river stop me, or the color of their skin. If they turn them women over to Mexicans, I don't reckon I'm gonna be able to tell the difference. Mexican, American"—he shrugged—"gonna be the same to me."

"You ain't gonna have nothin' to back you up if the Mexican government catches you. You know damned well those bastards in Washington're gonna deny ever havin' heard of you."

Malloy nodded. "Yeah, I know that, but it's somethin' I gotta do. Couldn't stand to look at myself in the mirror when I shave if I played it any other way."

Provo pushed Malloy's badge back across the desk to him. "I don't envy you, Gunfighter. Wish I could side you, but this job I'm doin' here is important, too."

"Yeah, I understand. But I'm gonna ask you to feed me any information you come across that might have a bearing on what I'm workin' on."

Provo smiled. "That's one thing I can promise."

Malloy drank the rest of his coffee, stood, shook hands with Provo, and headed for his cabin, where he wrote another letter to Turnbull. He had finished writing when Burston groaned, turned on his side, groaned again, and looked across the room at him. "Damn, my mouth tastes like I been eatin' cow droppin's. My haid feels like them same cows done stampeded right over every inch o' my skull." He put his hands to each side of his head and pushed. "Gunfighter, you better git outside. If my haid explodes like I figure it's gonna do, you might git hurt."

Malloy shook his head. "Naw, all you need is a couple o' beers to get settled down. Go on down to the Buckle, I'll be there soon. I got some thinkin' to do."

After Burston had gone out, closing the door softly behind him, Malloy sat staring at the bunk the rancher had so recently occupied. He reconstructed his thoughts of who might be responsible for getting women to move west and then having the stage on which they rode attacked. With what he knew of Burston, he dealt him out of the picture.

Maybe the outlaw boss, whoever he was, didn't have anything to do with getting the young women to move. Maybe he simply kept his eyes open for movement of any kind where women were concerned, and then set his henchmen on them. Malloy thought about that a few moments.

Finally he decided that someone in New Orleans had to be calling the shots, but how was he getting word to the *bandidos*? There had to be one man in charge of the whole operation, and there had to be a leader who could handle the outlaws—and, he thought, there might be separate men controlling each phase of the operation: intelligence, manpower, logistics, and the supreme commander. Malloy grunted, shook his head, took another sheet of paper, and wrote down the results of his thoughts. He studied the short sentences a while, folded the paper, and put it in his pocket. If the suspicions he'd come up with were true, this assignment was more complicated than any he'd tackled in the past.

Three days later, Turnbull sorted through his mail, most of which was Wanted notices, a few memorandums from Ranger headquarters—and two letters from Malloy. He opened them first, read them, studied the keys and saw they were for different rooms in the same hostelry. He put the keys in his pocket and went to his room.

He packed a couple changes of clothing, cleaned and oiled his weapons, wrote headquarters a letter telling his senior officer he had a lead on a man and was going to be gone from his office a few days, then went to the livery and selected a couple of horses from his string: one for packing, the other for riding. An hour later, he had thirty minutes of the trail to New Orleans behind him.

He thought to appear as a rough, unshaven man from the far reaches of the West, then changed his mind. He'd not packed a suit, but had well-fitting riding clothes in his bedroll. Three days later, clean shaven and bathed, he rode down Canal Street in the direction of the Jean Lafitte, turned off onto Bourbon Street, and went in the first bar he saw. Inside, he ordered a beer and, the place being nearly empty, talked with the bartender.

"Just in from Texas. Come over to see the sights. Know of any clean but cheap place to stay while I'm here?"

The bartender grinned. "Yeah, almost anywhere along Canal, or here on Bourbon, or maybe Basin; hell, man, just pick one out."

Bull frowned. "Man in SanTone wuz tellin' me 'bout a place." He scratched his head. "What'd he call it? Somethin' like John the Feet. You know of any place called by that name?"

The bartender smiled, then grinned, then broke into uncontrolled laughter. Finally, when he could control himself, he said, "Mon, I know of that place. It is Jean Lafitte. Nice, clean, cheap place, but some who stay there are not as honest as most would want to be around. What I'm telling you, mon, I don't think you'd want to stay there if you have any money on you."

Bull studied his drink a moment. "Ain't got much on me, just what I figgered to use for a good time. Then I gotta git back out yonder an' work a few more months fer another visit over here."

"Now, don' you go down yonder an' get your money stolen. Fact is, don't let anyone know you're packin' money from a few months' work. This's a rough town."

Turnbull smiled to himself. He'd been in rough towns before, and when he left, they weren't as rough as they'd been when he arrived. He knocked back what remained of his beer, tossed a coin on the counter, and left. He'd found out what he wanted to know.

Less than fifteen minutes later he stood in the office of the Jean Lafitte rooming house. The manager, not the type Bull expected to see running a boarding house, looked him up and down, then turned a hard stare on him. "You ain't from around here. Where you from, an' who sent you?" The man had a lean, hard look, stood about six foot, and didn't wear face hair, which let the scars around his eyes, mouth, and cheekbones show.

Bull deliberately put on a hard look of his own, one under which many men had wilted. "Gonna tell you somethin' might keep you from gettin' killed if you ever go out my way. Where I come from, we don't ask a man's name, an' we damned shore don't ask where he's from. Them two things in particular are a man's own business."

The manager studied him a moment longer, gave a jerky nod and said, "Yeah, I got a room. How long you stayin'?"

"Oh 'bout a week maybe. Figger I'll need to look for work by then."

He handed Turnbull a key with a large number 3 on it. "You decide to stay longer, I'll give you another key and a better room." His steel gray eyes never left Bull's face.

"When you decide to look for work, let me know. I might have something that'll interest you."

Turnbull shook his head. "Naw, I ain't one to stay in a town for very long. Reckon I'll ride back out the way I come."

The man nodded. "That'll be fine. I might hear of something out west of here. I'll let you know."

Bull nodded, signed the register as John Jones, paid the man, and went outside to turn his horses in the stable behind the building. While there, he checked the brands of the eight horses stabled there—all Texas brands with which he was familiar. Of course, that didn't mean a whole lot. There were many Texas men who came to New Orleans to get rid of months of trail dust and the long built-up need for a woman—but it was something to remember.

Turnbull stashed his bedroll and gear in the room, then sat back in the room's only chair to think. The manager, who had not offered his name, had not batted an eye at the name under which Bull had signed the register. In fact, he acted pleased and more trustful. Then Turnbull took out the two keys and laid them alongside the one he'd acquired a few minutes before. They could all have been cut on the same machine, but his key didn't have the place's name on it. He wondered if he took more permanent quarters, his new key would have the name. He thought it would. He'd have to wait a while for the answer to that question. Knowing he'd not get answers sitting around, he made ready to look like he was going out on the town. The one conclusion he'd come to was that the manager was a hard case from parts west of New Orleans. He figured he hadn't made the trip for nothing, and would find more when it was safe to check the rooms.

He went to the lobby. The manager was now dressed in a fashionable white suit with a swallow-tailed coat, highly polished western boots, white shirt, and tie. Bull looked down at his own slightly faded jeans and chambray shirt. "Man, I ain't never had no duds looked that good. You reckon I'm lookin' fit to go out on the town?"

The manager swept him with a glance. "Hell, yes. I don't usually spiff up like this, but I'm goin' to see my boss. He owns this here roomin' house, and I'm tellin' you true, Mr. Sotello don't like me comin' around in nothin' but clothes I could wear anyplace in town." He held out his hand. "Around here, they call me Anse Rugely." He grinned. "Reckon that's as good a handle as I need—for now."

Sotello—that was a name Bull had heard somepiace before. He figured he'd let looking at the rooms wait. He wanted to know what kind of business this Sotello ran. He'd follow Rugely to see if he could find out.

He walked out the door ahead of the manager, went to the corner, stepped around it, and waited. Soon Rugely appeared across the street, walking briskly. Turnbull let him get about a block ahead, then followed.

Rugely didn't appear to be concerned about anyone knowing where he went. He never looked behind. Then, in the center of the Canal Street business area, he slowed and pushed through the doorway of a store. The sign hanging out over the sidewalk identified it as an import/export business. Turnbull smiled to himself. Now there was a good line of work to follow if a man wanted to delve into more shady undertakings. Anything from smuggling contraband goods into, to sending items of the same stripe from, the United States—and what better way to keep contact with those outside the country who were interested in illegal activities? Bull walked another few feet and pushed through the door of the building next to him. It was a bar. He sat at a table by the window where he could watch the front of the Sotello store. He ordered a beer.

A couple of beers later, Rugley appeared and turned his steps toward the river, obviously not going back to the Jean Lafitte House right away. Bull downed the rest of his beer and headed back to his room. He'd find out what kind of man Sotello was later.

On the way back, he pulled the two keys from his pocket and studied them. Neither had a room number on it. He'd noticed that there were several rooms in the Jean Lafitte House with no numbers on their doors. He sighed. Hell, nothing was easy. He'd have to try the keys in each of those unmarked doors until he found the ones they fit.

Back at the rooming house, he walked past the desk in the lobby into the dark hallway—and came face to face with a man whose picture graced several Wanted notices resting in his desk drawer back in San Antonio.

The man hesitated only a moment, his mouth hanging open, before his hand swept to his side. Bull had the advantage. He didn't hesitate. His .44 came clear of leather and prodded the man in the stomach—hard—a second before the outlaw's hand could pull iron. "Turn around, go to room 3, step aside 'til I unlock the door, then go in ahead o' me." He pushed the barrel further into the hard-muscled gut.

The outlaw's expression never changed. He stared into Bull's eyes; then, frozen-faced, he said, "Now ain't it hell who a man can meet this far from home? What's the matter, Turnbull, the Rangers outta work in Texas?" His expression changed into a cold grin. "You ain't got no authority over here in Louisiana. You cain't do a damned thing to me here."

"Move it on down the hall. We'll talk once we get in my room." He prodded the outlaw toward his door again. A glance up and down the darkened hallway revealed no one. They came to his door, he unlocked it, and pushed the outlaw in ahead of him. "Gonna tell you somethin'. You raise yore voice even a little above what's necessary for me to hear you, an' I'll let this here little old Bowie hangin' at my side open you another mouth below yore chin." He pushed the door closed and twisted the key in the lock. "Drop yore gun belt and knife, then sit in that chair over yonder." He watched the man do as he was told, then stooped and kicked the knife and gun belt aside. He sat on the edge of the bed while he studied the hard-faced waddy.

What could he do with the man? He hadn't figured on this kind of complication. It wasn't in him to cut the outlaw's throat and try to dispose of the body after dark. He kept trying to think of the name printed on the several posters he had on the man. Then it came to him: Matt Beaulow.

Beaulow grinned. "Got you in a pickle, huh, Turnbull? What you gonna do with me? From what I hear, you ain't one to kill a man without givin' 'im a chance." His grin widened. "Even if I opened my mouth wide an' let out a yell, I don't figure you'd shoot me."

Turnbull's face felt like leather. "You try yellin', an' I'll let more daylight through you than the sun could shine through in a week of clear days." He pointed the .44 at Beaulow's gut. "Try me."

The outlaw's eyes flicked to the Colt in Bull's hand, and tightened slightly at the corners. "Don't reckon I'll yell. Figure what I heard 'bout you always givin' a man a chance only held long as it was 'tween you an' him. I yell, an' it'll be 'tween you an' a bunch—but I'll be gut-shot by then." He shook his head. "No, sir, I figger to do just like you done tol' me."

Turnbull's nerves relaxed only a little. "I didn't figure you as bein' smart, but you got the situation figured right down to a gnat's rear end. One peep outta you, an' you're a goner."

Turnbull studied the outlaw's hard face, ice blue eyes, lean, muscled body. Any break or letdown in his vigilance, and Beaulow would make a move. Bull mentally shook his head. He'd not allow that to happen even if he had to kill him.

After several minutes, he decided what he had to do— and how to do it, unless he stumbled onto others who lived in the Lafitte. He stood and walked to the back of the chair the outlaw sat in, raised his .44, and clubbed Beaulow on the back of the head. The outlaw slumped forward without a sound.

Bull looked around the room and found nothing with which to tie the man, so he pulled the top sheet from his bed and, using his Bowie, cut it into strips. He bound Beaulow's hands and feet and, using one of the strips, stuffed his mouth full. Satisfied he could get on with what he came here for, he eased the door open, checked the hall, and found it empty.

Turnbull walked to the first door in the darkened corridor, tapped lightly on it, waited a moment, and when there was no response, he tried each key. Neither opened the lock. He repeated this at each door until he found one that clicked open. He slowly twisted the white porcelain knob and pushed the door inward. He spent more than half an hour going over the room as only a lawman with years of service knew how to do. He looked under the bed, felt every inch of the mattress to determine whether anything might have been sewed into it, did the same to the pillow, and finally nodded, satisfied that the room was bare of papers, weapons, and personal belongings. He found no clue as to who the dead outlaw back in Laredo worked for. He closed and locked the door behind him when he finished.

He slipped back to his room, checked Beaulow, found him conscious and staring at him with hate-filled eyes. Bull

looked at the wrappings on the outlaw's ankles and wrists,
tugged at them, found them still secure, and went back into
the hall. He resumed his tapping on doors, then trying the
key in the lock. At the fourth room, he got a response.
"What the hell you want?" The voice sounded slurred, as
though the man had been awakened or was drunk.

Turnbull grunted, "Wrong door—sorry," then stood
there, Colt in hand, and waited to see if the man came to
the door. He didn't. The key fit into the next door he tried.

He went in, closed the door, stood in the middle of the
room, and sniffed the odor of a room long shut and unused:
dust and mildew. He made his search in much the same
way as he had in the first room. He found nothing of interest until he pulled open the drawer of the nightstand. A yel-
lowed sheet of crumpled paper came under his gaze. He
pulled it out, spread it on the top of the bedside table, and
read, "Go back to S.A. See S.B. He's got orders for you."
The note had the signature "G.S."

Turnbull folded the sheet of paper and placed it in his
shirt pocket under his bag of Bull Durham smoking tobacco. He went from the room to the stable, saddled his two
horses, then went back to his room. There he found
Beaulow, sweating like he'd been part of a haying crew,
trying to work his bonds loose.

Bull checked the sheet strips, found them secure, tilted
the outlaw forward so as to catch him over his shoulder.
He straightened, went to the door, opened it a crack, and
eased into the hall. He grunted. The damned outlaw
weighed a ton.

Even though he was carrying a man who he guessed
weighed about one hundred seventy pounds, Turnbull's
booted feet made not a sound as he moved to the rear door.
He went to the stable, threw Beaulow across the saddle on
one of the horses, and tied him in place.

Now black dark, he pushed the back door of the stable open, and led the two horses out. He had a real problem. He'd thought about what to do with Beaulow only far enough to get him out of the Jean Lafitte, but he had no idea about where to find the resident U.S. marshal, especially this time of night. Then, lacking any better idea, he rode his horse into an area of fashionable homes—antebellum, pillared, graceful structures of a day long gone in the South.

Turnbull tied his horse to a hitching post and strode to the door of the nearest home. A distinguished darky answered his knock. Bull introduced himself, showed his deputy U.S. marshal's badge, and asked to see the man of the house.

"May I ask yo business, suh?"

Turnbull nodded, then said he'd like directions to the U.S. marshal's office and home. "I got a prisoner out yonder slung on that led horse. I gotta git 'im stuffed away for safe keepin'."

The servant smiled. "Ain't no need to bother the mister. I can tell you what you askin' 'bout."

He gave Bull detailed directions as to how to find the man he looked for. His smile widened to a grin. "An' if he ain't at neither of those two places, you most likely to find him at Miss Delaporte's. She got the most pretty girls workin' fo huh of any place in town. The marshal, he spend a lot o' time there."

Turnbull thanked the man, went back to his horse, and led the other horse from the long, oak-lined drive.

Back out on the street, he pondered where to go first, then decided he'd try Miss Delaporte's establishment. He lucked out.

Bull waited only a few minutes until a tall, gentlemanly, white-haired man came to the foyer. He looked more like a banker, lawyer, or businessman than an officer of the law. Turnbull told him what he had, and who had deputized him. "Reckon what I'm askin', marshal, is for you to put this man away until we can clear up this case. I got plenty o' notices on him in my desk back in SanTone. Jest keep 'im an' don't let nobody know you got 'im. That woman-stealin' bunch has got some pretty strong ties to New Orleans. We don't want to let 'em know we're on to them 'til we get it all tied together."

The U.S. marshal buttoned his coat and led the way from Miss Delaporte's.

With Beaulow securely locked out of the way, Turnbull headed back to the Jean Lafitte House.

11

MALLOY, STILL THINKING of the jumble of possibilities he'd written down as to how the woman-stealing ring might be controlled, left the cabin and headed for the Silver Buckle.

The first person he saw upon entering was Burston. Megan Dolan sat with him. A twinge of jealousy pulled at Malloy, tightening the nerves at the back of his neck. He walked to the table and, without being invited, pulled out a chair and sat.

Megan stared at him a moment, a slight smile breaking the corners of her lips. "You should be ashamed of yourself, Mr. Gunfighter, leading Mr. Burston to sit up drinking with you most of the night."

Malloy's shrug did little to help his own aching head. "Ma'am, I figure he's a full-growed man, same as me. Reckon he done as much leadin' as I did." He gave her a sour grin. "So, ma'am, I figure that makes two of us as candidates for a foolscap. You gonna stand us in the corner for all the young students to laugh at?"

Megan chuckled. "No, I think you're both being punished enough. Sit still. I have a fresh pot of coffee brewing. As soon as it's ready, I'll get you a cup. You both look like you need it." She looked over her shoulder and said to one of the girls, "Bring two cold beers. These gentlemen can drink them while waiting for the coffee."

Two beers and three cups of coffee later, Malloy felt like he might live to see another sunrise, but he wouldn't go so far as to figure two sunrises were possible. He looked at Megan. "Ma'am, you got your stuff packed so Burston an' I can take it down to the cabin you're gonna occupy 'til we get this mess cleared up?"

"Do you really think that's necessary, Mr. Gunfighter?"

"Miss Dolan, if I didn't think so, I wouldn't have suggested inconveniencing you to that extent. Mr. Burston and I agree it's the only practical way we can do our utmost to keep you safe."

Megan smiled that Mona Lisa smile of hers. "You forgot to talk Texan again, Mr. Gunfighter. When are you going to let us know your secret?"

Malloy shook his head. "No, ma'am, I didn't forget. I wanted to make certain I used the right words to convince you. Will you agree for us to move you?"

She stood. "I'll have my things packed and ready for the two of you in a few minutes. Have another beer while I'm in my rooms."

True to her word, and before he and Burston finished their beer, Megan stood at the end of the bar and nodded that she was ready. Malloy shrugged, looked at Burston, and said, "Reckon we better git busy, an' get the lady situated in her new dwelling."

They stood and went to the end of the bar. "Ma'am, 'tween here an' that table we wuz sittin' at, I got to thinkin'. Why don't you just leave yore stuff where it is 'til closin'

time, then we'll take it back yonder to yore cabin. No need
to tell the whole town where you gonna be stayin'. I know
danged well they's eyes in this town would be downright
happy to know where they can lay hands on you."

Again that slight smile. "Whatever you say, Mr.
Gunfighter. Thus far you've taken very good care of me."

Malloy nodded. "Good. I have a few things to do, but
we'll be back in time to see you and the girls safely to your
quarters." He looked at Burston. "What you gonna do the
rest o' the afternoon?"

The rancher cast Malloy a sheepish look. "Gunfighter, I
ain't never made a habit of stayin' abed in the daytime, but
this is one time I'm gonna rest my achin' head against a
pillow until you come get me to help get Miss Megan
moved." He pulled his hat down on his forehead, and
stood. "You need me for anything else, come get me." He
stepped carefully toward the batwings. Malloy grinned,
knowing Burston's careful steps were to keep from jarring
his head.

"You should be ashamed of yourself, Mr. Gunfighter. I
don't believe that poor man ever drank as much, or felt as
badly, as he does right now."

Still grinning, Malloy glanced at her. "Ma'am, you
could say the same about me, but danged if it don't make
me feel better just knowin' they's one human bein' what
feels worse'n I do." He stood, and left the Buckle.

The bright sunlight made his head and eyeballs feel like
some sadistic bastard was beating a drum inside his skull.
He angled across the street to the marshal's office. He
vowed to himself that he'd never touch another drop of
whisky, but as soon as he made the vow, he knew he'd
break it by sundown.

In the marshal's office, he pulled his badge from his
pocket and placed it on the desk in front of Provo. "Like I

told you this mornin', if I have to, I ain't payin' no attention to no Rio Grande, or what country I'm in. Keep this 'til I come askin' for it. It'd get me, an' the U.S. of A., in a heap o' trouble south of here. If I don't come askin' for it, give it to yore grandkids, an' tell 'em a good story 'bout what a damned fool I was."

"Gunfighter, what I'll tell 'em will be the truth. You're already talked about at campfires over all the parts of the West I've been in." He smiled, but the smile didn't hide his somberness. "Gunfighter, they ain't a man in the world I'd rather see come back through that door to claim what he left with me. If you have to cross the river, you come back across it safe-like, you heah?"

"Marshal, you can bet your bottom dollar I'll do my best to get back, but only if I have those women with me." He stared at the wall a moment. "Provo, ain't nothin' or nobody gonna keep me from takin' 'em back." He stepped toward the door, and said over his shoulder, "Take good care of that badge. Polish it every two weeks. I'll be back for it."

Malloy, not used to idle time, walked about the town an hour or two, ate supper, went to the Buckle and played a few hands of poker, won abut ten dollars, then waited for closing time.

Burston showed up about a half-hour before closing time, then together they helped Megan close the place for the night. One in front and one in back of the girls and Megan, they escorted the little covey of females to their quarters, then helped Megan get situated in her cabin.

Burston headed for his bunk while Malloy made a couple of circles around the area, checking alleyways and any other place that might hide a man. Satisfied the area was as secure as he could make it, he turned in.

He heard Burston's snores while still ten feet from the

door. It took him only a few minutes to pull his boots and
hat off, and stretch out on his bunk. He and Burston had
taken to sleeping almost fully dressed so they could
respond to any commotion in only the time it would take
to pull on their boots.

Malloy felt as though he'd closed his eyes only a few
minutes when gunfire exploded somewhere in the middle
of town. He groaned, rolled to his side prepared to go see
what the shots were all about, changed his mind, and
turned onto his back. Hell, a few shots in Laredo weren't
unusual.

The next morning, Malloy and Burston escorted the
women to breakfast. They were through eating when Provo
walked in and came directly to their table. He tipped his
hat to the ladies and looked at Malloy. "Gunfighter, I need
to talk with you a little. C'mon down to the office after
you've had yore coffee, an' maybe gotten the ladies safely
into the Buckle."

Megan looked over the rim of her coffee cup at Malloy.
"Are you in trouble?"

He smiled. "Not that I know of, ma'am, but I don't figure to keep the marshal waitin' too long. He's been right
nice to me—wantta keep it that way."

His answer seemed to satisfy the Ice Lady. She daintily
sipped her coffee from the thick mug. Malloy worried the
idea around in his head that the shots he'd heard the night
before had something to do with Provo wanting to see him.

As soon as he could get the women up and out of the
café without appearing to rush them, he took them to the
Buckle. Megan handed him the key to unlock the door. As
soon as he leaned to put the key in the lock, he saw that
someone had jimmied the lock. He pretended to unlock the
door, stood in front of the raw wood while the ladies went
in to prepare for another day, then told Megan he'd better

get on over to Provo's office. As far as he could tell, she
hadn't noticed anything out of the ordinary.

He swung about and headed for the marshal's office, but
before leaving, he pulled Burston aside, told him what he'd
seen, and asked him to stay in the Buckle in case of further
trouble.

As soon as he walked in, Provo handed him a steaming
cup of coffee. Then, before the marshal could say anything, Malloy asked, "You wantin' to see me got anything
to do with the door to the Buckle bein' jimmied, or them
gunshots I heard in the middle o' the night?"

"You noticed that, huh? Well, you're right on both
counts. I had to go down to the Isle of Dreams to stop a
fight. That wuz after I figured all the waterin' holes had
closed." He rolled and lighted a quirly, then eyed Malloy.
"I wuz on the way back, walkin' in the street where the
dust kept me from makin' any noise, when I seen a man
slip out the door of the Buckle." He took a long drag on his
cigarette. "I knowed Miss Megan done closed up fer the
night more'n two hours before. I shouted at the man to
hold up.

"He drawed. My shot knocked 'im back into the doorway—into another man comin' out. That man fired, but his
shot went wide, thanks to the man I'd shot. Then I cut the
second man down an' went into the Buckle on the run. I
didn't draw no more gunfire, so I dragged the two I'd shot
into the saloon, searched 'em, checked through the buildin',
an didn't find nothin'. I went into Miss Megan's rooms an'
seen where they'd been in there: sheets throwed to the floor,
stuff pulled outta the closet, an' chairs overturned, as
though they wuz mad 'bout not findin' the lady. I reckon
they wuz through lookin' an' wuz leavin' when I seen 'em."

Provo took a sip of his coffee, dragged on his cigarette,
stubbed it out on the heel of his boot, then pointed to a pile

on his desktop. "That there's what I took outta their pockets. Go ahead an' look through it."

Malloy spent a few minutes examining the articles on the desk. None pointed to anything that would help him determine who the leader of the gang might be, nor was there anything like an old envelope with a name on it— nothing to tell him who the men were. He sat back, then stood and poured them each another cup of coffee. When again seated across from the marshal, he sat staring at the wall. Provo hadn't said anything about robbery. Everything he'd said pointed to an attempt to take Megan. Lord, how he wished he had a troop of riders at his disposal, but all he had was himself. He'd not draw Burston into it.

He looked at Provo. "You figure they were after takin' Miss Megan?"

"Ain't no other answer, Gunfighter. They didn't ransack the place lookin' for money. Hell, they didn't even steal a bottle o' whisky." He nodded. "You bet they wuz after Miss Megan." He stood and took a turn about the office. "Gunfighter, after I get through with my rounds at night, I'd be beholden to you if you'd let me help you an' Burston watch out for them ladies."

"Naw, I reckon you got enough to do without me loadin' more onto you." Malloy stood. "Reckon I'll get on back to Miss Dolan. Don't think any o' that bunch'll try anything in broad daylight, but I ain't takin' no chances."

Turnbull went back to the Lafitte House, turned in, and slept soundly the rest of the night. Before letting sleep take him, he pondered the meaning of the initials in the note, then decided to see what kind of man Sotello might be. After that, he would return to San Antonio.

The next morning, after a leisurely breakfast and the strongest coffee he'd ever put in his mouth, Turnbull walked down Canal Street until he spotted the sign over Sotello's door that depicted it as being an import/export business. He decided to go in and meet the man. Sotello didn't know him, so why not?

He opened the door to a variety of mingled scents: coffee beans, tea, leather, camphor wood, tobacco—many of the smells he liked when he was growing up. A rotund man of about forty stood beside a bale of dry goods. Turnbull thought the bale might hold silk from the Orient. The man came to meet him.

"Something I can do for you, sir?"

Bull shook his head. "Don't reckon so, mister. I ain't never been in a store like this before, just thought I'd see what it wuz like. I'm a cowboy. Come to town to see the sights." He grinned. "Reckon a country boy ain't got no business in a place like this, but it wuz somethin' different, so I wanted to see what it wuz all about."

The rotund man stuck out his hand and smiled. "Look as much as you wish, sir. I'm Grafton Sotello. I own this place, do a lot of business with the Far East, the Middle East, and, for that matter, right across our own border, with Mexico."

Turnbull wondered if he dared throw out some bait that might indicate he was looking for women to work in a dance hall down on the border. While pondering that thought, he let Sotello escort him around the store.

Finally, as he was about to walk out the door, Bull hesitated, pushed his hat to the back of his head, and looked at Sotello. "I got a friend down 'round Laredo way. He owns a saloon, an' needs dancin' girls. Ever' time he gets a good bunch, they up an' get married on 'im." He rolled a quirly, lighted it, and squinted at Sotello. "My friend knowed I wuz comin' over here, an' asked me to look around an' see wuz they any girls willin' to go down there." He grinned.

"Tell you the truth, sir, I don't even know where to start. You got any ideas?"

Sotello's eyes went flat and black. He shook his head. "I don't have any truck with loose women. I recommend your friend come get his own women when he can get away from his saloon."

From the look in the merchant's eyes, and the chill in his words, Turnbull knew he'd made a mistake. He wouldn't get information here, but on the plus side, he'd struck a chord of suspicion. The hate-filled but guarded look of Sotello was not the reaction of an innocent man.

Bull nodded and pushed the door open. "Well, I done what he asked me to do, now I can go see what this town's got that my town ain't."

He walked down the street, feeling the Frenchman's eyes boring into his back. His nerves tightened enough to pull a hard knot between his shoulder blades. He'd better watch his step from now on. Furthermore, the merchant had been warned, and from here on would be more careful. Bull shrugged mentally. To hell with Sotello. His reaction said he was involved with the woman-stealing ring—but Bull couldn't see him as the brains behind the gang, nor could he see him as the leader of a bunch of dangerous gunmen.

He walked about the town another half-hour or so, then went back to the Lafitte House. Before doing anything else, he cleaned and oiled his guns, honed his knife, and filled his cartridge belt. Finally, he packed and rolled his bedding. He'd get provisions on the way out of town, including another box of .44 cartridges. He figured he'd need them—soon.

Malloy went directly to Megan's rooms, knocked, and at her "Come in" turned the knob, opened the door, and removed his hat. Megan was almost through straightening up when he entered. She pulled the sheet tight, smoothed it with the palm of her hand, and faced him. "Did the marshal wanting to see you have anything to do with the mess I found here? When you made a show of unlocking the front door, I suspected something. I could see it had been forced, and when I found my rooms ransacked, I knew Provo had already seen the mess they made."

"Ma'am, he wanted to let me know what happened. He killed both of 'em when they tried to leave. Said he couldn't see no sign of robbery."

Megan held her hands at her side, clenched them, then opened them palms outward. "Mr. Gunfighter, then why would they break into my saloon? There's nothing here to steal except liquor, and I can't believe a man would go to such lengths for a bottle."

Malloy stared at her a moment, his face feeling like a dry creek bed. "Miss Megan, I don't want to alarm you, but this must be said. Those men were after something much more precious than money—precious to me, at least. They were out to steal the most beautiful woman ever to get to this border country. Ma'am, they wanted you."

Megan maintained an icy calm, but her face took on a deathly pallor. "Then you and Mr. Burston haven't been making an unnecessary fuss over something that might happen. You've been quite certain all along that it would happen."

Malloy nodded. "Yes, ma'am, I've never had a doubt but what it would happen, and I've never doubted what their ultimate prize was. They apparently will go to any lengths to get you."

"But why? Why would I be their idea of a special prize?"

Malloy shifted his gaze to study the neat way she'd rearranged some articles on her dresser, then looked into her eyes. "Miss Megan, I've already told you. You're not only a beautiful woman, you're blonde. You would sell for a wagonload of pesos below the border. Pardon me for the use of the word, ma'am, but I'm going to make damned sure they don't lay a hand on you."

Megan walked to him, one slow step at a time, then placed her hand on his forearm. "Mr. Gunfighter, besides being a gentleman, and abhorring the idea of a woman being molested, why have you seemingly taken a fatherly interest in keeping me safe?"

His gaze never broke from hers. "Ma'am, my interest in keeping you out of harm's way is anything but fatherly. Someday I'll tell you of my interest—but not now. This is neither the time nor the place. I hope you'll wait, and listen when that day comes."

Her hand still rested on his forearm. Her breath came in shallow pants. "Oh, Mr. Gunfighter, I'll wait, and I'll listen. Perhaps by then I'll have determined who you are, and where I've known you. I can't help but believe that if I really have known you, I'd remember you."

Malloy slipped back into his Texas drawl. "Ma'am, you've known me, but right now I gotta do all I can to keep you safe." He stepped to the door, put his hat back on, and said over his shoulder, "Gonna go see if I can find somebody to fix the door them rannies broke."

Megan stood staring at the door long after Malloy had closed it. Who was he? Why had he taken such an interest in her safety? Oh, that was a dumb question! She knew why he wanted her safe. He was looking at her as a woman, as the woman she really was, not as the Ice Lady. Somehow he'd looked through her facade and seen that she was a woman of fire, not ice; a woman capable of giving, a woman wanting the giving to be returned, a woman wanting a strong, brave man, a man of principle. Still staring at the door, she wondered if the rough, tough, fearless man who'd left her only a moment before was that man.

She shook her head to clear such thoughts from it. It was ridiculous to let her mind encompass such an idea. She hardly knew the man, had known him only in dangerous situations, had never seen him in a formal gathering of ladies and gentlemen. She smiled. She didn't care how he'd shape up in a formal gathering as long as he stayed as he was.

While walking about New Orleans, Turnbull had had the feeling he was followed; now, on the way out of town, he was sure of it. He was also sure that as soon as they were far enough from town, whoever followed him would try to kill him. He'd done more than make Sotello wary, he'd scared him into making a fool move.

Bull made no effort to evade the man, or men, who followed. He wanted them to know where he made camp that night, and he had no doubt they'd try to rid the earth of him as soon as possible—but not before he went to sleep. He smiled. Hell, he'd played this game before. Prior to becoming a Texas Ranger, he'd seen the elephant and heard the owl. Let them come.

A couple of times during the long, steamy afternoon, he rounded bends in the trail, then doubled back to make sure his quarry still followed, his main objective to find how many were after him. The second time he took a look, the same three men he'd seen still followed.

He rode into the sun until it sank from sight behind a thick, swampy growth of cypress. While it was still light enough to hunt for a good campsite, he cast about on each side of the trail, looking for a dry spot on which to spread his blankets.

Every time he thought of sleeping here in this swamp

country, a chill ran up and down his spine—alligators and cottonmouth moccasins were as plentiful as the trees surrounding him. No, he'd stay here only long enough to take care of those who followed.

Finding a dry spot of ground was more difficult than he'd thought. He left the trail three times looking for the right place before finding what he wanted. A slight rise in the land allowed for a thick growth of palmetto and a few feet of wet ground, free of standing water.

He spread his groundsheet, unrolled his blanket atop it, then, with a few strokes of his Bowie knife, he cut enough palmetto fronds to roll into a bundle and place under his top blanket. He built a small fire, then walked to stand in murky water almost to his boot tops. He glanced toward the trail, satisfied himself that the small fire could be seen from there, then started the nerve-stretching, gut-churning wait.

While standing there, he imagined snakes wending their way around his boots. His skin crawled at the thought. He pulled his taut nerves under control, and then went tight all over again. 'Gators. What if an old bull 'gator was hunting? What if it attacked him?

Turnbull had seldom been afraid, and never of a man, but here he was in unfamiliar surroundings, unfamiliar enemies—hell, it was a foreign world. He brought to mind a favorite saying, "A man fears only that which is unknown." He again pulled his nerves together. Boy! When he saw Malloy again, he'd shove that damned deputy U.S. marshal's badge down his throat.

12

TURNBULL STOOD THERE for over an hour. Twice he heard the roar of a bull alligator, and each time his muscles tightened. His scalp tingled such that he felt as though his hair stood straight up. He considered packing up, climbing aboard his horse, and riding for Texas. Each time, he pulled his nerves together enough to make the decision to stay a little while longer.

Finally, he heard horses coming down the trail from New Orleans. The sound of hooves stopped abruptly. Bull forgot his fear of snakes and 'gators. The men chasing him had seen his fire. Now his only problem was, could he handle three men in a swampy shoot-out?

He'd been holding his Colt fully cocked in his right hand; now his left moved to his belt and drew his Bowie. He saw a man flit from behind a tree to the shelter of another. His finger tightened on the trigger, then relaxed. He'd set the trap to get all three men. He had to wait until they stood in the small circle of firelight, or the advantage would be with them, in their own land, with him standing in water boot-top deep. Hell, they'd get him in only a few minutes.

The sound of water and mud sucking at feet came clearly to him. Time dragged so slowly. As he began to wonder if they were homing in on his fire, the first man appeared. He stepped to the small knoll Turnbull had selected, closely followed by the other two.

When they'd gathered about his blanket, the second man whispered, "Hell, let's shoot 'im in his blankets."

The man closest to Bull vetoed that idea. "Naw, I wantta tell Sotello how he looked when he took our slugs. Maybe we can make 'im squirm, or maybe beg to be let go."

The third man said, "I ain't waitin'." With his words the ratcheting sound of his handgun coming to full cock was followed by the sound of a pistol shot. Bull thumbed off his first shot from where he stood, then moved silently to his right.

The man who had fired into his blanket dropped his pistol and fell across the bedding he'd fired into. Both of the others spun toward the sound of Turnbull's shot, firing wildly into the shadows in which Turnbull hid. The deputy marshal fired into the man closer to him, then moved again. The dim light showed a red splotch spreading across the second man's shirt. The last of the three grabbed handfuls of darkness above his head. His six-shooter dropped into the mud at his feet.

"Don't shoot no more, mister. I done dropped my gun."

"Turn yore back to me, an' keep yore hands high."

Bull searched the surrounding darkness, on the slim chance he'd missed seeing them all. Then, satisfied there were no more, he stepped into the circle of light, picked up the bandit's six-shooter, and slammed it against the man's head, then took his time collecting the other men's weapons. He glanced at the outlaw he'd knocked out, then,

satisfied the man wouldn't stir for quite a while, went looking for the horses. He found them only fifty or so yards
from his camp.

After collecting all their gear, Bull slung the unconscious
bandit across the saddle of one of the horses, tied his hands
and feet, then rolled his own gear in his blankets. He
glanced at the two men he'd shot, went through their pockets, and left them where they'd fallen. By morning there
would be little but scattered bones to tell they'd been there.

Leading his captive and the horses, Turnbull headed
toward Texas, determined to travel until he could smell
dust from the surrounding countryside. He rode until the
sky lightened in the east, then pushed the dark shadows of
the night farther under the trees. After forever, the fiery
sun's orb appeared. The deputy marshal sighed, determined to never leave Texas again.

The bandit slung across the saddle groaned. He'd been
letting out that sorrowful sound for several hours. Now full
daylight, Bull reined off the trail to a small clearing free of
brush, under the shade of mammoth trees. He tied his horse
to a low-hanging limb, looped the reins of the led horses
over his saddle horn, and went to the groaning outlaw. He
untied him and let him slide to the ground.

The bandit looked up at him, his eyes wide with terror.
"You gonna kill me, mister?"

"If I wuz gonna kill you, I'd of done it 'bout the second
time you bellowed out that pitiful groan you been sendin'
my way most o' the night." While talking, Bull gathered
wood for a fire, then he set his coffee pot close to it,
dumped in water from his canteen, along with grounds,
and squatted at the side of the outlaw. "Why'd Sotello send
you after me?"

"Don't know no Sotello. Ain't nobody sent us after you."

Turnbull drew and raised his Colt above the bandit's

head. "You keep on lyin', I'm gonna give you 'nother headache on top o' the one I already give ya."

The bandit groaned again. "No, please don't. Sotello figured you for a badge toter. Didn't know if you'd found out anything, but wasn't gonna take a chance. Don't know what he was afraid you'd learned. The three of us wasn't in on what he was doin'. He just hired us to trail you, an' once outta town far enough, he said to get rid o' you. He paid us twenty dollars apiece. My twenty's in my left-hand pocket. You done got what them others had. Ain't none of us had no more money than what Sotello paid us."

Turnbull gave the man a jerky nod. He believed what he'd heard. He went about preparing breakfast, ate, and headed for the nearest town. He didn't feed his prisoner; he'd turn him over to the law as soon as he found a law-man. Then he'd head for San Antonio.

Megan told Malloy and Burston to go about their business, that she knew they had things to do other than sit in the Buckle and watch her and the girls. It was midafter-noon—no one would dare raid a place of business at that time of day.

Malloy and the rancher had been gone about an hour when her nerves tightened. At first she wondered at the tenseness gripping her, then realized that, one by one, several men had wandered in, men different from the hard-working cowboys and cattlemen who usually drank there. These men were dirty, unshaven, and boisterous, and obvi-ously all of them were hard cases. Of course they could have only now returned from a trail drive, but that thought didn't relieve her tension. She studied them a few moments, then went to her rooms, strapped a double-barreled derringer high on her right thigh, and to her left thigh she strapped a slim stiletto. She'd always worn these weapons when gambling on the riverboats, and had only recently discarded them because of the care The Gunfighter and Burston were taking of her. She dropped her petticoat and dress skirt down to cover her legs, and returned to the bar area.

None of the rough-looking men sat or stood with each other. Her gaze swept the saloon. One stood just inside the batwing doors; another stood by the entrance to the hall that ran to the back door; three had placed themselves about midway along each wall; and two others stood at opposite ends of the bar. All held a drink in the hand on the side opposite to their holster.

She frowned. Most men would hold their drink in the hand they used to write, eat—or handle a gun. Trying to appear nonchalant, she walked slowly toward her big bouncer. When she was close enough to whisper, she said, "Jim, I believe we have trouble about to happen. Is your Greener handy?"

"Yes'm. I seen them rannies, an' figgered jest like you do. I got both barrels o' that Greener loaded with buckshot."

"If trouble comes, Jim, please don't hurt any of the townspeople or cowboys. I'll try to get the girls together so we can keep them safe."

"Ma'am, I wuz you, I'd leave 'em scattered around the room like they are. Be harder fer anybody to gather 'em in."

Megan, in the middle of agreeing with her bouncer, stopped. A soft voice, only loud enough for those in the room to hear, said, "Now all you folks stand steady. Ain't nobody gonna get hurt."

Megan swiveled her head toward the voice. A big man, taller than any man close to him, stood at the end of the bar closer to the door. He held a six-shooter in his right hand, and his drink in the other. A glance at the others of his kind showed each of them holding a gun.

"Now folks, jest stand fast—all 'cept you women. Y'all come over here by me. Don't raise yore voices. Don't none o' you scream, or I'll put a slug through yore head, you heah?"

His voice stopped while the women edged over to him. Megan stayed next to her bouncer. The man who'd done all the talking looked at her. "You, too, ma'am, you the one we want most of all. Git over here."

Megan walked toward him, hoping Jim didn't try to use his shotgun. She'd almost reached the outlaw when her hopes died. The bellow of the Greener shattered the silence inside the saloon—then the other barrel belched along with the sharp crack of handguns coming to life.

Everything in Megan's mind and vision slowed. Jim fell, his chest blossomed red. Other guns about the room barked, and men fell. The outlaws pushed and herded the women toward the door. Megan moved as though the nightmare that enfolded her belonged to another world. She tried to keep the girls together, tried to keep them safe—but what did "safe" mean? Then, the women bunched, the outlaws gathered around them. All gunfire ceased. The saloon's customers were obviously fearful of hitting the girls.

Pushed, shoved, and then picked up and thrown into saddles, the women were outside and headed toward the Rio Grande before any of the townspeople could comprehend what had happened.

Megan's thought went to The Gunfighter. Where was he? Would he come wading into these ruthless bandits single-handed? She had no doubt he'd come, but when? Where? Would he find them soon enough to keep the women from treatment worse than death? It never entered her mind that he wouldn't be able to handle the situation. Why was she not terrified? Her only answer was that The Gunfighter would come. She knew he would.

Before any organized pursuit could be pulled together, the horses of the bandits and girls sloshed across the river—beyond the safety of United States law.

Malloy picked up his coffee cup, about to take a swallow, then stopped and lowered the cup to the table. That twin roar he heard was from a shotgun. A cowboy raising hell would use his handgun. He stood, his chair crashing backward into the wall. On the run toward the door, he yelled to the café owner "Pay you when I get back."

On the street, shots coming from the direction of the Buckle now sounded like a full-scale shoot-out. He headed that way, but came up short when several horses came at him, all mounted, all running like somebody lit a fire under their tails.

He pulled his Colt, thumbed back the hammer, then lowered it. There were a number of women astride the horses in the middle of the group. He dared not fire. In the lead of the women rode Megan. He dropped his handgun back in its holster and sprinted toward the saloon.

Inside, men lay bleeding on the floor, some groaning, others staring with sightless eyes at the ceiling, others cursing and yelling at each other to collect a posse. Malloy wheeled and headed for the cabin he shared with Burston.

He burst in on the rancher, who was just rolling out of his bunk. "What's goin' on? I thought I heard a whole bunch o' shootin'."

"You did. They got Miss Megan and the girls." Malloy threw clothes and trail gear into a blanket while he talked. "Go to the livery and saddle my horse, then bring me a packhorse. I got a idea this here's gonna be more'n a day or two's ride."

By now, Burston duplicated Malloy's actions. "Saddle yore own horse. You an' me are gonna ride together."

"You damned fool, you'll get yoreself killed. Stay here—I'm goin' alone."

"Like hell. You'll have to shoot me to keep me here. I'm goin'."

Malloy didn't argue further. When he had his blanket rolled, he grabbed a coffee pot, a cooking pot, a slab of bacon, a few tins of beans, tins of peaches, flour, coffee, and other things he knew he'd need. The last things he packed were three boxes of .44 shells. He looked at Burston. "If you ain't ready, I'm leavin' you."

"I'm ready. Let's go."

Loaded down with the gear they'd just packed, the two men headed for the livery. There they divided the stuff, packed the packsaddle, toed the stirrup, and headed south.

The Rio Grande was low; any runoff from the rain the other night had long since flowed downriver. They crossed the shallow ford at a run. On the other side, a small Mexican boy yelled and pointed. "They go that way, señores. Many riders. Many señoritas with them."

Malloy pulled rein, dug in his pocket for a cartwheel, and tossed it to the urchin. "*Gracias, niño.* Did they not go into the town of Nuevo Laredo?"

"No, señor, they ride around the town, and continue on."

Malloy thanked the boy again, and nodded his head in the direction they were to ride. Burston kicked his horse into a run.

"No, amigo, slow down. We'll only kill our horses if we try to catch them."

Burston pulled rein, and slowed for Malloy to catch him. "You're right, but if we let them get too far ahead, they might have a chance to turn the girls over to others of their gang."

Malloy stared between his horse's ears, then shook his head. "No. I figure they got the prize they been after all along. They ain't gonna turn her over to nobody 'til they can collect the full price for her. Whoever's runnin' this show probably told them to do just that. An' if he ain't with 'em, he's told 'em to bring the money directly back to him." He pushed his hat to the back of his head, mopped his brow with his bandanna, then pulled his hat down over his eyes. "I figure we gonna have a long, hot ride. You bring them four extra canteens?"

At Burston's nod, Malloy urged his horse to a faster pace. They circled Nuevo Laredo and picked up sign of a large body of horses being ridden at a fast pace, but not fast enough to wear them down in a hurry.

Malloy looked at Burston. "Gonna tell you how it is, cowboy. I'm runnin' this show from here on. Gonna tell you why. Manhuntin' is my game. I been doin' it for quite a spell now, an' I know how they think, act, and smell. You cain't accept that, turn around an' head back."

The rancher nodded. "That's the way it'll be, but I'm here to tell you right now, I ain't no tenderfoot. You gonna have to trust me to know what to do in tight jams."

The Gunfighter nodded. "All right, partner. Let's get on with it."

The tracks were easy to follow. The bandits didn't ride like they expected pursuit, but kept up the long, ground-eating pace with which they'd crossed the border. Malloy reined in and studied their tracks. "Looks like they're headed for Monterrey, an' maybe from there to Saltillo." He rolled his tongue around in his mouth to collect the dust, now mud, that had collected during the hot afternoon. He spit, frowned, and continued staring at the tracks.

If he'd made a raid like those in front of him, would he assume there would be no one following? He thought about that for a moment, then shook his head, and twisted in his saddle to look at Burston. "Cowboy, we ain't gonna stay on this trail, we're goin' out in the chaparral. Gonna be hard ridin', but I figure it might keep us alive. They might send a couple o' riders back to cover their backsides."

Burston grinned. "Got to thinkin' the same thing a while ago. Let's go."

They reined off the trail into the thick brush. Roan Malloy snorted to clear his nose and throat of dust, then made another decision. "Burston, ain't gonna tell you my whole name, but for now you can call me Roan." He grinned. "I tell you my last name, an' you'll remember where you knew me. Fact is, the less you can admit to knowin' 'bout me, the better off you'll be. It might keep them varmints from killin' you—if they get ahold o' you."

Burston nodded, then, his voice only a croak from the dust collected in his throat, said, "Okay, Roan. That's how it'll be."

They wended their way through the chaparral the rest of the man-killing hot day. Then Malloy called a halt. "Gonna fix some supper. Then we gonna move our camp a good mile from where we do our cookin'."

"Why? You think they can follow us since we cut off the trail?"

"Ain't no doubt about that. We ain't the only ones who grew up fightin' Injuns, rustlers, and pure-dee mean outlaws."

Roan used water sparingly, but tonight he figured to have a good cup of coffee. He filled the pot and set it beside the small fire Burston had made. "While you rustle us up some supper, cowboy, I'm gonna backtrack a ways. See if we might be followed." He twisted to move around the fire.

That movement saved him. A shot split the air and cut ears off a prickly pear cactus. Malloy hit the ground, rolled, and came to his knees with his .44 in hand. Burston was nowhere to be seen. Then, from behind a huge old yucca, a .44 bellowed. The bullet came nowhere close to him. Burston had entered the fight.

When Malloy rolled to his knees, he found himself behind a clump of prickly pear. He glanced to his back, saw nothing of danger, then brought his gaze back to the side of the camp from which the shot had been fired. There had been only the one shot. His search for telltale powder smoke came up dry. He swept the area again, but saw only the tangle of brush.

Malloy was not a patient man, but he'd learned to squelch his urge always to keep moving, keep doing. Now was a time for staying still, waiting the other men out. He hoped Burston would stay where he was until the outlaws made a noise, or moved.

He squatted on his knees. They first got sore, then numb. Sweat ran in rivulets down his face. His shirt and jeans were soaked, and the moisture felt good on his sunbaked body. After about an hour, he grinned to himself. He'd been worried that Burston would make a move or do something dumb. Not that cowboy. He hadn't given a hint as to where he went to earth. Malloy's opinion of the rancher went up several notches. Burston was not only a fighting man, but he knew how to do it the right way.

Another half-hour passed, then Roan thought he saw a bit of red cloth behind a yucca about twenty-five feet away. Hoping for more of the man to show, Malloy combed his memory for what color clothes Burston was wearing. He shook his head. He couldn't remember. He'd have to wait until he knew who he was shooting at.

A few minutes later, the splotch of cloth withdrew, then an arm came into view. Malloy waited. The man apparently shifted his weight again, and his shoulder and part of his chest came into view. The shoulder did not have the square look that Burston's had.

Malloy took careful aim, inside the shoulder and as far down on the chest as he could see plainly. He had been holding his Colt cocked; now he squeezed the trigger. A blue hole appeared below and inside the shirt pocket. Malloy saw red ring the hole as he threw himself to the ground.

Two rolling shots knocked holes in the large ears of the prickly pear, then three shots, sounding almost as one, came from where the first two shots sounded. A man—a Texan, judging by his dress—lurched from the brush, firing his handgun as fast as he could pull the trigger. His shots kicked up dirt not far from his feet.

"Looks like we got 'em both, Roan."

"Stay where you are. There might be more of 'em."

"Nope. That's all of 'em. I seen 'em when they took that first shot at you."

Malloy didn't doubt what the rancher said. His actions in the last couple of hours had convinced him that Burston would do to ride the river with. He stepped into the open. "Okay, cowboy." He glanced at the coffee pot. The coffee simmered in it, sizzling when it hit the hot, dry sides of the pot. "Reckon we can have our coffee now. Then we gotta move on."

Burston stood staring at Malloy. "Roan, you'd a made a damned good Apache. I wuz hopin' you'd stay still 'til they made the first move." He nodded. "You did."

Malloy grinned. "I was hopin' the same 'bout you. You'd a made a good Ranger."

Burston shook his head. "Naw, I tried that. Decided a man could get killed doin' that kind o' work. Figgered ranchin' wuz a lot tamer. Them longhorns give a man a little warnin' 'fore they hit the end o' yore rope." He glanced at the coffee pot. "Let's drink and get the hell outta here."

Two hours later, riding parallel to the Monterrey trail in the dark, Malloy pulled up. "We gonna stop, cook ourselves some supper, get a good night's sleep, then hit the trail 'fore daylight.

Burston nodded.

Any inclination Megan Dolan had to let fear overcome her drowned in the hot blood flooding her veins. Anger forced out fear, leaving only hatred and contempt for the bandits. Her greatest concern now was her girls. If any of that trash touched one of them, she might lose her chastity, her life, but she'd protect them as far as she could.

The derringer riding on her thigh caused a raw, chafing discomfort, as did the stiletto, but they also gave her a small feeling of security. While they rode, she studied the bandits. They all spoke English, if what they spoke could be called English. It was a mixture of Texan and southern white trash, along with the most horrible profanity she'd ever heard. Looking at them made her ashamed to be an American, for that's what they were—the riffraff of the Southern States.

She ignored the heat that pounded at her back all the long afternoon. Perspire? No. She sweat, despite being a lady.

The sinking sun gave no respite from the heat. The lower the sun, the more a slight fear grew that they'd camp somewhere along the trail in the chaparral. And if the men had anything to drink in their saddlebags, it would not take much whisky to bring out the animal in them. What would she do then? That small gun on her thigh could take care of no more than two of the beasts.

The sun, about half swallowed by the horizon, brought a scorched, sunbaked look to the terrain, a grayness that burnished the yucca, prickly pear, and ocatillo. If anything could bring depression down on her more than this land, she couldn't think what it would be. Then, right in the middle of this horrid land, a town rose out of the distance. It showed white against the gray of the desert. Megan's hopes rose. Surely there would be some decent people there, people who would perhaps question the lawlessness of these ruffians herding women about as though they were cattle.

The closer they drew to the town—she'd heard one of the bandits call it Naranjo, the more her hopes died. The town was only a collection of jacales huddled around a square, with a few broken-down benches under some scraggly trees. The townspeople were mostly peons: ragged, dressed in a material that looked like white canvas. None of them appeared to be armed. Her hopes for help hit bottom.

Her gaze swept the square. One building looked as though it had care, and money behind its ownership. A sign painted on the adobe wall read La Paloma, Tienda Y Cantina—The Dove, Store and Saloon. Megan's spirits rose a little.

The band reined in at the front of the saloon, pulled the women from their horses, and pushed them inside. The smell of peppers, meat frying, coffee, and leather goods permeated the interior. Hunger pushed its way past the concern Megan had been feeding on for the past few hours.

A good-looking, red-haired woman, with big brown eyes a person could drown in, came to meet the outlaws. "Ah, vaqueros, it has been a long time since you visit my humble business. What is it you need—tequila, food, women? I have whatever you hunger for."

The big American, whom Megan had identified in her mind as the leader of the outlaws, nodded. "*Si*, Señorita Ulla, we want it all. As you can see, we have women with us, but we are not allowed to take them to bed. The boss will kill any of us who touches one of them, especially that blonde bitch there in the middle."

The leader spoke as though he thought none of his captives spoke Spanish. Megan did, as did most of the women with her. They'd all grown up in New Orleans, and spoke French, English, and Spanish. When the man said they were not allowed to touch any of them, Megan felt much of the tension leave the girls. She hadn't realized it, but she, too, had been holding herself tense since entering the cantina. She whispered, hoping no one but the girls could hear, "Do not any of you let on you can speak Spanish. *Sabe?*"

The bandit leader slapped Ulla on her well-shaped rear. "First get us a *cerveza*, two of them for each, then we can start on the tequila. I want these women in a room for the night. Feed them, and give them whatever they want to drink—but put them where they can't get away. If one of them escapes, I'll take you along with them. *Comprende?*"

"Ah, vaquero, you have stopped here many times, and never has one of your little doves flown away. Do not worry, señor, none will escape."

Megan's hopes plummeted. She had hoped she'd find at least a small amount of sympathy in another woman, but Ulla was as good as an accomplice. Any chance to escape rested within the small group of women—or perhaps The Gunfighter would get to them in time. Her mind wouldn't accept the idea that he might not come.

Her thoughts shifted to the proprietress of the saloon. Ulla, that was a German name. What was a German woman doing in the middle of the Mexican desert? Yes, she was running a bordello, but why here? She pondered that puzzle until two beautiful señoritas brought trays loaded with food. They left and returned with wine, beer, and tequila.

The food was delicious: tortillas, beef, goat, frijoles, and a vegetable that was unknown to Megan. At least the bandits did not intend to starve them.

The room in which the girls were placed was devoid of furniture. The air was stale, there were no windows, and the floor was of packed dirt. Ulla brought them each a blanket to sleep on, hesitated, and, obviously wanting to talk, looked at Megan. "I don't want you to get up any false hopes, señorita. I will not help you." She spoke in Spanish.

"Miss, do you not speak English?" Megan shrugged. "That is the only language I have at my disposal."

Ulla gave her a long, studied stare. "I do not believe you, lady, but yes, I speak English. I'll lay it out for you in your language. I will not help you. I'm allowed to stay in business here only because I help men like those who brought you here. When Maximilian's forces overran Mexico, my parents were killed. When Juarez won the war, I was allowed to stay, provided I stepped on no toes. And since his death, I have found that I can survive quite well by helping men satisfy their animal hungers." She shrugged. "I've found that men everywhere are the same: satisfy their stomachs, or what lies between their legs, and I can get along with any of them."

Megan stared at her a moment. "I feel sorry for you. If you've never met a man who liked you for your heart, your mind, your spirit, and your personality, you've missed a great deal in life."

A sad but hard smile broke the corners of the madam's mouth. "You might consider that perhaps I've never met a man I *wanted* to care for me."

"I hadn't either, until very recently. Now I know there are men, or at least one or two men, I trust. They aren't my friends just for what they think I will give them."

Again that hard smile creased the madam's face. "Don't

bet on it, lady. All men want something from a woman while they don't give much, if anything, in return." Ulla walked from the room. When the door closed, a lock rattled against its bulk.

Megan stood a moment, staring at the door, then turned her attention to the girls. "Keep your courage, my friends. If there is anything we can do to slow those animals out there, we'll do it."

"But what will slowing them get us, Miss Dolan?"

Megan shook her head. "I don't know. It might give some of us a chance to get away—or it might give The Gunfighter a chance to catch up with us." She shrugged. "I don't know what one man could do to free us, but somehow I have faith that he will come, and that he'll find a way."

Morning came with no letup in the heat. While Malloy scouted the area, Burston cooked breakfast. After eating, the marshal and rancher saddled, packed, and rode.

The sun, almost straight overhead, eliminated any semblance of shadows. Snakes, lizards, all forms of life disappeared under rocks or into holes, taking shelter from the heat. The only moving things were the two men, their horses, and their pack animals. Burston pushed his hat back and mopped his brow. "Gunfighter, you get the idea we're the only two damned fools in this piece o' hell we're ridin' across?"

Looking into the distance, trying to see through the shimmering, ghostly dance of heat waves, Malloy nodded ahead. "You know of any town down here we oughtta be gettin' close to?"

"Yeah, they's a place, not much of a town, called Naranjo. We outta be comin' up to it right soon."

Malloy looked down the trail and said, "You reckon that's it?"

The rancher pressed his lids together, obviously trying to rid his eyes of sweat. He grinned. "Yep, that's it. They's a cantina there, run by a German woman. Don't trust 'er. Them who spend time in this country say she has a special tie-in with every Mexican *bandido* in these parts."

"You know 'er?"

Burston shook his head. "Cain't say as how I do. I met 'er once when I wuz down this way to buy some cattle. She might remember me."

Malloy's face creased in a grin wide enough to break the crust of sweat-laden dust on his cheeks. "Good. That's our excuse for bein' here. We come down here to look for a good buy in cattle. I'm your *segundo*. I ain't gonna let on I can talk Mexican. She pro'bly knows you do."

Burston nodded. "Good, we'll play it that way. Now let's go get a beer an' see what we can learn."

When they pulled rein in front of La Paloma, Malloy nodded to the ground. "Notice anythin'?"

"Yep. They wuz a bunch o' horses at this hitch rack not more'n a day ago. Them horse apples ain't even had time to dry out."

"Wantta bet them horses wuz rode by a bunch o' men with women ridin' along against their will?"

After tying their horses, they walked to the veranda, slapped dust from their clothes, and pushed through the batwings.

A voice from the end of the bar said, "Welcome, Señor Burston. Have you come to buy more cattle?"

Burston's eyes, only then allowing him to penetrate the darkened interior, sought and found Ulla. "*Si*, señorita. I have taken on a partner an' more land since I last saw you. We need more cows." He spoke in broken border Mexican.

Burston looked at Malloy and, speaking in English, said, "This here's Bart Mabin, my partner an' *segundo*.

Bart, that's the handsome woman I wuz tellin' you 'bout. That's Ulla. She ain't got no other name I know of."

Ulla walked to meet them. "Ulla's good enough." She stepped back and scanned Malloy from head to foot. "My, but you're a big un, and handsome as any man I ever saw, despite that beard hiding your face."

"Aw, now, ma'am, you can quit joshin' me. I ain't got nothin' to buy no cows with, Mr. Burston's the one with it. All I got is cow savvy."

Smiling, but her voice serious, Ulla looked at Malloy. "Señor, I hope you have some woman savvy. I got the idea we could become close friends."

Malloy nodded. "Friends never hurt nobody, ma'am, but a good start would be somethin' to eat, an' a cool *cerveza*."

Ulla turned to one of her girls and spoke in rapid Spanish. Within minutes, food and beer were served. Ulla, without an invitation, sat at the table.

Malloy glanced around. "Figured they'd be a whole bunch o' vaqueros in here outta the heat."

Ulla gave an exaggerated sigh. "No, hombre, business is bad." She shrugged. "But it is always like this when the vaqueros have not been paid for a few weeks."

Malloy did not look at Burston, afraid the madam would see it, and know she had been caught in a lie.

13

MALLOY TOOK A swallow of beer, then a huge mouthful of beef, and used the time to think. Should he take the chance and ask the madam questions, or perhaps try to get her talking about herself and hope she'd divulge information about the person with whom she did business, and maybe what kind of business?

He decided to withhold any questions he might ask. Maybe he could lead her into talking. "Ma'am, this here's some small town, yet you seem to have a right nice bunch o' customers. What made you figure they'd be enough money comin' in to let you stay in business?"

She raised her eyebrows. "Let's say I just got tired of large cities. Monterrey was growin' too fast, an' most of the people there were poor. The men with money to spend were businessmen, and most of them were married." She laughed. "I thought a place where there were hardworking, lonesome vaqueros who would want good food, drinks, and women might be a smart place to build. It's worked out."

Burston nodded. "Told you Ulla was not only a good-lookin' woman, but smart, too."

They ate mostly in silence after that. Malloy didn't push his luck. He figured before Ulla would say much about the real reason she was out here, he'd have to get to know her a lot better. His mission was to get the girls and Megan back, and then to find who ran the operation and eliminate them. One thing at a time was all he could hope to accomplish—and Megan was first priority.

They finished eating, drank another *cerveza*, and told Ulla they'd better get moving. They wanted to buy a herd and get them north of the border before winter set in. They left, and outside, Burston allowed as how the madam would be a complicated puzzle. Malloy gave him a hard smile. "Well, partner, we found out a couple of things. She's a helluva good liar, an' whatever her hookup with the bandits is, she ain't tellin'."

Ulla watched Malloy and Burston push through the doors, untie their horses, and lead them to the watering trough. That big man roused unwanted stirrings in her. If she let herself, and he was going to be around long enough, she'd get to know him better. Along with those thoughts, a small warning bell sounded in the back of her mind. She held onto the La Paloma by not seeing anything, knowing anything, or talking about anything. If she did, the man who'd put her in business would not hesitate to have her killed. She feared him like Satan himself. He had men everywhere, and to her mind knew everything that went on from San Antonio to Mexico City. She shivered despite the heat. She feared the man north of the border, but it would be mighty nice to get to know that big devil who only moments ago walked out of her cantina.

• • •

The middle of the afternoon, Malloy reined in alongside the trail. "You notice anything strange, partner?"

Burston frowned. "You mean them we're chasin' don't seem to be in no hurry to git where they're goin'?"

Malloy nodded. "Not only that, they done changed directions. Ain't nothin' out this way I ever heard of."

"Yeah, there is. They's some mighty fine ranchos out this way. They got haciendas on 'em like I hear them rich folks back east have, or like the plantation owners had before the War 'Tween the States. Fact is, I bought a herd o' pretty good cattle out this way once."

"You don't b'lieve they tryin' to throw us off the scent by wanderin' around out here?"

Burston grinned. "Nope. They got no reason to try to throw us off. All they gotta do, if they figger we're fol-lowin' 'em, is send back enough men and eliminate us. Fact is, they pro'bly figger them two we killed back yon-der already got rid o' us."

Malloy nodded. "Reckon we better keep followin' 'em then. Hope them women are still all right."

"Only way we gonna know that is to get close enough to see how they're bein' treated."

Getting close, that was what worried Malloy. These ranches out here were like fortresses: high adobe walls around the haciendas, armed vaqueros, and sentries. These old Spanish dons were like feudal lords.

Malloy and Burston followed the easy-to-read sign the bandits left. Malloy scanned the horizon every few min-utes. The rancher cast him a frowning look. "What you keep lookin' off in the distance for?"

"Dust cloud. Reckon a dust cloud would tell us when we're gettin' too close. That many horses we're followin' would sure as the devil raise a right nice cloud. I ain't anxious to get too close to them varmints yet. We do, an' we won't be seein' them women—or nothin' else—ever again."

Riding off the trail a couple of hundred feet, the two wended their way around greasewood, cactus, and yucca. Malloy pulled his canteen from the saddle horn, hefted it, shook it, then shook his head. They'd filled four canteens apiece before leaving Ulla and La Paloma. Neither of them had emptied the first one—and didn't intend to, unless they found another place to fill them. Malloy ran his tongue across his lips, tasted the bitter alkali dust, and felt the cracked skin. Then he ran his tongue around the inside of his mouth, spit cotton, and hung his canteen back on the horn.

He slanted a look at Burston. "In yore travels down here, you ever hear of a stream, or a pothole of good drinkin' water?"

The rancher nodded. "Up ahead 'bout ten miles, they's some rocks. A spring wells out from under one o' 'em. That is, it did the last time I wuz out this way." He shook his head. "Hot as it's been, with no rain, I ain't countin' on there bein' anythin' there." His face hardened. " 'Sides that, them *bandidos* might take a notion to camp there for the night. Don't know of any rancho they can reach this afternoon."

Malloy studied on that a few moments, then decided there was something good about everything. If they couldn't have a wet camp, they might be able to scout the bandits and see how many there were, and how well they guarded the women. They'd also see how the women were being treated. The thought of them touching Megan brought hot blood to his head.

Sweat that earlier had soaked their shirts now dried to a muddy crust. The bandanna with which Malloy mopped his brow wiped more dust across his neck and face. They rode another two hours before the sun dipped its bottom edge into the distant mountains.

Burston glanced at Malloy. "Roan, we gettin' mighty close to them rocks I wuz tellin' you 'bout. We better git down an' walk 'til we see a fire, or git close enough to scout the spring an' see if we get to sleep by it tonight." He squinted ahead. "We stay on our horses, we gonna be high enough for them to see us skylined 'fore we see them."

Malloy stepped from the saddle and led his horse forward. He'd not gone ten feet when he stopped, shook his head, frowned, and said, "If we're that close, you stay here with the horses. I'll slip on ahead, an' see what I can see." He passed the reins of his horse to Burston, pulled his Winchester from his boot, and, the thick dust of the desert floor cushioning his steps, moved ahead.

Careful to avoid stepping on dried greasewood, and sticking to ground clear of cactus rubble, Malloy scouted for twenty minutes before he heard voices talking in what some would call English. He eased to his stomach and inched forward. The man who was talking said, "Wonder why Buck an' Dudley ain't caught up with us by now. Reckon they run into trouble?"

Another voice. "Naw. They ain't nobody crazy enough to follow us into this here country. Figger them two stopped at Miss Ulla's place to suck up some o' her beer, an' maybe satisfy some o' them cravin's that got started in their stomachs by lookin' at these fillies we brung with us. Boss won't let us mess with them, so why not mess with the ones what ain't gonna git us killed?"

"Yeah, reckon you're right."

Every movement slow, Malloy took off his hat and moved around a Spanish dagger that spread its needlelike thorns in a circle of about seven feet. He peered around its base, then quickly drew his head back. The bandit's camp spread along the base of the rocks. Close to the middle boulder, which he figured stood about eight feet high, the women were bunched in a tight little circle. Megan sat in the middle. None talked; they only sat and stared, hollow-eyed, from one bandit to another. Megan was the only one who looked as though she sought for a way out of their mess. Her eyes swept the bandits, who were sitting close enough together that each could reach the bottle being passed around when it came his way. Her eyes then looked as though they studied the surrounding brush. They moved slowly from one clump of desert growth to another—then stopped. She stared directly into Malloy's eyes, then quickly looked away. Even under the deadly burden of what was planned for all of them, a slight smile broke the corners of her mouth.

Pride swelled Malloy's chest, his throat tightened around the knot that formed in it. If God had ever made a perfect woman, she sat there in front of him, surrounded by the other captives.

He eased back from where he lay. He'd found what he came for. The women were all right, but the bottle being passed around bothered him. Would the outlaws get drunk enough to let their passions control them? He could only hope not. He and Burston would have to wait for a better time, perhaps when the women had been delivered to who-ever was to receive them, a time when perhaps only one or two bandits guarded them.

Knowing where the camp was, and that he and Burston would have a dry camp that night, Malloy recaptured his hat and returned to where Burston held the horses in only half the time it had taken him to slip up on the outlaws. Twilight had settled in when he walked up to Burston. "We

ain't spendin' no time around that spring tonight, partner."
He pushed his hat to the back of his head. "For now, them
girls an' Miss Megan are all right. Don't seem like the ones
who have them are of a mind to mess with 'em. Let's back
down the trail a ways an' make camp where we can have a
fire an' some hot food."

Burston studied Malloy through hot eyes. "Roan, we
gotta try to git 'em free. Ain't no tellin' when them bastards gonna git to lookin' at 'em, an' maybe let themselves
ferget any orders they got." He slapped his thigh. "We
gotta do somethin'."

Malloy shook his head. "We go bargin' in there an' git
ourselves killed, we ain't gonna do them women no good
whatsoever. Know how you feel, partner. I felt the same
way when I looked at 'em, all hot, dusty, and tired, but we
gotta wait for the right time."

Burston's shoulders drooped. "Damn, Roan, don't know
if I can stand to wait for that time."

A hard smile broke the corners of Malloy's lips. "We
gotta."

Even with the torrid temperature, Megan felt a chill go up
her spine that almost pushed a sound of joy from her lips.
Her eyes held The Gunfighter's only a second, but affirmed
what she'd known all along. He would be there when the
right time came to get her and the girls away from the vermin that held them. She leaned toward the closest girl to
tell her there was hope, then pulled back. If she told one of
them, soon they would all know, and there was a good
chance some would change their attitude enough to alert
the bandits. She leaned back against the rock, the slight
smile lingering.

She listened to every word the bandits said, knowing

that some of it would be of use to The Gunfighter when—
and if—he managed to break them free. The name she
heard most often was Bentley. The name meant nothing to
her, but she felt certain he was in some position of leadership, and the name might mean something to The
Gunfighter.

She thought on the name "Gunfighter" for a moment. It
was a hard name, a name most avoided, even those who
deserved it, but the tall man she knew seemed not to mind.
She found that she thought of it as a somewhat endearing
term after knowing the man who wore it. She smiled again.

She knew Burston cared for her, and she liked him—a
lot—but liking was all it was. She also knew that she had
feelings for The Gunfighter, much stronger feelings, but
was not ready to admit to anything more than gratitude and
admiration for a brave man. She shrugged mentally. Time
would tell. After all, he'd shown only an attitude of respon-
sibility and liking for her as a strong woman. For now that
was enough.

New Orleans was mentioned by one of the outlaws. Her
mind returned to listening to what they talked about. This
time she heard only the city mentioned, but no names to go
with it. One of the bandits broke into her thoughts when he
brought a plate of food, untied her hands, and placed the
tin plate in her hands.

Soon after eating, she and the girls were again tied, and
tossed a blanket. Megan had watched the men consume several bottles of tequila, and had been worried about what the
alcohol would do to their desire. The tossed blankets calmed
her fears. After curling up under it she heard more talk.
From it she gathered that on the morrow they would arrive
at some place important to them. She snuggled down under
the blanket. The desert had cooled with the coming of night.

• • •

Malloy pushed his blanket down, and crawled from under it. Burston was up, and had gathered enough wood from the desert scrub oak to have a small smokeless fire.

The rancher opened a couple of tins of beans, placed them close to the coals, and waited while Malloy sliced a few strips of bacon and readied the coffee.

During breakfast, Malloy looked from under his hat brim. "Burston, we gonna drop back a ways today. Ain't gonna take a chance on our dust givin' us away. We'll wait'll they get well away from the spring, go set by it while that thin stream fills the sump, then fill our canteens, water the horses, and follow whatever sign they leave." He took a good bite of bacon and a forkful of beans, chewed a moment, then took a swallow of coffee to wash it all down. He made a swiping motion with his fork. "I got a feelin' they gonna reach some sort o' town or a rancho 'fore sundown. Hope it's a town; we need to give these horses a rest and a good bit o' grain if we gonna keep goin'. Stoppin' at a rancho ain't gonna give us a chance to do neither."

Burston stared at his boot toes a few seconds, then looked straight at Malloy. "Roan, all you an' me been thinkin' of is gittin' them women free. We better be worryin' 'bout gittin' some extra horses—twice as many as we got bodies to fill saddles, so's we can run when the time comes."

Malloy shrugged. "Reckon we gonna have to figure a way to steal some. And, like you said, we ain't been thinkin' past the end o' our noses. We gotta have them horses ready to travel when we git the girls."

They finished eating, saddled, and headed for the spring. Before getting there, Malloy dismounted and went ahead on foot to see if the bandits had left. They had. He climbed to the top of the largest boulder and scanned the horizon. Far out, seven or eight miles by his best guess, a dust cloud billowed. He cupped his hands and yelled for Burston to come on in.

At the spring they waited for the sump to fill, watered the horses, then filled their canteens. Malloy glanced from the horses to the rancher. "Where you reckon they're headed?"

"They's a few ranchos out here, but I know most o' these people, an' don't figure they gonna help a bunch o' outlaws steal women." He pushed his hat back and squinted into the distance. "A town of sorts is farther down, real small place, maybe a cantina, a place to get somethin' to eat, an' a 'dobe shack to bed down in. The settlement is called Candela. I'd say that might be our best chance o' gittin' close enough to maybe try somethin'."

"What 'bout horses?"

"Nothin'."

"You know anythin' 'bout what's on the other side o' that town?"

Burston shook his head. "Nope. Never made it that far down. Way I got it figgered, we better git somethin' done at that town, or we ain't got much hope after that."

"Reckon we'll do what we gotta do." Malloy stood, tightened the cinches on the horses, toed the stirrup, and waited for Burston to fall in alongside. After a while, he looked across his shoulder at the rancher. "I'm gittin' a idea 'bout horses, an' how we gonna get them women free, but first I gotta see the town. We can plan from there.

Turnbull rode into San Antonio tired, dusty, hungry, and thirsty. He figured if he had anything to say about it, he wouldn't be going back to New Orleans anytime soon—or ever. He decided to satisfy his thirst first, then eat and take a bath.

After a couple of cold beers, Bull sat sipping the third,

staring into his glass. There was a tie between New Orleans and San Antonio in this woman-stealing ring. He knew it, but he had only one end of the puzzle in his grasp. There had to be someone here who Sotello contacted when a good-looking bunch of fillies grabbed a stagecoach for San Antonio—but who? Then he thought of the telegram he'd found in the Lafitte House. He took it from his pocket and studied it a few moments. The initials stood for something—places, names, what?"

Now, food forgotten for the moment, Bull downed the rest of his beer and stood. He'd go see Barge, the telegraph operator and train station agent.

In only a few minutes he stood in front of the depot. He glanced at his watch. Train time was still hours away. Through the window, he saw no one in the station except Barge. He went in.

Barge looked up from some paperwork. "Somethin' I can do for you, Ranger?"

Bull nodded. "I want a copy of every telegram you got comin' in here, an' I want all them you got for the last two weeks."

Before he finished talking, Barge was shaking his head. "Cain't do that. What's on the wire is the business of only them who sent it, an' them who gets it."

Bull's eyes felt hard and mean to him. He wondered how they must look to Barge. "Gonna tell you somethin', mister. I didn't ask you to let me see all that paperwork, I told you I'm gonna see it." He placed his hands on the desk and leaned across to stare directly into the agent's eyes. "This here's law business. I'm gonna see them pieces o' paper, an' you ain't lettin' it go outta this depot that I'm seein' 'em. It works that way, or you go to jail right along with the ones I have to send to prison. *Sabe*, amigo?"

Barge swelled up like an old toad. Then, spitting and blustering, he said, "Don't you threaten me, Ranger. I'm a respectable citizen."

Bull looked at him a moment, then softened his voice. "You're respectable only so long as you stay within the law. Now I'm tellin' you, *no one, especially those who received them telegrams, is gonna know I'm lookin' at 'em. Sabe?* Now, hand 'em over."

While Barge went to a drawer and pulled a couple of sheafs of yellow paper from it, Bull watched the windows to make certain no curious person might be peering in.

The agent shuffled the papers together, making them as neat as he could before Turnbull took them from his hands. "I'm gonna need them papers back soon's you're through lookin' at 'em."

Turnbull nodded. "I'll be keepin' 'em a while—but you'll get 'em back." The ranger stepped toward the door, then looked back. "Tellin' you again, don't you tell nobody I got these."

He went out the door, walked to the nearest alley, and stepped into the darkness. A few moments later, Barge walked out the door, locked it, and went up the street. Bull followed.

The telegrapher went directly to Brent Clausen's general store. Bull waited for a good fifteen minutes before the agent reappeared, opening a fresh bag of Bull Durham tobacco. Turnbull shook his head. He had hoped the telegrapher would report to someone what had happened at the train station, but apparently he only needed to replenish his smoking tobacco. Bull turned toward his office. He'd spend the rest of the night, if need be, going through the stack of telegrams.

• • •

Malloy and Burston topped a knoll above the town of Candela a little after sundown. Lantern light painted the dirty windows of one adobe building. Malloy nodded to himself. That building had to be the cantina; everything else would be closed this time of night. While that thought passed through his mind, lights appeared in a window of another building. In the murky half-light he made it out to probably be the hotel: long, narrow, one-story adobe.

He looked at Burston. "Gonna go down there. See if maybe that long 'dobe is the one where they're holdin' the womenfolk." He removed his hat and hung it on the pommel. "While I'm down yonder, I figure to look the place over pretty good, find out where the horses are, an' about how many others in the town we might have to deal with." He grinned. "Reckon it ain't gonna hurt none if I find out how many of that trash is guardin' the women."

"Roan, you be damned careful down yonder. They get you, an' the women's chances gonna be cut right in half. Don't you want me to go with you?"

"No. You gotta hold the horses. Don't come down there 'less you know I done tied into more'n I could handle. Even then, stay outta it. You'll be the only one the women'll have left to get 'em outta that mess."

"All right, but I'm tellin' you again—be careful."

Roan stepped from the saddle, handed the reins to Burston, drew his Colt and shoved another cartridge into the cylinder, then headed down the hill toward the settlement.

He walked into the place behind what he discovered was the livery. The stable was full of horses munching hay and making new piles of horse apples. He'd found the horses— now to find the women.

The riders who'd stolen the girls were Texans, all dressed much as he was, so he made no effort here in the darkness of night to hide his movements. He walked down the dusty street, stepped around a dog who curled up in the middle, then headed toward the hotel.

Every nerve pulled tight as a bowstring, every sense seeking danger before it could hit him, Malloy walked as though he belonged here. He passed the hotel as though going to the edge of the settlement to relieve himself, then turned back to the side of the long adobe bulding.

Now every nerve stretched farther. He came alongside the building, searched for windows—and found only holes through which the hot desert air could pass. Now the tendons in his neck pulled tight on his head, his shoulder muscles tightened until they hurt, his gut churned. If the windows were not covered, there must be a guard outside to prevent the women from escaping through the openings. He froze, held his body tight against the wall, and waited. The guard, if he was doing his job, would be walking the length of the wall. Malloy would wait for him to come to him.

His hand sought for, and found, his Bowie knife. The next second a dark shape loomed out of the darkness. The man had come abreast of him when Malloy swung the arm holding the Bowie. He'd gauged where the man's throat would be and prayed his estimate was right.

The knife made contact. Malloy held it tight against what it had found and drew it toward him. A warm gush of fluid poured over his arm and hand. Malloy knew he'd found the man's jugular. He caught the slumping body and eased it to the ground. Gurgling, sickening sounds came from the man's neck.

Malloy knew he'd better get rid of the body now. The moment it was discovered, every outlaw in the cantina would be combing the area for who did it. If the guard was simply missing, they'd figure he'd abandoned his post to go lay with one of the whores. But—he wanted to find exactly where the women were bedded down. He left the bandit where he'd fallen and went to each window, peered in, and went to the next.

The fourth opening he looked through, the dark bulk of several bodies showed, all lying in a row. He wanted to whisper a word of encouragement, but squelched the thought. He knew where they were. That was good enough for now.

Malloy dragged the body of the guard out into the chaparral, at least a half-mile, by his best guess, and left it for the coyotes. He went back to town and walked boldly down the trail to the front of the cantina. There he counted only three horses at the hitch rail; they probably belonged to vaqueros from an outlying rancho. He scanned the street and, seeing no one, walked to the edge of the settlement at a leisurely pace, then hit a long, ground-eating stride toward where he'd left Burston.

Before walking up on the rancher, Malloy silently slipped close enough to see the outline of the horses and one man etched against the night sky. "Burston, it's me, Roan. I'm comin' in."

It took only a few minutes to tell Burston what he'd found in the town, where the horses were being kept, and where the women were located. Then he laid out his plan of how they would try to rescue them.

Burston pushed his hat to the back of his head, then squatted and rocked back and forth on his heels. "Man, you got a lot o' faith in what two men can do aginst a bunch o' hard cases." He chuckled. "But reckon I never figgered to live forever. When we gonna do this?"

Malloy squatted by the rancher's side. "We gonna do it

tonight. We might not have as good a chance again." He reached out and touched Burston's arm. "An' cowboy, we gotta live long enough to get them women back north of the Rio Grande."

14

TURNBULL HUNCHED CLOSE to the lantern he'd placed on his desk, shuffled through the telegrams, made two piles of them, then pushed one of the stacks to the side. The telegrams he pulled in front of him were all from New Orleans. He would give the other stack a closer look later, but for now he wanted to look for a tie-in with the river city.

Several of the messages told of shipments of goods being sent to San Antonio, a few were from family members advising of impending visits, and fifteen were written in the same kind of code as the message he'd found in the Lafitte House.

After about an hour, he pulled his heavy, silver railroad watch from his vest and glanced at it; twelve o'clock. He sighed. He'd give these a closer look after the sun came up; reading by lamplight would put a man's eyes out right soon.

As he was about to shove the telegrams in his desk drawer, heavy footsteps sounded out on the boardwalk, and the door swung inward. He turned the stacks of telegrams over. Shug Bentley, the town marshal, slouched over to stand in front of Bull's desk. "Workin' late, Ranger?" Then, without being invited to take a chair, he sat. "Wuz makin' my rounds an' seen yore light. Thought you might have a pot o' coffee brewin'." While he talked, his eyes never strayed from the stacks of telegrams. "Them looks like the kinda sheets the telegraph operator uses. What good they to you?"

Turnbull felt a rush of impatience, and a slight burst of anger push blood to his face. He looked into the town marshal's eyes. "Let's just say I didn't have nothin' else to read, so, to kill time, I figured to read these. I'm tired o' readin' all them Wanted notices."

Bentley's eyes still focused on the stacks of messages, almost as though trying to see where they were from. When Turnbull deliberately picked up each stack, put one on top of the other, and shoved them into the top drawer of his desk, it was the town marshal's turn to show anger. His face stiffened, flushed in the lantern glow, and his jaw muscles knotted. "If them pieces o' paper got anythin' to do with the law, I'm gonna tell you right now, I'm the law in this here town."

Bull stared into the marshal's eyes, then cut him a hard grin. "Bentley, you ain't tellin' me nothin'. You got law problems, then they're yours an' SanTone's. What I do ain't none o' your damned business. Got that? Now get the hell outta my office, an' come back after the sun's up. I'm goin' to bed." He stood, letting the town marshal know that if he'd any business in here, it was over.

Bentley's face turned even redder, his shoulders stiffened, and he stomped from the office, slamming the door as he left.

Turnbull stared at the door a moment, frowning. Why had Bentley gotten so angry when he refused to discuss the telegrams with him? Why had he dropped by this time of night for a cup of coffee? They never drank coffee, or anything else, together. Besides, the café down the street gave any officer of the law free coffee. They made good coffee, and it was always freshly brewed.

Still frowning, he went to the window, drew the blinds, then went back to his desk and removed the telegrams. He pushed a .44 shell from his belt and placed it on top of other papers in the drawer. He then pushed the stack of telegrams inside his shirt, pulled out his chair, and sat staring at the wall a few moments. Despite his orders, that damned Barge had spread the word that the Ranger was looking at all telegrams. He stood, turned the lantern down and then out. He left the office, locking the door behind him.

Malloy and Burston reined in a few yards deep into the chaparral. Candela's closest building, the livery, stood within rock-throwing distance. Malloy put his face close to Burston's. "Gonna help you saddle them horses, then we gonna fill every canteen we can find on them saddles, then we gonna ease every horse in the stable out in the brush a little distance from the hotel. I want you to stand by the horses. I'm gonna put the new guard outta his misery, an' hope like the devil they haven't got excited 'bout that one I killed disappearin'. An' while I'm doin' all this hopin', I'm gonna hope they ain't increased the guard. If they have, I got a whole lot o' trouble."

"You sure you don't want me to go with you?"

Malloy shook his head. "Two of us'll maybe make a noise, an' be easier to see movin' around. Besides, if it comes to shootin', the horses might get skittish and bolt. They do that, ain't none o' us gonna get outta here alive. You stay with the horses."

They slipped into the stable and looked for the hostler. After a few seconds he came from the front to meet them.

"What you hombres want? I thought you'd all be swillin' that hog slop they put out down at the cantina."

Malloy frowned. The livery man spoke English. Maybe the whole town was run by Americans. In the dark, he stepped toward the hostler, drawing his Colt at the same time. Without even a "howdy-do," he swung his handgun up, then down. A good solid thump, and the man fell at his feet, his head bashed in.

"Think we oughtta tie 'im up, Roan? He wakes up, it's gonna be hell to pay."

Malloy bent, slipped his hands under the livery man's shoulders, and dragged him toward one of the stalls. Over his shoulder he answered Burston. "He ain't never gonna wake, cowboy. Now let's get these horses saddled."

They saddled enough horses for all the women and themselves, so they could give their own a rest. They put lead ropes on those horses that weren't carrying a saddle. Then, as though they belonged in the town, they slung canteens over their shoulders and headed for the well.

They had filled all but two of the canteens when a guttural voice sounded from the dark behind them. "What y'all doin' workin' out here this time o' night?"

Keeping his back to the voice, Malloy said, "Boss wants 'em filled, I do it."

The man made no noise leaving. Malloy didn't figure they'd have any trouble with him. They finished filling the canteens, then went back to the stable. They slung two canteens from the horn of each saddle, then led the horses into the brush.

Satisfied they were far enough from town, Malloy stopped. "Hold the horses right here, 'less you hear shootin'. If you do, wait a few minutes, an' if I don't show up with the women, head straight west about a mile, then wait. If I'm in a lot o' trouble, an' can fight my way outta it, I'll meet you there. I don't want these horses back in the hands of those outlaws. Our best chance is to set 'em afoot an' keep 'em there."

Impulsively, he gripped the cowboy's shoulder. "Partner, thanks for yore part in this." He released Burston's shoulder and turned his steps toward the town.

In less than ten minutes Malloy stood at the side of the hotel. He pressed his shoulders against the adobe wall and waited. His ears searched for man-type noises: the scrape of a boot against a rock, breathing, a cough. Then he tested the air for whiskey fumes, cigarette smoke, or the sour stink of an unwashed body. Finally, satisfied that there was no one close to him, he slipped silently along the sunbaked wall, careful to keep his jeans from scraping the rough surface.

After about ten feet, he stopped and listened again. Nothing. As he was about to move again, there was a slight scraping sound and the flare of a match.

The guard cupped the light in front of his face, puffed his cigarette to a glowing coal at its end, then blew the flame out. Now was the time to attack. The sentry would be blinded momentarily from the match flare. Malloy, holding his Bowie, glided silently to the side of the bandit and, pushing the knife straight out in front of him, slipped the blade hilt deep into the man's gut, worked the handle up and down a few times to cut everything the blade could reach. Then, holding the bandit spitted on his blade, he lowered him to the ground. He made no noise.

Leaving the man where he lay, Malloy straightened, stood for a moment, hoped there wasn't another sentry, and then waited a few moments more. Each moment seemed an eternity. He wanted to get on with getting the women out of their prison, but to rush things now could mean his and Burston's death, and eternal hell for the women.

He lifted his foot to step toward the opening through

which he'd last seen the women. Not five feet from him a man coughed, hacked, and spit, then said, "What the hell you doin' away from where you s'posed to be? Stay down there at the end o' the buildin' like you wuz told."

Making his voice as gruff as he could, and still be understood, Malloy grunted, "Need a lucifer."

In the murky darkness the man's hand went to his shirt pocket. That one moment gave Malloy the time he needed. His Bowie sliced through the night—and again a man died, his hand pinned to his pocket by Malloy's long blade.

Hoping there would be no more guards, Malloy went straight to the window through which he'd seen the women. A glance in both directions, and taking only a second to listen, he swung his leg across the thick wall framing the opening and, placing his finger to rigid, dry lips, said, "Shhhh."

Megan must have been waiting for the moment. In a quiet voice, little above a whisper, she told the girls to not utter a sound, but to do as they were told, quickly and quietly. Malloy's pride in her almost burst buttons from his shirt.

"I'll be outside the window and help the girls down; you get them to the opening as fast as you can. No noise." He slipped through the hole in the wall and held out his arms. Gently, he took each of the women in his arms and lowered her to the ground. Then came Megan.

Through all the dirt, sweat, and trail dust, her perfume told him he held her in his arms. He pulled her close for only a moment, every nerve, every ounce of flesh yearning to hold her forever. He swung her to the ground.

"Stay close. I don't know when the guards will be coming to relieve the ones that were there. Walk with as little noise as you can. No talking. All right, let's go." He moved toward where Burston held the horses, then stopped. "If I take a turn, right or left, y'all do the same. I'll lead you around the thorny, spiny plants out here. Megan, you bring up the rear and keep them close. Let's go."

At the horses, he and Burston lifted each girl to a saddle. "You women gotta be sore, and I know you're tired, but that ride down here prob'ly got you so you won't be as sore as the first day you left the border. We gonna ride fast and hard. Stay single file an' follow Burston; he'll get you outta the chaparral soon's he can. I'm gonna bring up the rear."

The words had barely left his mouth when a yell, and some of the foulest cursing he'd ever heard, came to him from the direction of the hotel.

"*Vamanos*, amigos, let's ride. Them *bandidos* back yonder are madder'n a nest o' hornets. They'll follow on foot if they have to." Malloy toed the stirrup, and pushed close to the last woman in line, Megan. "Keep it close, pretty lady. Gonna get you north of the Rio Grande without much rest."

Malloy stopped them after about an hour to blow the horses and let the women rest a few moments. He walked to where Burston held the reins of the unmounted horses. "Know what, partner? We gonna be followed right close."

"How you figger? We left 'em afoot."

Malloy chuckled. "Almost, but not altogether. Remember them three horses in front o' the cantina? Well, I figure them bandits took over ownership of them horses."

"Oh, damn! You reckon they'll catch us?"

"Yep. Ain't no doubt about it." He packed his pipe, put fire to it, then puffed quietly for a few moments. "Tell you what I'm gonna do. You keep headin' toward the river while I drop back a ways and see can I tie a can to their tails."

He lifted his leg to toe the stirrup, stopped, and looked at Burston. "Partner, case I don't join up with you 'fore

you cross the river, take these fillies to yore ranch, an' set
guards to protect them in case this scum follows."

Burston nodded. "You got it, Roan. Git back with us
soon's possible."

Malloy toed the stirrup and headed in the direction from
which they'd come. He hadn't ridden more than a quarter-
mile when the sound of horses being ridden fast overpow-
ered the sound of his own horse. He slowed, then dropped
off the side of his horse and pulled his Winchester from its
scabbard as he hit the ground running.

A glance showed no place to hide or protect himself
except old yuccas. At a trot, he led his horse to the plant he
selected to hide behind, pulled him to the ground at his
side, and leveled his rifle toward the fast-approaching
sounds.

Three riders, bent low over their horses' withers, pounded toward him. They were already well within range.
Malloy jerked his Winchester up and fired at the close-
grouped bunch. One of them flung up his hands, fell to the
ground, rolled, bounced a couple of times, then lay still.
The other two left their horses as though they'd been hit.
Malloy knew better. He hadn't fired at them, and neither
had been in line with the shot that knocked the first rider
off his horse.

The Gunfighter had a notion to change his position, then
decided not to. The bandits had been riding too fast to take
a bearing on where his shot came from. He held his position. Only his eyes moved, constantly searching the brush
about him.

For minutes that seemed to drag into years, he held his
stance and position. Nothing moved. A breeze rustled the
spiny plants around him, a puff of dust stirred about twenty feet out. His horse heaved a great sigh. With the sigh,
one of the bandits stepped into the open, and levered a shot

at the yucca in front of Malloy. The soft, pulpy wood did little to slow the bullets.

The bandit fired three times before Malloy's rifle began to spit lead. The outlaw was faster than he was accurate. Malloy put two slugs into his chest before he could get off another shot. Dust jumped from the bandit's shirt, and two holes close together told Malloy where his slugs had hit. He turned his attention to the last of the three.

The remaining outlaw stood out in the open only about ten feet from Malloy. He'd dropped his rifle and held a revolver in each hand, and each of the handguns spewed flame toward the marshal.

A heavy, pounding jolt hit Malloy in the side, another took his left leg from under him. While falling, he triggered his rifle, fired, jacked another shell into the chamber, and fired again. His attacker's weapons kept spewing lead, but now the shots went into the ground closer to his feet, then closer, until his body lay on top of his hands, still pulling triggers. He shuddered, straightened his legs, and lay still.

Malloy, numb from his shoulders to his knees, stared at the last man he'd shot. Then, without moving his body, his eyes found the others. None of them moved. Malloy tried to move, but he remained on the ground.

From experience, he knew this inability to make his muscles do his bidding was only temporary. But he also knew that with the return of control over his muscles, gut-wrenching pain would rob him of much of his strength and will to move. To give in to the pain and weakness meant giving up. He'd never given in to pain, but weakness was something else. He'd just have to do his best.

While lying there, waiting for muscle control to return, he watched the red stain cover more and more of his side. He couldn't see his leg, couldn't tell how bad it had taken lead; but if he didn't stop the bleeding from his side soon, it wouldn't make much difference how bad his leg was.

His stomach muscles spasmed, causing his arms to pull in close to his chest. Now he could use his arms. He pulled his bandanna from his neck and stuffed it inside his shirt. He felt his back and couldn't find a hole where the bullet had gone through. He lay back, exhausted.

He figured he'd never make it to the border, but where could he hole up? The only place he could think of was La Paloma, and the redheaded woman who ran it. But she was owned by the outlaws and the man who controlled them— whoever he was. He glanced at his side again and shrugged mentally. His alternative was to lie out here in the desert and die. He wouldn't accept that.

About thirty minutes later, Malloy sucked in a deep breath, crawled to the side of his horse, grabbed the saddle horn, and urged his horse to get to its feet. The big dun rolled, got his feet under him, and stood, dragging Malloy up with him. Roan had put his right leg across the saddle before the dun had rolled to stand. Now he sat the saddle.

His head swam, his eyes refused to focus, waves of pain washed over him. He grabbed the saddle horn and gripped it until his knuckles ached. He fought off nausea, swallowed several times, squeezed his eyes shut for a moment, then looked at his leg. The holes, front and back, were about four inches above his knee. It still bled but was not a gusher. He nodded, pulled his Bowie from its scabbard, and cut through the pant leg above the wound. He stripped the pant leg off and made a bandage of it.

The next hours were more hell than Roan believed a man should have to ever go through. Every step the dun took jarred his side, shooting pain through his body and setting off waves of nausea. Then the sun rose.

Through heat, pain, nausea, and fading in and out of consciousness, Roan stayed in the saddle, often reeling from side to side, threatening to fall, but knowing if he did, he'd die out here and only the coyotes, javelinas, and buzzards would know where he fell, or what happened to him. Through all of this, at the core of his thoughts, nightmares, and hallucinations, Megan seemed to urge him to hang on. She sat the saddle behind him, and when he felt certain he'd fall, she'd steady him until he could hold on. Then she'd disappear until his next need for her.

Malloy stayed in the saddle all through that day of sun hell, pain hell, and loss-of-awareness hell. Night, and a desert coolness set in to assuage some of his misery. He rode another few hours, then, not knowing whether what he saw was a mirage, the buildings of Naranjo rose out of the desert.

He reckoned daylight was not too far in the offing. He'd best get to La Paloma and see if he could rouse Ulla without stirring her entire staff into wakefulness. If he could keep his presence between only himself and the madam, she might have enough decency left in her to help him. No matter the consequences, he needed help.

His tired horse, head hanging, walked slowly to the rear of the cantina. Malloy sat there, afraid that if he tried to dismount, he'd fall and lie there until the town wakened. He muddled the thought around to call out—maybe he'd luck out and Ulla would be the one to answer.

Finally, his mind made up, he opened his mouth to try and get words past his dry, dust-crusted throat. No words came. He tried again, and all he could manage was a croak. Then the thing happened that he wanted least: someone other than Ulla found him. An old Mexican came around the corner of La Paloma, unbuttoning his trousers to relieve himself after sleeping.

The old man stopped, stared at Malloy a moment, rebuttoned his trousers, and hurried to his side. "Oh, señor, you 'ave been 'urt. Let me help you."

His voice sounding to him like it pushed past sharp stones, Malloy said, "Señorita Ulla—need her."

The man's look swept Malloy, then pinned him with a sharp look from eyes not dimmed by age. "The señorita has Americanos, bad men who come and go. It would be dangerous for you if they saw you. I recognize you from the other day. I don't think you are one of them."

To Malloy's pain-fogged mind, the man seemed not unfriendly. "Can you hide me?"

The old man reached for the dun's bridle. "*Si*, I will do what I can. We go now to my *jacal. Mi nombre es* Emilio." Leading the dun, the old man shuffled past the backs of the three stores, then out into the chaparral a few yards. Malloy saw an adobe shack, not much more than four walls with holes in each side to let what breeze blew go through the shanty. Its roof was of desert brush.

Emilio, using care not to hurt him, lowered Roan to the ground, took him by the shoulders, and dragged him into the shack. "I go now to 'ide 'orse."

He disappeared for about fifteen minutes, and when he returned, he had a handful of spikes from one of the desert plants. Malloy had heard them called aloe vera. Supposedly they were good for healing.

Emilio broke the spines and pressed the gooey sap inside them into the bullet holes, then he tore Malloy's shirt into strips and bound the wounds. Roan thought that if infection from all the filth Emilio bound to his wounds didn't kill him, he'd live to be a hundred.

The old man took a gourd from beside the door, dipped it into a rusty bucket, and brought Malloy water. He replaced the gourd and looked at his patient. "I go now to clean the cantina. Bring food when sun is low."

Malloy lay there and sweated throughout the long afternoon. Despite the filth, the heat, and loss of blood, he felt better toward sundown, but was thirsty enough to spit cotton by the time Emilio returned. The first thing he did was go to the water bucket and bring Roan a drink, then, squatting on his heels by Malloy's side, he told him that all the Americanos had left, but he thought they'd be back in a couple of days. He said they headed toward the west. Candela lay to the west. Roan hoped that by the time they could get horses for their friends, Burston would have the women at his ranch.

Emilio touched Malloy's shoulder. "Señor, the señorita say she come after all vaqueros are gone from the cantina." Roan opened his mouth to ask if she could be trusted. The old man, apparently reading his thoughts, nodded. "The señorita does what she must for the hombre in Norte America. She will not tell of your 'iding place. She will know more how to take care of you than do I."

Roan took another few swallows of water, then muttered, "Sleepy—very sleepy." He closed his eyes, wondering that he trusted Emilio and Ulla. A strange pair at best, one a peon and the other a whorehouse madam. Regardless of his reservations, his life was in their hands. He went to sleep.

His first awareness upon awakening was of a cool cloth pressed to his forehead, then a soft hand—a woman's hand—replaced the cloth. He recognized Ulla's voice. She spoke in Spanish. "Emilio, he has no fever. Whatever you did for him was good. I need help getting him to my rooms in the cantina. Will you help me?"

"*Si*, señorita, but it will be very dangerous for you if 'e is found there."

"No one, not even the Americanos, comes into my rooms. I will take care of him. You will say nothing of this, *comprende?*"

"*Si*. There are many good hombres from north of the border, but your friends are not among them."

"Old man, they are not my friends. I'm very afraid of them, so afraid that I know I'm letting myself in for a great deal of misery if I'm caught doing this. This hombre may be a rancher, but I sense that he is also a very dangerous man."

"*Si*, the way he wears that big gun of his tells me that, too, señorita. We will be careful."

"Miss Ulla, I listened to you and Emilio. Don't put yourself in a bad position for me. Let me rest here with the old man a day or two, then I'll head for Laredo."

"Nonsense. I've made up my mind. You'll be cared for by me, in my rooms. When you are well enough, and there are no border trash to contend with, Emilio will bring your horse." She gave him another drink of water. "When all is quiet after I close the cantina, I'll be back for you."

When she'd gone, Roan lay there, wondering how an old man and a woman could manage to get him to the saloon. He didn't sleep. Time dragged, and after hours— Malloy figured it to be about three in the morning—a scraping sounded outside the jacal. He slipped his Colt from its holster, which Emilio had placed at his side. He waited.

"Señor, it is us, the señorita and me, Emilio. We have come for you."

The dragging sound again, and the old man ducked through the low door, dragging a travois. Roan wondered if the two of them planned to drag him to the cantina on the blankets slung between the two poles. They dragged it a few feet from the doorway of the shack, then tied the ends of the poles to a saddle mounted on the back of the smallest burro Malloy had ever seen. He thought he should be carrying the burro rather than the small animal dragging him. But it worked.

They got him to the back of the cantina, then, with both

of them grunting and swearing, they got him through the door and into Ulla's rooms. "Damn, big man, I don't know why I admired your size so much. Probably wouldn't have if I'd known I was gonna have to half-carry, half-drag you so far."

"Miss Ulla, reach in my pocket, left-hand one, an' give Emilio two or three dollars for all the work and worry he's gone to. I'll find some way to pay you later."

Ulla lighted a lamp and, smiling, looked him square in the eye. "Big man, you let me worry about how you can pay me. The fact is, I've got a pretty good idea how that debt will be paid."

Looking at her smile, and the glance she passed down his body, pulled Malloy's nerves tight. Maybe he'd been better off trying to reach the border on his own. But his glance also took in her lush figure. He sighed. What a man might have to go through to pay his debts! He, too, smiled.

15

TURNBULL PUT THE coffee pot on the stove, raked the ash-coated coals to life, then picked up the stack of telegrams. He laid the one he'd taken from the bandit's room in New Orleans by the side of each of those written in the childish code. He found it easy to determine that the SA referred to San Antonio because the letters were always used in conjunction with "go to" or "leave," but the other initials bothered him. The GS he assigned to Grafton Sotello, but he hated to give in to his suspicions about the SB. He didn't like Shug Bentley, but hesitated to lay the crimes around here at the door of a man wearing a badge.

He pondered the way Bentley had stared at the stack of telegrams the night before. Finally he nodded. All right, he would assume that the town marshal was part of the gang—for now—but he wasn't ready to give Bentley credit for having enough sense to run and control a gang of outlaws like the one stealing women.

He studied the GS, shook his head, and cursed. Sotello might have the brains, but he was too far from the center of action. He finally decided they both worked for someone, and that someone was in, or close to, San Antonio. He wished for one other set of initials—those of the boss bandit.

Before he could get tangled up in the puzzle further, a knock shook the flimsy door of his room. Bull yelled, "C'mon in, it ain't locked."

Barge stepped inside. "Gotta telegram for you, Ranger." His demeanor suggested that he was pleased with the message he brought. He tossed the telegram to the desk in front of Turnbull but his eyes swept the stack of those he'd given the Ranger the night before.

Bull tore the envelope open, read the words on the yellow sheet, and swallowed twice to try to rid himself of the anger swelling his throat. The message read: "Mr. Brent Clausen reports you are bullying the town's most prominent citizens. Stop. Headquarters does not condone behavior of that nature. Stop. Any further report of actions such as these and disciplinary action will be taken. Stop." It was signed "Captain Rawlins."

Turnbull glanced up at Barge, who stood there trying to smother a huge grin. "What the hell are you grinnin' at? You find somethin' about this message you like? Well, gonna tell you, what it says don't mean a damn thing to me. I'll do what I have to do."

Barge motioned to the stack of telegrams he'd reluctantly given Bull the night before. "I'll take them sheets I give you last night. I need 'em in my files."

Turnbull shook his head. "Nope, you'll git 'em back when I'm through with 'em. I ain't through with 'em. Now get the hell outta my room." With his words barely out of his mouth, Bull pushed to his feet. Barge hurriedly backed through the door.

Bull stared at the door a moment, went to the coffee pot,

and poured a cup of coffee, a little ashamed of bullying the worm who had brought him the telegram. He looked at the stack of messages, shook his head, and wondered how he'd determine the real leader of the gang. Whoever he was, he'd woven a pretty good web of deception. He'd have to think on it.

Burston headed the ladies toward the border at as fast a pace as he dared. They had all of the outlaws' horses, so they changed to fresh horses about every hour.

He noticed Megan casting a look to their back trail every few minutes. He knew she looked for Roan. He tried to tell himself that her concern was no more than what she'd feel for any friend—but in his heart he knew better. He rode up alongside.

"Miss Megan, The Gunfighter's gonna be all right. He might even be leadin' them outlaws away from us at this very minute." He nodded. "Yep, that's what I figger he's doin'. He thinks that way."

Megan looked across her shoulder at him. "Thanks, Mr. Burston, I know you're trying to make me feel better. But The Gunfighter isn't the sort of man to dodge trouble. If they do manage to get horses and trail us, I wouldn't put it past him to ride right into the middle of them, shooting with one hand and swinging that big knife he carries with the other."

Burston tried to force a grin, but knew he failed. He nodded. "Yes'm, reckon you're right. The heck of it is, he don't never know when he's up against bad odds. He'd charge hell with a beer mug full o' water."

Megan glanced to the rear again. "Mr. Burston, next time we stop to rest the horses, why don't you draw me a map of how to find your ranch, and you go back to see if you can help him?"

Burston swallowed hard. She was willing to put him in

jeopardy to help Roan. He was coming up a bad second in his hopes for winning her hand. He shook his head, and urged his horse to a faster pace. "No, ma'am. The Gunfighter told me to get y'all safe to my place." His jaw muscles tightened. "That, ma'am, is exactly what I'm gonna do. Then, if he ain't showed up, I'll head back down here to find 'im." Neither of them said anything more. Then he eased his horse closer to hers. "Ma'am, we done knowed each other quite a spell now. Don't you reckon you could call me Clint?"

"Why, of course, Mr., uh, Clint."

Burston drove them mercilessly for the rest of the afternoon, and well into the night. They crossed the Rio Grande about eleven o'clock by his reckoning. Then, on U.S. soil, he led them into the chaparral until he found a clear area to make camp. He reined in, looked at the girls, and felt a twinge of regret. They sat their saddles, heads drooping, holding onto their saddle horns to keep from falling off.

He stepped from the saddle and helped each of them to the ground. "Ladies, I'm sorry I drove y'all so hard, but what waited for you down yonder was a whole lot worse. Stiffen yore backbone a little, and feel good 'bout bein' this close to home."

"How close are we, Mr. Burston?"

The rancher pushed his hat to the back of his head, squinted into the distance to the west, then nodded. "Well, ma'am, I reckon if we rode another hour, we'd be there, but I ain't gonna ask a single one o' you to climb back in the saddle, not tired as y'all are."

Megan turned to look at the girls. "You heard Mr. Burston. His ranch is about an hour from here. We're an hour from a hot meal, a bath, maybe a bed. You think we might be able to climb back in those saddles and ride another hour?"

Without a word, each girl walked to her horse, pulled herself to the saddle, and in unison they said, "Let's ride." Their voices sounded like they'd not ridden a mile. Burston smiled into the darkness. Hope was a wonderful thing. It gave a person a wellspring of strength he didn't know he had.

He pulled his horse alongside of Megan's, toed the stirrup, swung up, and looked at her. "Gotta tell you, ma'am, I'm gonna add 'bout a half-hour to our ride. We'll ride right into Laredo so our tracks'll lead any who follow to the livery—then we head for my ranch. Once there, I've got enough men to take care of 'em."

After that they rode in dead silence. The spurt of energy following his promise to get the girls to his ranch soon lasted only about a half-hour. They rode as though half dead.

Burston led them into the dark maw of the livery, changed saddles to fresh horses kept there by his *segundo*, and they headed out.

Even though the saloons were running full blast, an American, half drunk and stumbling toward another watering hole, saw them enter the livery. He changed route to report what he'd seen to his boss.

Malloy wakened tired and hurting, but he felt like he already healed faster than he figured Ulla would admit possible.

He thought about the redhead. She was a luscious, desirable woman, and had already as much as told him he didn't have to worry about the *bandido*—as long as he paid her the kind of toll she would demand. Of course she hadn't said it in so many words, but even an idiot could have read her meaning.

His thoughts shifted to Megan Dolan, a woman nothing like the madam he now stayed with. She had let him see the real woman under the icy facade she showed the world. She could laugh, cry, have feelings for people—as she had shown she had for her girls—and he had a hunch a slow, glowing fire burned in her, waiting for the right man to bring the fire to an inferno. He intended to be that man. But for now he had to deal with Ulla, and he had no idea how to accomplish letting her down easy enough that he wouldn't hurt her feelings. He suspected she could be as vicious as she was desirable.

He rolled over. The bed was soft, too soft; he was accustomed to sleeping on the ground, and liked a hard surface to sleep on. The bed was one he would have picked for Ulla after seeing her only once. It was as soft and embracing as he imagined her arms would be, one that would be hard from which to escape once it wrapped itself around a man. The thought sent chills down his spine. He might be in as bad a situation as he would be if the *bandidos* had him in their grasp. He struggled to his side and swung his feet to the floor. A moan escaped him.

Light footsteps sounded outside his door. He grasped his side and leaned into his wound. Ulla found him sitting like that. "Here, now, what're you trying to do?" She rushed to his side, thrust one arm under his legs, lifted, and swung him back into bed. "You're not in any shape to try sitting or getting out of bed. Now you lie still until I can prepare breakfast for you." She turned toward the door. "I'll tell my cook I'm getting breakfast for myself and will eat in my room." She laughed. "She'll like that. She has enough to do, cooking for the women who work here." She stepped to the door, peered around the casing, looked over her shoulder, and said, "Stay in bed. I'll be back as soon as I can." She left, closing the door softly behind her.

Malloy grimaced. He'd faked pain when she came in. It

had not been hard to do, though he had been hurt many times and had made a habit of concealing his feelings. Hell, it almost felt good to give way to them.

Her visit had reinforced his opinion that it might be harder to get away from her than he wished. And he had no idea where the old man had stashed his horse.

Now his mind began to function the way he'd trained it to do for many years. His eyes swung from the bed to the rest of the room. It was furnished in good taste, not what he expected a madam's taste to be. The style of the day was massive, heavy furnishings. The chairs and settee were of that style. Curtains of heavy brocade bordered the only window. A washstand with a heavy, white porcelain bowl and pitcher sitting atop it stood in a corner. A small room, the door open, had a four-footed bathtub in its center. He could see no window there, and assumed there wasn't one due to the darkness of the area. His eyes swung to the chair at his bedside. His belt holding his holster, handgun, and Bowie knife hung from the arm.

Malloy stared at his weapons a moment. Where was his Winchester? He thought on that a moment, then decided the old man had left it in its saddle scabbard. He thought about the old man a moment. How far could he trust Emilio? Then he grinned. A few silver pesos should solve that problem—if the old man was not too loyal to Ulla. The light tread he associated with Ulla approached.

She came in carrying a tray loaded with food: eggs, salsa, tortillas, ham, jelly, and fried potatoes. Malloy stared at the tray a moment, then looked into Ulla's eyes. "Ma'am, you feed me like this, I'll grow to be big an' fat as a old sow I seen once."

She pushed a couple of tsk-tsks through her pretty lips. A smile showed behind her eyes. "Now, vaquero, that would purely be a shame. A shame to put fat on that big, beautiful body." She shook her head. "No, you can bet I'll not fatten you. I like what I see right now."

She placed a towel across his chest, smoothed the sheet around him, and sat on the edge of the bed. "I'll feed you. Moving your arm might pull on your wound and start it bleeding again."

"Aw, now, ma'am, ain't no need for you doin' such. I'll feed myself."

"You'll do nothing of the kind. Now behave, and open your mouth."

Ulla insisted on this routine for the next couple of days. During that time Malloy wondered when the outlaws would come back, or at least come this way hunting him. They had surely found the ones he had killed, and would be searching every inch of the desert for him. And, during that time, when Ulla had other things to do, he stretched, flexed, and moved his shoulder, stomach, and side muscles until they pained so bad he had to stop—but he was healing and regaining the strength that loss of blood had taken from him. He was careful when the madam was with him to act as though he still hurt badly.

Then on the third day Ulla, when she came from the room in which she had slept since giving up her bed to him, moved to the side of his bed, pulled the sheets back, and looked at his wounds. He'd long since gotten over the modesty inherent in him. He lay there, stripped of all clothing and sense of shame, while her long, slim fingers tenderly traced the scabbed-over holes. Her eyes lifted from inspecting the wounds to lock with his. "You're about well enough that I can move into my own bed again." The slight smile that crinkled the corners of her lips left no doubt in Malloy's mind what she intended. He chose to put a different meaning on her words and look.

"Ma'am, I shore am sorry to have put you out so much.

I reckon I can get ahold o' Emilio, get my horse, an' head for home."

Ulla's smile widened. "You'll do no such thing. You'll stay right here. This bed is plenty large enough for the both of us."

Malloy's gut tightened. Heat flooded his body. His sense of decency fought against desire. How was he to get out of this? He wanted to go to Megan with no sense of guilt. He wanted to court her, let her know he loved her in the purest sense. He couldn't do that if he gave in to the desire showing in Ulla's eyes. He'd have to feign pain as well as some of those actors he'd seen in New York.

"Ma'am, I reckon I ain't ever had such a tempting offer in my life, but I just flat don't think I can manage to do what I reckon we both want—yet. You reckon we can wait a couple more days?"

The smile still showing behind her eyes, but disappointment shadowing it, Ulla traced her fingers down his body, settled on his scars, then curled the hair on his chest around her ring finger. "Big man, I think it'll be a hard thing to do, but yes, I'll wait. I want nothing to intefere with the quality of what you have to give." She stood. "But I'm tellin' you right now. I'll wait two more days, and during that time I'll share that bed with you. I'll not insist that anything happen, but at the end of two days, I believe you'll be healthy again." She stepped toward the door. This time her tread was not as light as before.

Burston led the women from the livery at as hard a pace as he dared. They could not stand more. Although Megan had tried to hide her fatigue, he knew from the weariness his own muscles were feeling that she must be on the verge of dropping. But a bullet would permanently end all feeling. He had to get them safely to his ranch. He had no doubt that, the saloons being crowded with the rough bunch, one or two prying pairs of eyes had seen them either enter town or leave.

After about an hour and a half, he strained to see the soft glow of lantern light, although he doubted there would be a lighted lantern this time of night. All of his men would be in their bunks resting for what the next day would bring. The life of a cowboy was never an easy one.

They topped a hill, and even though he couldn't see his ranch buildings in the dark, he knew they were there. He recognized the hill. "Ladies, a few more minutes and we'll be home. No baths tonight; just fall into bed as you are, and sleep as long as your tired bodies demand. I'll have bathwater ready for all of you when you waken."

A few minutes later, a challenge came from the dark alongside the trail. "Who rides this time of night? Sing out. Who are you?"

"It's me, Burston. Stay here on watch while I take these tired ladies to the house."

Only a few moments afterward, he escorted the women into his home. "Like I said, ladies, crawl into bed as you are. The bedrooms're right down that hall. Double up however you want, get up after you've gotten your bodies rested." He turned to look at Megan. "That there room's yores." He pointed to the first room off the big living area.

She looked at him a moment. "You're not going back to find The Gunfighter, are you?"

He shook his head. "No, ma'am. He told me to get y'all back here to my ranch, and to keep you safe. That's what I'm gonna do."

Her shoulders slumped even more. She looked into his eyes, hers swimming behind a veil of tears. She nodded and headed for the room he'd indicated as hers.

Megan shut the door behind her, glanced around the

room at the massive bed, chest, and chifforobe. Then her eyes came to rest on the large porcelain pitcher and bowl beside it. Tired as she was, she stripped to the waist and sponged her body and face to rid them of some of the trail dust and sweat. Then, feeling only a bit cleaner, she went to the massive bed and fell into it, asleep before she could pull the sheets up to her chin.

The next day, noise from the front of the house awakened her. Light in the room was dim. She wondered that she'd wakened so early after the hard ride. She rolled to her side, then sat on the edge of the bed, for how long she didn't know. When she cast her eyes about again, the room was darker. Feeling drugged from the hard sleep, she realized the sun was setting, not rising. She'd slept through the day.

Standing, Megan slipped on the dirty clothes from the day before, then went into the hall. A young Mexican girl almost bumped into her. "Ah, señorita, you are awake. Do you wish to eat first or have your bath? The water is already warmed."

Megan smiled. "I don't think, even as hungry as I am, that I could eat until I get this dirt off of me and get dressed in clean clothes." She nodded. "Get me the bathwater first."

She'd said "clean clothes." Whose clothes? She decided that maybe Burston had sent someone to the cabins to gather clothes for all of them.

She sat in the warm water, letting it soak into her tired body. Her mind was on The Gunfighter. Where was he? Had he been hurt? That thought caused her chest to tighten, and her throat and mouth to dry. Maybe he'd come in during the night. That thought caused her to hurry and finish her bath. As she stepped from the tub, scattered gunshots broke the stillness of nightfall.

Without bothering to completely dry her body, she

dressed and rushed into the living room. Men stood at each window; all had rifles, and all peered through the gun slots of the lowered wooden shutters. None of the men fired randomly. Each watched carefully before squeezing off his shots. Megan walked to the gun cabinet, pulled an 1873 Winchester from it, checked it for loads, and scooped up a handful of shells. She dropped them into her pocket and went to a window.

The first night Ulla crawled into bed beside him, Malloy moved far enough to the side of the bed to worry that another inch and he'd fall to the floor. Ulla followed. "Big man, I'll not insist that we have more than this—tonight or tomorrow night, but after that we *will* act as two healthy humans would. Now move back to take the space you need to be comfortable."

Every muscle tense, Malloy did as he was directed. He knew that to spurn her would mean instant retaliation. Any of the bandits in the area would be directed to him. He lay awake long into the night, long enough for Ulla to go to sleep, and later to drape one shapely leg across his body. He made up his mind then to take a chance on Emilio helping him.

The old Mexican cleaned his room every morning. That would be the time for Malloy to see if he could be bought.

The next morning, Ulla opened her eyes to stare into Malloy's, which had hardly closed all night. She smiled a slow, lazy smile, ran tender fingers down his beard-stubbled cheek, then kissed the tips of her fingers and touched them to his lips. "Now, big man, one more night like this and then . . ." Leaving her sentence unfinished, she swung her feet to the floor, not at all shy of showing her nudity. Malloy stared at the wall. She laughed a throaty, low chuckle and reached for her robe.

By now Malloy knew her routine. She'd bathe, dress, and go into the cantina for the rest of the day. Emilio should be coming to clean soon after she left the room.

An hour later, Ulla went through the door and Emilio, who must have been waiting outside, came in. Before he could take the damp mop to clean the dust from the tile floor, Malloy crooked a finger at him. "Amigo, come, we must talk."

"Señor, if I do not get this room clean and get back into the cantina, the señorita will have my hide."

"Emilio, what will it cost me for you to get my horse and put him, saddled and ready to ride, at the back of the cantina after it closes?"

Before he finished, the old man was shaking his head. "No, señor, if I do that without the señorita telling me to, she will have me killed."

Malloy thought a moment, then pinned Emilio with a gaze. "You are from around here, old one?"

"No, señor, I come from the mountains to the west. My people are Yaquis. I come here to make *dinero* to buy the things we cannot make with our hands." He shrugged. "It is a hard time we have of it, señor. By the time I pay for my food, there is little left for my people."

Malloy stood, walked to where his clothes rested on the seat of the chair from which his gunbelt hung. He picked up his trousers, unbuttoned a flap in the waistband, and ran his finger down into the pocket. Several days before, he had checked to be sure his money was undisturbed. His finger rolled an American double eagle into his palm, then another, and another, until he had six.

He held his hand out so the old man could see what lay within its grip. "How long it take you to make this much?"

Emilio's eyes bugged, he looked from the shiny coins to Malloy. In a hushed tone he said, "Señor, three, maybe four years I work for that much, and little of it gets to my people." He shook his head. "I will not live long enough, two times over, to make that kind of money."

Malloy closed his fist around the coins. "These will be yours—if you do as I say." He slipped the coins back into the waistband pocket, then looked at Emilio again. "You must steal yourself a *caballo*, a good one to ride to the mountains. Bring my horse and yours to the back of the cantina after it is closed. I will pay you then, and you can ride toward your home. I'll take my horse toward *Norteamérica*.

"If I do as you say, amigo, we may both be killed."

The use of the word "friend" gave Malloy hope he'd convinced the old man to do as he said. "Amigo, what is life worth as we are now living it?" He spread his hands. "*Nada*."

Emilio backed toward the door, his eyes fixed on where Malloy had stashed the gold coins. "How do I know I can trust you, señor?"

Malloy had considered the same question, as to whether he could trust the Mexican. He shrugged. "Old man, we are both in a situation where at some point we have to trust someone. You have my horse, I have gold you can use. I say we are both gambling that the other will do as he says."

Before reaching the door, Emilio stopped, frowned, still staring at the trousers where the American had stashed the gold. Malloy's heart beat a little faster. He'd caused the old man to think.

Emilio hesitated another few moments, then returned to the center of the room, picked up the mop, and swung it across the tiles. He stopped and looked at Malloy. "Tell me your plan, señor."

"It is a simple plan, old one. Work just as you do every

day. Then, when all have left the cantina, leave for your home as usual. Instead, go to my horse and bring him. There will be horses, good horses, at the livery belonging to those who will spend the night here. Take the best of those there and bring him to the back of the cantina where you have left my *caballo*. I'll be there to meet you. I pay you, and we ride away."

Emilio frowned. "It sounds too easy, amigo. What if something goes wrong?"

"Anything goes wrong, I'll give you the money. You climb on the horse you have taken, and ride like the wind from here. Any fighting needs to be done, I'll do it. *Comprende?*"

Emilio hesitated only a moment longer, gave a half-scared smile, and said, "It will be as you say, amigo." He dipped the mop in the bucket, wrung it out, and looked at Malloy. "Now, I must get this room cleaned, or the señorita will know I've been lazy."

Megan peered through the first gun slot she came to. Whoever attacked the ranch was not as selective about where they shot as were those inside. They sprayed bullets toward the house as though willing them to find a target on their own. Most shots went into the thick adobe walls, a few hit the wooden shutters, and fewer of them penetrated to send splinters about the room.

Megan picked a steady flash of gunfire as one she'd fire at until she silenced it. She marveled that the feeling she had in the pit of her stomach and the exhilaration that caused chills to traverse her spine weren't what she thought she'd feel if afraid. Then it dawned on her. She wasn't afraid. She welcomed the chance to fight back. Running as they had been had never been part of her makeup.

She'd fired three times, the smell of cordite penetrating

her nostrils, leaving an irritating, choking, tickling in her throat. If less heavy, the smell would have been one she enjoyed. She jacked another shell into the chamber, pushed the barrel through the slot, and fired, then peered through the hole in the shutter. Either that gun was silenced or he was reloading.

A heavy, calloused hand closed over the magazine of her rifle. She twisted to look into Burston's eyes. "Lady, put that gun down an' git behind some o' that furniture. A sliver from one o' these here shutters'll tear you apart."

She opened her mouth to protest. Burston's next act was to take the Winchester from her grasp. "No arguin'. Git."

Megan moved to stand behind adobe rather than in line with the shutter. "Mr. Burston, you and your men are defending me and the girls. I'll do my part. Now stand aside." She retrieved her rifle and again poked it through the slot.

She wondered how many men Burston had inside the house. Most of the men working cattle should have returned to the ranch by sundown, except those who would spend their time at one of the line shacks scattered about the ranch. They were the men working too far from headquarters to ride back and forth every day. They'd probably come in for pay day. Most of those who had returned would be doing their fighting from somewhere outside.

Megan stood to the side of the window and glanced about the room. Four men manned the windows, and the sharp crack of rifles sounded from different parts of the house. It seemed Burston had managed to get several of his men inside before the outlaws attacked.

Outside, the gunfire slackened, then ceased. Almost immediately the sound of a large band of horses being ridden fast broke the sudden stillness. The hoofbeats retreated into the distance, then died out.

Megan pulled her rifle from the gun slot and looked at Burston. "Do you always awaken your guests in such an exciting manner, sir?"

He only stared at her, his mouth twisted in a sour grimace. "Ma'am, this here is not a jokin' matter. Them men who just rode away wuz madder'n hell that we beat 'em outta you women. They had killin' on their minds." Tiredly, he stood his weapon against the wall. "Hope you'll excuse me fer cussin', ma'am."

Megan, forgetting to use her icy smile, gripped his forearm. "Clint, I know they meant business—you go ahead and cuss as much as you want. I'll join you."

He stared at her a moment. "That's the first time you used my first name. I'd shore like to call you by yore first name, too."

She tightened her grip on his arm. "I'd be pleased if you would. After all, we've been through a lot together."

He laughed. Megan thought he seemed as joyful as a small boy getting a new toy. "Let's clean our weapons, then see if Cookie has kept supper ready while we scared off the attackers." He took her arm to lead her to the dining room, then looked at a couple of his men. "Light a torch an' go see how many o' them critters won't be goin' home. Be careful. Make sure they're dead, or crippled up enough they cain't shoot at you." He led Megan to the dining room.

Ever since arriving at the ranch house, Megan had wondered at the careful planning that had gone into the building of the structure, but also thought it needed a woman's touch. Everything was masculine, austere. Clint needed a woman. As he seated her at the table, she looked up at him. "Do you think they'll be back, Clint?"

He shook his head. "Don't know. Depends on how many they had to leave behind. If we hurt 'em bad enough, reckon they'll stay away long enough to lick their wounds," he nodded, "but, yeah, I reckon we ain't done with 'em yet."

"Where do you suppose The Gunfighter is?"

Pain filled Burston's eyes, then he shielded them with a quick droop of his eyelids. "Ma'am, I don't know where he might be. Cain't go runnin' off down there to try an' find 'im. He could be anywhere."

"Do you think he's hurt?"

Then Burston, knowing he couldn't squelch the roughness of his voice and words, said, "Ma'am, he could be hurt, he could be runnin'—hell, he could be anything. He could even be lyin' out yonder dead. I got enough troubles tryin' to take care o' all you women without worryin' 'bout him."

Megan frowned. "But of course. Any of those things are possible. And I'm sorry we've so inconvenienced you."

His head snapped around to study her. He'd let his feelings force words from him that he wished he could take back—but it was too late. He and Roan had discussed this, and both knew they'd be vying for Megan's affections. He had thought he could accept whatever decision she made, but now he was unsure. He had to face the fact that Roan was a dashing, commanding figure of a man, and younger than him by maybe ten years. Burston swallowed, grimaced, and looked her in the eye. "Aw, ma'am, I'm sorry for them rough words. Reckon sometimes a gunfight makes me use words that're too rough for ladies. You, nor none o' yore girls, has put me out no more than I am happy to be put out." He passed a plate of fried eggs to her. "Ma'am, The Gunfighter an' I talked 'bout this. We figgered what each o' us had to do to keep y'all safe. He took the job he figgered he wuz best fitted for. I gotta admit he wuz right. I ain't gun-quick like him, an' I ain't as sudden on fightin'." He gave a smile that he thought was sheepish.

"Megan, I reckon wherever he is, an' whatever he's doin', he's all right."

His foreman came into the room, hat in hand. "Boss, we got eight o' them dead; two took lead but will make it. What you want me to do with them what didn't?"

Burston looked over his shoulder. "Find a dry wash an' bury 'em. Fix them two what ain't gonna cash in their chips so's they won't bleed to death. I wantta talk to them later."

Malloy watched the old man quietly close the door behind him when he finished cleaning the room. He felt like a bucket of worms crawled in his guts. Could he trust the old man? Would Emilio let fear change his mind? If the Mexican did as he agreed, how was he going to get from his room to the back of the cantina without being detected? What was he to do with Ulla? He couldn't knock her out, knife her, shoot her. It wasn't in him to treat a woman as anything but a lady.

He wished for a rope or pigging string to tie her with, then shook his head. Rope would be too harsh. Then the idea hit him. He pulled his Bowie, stripped the sheet from the bed she'd been using, and cut it in strips. He remade the bed as best he knew how, then pushed the strips of sheet under the covers of his bed and smoothed the top cover.

He checked his Colt. It had not been cleaned since he came in from the desert. He wished he had some patches and gun oil, but that equipment was in his saddlebags. He'd have to do without the gun oil. He would use a thin strip of the sheet for a patch. He searched the room for something to push it through the barrel. A quill lay on Ulla's desk. Using his Bowie, he sliced the feathers from the quill, then pushed the dry cloth through the barrel and through each cylinder. Satisfied he'd done his best, he'd have to trust the job he'd done. If the bandits came back, they'd drink and bed every woman in the place before they settled down for the night. A chill ran up and down Malloy's spine again. His back and neck muscles tightened. He dropped his Colt into the holster. He shrugged. It wasn't his nature to borrow trouble. He'd have to meet it head-on if it came. Then hoofbeats of a large band of horses broke the morning stillness of the small town.

16

MALLOY SLIPPED INTO the hallway and onto the balcony overlooking the bar area. Standing in the shadow, he counted the bandits when they came in. Fourteen. He studied what that number of men would do to his plans. Finally, he forced a cold smile. If anything, the large number might enhance his chances of getting away undetected. They'd keep every woman and bartender busy into the early morning hours. He went back to his room to await the right time.

Hours dragged by, then about ten o'clock that night the noises from below lessened. Some of the bandits had drunk themselves senseless, and others had taken a woman to bed. Then, as more time passed, the noise abated to a hushed silence. Malloy climbed back into his bed and awaited the coming of Ulla. He didn't have long to wait.

The doorknob rattled. The door swung inward. Ulla stepped into the room, looking as fresh as she had when she left to run her saloon and bordello. The sparkle in her eyes said she'd been looking forward to this night for longer than she wished. Malloy pulled farther down under the covers.

The madam closed the door and stood there a moment, then slowly unbuttoned her blouse. Feeling a traitor to Megan, Malloy couldn't move his eyes from Ulla's ripe, pink-tipped breasts, then on down to take in her entire body. He fought it, but his body betrayed him, responding to every article of clothing she removed. He tore his eyes from her and looked toward the wall.

A deep-throated, sensuous chuckle erupted from her throat. "More than you can stand, big man? Well, this is only the beginning. Move over in that bed." She let the last article of clothing drop to the floor around her ankles. "I've heard some of these Americanos use the expression, 'This is my night to howl.'" She grinned. "Well, big man, this is my night, and I'll tell you right now, I'm gonna do a lot more than howl."

Malloy moved over, hating himself for what he was about to do. He'd never hit a woman in his life, and he especially hated to hit a woman who'd been good to him, but his, as well as Megan's, life might depend on his getting out of here.

Ulla stepped toward the table to blow out the light, then, smiling, moved toward the bed. "Think I'll let the lamp burn. I want to see all that goes on, see your every expression." She pulled the covers down, looked at the shredded strips of sheet and then, her eyes wide, looked at Malloy. "What the . . ." That was the moment Malloy pushed himself up. His right fist whistled to the point of her jaw. She fell, her legs dangled from the edge of the bed and her upper body lay across Malloy. She moaned, then didn't move.

Malloy pulled himself from under her, reached for the strips of sheet, and bound her legs, wrists, and mouth. He thought to make her bonds loose enough so they wouldn't hurt, then decided that would be a fool move. She'd have them off and be screaming for help before he could clear the building.

He dressed, swung his gun belt around his waist, and stepped toward the door, then thought of the lamp. When he bent and cupped his hand around the chimney to blow out the flame, he looked toward Ulla. Her eyes, wide, sent darts of poison at him. "Awake, huh? Sorry I had to do that. You've been mighty good to me, but a lot depends on me gettin' back to Texas, so I'll have to tell you adios." He blew out the lamp and opened the door a crack.

He checked the hallway. It stood empty and silent. He slipped out and headed for the back stairs. If Emilio had not carried out his part of the bargain, he was a dead duck. Then Malloy thought that if the old man had cut out on him, he could still take one of the outlaws' horses and head for the border.

He hoped the stairs were well built, and that the boards would make no noise. He could have saved himself one hope. The stairs, down the outside of the back of the building, were of stone. He descended lightly to each step.

When he reached the ground, the splash of water stopped him. Then a drunken voice said in English, "C'mon, join the party. They's three of us here. Reckon the whole outfit might come down to relieve themselves."

Malloy wondered how to play his cards, then grunted, "Sick, real sick." Then he forced gagging noises, and made like he threw up. The sound of about three voices came to him, then laughs, and heavy steps ascended the stairs. Malloy waited a few moments, then looked for a shadowy form that would tell him where Emilio might be.

"Hey, señor, over here." The old man's whisper came from Malloy's left. He pulled his Colt as he moved toward the words. Emilio might have decided to take the gold and leave without doing his part.

"No need for the *pistola*, señor, I have done as I said."

Malloy, his eyes now adjusted to the night, could see the old man standing by two horses. He unbuttoned the pocket inside his waistband and counted six coins into his hand, then raked his finger deeper into the pocket and took out two more. "Old man, you have done your part. Here are two more coins than I promised."

Emilio bent at the waist, bowed two or three times, and held out the reins to Malloy. "*Gracias, muchas gracias.* You are a man of your word." He pushed the eight double eagles into his pocket. "Señor, if you will permit, I'll make a suggestion. Ride with me to the west. These men will think you ride to the river, and will go straight there." He toed the stirrup while talking. "They will not think you take to the desert west of here."

While climbing to the saddle, Malloy considered what the old man said. Settling into the kak, he nodded. "Think you're right, old one. Let's go."

They'd not ridden a hundred yards before an infuriated scream came from the cantina. To Malloy's surprise, Emilio switched to English. "I theenk we get the hell outta here queek, amigo. All hell's gonna break loose soon's the señorita tells 'em what you done." Before he finished speaking, lanterns sprang to light in the cantina. They urged their horses to a run.

They put about a mile behind them before pulling the horses down to a walk. Now knowing the old man understood English, that's what Malloy spoke. "Old one, if they follow our tracks, it'll get you in more trouble than you ever seen."

The old man chuckled. "De nada. Eet ees nothing. We get to my mountains, I cannot be found there. My people weel see to that."

Malloy nodded. "Good. I don't want to cause you more

trouble. Once I know you're safe, I'm gonna head for the border."

"Eet ees good we ride together, señor. Eef they follow, we weel have two rifles against them."

"You have a rifle, Emilio?"

The old man chuckled. "*Si*. I pick the horse and saddle weeth a gun in the scabbard. I look for just such a horse and saddle, amigo." He looked toward the east. "I theenk eet weel be daylight soon." He nodded. "They weel track us then."

Malloy had nursed the hope that the outlaws would saddle up and head for the border, thinking to catch him before he reached the Rio Grande. That hope was in vain. Not long after full daylight, perhaps four or five miles to the rear, a great dust cloud boiled above the brush. He slanted a look at Emilio. "They done picked up our trail, amigo." The old man nodded.

They rode perhaps another fifteen minutes, then Malloy rode his horse closer to the Yaqui. "Don't want to get you in no more trouble than I already have. Think if I cut out for the river now, they'll follow me. Maybe you can get to yore mountains safely that way."

Emilio shook his head. "I weesh to stay weeth you, help you fight them. Those gringos 'ave been bad to me for a long time now. This my chance to even theengs." He wiped sweat from his brow, then gave Malloy a toothless smile. "The señorita, she tell me you are *mucho* hombre, she tell me you're the one they call The Peestolero, a hombre much feared in Norte America." He nodded. "*Si*, I theenk I stay weeth you. Have beeg fight."

Roan measured the dusty desert ahead, gauged how far to the river if they cut for it now, then decided the mountains were their best chance. "*Bueno*. We'll ride together. We go to your mountains."

All that day, the dust cloud drew no closer—and it didn't drop farther behind. Malloy peered squint-eyed into the sun. What had appeared to be a thin line of dark clouds on the horizon now stood higher. Another day's ride, and they'd probably take shape as rugged, rock-strewn hills. He slanted Emilio a look across his shoulder. "How many days ride past them hills 'fore we reach yore home?"

The old one shrugged, and grinned at Roan. "We reach heels, find rocks to hide behind, wait for *bandidos*, have fight, keel many of them, then ride to my people in peace."

Malloy grunted under his breath, "Wish to hell I had as much faith we'd ride in peace, in fact be able to ride at all after we tangle with that bunch. They're salty."

Despite being followed, Roan set a pace intended to save the horses. Judging by the dust cloud behind, the outlaws did the same. Malloy glanced to the rear and felt a sense of hope tingle his nerve ends. If they weren't pushing their horses, they hadn't brought extra ones. Roan's hope increased, and with it a tightening of his throat muscles. Then he wondered if they had brought extra canteens—or if they had any. Emilio had stolen several of theirs, filled them, and hung them from his and Malloy's saddle horns.

As though the old man had read his mind, he said, "*Bandidos* have dry mouths soon. They don't know where water holes are, an' we have most of their canteens." They rode a while longer, then he said, "I make sure we don't ride close to water."

Malloy studied what the old Mexican told him. Those outlaws weren't damned fools. They probably had long since realized the hopeless situation they were in, and after dark would most likely continue to push toward him and his amigo.

He drew his horse abreast of Emilio's. "*Compadre*, I

think we best find a good place from which we can fight, pull in, make camp—and wait."

"*Si*, I theenk you are right, but first we must make sure they don't come up on us while it's still dark. We must ride until they weel have no chance of doing that. There are many places ahead which weel geeve us a place to shoot from."

Malloy mulled that over for a while. What the old one said made a lot of sense. He considered himself a pretty good Indian when it came to stalking, tracking, and gun-fights, but now he had the real thing with him. He'd play it the way the Yaqui called the shots.

Holding the horses to a slow walk, they rode until Emilio pulled off into some large boulders. "We make camp, build fire, then pick good place to shoot at those who come in on the fire, *si?*"

Malloy didn't even try to hide his grin. "Yep. Figure you got it down to where we ain't gonna take many chances. By the time they get here, the sun's gonna be toppin' the horizon. We gonna be able to see 'em pretty good." Still grinning, he slapped Emilio on the shoulder. "Glad you're on my side, amigo."

Those words brought a toothless smile from the old man. "Get old, still know how to fight."

Malloy looked at the Yaqui. Damned if Emilio wasn't looking forward to being a warrior once again. Putting himself in the bandits' minds, he knew they'd think that he and the Indian had ridden until, feeling safe from pursuit, they had pulled off to cook a meal and rest a bit.

They built a fire, made certain it gave off smoke by put-ting a couple of branches of greasewood on it. Emilio led the horses off a couple of hundred yards and tethered them so they'd not be in harm's way. Then he and Malloy select-ed a couple of boulders higher than the rest, and settled down to wait.

Roan looked from his vantage point to where the Yaqui lay atop a smooth boulder. "Don't let the sun reflect off your rifle barrel."

"Got serape wrapped around it. It no geeve us away."

Malloy, satisfied the old man knew what he was doing, began to feel the effects of the coming fight. He sucked in a deep breath to try to relax, then stifled a sneeze from inhaling dust.

He pulled his bandanna from about his neck and wiped sweat from his eyes. Then he saw the dust cloud stop— about three hundred yards from where he and Emilio had set up their fake camp. He motioned to the Yaqui.

The old man nodded, a grin splitting his toothless mouth. "Warrior now. No clean white man's dirt."

Malloy looked down on every move they made. For the first time, he knew how many men they faced. He counted nine of them when they left their horses. Not bad. He'd faced worse odds several times. He and the Yaqui had agreed they'd wait until the last man was in accurate rifle range. He waited.

About a hundred yards out, every outlaw dropped to his belly and snaked toward the fire. Malloy looked toward the Yaqui and winked. He got another grin. Then he brought his Winchester to his shoulder.

Firing down at a target was never as accurate as a straight-on shot. He drew a bead on the head of the man farthest from him and squeezed off his first shot. The sharp crack of his rifle sounded simultaneously with that of the Yaqui.

The man he'd fired at raised up on his elbows, then slumped to lie still. The one the Yaqui fired at never moved. Malloy thought the old man had missed until he saw the gory mess where the bandit's head had been. Now the remaining seven scattered to find shelter. Four found

small rocks behind which to hunker; the other three settled
for large yuccas.

Roan picked one of the men behind a yucca for his next
target. He bracketed the yucca with two shots, and when
the outlaw tried to squirm to the side, he put a shot between
the man's shoulders.

Now bullets whined off the hard surface of the boulder
on which he lay. Rock slivers stung his cheek. He rolled to
take up a better position. The Yaqui's rifle was talking a
steady, resounding stream of noise. Abruptly, all firing
ceased. The Yaqui looked toward Roan and held up four
fingers. Malloy nodded. The only ones of their attackers
left were those behind the rocks. He settled down to wait
them out.

The sun beat down from a brassy, cloudless sky. The
boulders Malloy and the Indian had chosen for protection
only kept them safe from bullets. They acted as reflectors
for the relentless heat. Roan moved only enough to swab
his face and neck again.

High noon came and went. Malloy didn't like the idea
of trying to hold their position after dark. He studied the
terrain, looking for a good route to slip up on the bandits.
When he had each target charted in his head, he glanced
toward the Yaqui. The Yaqui was gone.

Had the old man deserted him? He thought on that while
he continued watching the hiding places of the four outlaws. He couldn't believe the old man would leave him
high and dry. Nope, the Yaqui was too proud of being a
warrior once again. He was probably doing the very thing
Malloy planned. Then he saw a flash of white, a little
whiter than the grayish-white alkali soil of the desert. He
pinned his eyes to the spot, then he saw it move, then flit
to another nearby rock. The Yaqui had not deserted him.
Shame flooded him for thinking such of the old man, who

had stuck with him through the danger of getting away from the cantina.

The Indian moved again, this time to the rear of where one of the bandits had taken refuge. A flash of sun on steel, and Malloy figured the bandits now numbered three.

He watched where he knew the Yaqui to be, and at the same time kept the hiding places of the others in his peripheral vision. Then the one behind the boulder closest to the Indian swung toward the old man, raised his rifle to fire; Malloy could see his upper body. In one smooth motion, Roan swung his rifle to sight on the bandit and squeezed off a shot. From where he crouched, Malloy saw red blossom high on the bandit's ribs in front of his arm. He toppled to the side.

The old man slid to the ground at the side of the boulder and lifted a hand toward Roan. Now the odds were even.

The marshal studied the two remaining rocks. There was no indication they hid anything, but he'd seen the bandits go to ground behind them. He reloaded his Winchester and shot to each side of the two rocks. Maybe he could keep their attention on him so the Yaqui would have a better chance. He had a hunch that neither of the outlaws knew their partners had been taken out. Then the one behind the farthest boulder proved him wrong.

The bandit behind that boulder crouched low, ran toward the horses. Malloy sighted between the man's shoulder blades and squeezed off a shot. The bandit threw up his arms, his rifle arcing into the air ahead of him. He fell facedown and never quivered. Now there was one.

The Yaqui, stooped low, ran toward the remaining hiding place. The outlaw stood, tried to bring his rifle to bear on the Indian. Emilio ran with knife in hand. He was obviously too close for the outlaw to get his rifle in action. The bandit dropped his long gun and made a sweep toward his handgun. He never made it. Emilio's knife was faster and more deadly. The knife went across the bandit's throat, and Roan watched as a gusher of red spouted out to cover the man's shirt.

Emilio faced Malloy, raised both hands in the air, and motioned that he was going to collect the bandit's horses. Roan watched the old man take the reins of the horses, lead them to where each outlaw lay, collect the rifles and handguns of each, hang them over the saddle horns, and come toward camp.

"Old man, you took a helluva chance going out there alone."

"Not old man now. Warrior. Never clean bad men's mess no more forever."

Malloy smiled at the Yaqui. "Yep, Emilio, you can stand tall with the best of your people." He frowned. "Did you go through the pockets of them we killed?"

"*Si.* I got *mucho dinero.* Now Emilio rich warrior. My people listen to my telling of what happened many times, then they tell all who are about. I have many wives again."

Malloy studied the old man a moment. The Yaqui stood straighter, his face was less wrinkled, he held his head prouder. Yes, the old man was again a warrior. "Come, Emilio, we'll fix some o' them victuals you brought. I'm hungry. Been a long time since we ate."

Soon the mouth-watering smell of frying bacon settled over the camp. They fried tortillas in the bacon grease, and made a meal of what they had.

Malloy looked across the fire at his friend. "Amigo, if you think they won't be no more fightin', reckon I'll cut north, cross the river at Piedras Negras, an' get on back to Laredo."

The old Yaqui stared into the fire a moment, then pinned Roan with eyes that a much younger man would be proud of. "Señor, I weel 'ave no more fightin'. You weel. Those *bandidos* weel send men to each border town. They weel be there to wait for you." He nodded. "I hear them talk. They don't pay attention to an old Indian. They say theengs they weel not say to gringos."

Malloy's senses sharpened. The old man was about to tell him something, perhaps something about the outlaws. "What do you hear, amigo?"

"Ees maybe nothing, but maybe eet ees something you want to know." He took time to roll a brown paper cigarette, lit it, then looked at Malloy. "I don't theenk you fight these *bandidos* for nothing, or maybe only because you like the beeg fight. I theenk you maybe belong to the law up there in Norte America." He took a drag on his cigarette, blew the smoke toward the fire, then frowned. "Señor Peestolero, you maybe theenk the hombre who bosses these *bandidos* ees een Laredo." He shook his head. "The one you want ees in Ciudad San Antonio."

A surge of energy flooded Malloy's chest. Was the old man going to tell him the name of the man he wanted? Even if not, he was much closer to finding him. He could eliminate New Orleans and Laredo. "You know the name of this man?"

Emilio shook his head. "I never hear it. I theenk only the Señorita Ulla know hees name, and she would never speak it. She was much afraid of heem, afraid he would keel her."

Malloy nodded. "You have helped me a great deal, Emilio. Yeah, I'm a lawman up there, but that don't hold no water down here." He packed his pipe and lit it. "I reckon you're right. I figure they's gonna be bandits waitin' for me wherever I go along the border." He shrugged. "But if you think you won't have any more trouble, I'm gonna head on up that way."

"You want me to go weeth you, señor? I can watch your back."

Malloy got all soft inside. He'd really made a friend. He touched the old man's shoulder. "Emilio, you go on back to your people. You bein' willin' to side me in another fight tells me I've made a friend, but bein' your friend, too, I ain't gonna put your life on the line again. *Muchas gracias*, amigo, but this is my fight. You go on back and tell all them brave warriors what a really brave warrior does when the chips are down." He took a drag on his pipe, then nodded. "Come daylight, I'm headin' for the border—alone."

Daylight found Malloy an hour away from the camp of the night before. Emilio had stood by the fire and watched him go into the darkness.

Roan tracked almost straight north to Piedras Negras and crossed the river into the small settlement of Eagle Pass. He went to the only hotel, got a room, and told the clerk to bring up bathwater, a lot of it.

While waiting for water to be brought to the room, he went to the general store and bought new clothes from the skin out. Then he went to his room and cleaned his guns until not a speck of desert dust remained in the cylinder or barrel.

While bathing, he decided on having a beer, maybe a couple of them, before hunting up the café and eating a steak big as the plate.

Outside the saloon, he thumbed the thong off his Colt. Emilio was right; each of these towns would have members of the woman-stealing gang posted to get rid of him. He'd been too much of a thorn in their side. As he was about to push through the batwings, his back muscles tightened such that they pained through to his chest. The tendons in his neck pulled against his head until his head hurt. He stepped to the side, took a deep breath, then another, until his senses relaxed. Only then did he push through the doors.

It was dark, cool, and filled with danger inside. He stepped to the side to wait for his eyes to adjust to the changed light, hoping he had time for that before he was seen. That hope was in vain. He'd stood there only a moment when the usual noise and loud talk hushed to a thick, knife-cutting silence.

The one thing the tenseness couldn't erase was the smell of sour whisky, beer, and stale tobacco smoke. Regardless, Malloy had come in for a beer, and he would see them all in hell before they got in his way of having one. His eyes were now seeing what he wanted to see. The room was filled with punchers, ranchers, and hard cases. The difference was easy to spot. The cowboys' and ranchers' sidearms were not tied to their thighs. The hard cases all had their guns tied down, and their hands never got too far from the walnut or bone grips.

Those after his hide would have been smart to take advantage of his thwarted vision when he first came in. But like most, those who wanted him had to bolster their courage with talk.

Malloy edged his way around the wall toward the bar. All eyes followed him. The Gunfighter was known in most of the border towns, but was feared only by those who had a reason to fear him. When he got to the bar, he knew it by the feel of the smooth surface against his side. He put his back to the wall and stood, waiting. He knew it would come. The man in San Antonio would have covered his every chance to get rid of the one man who had thwarted his operation.

Without looking at the bartender, he said, "Beer, cold; then go to the other end o' the bar."

In only a moment, he heard the glass put on the surface at his side. Those he figured to be cattlemen and punchers had all moved to the walls. One wall was significant for the lack of men standing along it. That was the direction from which the hard cases would come at him. To his surprise, he saw only three men to stand against him.

The one slightly ahead of the other two stopped and stood spread-legged. The other two came to stand at his side. They were all clean shaven, in clean clothes. The two standing by the obvious leader were slim, hard-faced men. The leader was huge. Malloy thought if he flexed his arms and chest, he'd split the seams of his shirt. That man was the first to speak.

"Looks like we got you boxed, Gunfighter. Figured we might need odds on our side."

Malloy figured that regardless how fast he might be, three men could take him easy. He stared at them a moment, then cut them a cold smile. "You got the odds, but which one o' you is willin' to die first?" His smile obviously took them by surprise, and his words caused them to huddle closer together. Malloy didn't wait. He drew, perhaps the fastest draw of his life, and thumbed off shots as fast as he could pull the trigger.

Each gunman swept his hands to his sides. The first to take a slug was the big man. It went through his cheek and into his head. The second was the man to his right. He caught a slug in his chest. The bullet knocked him backward, but he caught his balance, stepped forward, and fired.

Malloy, still firing, felt a burning along his arm, then a jolt against his right foot. It knocked him off balance. He fell to the side, put another slug into the chest of the man still standing, then turned his Colt on the second man, who was trying to get off another shot, and put two more slugs into him. His gun, smoke curling from the barrel, clicked on a spent shell. His gun was empty. He pulled his Bowie.

The third man teetered on rubbery legs, pulled the trigger again, and put his slug into the floor at Malloy's feet. Roan stepped toward him, within arm's length, and swung his blade. It took the outlaw across his face, down his neck, and across his chest. Malloy stepped back, then with his knife held straight out, stepped into the man who was still standing. His blade went in up to the hilt—but it went into a man already dead. Staring from blank eyes, he fell into Malloy's arms.

Roan pushed him aside, stepped to the bar, picked up his beer, and drained it. "Bring me another, and a glass of whisky." Maybe the whisky would wash the taste and smell of cordite from his throat.

He wanted to look down and see where he was hit, but would put that off until he'd finished his drink. He didn't feel blood, and could still walk on his numb foot, although he had a limp.

The bartender slid a glass of whisky down the bar, followed by a beer. Then the room erupted into an uproar. Among the words Roan heard were "Three men. I never seen the like. I heered 'bout The Gunfighter fore, but this is the first time I seen 'im in action. All I heered is true."

Malloy, sick of killing, sick of his reputation, and sick of hearing men voice their opinions, knocked back his drink, stepped toward the door, and almost tripped. He looked at his foot. The boot heel had been shot away. Then he glanced at his burning arm. It hardly bled. He shrugged and headed for a bootmaker. He'd get his arm looked at later.

Outside the saloon, he reloaded his Colt, filling all six chambers. There might be more trouble, although he hoped not. He was bone tired and hungry. He intended to take care of those two problems before he gave anyone another chance at his hide. Also, he wanted to leave for Burston's ranch as soon as possible. He wanted to see the sun in

Megan's hair, see the smile on her face. He hoped it would be a special smile for him.

The days, seeming like years, dragged by. Not an hour passed without Megan's walking to the veranda to look down the dusty trail toward Laredo. Then she'd sweep the direction toward the river with a long searching look. Her inner voice screamed, *Where are you, Roan? Are you all right? Have you been horribly wounded? Is there anyone to care for you?* She now thought of Malloy as Roan most of the time, ever since Burston had told her The Gunfighter's first name. But deep within her, she still thought of him as The Gunfighter, a name she held dear for the man she thought so highly of.

She wondered at herself. She'd known many men, any one of whom would have given everything, anything to have her think of him in a special way. But those men stood in Roan's shadow. None of them fit her idea of what being a total man should be.

Then, on her latest walk to the veranda, the thought hit her, stopped her in midstride. Was she in love with the big, rough man? She shook her head. Impossible. She hardly knew him—but deep inside, she knew it was not impossible. She knew she thought more of him than of any man she'd ever known.

Burston walked to her side and put his arm about her shoulders. "Little one, he'll be comin' soon. I know you're worried sick about 'im. You've lost weight. I can tell by the hollows in yore cheeks."

She looked across her shoulder at Burston, who seemed almost like a brother. She thought about that a moment. Why was she more interested in The Gunfighter than in Clint? Burston was more stable, had established himself as a rancher, and was well thought of in Laredo. Roan seemed to her like a tumbleweed, never still, showing no inclination to put down roots anywhere, yet her deepest feelings went out to him.

"Clint, he's been gone such a long time. Do you really think he's all right?"

To see her worry so, about a man he thought of as a friend—but also the man who he was now certain had stepped between him and Megan—caused Burston heartache he never dreamed possible. Heartache? Yes. He actually hurt deep in his chest, and that hurt became an almost constant dull headache.

What did Roan have that he didn't? He considered that a few moments. He could never compete with The Gunfighter, who was younger and, he suspected, better looking if he'd shave that beard. On the other hand, he had stability, a ranch, money. Yet material goods had never made a difference where the heart chose to lead a man or woman.

17

MEGAN TILTED HER head to rest it on Burston's shoulder. He wished he could take that as meaning she considered him the one to comfort her, love her, but he knew better. He'd seen the misery in her eyes when she searched the trail and chaparral for the sight of another man.

The soft clop of a horse's hooves drew his look toward the gate. His eyes widened. He twisted Megan so he could look into her eyes. "Little one, if you'll look out yonder a bit, you'll see that I'm right most o' the time."

She turned, looked, and twisted her shoulders from under his arm. Then she was running.

Roan came abreast of her, reached down, caught her under her arms, and pulled her to the saddle with him. "Just sit there, Megan, don't get too close. I ain't had a bath in some time. Figure I smell right ripe by now."

"Gunfighter, I don't care if you smell like a wet dog, pull me close to you." He did.

When he reined his horse in by the veranda, he lowered her to the ground, looked at Burston, and grinned. "You gonna hug me, too, or you gonna have somebody bring some bathwater to my room, or the bunkhouse, or wherever you gonna let me sleep?"

Burston studied him a moment, his eyes showed worry. "Roan, you all right? You're lookin' kinda gaunt."

Malloy's grin widened. "Considerin' I been shot three times, suffered almighty hell at the hands of a good-lookin' woman who right now prob'ly wants me dead, an' rode across half o' Mexico tryin' to get here, I reckon I'm doin' right fine."

He neck-reined his horse toward the stable. "I'll take care o' my horse. Then we can talk."

Megan took the reins in her hand. "You'll do no such. I'll take care of your horse."

Burston looked out into the yard. "Hey, Spike, come git The Gunfighter's horse an' put 'im in a stall with grain, water—aw, hell, take care o' his horse."

Spike took the reins from Megan's hand, looked at Malloy, and grinned. "Howdy, Gunfighter. Looks like you done been rode hard an' put away wet." He pushed his hat back off his forehead. "Don't seem like nobody else's gonna say it, so I will—git down an' rest yore saddle."

On the way into the house, Megan walked as close to Roan as she could without tripping him. Then inside the thick, cool adobe walls, she twisted to look at him straight-on. "You've been shot? Where? How?"

Malloy laughed, pleased that she cared, and hoped the caring was more than that of a friend. He took her shoulders in his big hands. "Gonna tell you somethin', lady. We gonna talk way into the night if you want, but first, if Burston'll pour me a drink, I'm gonna take it to my room, drink it, an' then take a bath." He looked at Burston. I got clean clothes in my bedroll out yonder."

The rancher nodded. "I'll have one o' the boys fetch

'em." While talking, he poured Roan a glassful of whiskey, then handed it to him. "Now go on. Get cleaned up. Yore room's second door to the right down the hall."

After supper, sitting with a drink, Malloy told them about the happenings since he'd last seen them. He skipped what Ulla wanted in payment for her kindness. Then he looked at Burston. "They's a whole bunch o' them woman-stealin' bastards lookin' for me. Whoever their boss is, has got 'em scattered in every town along the border from here to Brownsville, if I can judge by what happened in Eagle Pass."

Burston nodded. "I figger that'd be a pretty good guess. They don't know what you know, an' they damn well want to close your mouth—for good."

Megan glanced from one to the other, then centered her look on Malloy. "Roan—yes, Clint told me your first name—these bandits are not your business. Let the law handle it."

Malloy wanted to tell her that he was the law, but thought the time wasn't right. "Megan, I figure it *is* my business. I've hurt 'em with costin' 'em men, as well as almost uncovering who's runnin' the show. They can't let that go without tryin' to shut me up." He spread his hands, palms up. "They got too much to lose."

Pain showing in her eyes, she leaned toward him. "What does that mean, Roan? Are you going to try hunting them down? Are you going to put yourself in a position to get shot again?"

It was in his thoughts to tell her he had to do it, that it *was* his duty, but Burston saved him. "Megan, even if Roan walked away from it, they'd stop 'im. He ain't safe in no town along the Rio Grande."

Her eyes swimming, she squeezed them shut to rid them

of tears that only trickled down her cheeks. "Th—this is a horrible country. M—men killing each other. No one stopping it or protecting those who are innocent."

Malloy frowned, knocked back his drink, and held the empty glass toward Burston for a refill. "Megan, it's not only this country. These things happen everywhere—New York, Boston, New Orleans, San Francisco." He shook his head. "It's just that in most o' those places, the culprits sneak about in the dark to do their dirty work. Men who care have to step forward and do the right thing."

She sniffled. He held out his handkerchief to her. Through her tears she said, "Mr. Gunfighter, there you go again. When you're dead serious, you use correct grammar. You've done it several times. When are you going to tell me who you really are?"

He smiled. "Ma'am, I'm gonna surprise you one o' these days, an' I'm bettin' you gonna be flabbergasted."

"I'm bettin' I'll be, too," Burston said. "I know more about you than Megan does, but I got it figgered they's a whole lot more to you than either of us knows."

Malloy smiled, looked into his empty glass, and said, "A man could just flat die of thirst if he had a host who wasn't tryin' to make him welcome."

"Does this mean you're going to get right back into the middle of things, put yourself in places to get shot again? I don't think I can stand the thought of it. Besides, what are you going to do with us while you're off picking gunfights with people?"

"Ma'am, I want you to know, I never picked a fight with any man." Malloy shrugged. "If they bring it to me—I have to fight, run, or die. It's that simple, an' two o' them choices ain't acceptable."

Megan opened her mouth to say something else, but

Roan cut her off. "As for you and the girls"—he looked at Burston—"I reckon you're gonna have to accept Clint's hospitality for a little while longer."

Burston shook his head. "I'll leave the boys to guard 'em. I'm tellin' you right now, I'm goin' with you."

Malloy studied his friend a moment, decided it would do no good to argue, then nodded. "All right. I figure I'm gonna need somebody to watch my back." He looked at Megan. "Soon's this is all over, I'll be comin' to take you home. By then you might decide home is in Laredo, or maybe New Orleans. Whichever, I figure to see you get there safe." He knocked back his drink, studied the empty glass, decided he didn't need another, and put the glass on the table at his side. "Clint's men'll keep you safe while we're gone."

"It's not my safety I'm worried about."

They talked long into the night; most of the talk Burston and Malloy tried to convince Megan they'd be safe and wouldn't take any unnecessary chances. Before going to bed, Malloy decided they better leave for Laredo or San Antonio the next morning.

Three days later, again hot, dirty, and wanting a cold beer, Malloy glanced at Burston. "Oughtta be in Laredo come sundown. You figure they gonna have somebody waitin' there for me?"

Burston grimaced. "Gunfighter, anybody who'd bet they won't would be a damn fool."

Malloy gave a jerk of his head that passed for a nod. "Way I figure it, too. But I'm tellin' you right now, stay outta it unless they's somebody gonna try a back shot at me."

Burston nodded.

They rode another three hours before they raised the rooftops of Laredo's buildings. As soon as they settled into their rooms, Malloy told the rancher he needed to see Provo, the town marshal. "See you in the saloon soon's I can get cleaned up."

When he pushed through the door of Provo's office, the marshal looked up, grinned, reached into his top drawer, and pulled out something he handed to Malloy. It was the highly polished U.S. marshal's badge he'd left with Provo. "Damn, man, looks like you just about polished the silver off it."

Provo gave him a jerky nod. "Didn't do it like you said, polish it every two weeks—I done it every day. You have any trouble down there?"

Straight-faced, Malloy shook his head. "None to speak of, marshal. Reckon you know we got the womenfolk back."

"Yeah, one o' Burston's men come in an' tol' me." He frowned. "Gotta tell you, Gunfighter, yore troubles ain't over. I'd say they's six, maybe seven, rough-lookin' customers been hangin' round the saloons lookin' for someone. I figger that someone's you."

Uninvited, Malloy poured himself a cup of Provo's coffee, then nodded. "Figure if I went into any town from here to Brownsville it's gonna be the same. Yeah, they're lookin' for me."

Provo pulled his six-shooter, looked down the barrel, and put it back in its holster. Then he stood, went to the gun rack, took a sawed-off Greener from it, broke the action, and stuffed two shells in the magazine.

"What the hell you think you're doin', Provo? This here's my fight."

Provo grinned. "You figger to stop me?"

Turnbull thought on his problems a few more moments, drank another cup of coffee, and looked through the telegrams again. He admitted to himself he didn't like

Shug Bentley, the town marshal, or Barge, the telegraph operator. He had to be careful to not let his likes or dislikes cloud his thinking. Then he again came to the message from headquarters. He twisted his lips in a grim smile. Brent Clausen was a different kind of problem. The store owner had an inflated opinion of himself and where he fit into the town's leadership—and he did have influence, and was brash enough to try to swing his stick in all directions.

He sighed, pushed the stack of papers into a neat pile, and stuffed it inside his shirt. He wondered what triggered that move. Surely he could have left the telegrams in a drawer. He shoved his hand inside his shirt to remove the papers, then left them where they were.

That afternoon, he received another telegram from headquarters. "Your duty is to support local law officers. Stop. Any more harassing of local law brings suspension. Stop."

Bull stared at the message. He had no doubt that Bentley had reported his refusal to share what he knew of the woman-stealing gang. He studied the message a while longer, then dropped it on the pile of other messages. His suspicions and the evidence, slim as it was, would not permit him to draw the town marshal into his confidence. Hell, Bentley was the only prime suspect he had.

He stood, went into the front cell, and pushed the stack of telegrams under the straw mattress. Then he left, locking the cell door behind him.

He'd no more than returned to his chair behind his desk when Bentley walked in the door. His face wore an oily smirk. "Well, Ranger man, you got your orders from headquarters, now let's you an' me go over them messages together." He pulled the chair from the other side of the desk and straddled it. "Me bein' the local law around here,

I wantta know everything you done found out, an' what you've made of it."

• Bull gritted his teeth and got a tight rein on his anger. The sorry town marshal got the word on every message that came over the telegraph wires. He'd apparently read the telegram from Ranger headquarters before Turnbull got it. The blood surged to his head, then subsided. He stared a moment at the marshal, grinned a tight grin, and shook his head. "Uh-uh, you ain't gittin' nothin' outta me." His grin widened. "Tell you what. Why don't you take your sorry butt outta my office, hightail it back to the depot, send another telegram to Ranger headquarters, an' see kin you git me suspended." He stood. "An' I'm gonna tell you somethin' more. When I finish the job I'm on, I'm gonna take you down behind the livery an' clean yore plow good." He stared straight-on into Bentley's eyes. "You got that? You know what I'm tellin' you?"

Bentley stared back, apparently not understanding a man who would do his job despite any kind of obstacles. Finally he shook his head, stepped toward the door, and said over his shoulder, "Gonna do jest what you said, an' I'm gonna be right here to put a lock on the door o' your office."

"Git!"

At Turnbull's roar, Bentley rushed out the door. He slammed it behind him and slanted across the street toward the general store. Bull watched him make tracks, then frowned. Why would the marshal head for the general store when he was obviously set on sending another telegram to Ranger headquarters? He wondered about that a moment, then decided that another message from Clausen, or one cosigned by him, would carry more weight. He shrugged, stuck his hand in his pocket, and rubbed his thumb over the smooth surface of the deputy U.S. marshal badge.

Provo held the Greener in his left hand, eased his Colt in its holster, looked into Malloy's eyes, and grinned. "Ain't had no fun like this in a month, Gunfighter. You aimin' to stop me?"

Malloy slanted him a tight grin. "Hell, no. If you're dumb enough to step out that door with me, knowin' all hell could break loose any moment, an' it's gonna be centered around wherever I am," he shrugged, "reckon you're welcome to the party."

Provo frowned, then shook his head. "Let's don't play it that way, Gunfighter." He shifted his gaze to the wall, frowned deeper, then looked at Malloy. "They gonna be watchin' all the waterin' holes in town. I figger they'll have one or two men in each." He smiled. " 'Cordin' to my figgerin', you could take any two of 'em in a straight-on, stand-up gunfight, but there might be more'n two. That's where I come in. I ain't gonna let nobody back-shoot you."

"I already got a partner to watch my back. Burston's sidin' me."

Provo shook his head. "Nope. We ain't got enough good men in this town. I wantta keep 'em all safe. It's my job." He gave Malloy a jerk of the head that passed for a nod. "You an' me's gonna do it."

Malloy shrugged. "Let's go."

When they stepped out the door of Provo's office, Provo waved the barrel of the Greener to indicate that they should turn down the alley and go along the backs of the stores. Malloy melted into the darkness, Provo was slightly behind him.

At the back of the first store, the town marshal came

alongside. "Third buildin' to our right is the Horseshoe. You go in first, let 'em see you. We'll see what they do then. I'll be to your left once we get inside."

Malloy ghosted his way down the store backs. Neither of the two men made more noise than the tinkle of the tin-panny piano drifting to them on the night air. At the back of the Horseshoe, Malloy found the door, twisted the knob, and went into a darkened hallway. He wasn't surprised the back door had been unlocked; the bartender would use it to dump trash until closing time.

He stepped smoothly and silently toward the rectangle of light showing about ten feet ahead. Reaching it, and before going in, he stood back in the dark and swept the room with a glance.

Inside the saloon, and not more than fifteen feet from him, stood two of the men he figured to belong to the gang. They weren't cowpunchers for sure. The way they wore their guns told him that. At a table along the back wall sat two more he pegged as part of the same ilk. Malloy stepped farther into the darkness of the hallway. "Provo, I figure my trouble's gonna come from them two against the wall." He took the marshal's shirt between two fingers and pulled him toward him so he could see.

"Got 'em in my sights, Gunfighter. Go ahead an' see how them two at the bar act when they see you."

Malloy took a breath of the musty, sour, beery air, rolled his shoulders to relieve the knot in his back, then stepped into the empty area at the end of the polished bar stretching the length of the room. From the moment he stepped into the light, his eyes never left the two at the bar.

Several men—cattlemen and cowboys, by their dress and the way they wore their handguns—apparently saw Malloy before the bandits did. They picked up their drinks and stepped into the crowd behind them. Then others, at tables and standing talking, pushed to get far from Malloy and the two remaining to face him. It was only then that the two gang members pinned Malloy with a gaze.

Both were tall—one heavy and beefy shouldered, the other slim, big-eared and big-nosed. They smiled at the Gunfighter as though they expected him. Neither seemed concerned that he stood there. Malloy figured they counted on their friends at the back wall to make their play a cinch.

"Heard up the river a ways, they was border trash in every town on down to Brownsville lookin' for me. Figure you're some o' that trash they was speakin' of. If I got you pegged, reckon you gonna make a try for them guns you're wearin'."

The heavy-shouldered man carefully placed his drink on the bar alongside his partner's and lowered his hands to his sides. He nodded. "Reckon we some o' the bunch you heered 'bout, but from what they say, I figgered you for more sense than to brace the both o' us."

Malloy shook his head. "Naw now. What you heard is all wrong. I ain't got enough sense to get in outta the rain, so it looks like I mighta made a mistake. You figure to talk all night—or you gonna fill your hands?"

The thin one's eyelids slitted, and his hand swept for his side. Too late. Malloy's first shot caught him in the neck. The Gunfighter swung his Colt to center on the heavy-shouldered one and thumbed off a shot at the same time he heard the belching roar of the Greener at the back of the room. Two shots close together.

The heavy-shouldered gunfighter staggered backward, caught his balance, and stepped toward Malloy at the same time Malloy's second shot caught him in the center of his chest. Staggering, he walked toward Malloy, thumbing off shots with each step. Every one of his shots went into the floor at his feet. Finally, only a couple of steps in front of Malloy, his handgun apparently got too heavy. It rotated around his trigger finger, then fell to the floor. He stood there. His eyes bulged in an insane stare at the man who only moments ago had put two slugs into his chest. Then his knees buckled, he bent at the waist, and toppled face-down into the sawdust beside the bar.

Through powder smoke and the acrid smell of cordite, Malloy glanced at the first man he'd shot. When he'd seen where his bullet hit, he'd shifted all of his attention to the second man. That bullet had opened a hole that let blood spurt in gushes. Both men needed burying.

Only after making certain he had no worry about the two he faced did he turn his attention to the back. Provo stood sweeping the crowd with a searching look, then, stiff-lipped, said, "Anybody else b'long to this here bunch?" No one answered. He nodded and looked toward Malloy. "You catch any lead, Gunfighter?"

Malloy shook his head, turned his eyes toward the bar-tender, and made a sweep toward those on the floor. "Send a man for the undertaker. Git 'em buried, an' send the town the bill."

Provo walked to his side. "This ain't all o' 'em, Gunfighter. You want we should hunt 'em down now?"

Malloy again glanced at the four bodies, then turned his look on the marshal. "I reckon by now they done got word what happened here an' are on their way to elsewhere."

Provo turned to the bartender. "Four water glasses full to the brim o' yore best whisky."

A slight smile cracked the corners of Malloy's mouth. "You gonna let me have one o' them drinks, marshal, or you gonna drink 'em all?"

Provo chuckled. "You take two, I'll take two. Then, if we want more, I got a bottle in my desk drawer." He shivered. "Hate killin', Gunfighter, hate it worse'n poison." There was no chuckle in his voice.

They knocked back their drinks and headed for the marshal's office.

They'd been there only a few minutes when Burston slammed through the door. "What the hell you bring me along for, Roan? I waited in that there saloon, the Den, an' you never showed. Next thing I know, a bunch o' cowboys come in tellin' 'bout the gunfight you an' the marshal had." He walked to a chair, pulled it out, and sat. He looked like a spanked kid. "Didn't you trust me to cover yore back, Gunfighter? Hell, I'm yore friend. I want to help protect you."

Malloy put his hand on Burston's shoulder. "It's for that very reason Provo insisted on coverin' my back. He said they ain't very many decent folks around here, but you're one of 'em. He wants to keep all you good ones alive."

Burston frowned, then apparently sighted the drinks in front of his two friends. "Hell, I ain't much of a friend if I ain't offered a drink right soon."

While Provo poured him a drink, he asked Malloy what his plans were now.

"Well, tell you like it is, I figure to head for SanTone." He looked into Burston's eyes, "And, my good friend, you ain't gonna go with me."

The rancher opened his mouth obviously to argue, but Malloy cut him off. "Tell you, we go on together, we both might buy the farm. What would Megan and the girls do then? One of us has to stay healthy to see they're taken care of. The one to stay in the game and do the fightin' is me." He looked at both of them. "You know my job, both of you. You know it's my assignment to gather up this bunch, or put 'em all in the ground." He tossed his hat to the desk. "Gonna tell you, when I come back, I expect to see Megan and her little flock of chicks all healthy and doin' well."

He poured himself another drink of Provo's whiskey, took a swallow, and eyed Burston. "And, when I get back, we gonna give all them women a chance to go back to New Orleans if they want. There might be one or two o' them who'll go."

Burston, his face chalky white, locked eyes with Malloy. "Roan, you gonna give Megan a chance to leave?"

Malloy glanced at Provo, wondering if he should answer that question in front of the marshal, then decided to do so. "Yeah, Clint. Ain't neither one of us had much chance to court her, but when we do, I hope, regardless who wins, that we can remain friends."

Burston's face still showed white around the gills. He never took his eyes from Malloy's, and finally he nodded. "Done give that a lot o' thought, Roan. Had a chance to watch Megan when you come up missin' down yonder in Mexico." He shook his head. "I ain't never had a chance with her. I reckon she's yore woman when you want 'er."

Malloy opened his mouth to protest, but Burston cut him off; he held up his hand. "Don't say nothin', Gunfighter. I know what I'm talkin' 'bout, an' I'm gonna have one say in this that you ain't gonna change one bit." He poured himself another drink, knocked it back, and frowned at Malloy. "When that little girl says she'll marry up with you, you gonna turn in that badge you been totin'. She ain't gonna lose her man, an' I ain't gonna lose a friend. You got that?"

A slow smile cracked the corners of Malloy's lips. "Clint, I wouldn't have it any other way."

Provo glanced at each of them. "Well, by damn, reckon that calls for a drink."

"Provo, the only reason you're offerin' us more of your whisky is 'cause that bottle ain't got but a small swallow left in it." Malloy pushed to his feet, felt like the blood rushed from his head, and again claimed his chair. "Figgered to go get us another bottle, but damned if I ain't already more'n a little drunk."

Burston stood. "I'll get us another bottle, but I'm here to tell you, I'm the only one in this room who can stand another drink."

Owl-eyed, Provo looked at Burston. "Reckon you're right, cowboy, but I've seen the Gunfighter here have to kill before. Done seen 'im git sick to his stomach 'cause of it. I git the same way, so I figgered to sort of head that off 'fore it could git started." He grinned a sickly look at them both, his mouth slid off to the side. "Reckon it worked pretty good." He glanced at the door. "When y'all head for the barn, lock the door behind you. I'm gonna sleep in one o' them cells." He leaned forward, put his head on his desk, and snored before either of them could get around the desk to him.

"Reckon we can carry 'im into that cell, Clint?"

Burston glanced from the sleeping Provo to the unsteady Malloy. "Sit. I'll get 'im in there, then I reckon we better get to our rooms."

About fifteen minutes later, they walked from the marshal's office, locked the door, and stepped onto the boardwalk—into the face of gunfire.

Malloy grabbed Burston's arm and jerked him to the rough boards. Instantly sober, he shielded Burston's body with his own while he pulled his Colt. He lay there a moment, waiting for another shot. None came. "You take a hit, Clint?"

"Naw, but I might as well have. You damned near killed me throwin' me to the boardwalk like that."

"You see where them shots come from?"

"I didn't see nothin'. You didn't give me a chance to.

You reckon they're still out yonder waitin' for us to make a move?"

Although he figured Burston couldn't see, Malloy shook his head. "Nope, I think they'll be long gone 'fore we find where they shot from." He stood. "Right now I'm gonna get a good night's sleep, then in the mornin' I'm headin' for SanTone. You're goin' back to the ranch an' make damned sure them women are safe, and stay that way."

Burston crawled to his feet. "Yep. Figure you're right. Them woman-stealin' bastards want two things. First off, they want you dead, an' second, they want them women. I aim to see they don't git their second want. Reckon you gotta see they don't git their first one."

Despite an aching head, Malloy was an hour out of Laredo when another hot, brassy sun inched above the horizon. He sighed. Another day ahead like the one before. He figured two and a half days would put him in San Antonio.

While riding, his thoughts went alternately from Megan to Turnbull. He felt certain Megan would be safe. Burston's ranch house was built like a fortress, and he had enough men to take care of the ranch work and the safety of the women.

He wondered if Turnbull had found out anything about the bandit gang. He mulled that over a while, shrugged, and decided the only way he'd know that was to talk to the ranger.

Two days later, the sun straight overhead, Malloy rode his horse through the back doorway of the livery in San Antonio. After telling the hostler to rub the horse down and grain-feed him, he pulled his Winchester from the scabbard, hung his bedroll over his shoulder, and headed for the hotel.

He'd no more than stepped to the rough wooden surface of the boardwalk when he met Turnbull. Bull took a step back, and studied the U.S. marshal. "Damn, Malloy, don't reckon they's anybody I'd rather see than you right now. Come on over to the office."

"Can't it wait 'til I put my gear away?"

"Nope. We need to talk right now." His look traveled over Roan's lean length. "You done lost some weight since I seen yuh last." Then he glanced at the gear Malloy toted. "Shift that gear to yore left shoulder, loosen the thong off'n yore six-gun, an' keep yore eyes peeled for trouble. You ain't got many friends in this here town." He chuckled. "Cain't say as how I got any more'n you. Reckon 'tween Bentley an' Clausen, they done managed to turn the whole town agin' me."

"Why?"

Bull nodded his head toward his office. "C'mon, I'll tell you all about it."

Despite Bull's warning, they made it through the front door of his office without trouble. The Ranger poured them each a cup of coffee, motioned for Malloy to sit, and then sat on the corner of his desk. "Malloy, gonna tell you what I got, then want you to go over everything I have, then we gotta talk. I think I have one of the links in this here chain pegged pretty tight—but I figger I ain't a damned bit closer to knowin' who the big cheese in the gang is than I was when you left here. Need your thinkin' on it. Maybe you can figger it out."

18

MEGAN STOOD AT the window until Malloy and Burston rounded the base of a hill and disappeared from sight. She sighed, tried to remember if there had been a time she'd not worried about The Gunfighter when he wasn't within sight. She shook her head. If there was trouble, he was always in the middle of it. Then she wondered why she still thought of him as The Gunfighter. She smiled. That name had lost the horrible connotations it had originally had.

She turned from the window, poured a glass of water from an olla by the door, and stood drinking it. She frowned. Why should she and the girls sit here, protected by over half of Burston's men, and let the two men she cared most about ride off to battle for her? Why couldn't she and the girls help? She thought on that a while and came to the conclusion that if they were where the fighting would take place, they'd only get in the way; might hamper the way the two men reacted to assailants; might get one or both of them shot, maybe killed. Her shoulders drooped. She took another swallow of water, squared her shoulders, and went to her room. She would not stay here and wait for someone to take care of her. She'd taken care of herself since the day her father died.

But she found that convincing Rance Singleton, the ranch foreman, to send her to Laredo with the girls and an escort of riflemen was nigh on to impossible. When she told him what she wanted to do, his jaw knotted, he frowned, and shook his head slowly, the way she'd seen one of the old bulls do while being held in the holding pen.

"Miss Megan, even if the boss hadn't told me to keep you here—and safe—I wouldn't take you to Laredo." He made a quirly and lit it before going on. "Why, ma'am, do you realize they's a whole bunch o' critters out yonder wantin' to take you into Mexico an' sell you into a life I wouldn't wish on nobody? 'Sides that, if I took you away from here, chances are we'd be in a gunfight 'fore we got ten miles. Some o' you womenfolk might get shot." He shook his head. "Don't reckon I wantta carry that around on my conscience the rest o' my life."

An idea began to bloom in the back of Megan's mind. She nodded. "All right, then, I want you to give each of us a rifle and some bullets. Then I want you to have one of the riders teach us how to shoot. If this place gets raided again, we need to be able to help defend it."

Singleton frowned, chomped down on the gigantic cud of tobacco he kept in one cheek or the other, whether he had a quirly hanging from his lips or not, then nodded. "All right. I figure that's a good idea." He walked to the gun cabinet and pulled several 1883 Winchesters from it. "Go git the womenfolk. Then we can git started."

Two hours in the morning, and two hours in the afternoon, Singleton worked with the women. The morning of the tenth day, the rawboned old foreman grinned. "Ladies, if'n I hadn't seen it with my own eyes, don't reckon I'd of believed it." He pulled the chew from his mouth, tossed it into the corral, and bit off another. He shook his head, as if in disbelief. "Why, hell, I'd put you womenfolk up agin the best shots we got—an' bet you'd come out on top."

Megan came softly to his side. "You mean you'd take us into a firefight, and feel good about it?"

He shook his head. "No, ma'am, don't reckon I'd ever feel good 'bout puttin' womenfolk where they might git a chunk o' lead in 'em, but I'm here to tell you right now, if'n it happened, we couldn't git outta it, I'd just soon's have y'all on my side as any man." He chewed a moment, switched his cud to the other jaw, frowned, and looked Megan straight in the eye. "But, gonna tell you, missy, it's one whole lot different shootin' at a target than it is when you gittin' shot at at the same time."

During the ten days Singleton had spent with them, he and Megan had bonded in a tight friendship. She took him by the arm. "Rance, are you saying we don't have just as much gumption as a man?"

His face showed red through the deep saddle-leather tan. "Aw, now, Miss Megan, I ain't sayin' that a-tall. You an' yore ladies done showed me you got what it takes to stick." He pushed his hat back from his brow. "Why, heck, ma'am, hot as it's been, along with blisters on yore hands, sore shoulders, sore muscles, an' chances we'd git shot at from the chaparral, y'all stuck to it without a whimper." He shook his head. "No, ma'am, I figger y'all would do to ride the river with."

She squeezed his arm. "Why, Rance, that's a mighty nice thing to say." She realized then that she'd taken to talking a lot like the Texans—and felt a bit of pride in it.

They called it a day after the last girl fired her weapon and received praise from Singleton. They all went to their rooms to bathe and change clothes.

250   *Jack Ballas*

Stripped, and splashing the tepid water over her warm body, Megan wondered how to again bring up the subject of going to Laredo. She pondered the problem during her bath and while dressing. When she walked into the living area the soft clopping of a horse's hooves caught her attention. Then she heard Singleton's voice, "Climb down an' set a spell, marshal. Supper'll be on the table right soon."

Then the sound of footsteps on the veranda, and Marshal Provo's voice. "Came out to tell y'all how things're goin' in town."

"Aw, come on in, we can talk while we eat."

When they walked through the door, Megan stood facing them. "Marshal Provo, Rance Singleton doesn't speak for me. I want to know now, before supper, how and what Mr. Burston and The Gunfighter are doing."

Provo pushed his hat to the back of his head, then removed it and placed it on a nearby table. He frowned. "Ma'am, don't rightly know how *they're* doin'. Burston's in Laredo, an' The Gunfighter's done gone to SanTone. 'Fore he left, he shot two more o' that bunch that's been causin' you all the trouble, an' I'm here to tell you they wuz a whole bunch more of 'em left town after that." He grinned. "Laredo's a right peaceful town now that he run most of 'em outta town."

Megan's stomach turned over. A chill ran up her spine. "Do you mean to tell me The Gunfighter left town alone, and has gone to seek more trouble in SanTone?"

Provo, obviously surprised at her concern, stepped back. He looked at Singleton, shrugged, and returned his eyes to Megan. "Reckon that's the size of it, ma'am." He shook his head. "That man don't seem to know when to quit. He got his teeth into this problem what's rightly mine an' the

Texas Rangers', an' he ain't 'bout to turn loose."

Megan stood there a moment. Fear tightened her back muscles while pride swelled her throat until she could barely swallow. She looked at Singleton. "I'll not hear an argument against it, Rance. The girls and I are going back to Laredo with Marshal Provo."

The old foreman chomped hard on his tobacco, his eyes slitted. He shook his head. "No, ma'am, you ain't. I done got orders to keep you here safe, an' that's 'zactly what I'm gonna do."

Provo, obviously seeing a no-win situation coming on, cut in. "Tell you what. Laredo's 'bout safe as any place them womenfolk could be right now, an' I don't think the fight'll be comin' back there. I figure The Gunfighter'll wind things up in SanTone. Why don't you give me four men, I'll deputize 'em, an' we'll take the women to town? Ain't nothin' there to harm 'em now. I'll see to that."

Singleton apparently hated to give in. He chewed furiously on his chew, opened his mouth to say something, clamped his jaw tight again, and shook his head. "All right! But I'm tellin' you right now, if Clint Burston fires me, you gonna make me a deputy an' pay me the same wages I'm makin' here."

Provo placed his hand on the old man's shoulder. "Old-timer, I got no money to pay a deputy. Hell, them four men you gonna give me'll still be drawin' ranch wages from Burston. But tell you what I'll do; I'll take full blame for lettin' them women come to Laredo. Then The Gunfighter an' Burston'll have to have it out with me."

Singleton looked from Provo to Megan, chomped a couple of times on his cud, then gave a jerky nod. "Let's eat. We'll go in town with you in the mornin'."

• • •

On the way to town, they met Burston heading for the ranch. The rancher looked steely eyed at his foreman. "Thought I told you to keep the womenfolk at the ranch—safe."

The old man returned his look. "Clint, ain't no man alive coulda kept Miss Megan at the ranch. The marshal an' me done figured the best thing to do wuz to take all them women to town, but to stay with 'em so's they'd be safe as we could make 'em."

Burston shifted his look from his foreman to Provo. "Thought you had enough sense to keep 'em outta town."

"You try it, Burston. We done our best, so we took the next best thing. Singleton's done tol' you how it is."

"Clint, they did everything but hog-tie us to keep us from leaving. If they had refused to take us to town, I'd have taken the girls and gone alone." She gave him a brief smile. "Of course we'd have borrowed a few of your Winchesters to keep us company."

To Megan's thinking the look he showed her dripped sarcasm—mouth crooked, eyebrows raised—then he said, "And what the hell you figure you an' them women would do with them rifles?"

"Why, Clint, why don't you ask Rance what we would do with them?"

Singleton cut in, "Boss, them women can shoot with the best shots in yore crew, an' I'm gonna tell you right now, they got sand."

Burston swept them with a look that did little to hide his chagrin at being out-argued by Megan, Provo, and his foreman. "All right, you've made up your minds, so we'll go back to town—then what?"

Megan's shoulders slumped. "I don't know, Clint. I guess I hoped there might be something we could do to keep The Gunfighter from getting killed."

Burston looked at Provo. "You ain't told 'em that he's already left town? You ain't told 'em 'bout the gunfight you an' him had in town? You ain't told 'em that every bit o' the border scum in Texas is hell-bent to put him under six foot o' this Texas soil?"

"Burston, I figure these here ladies already know the answer to all them questions. But you know as well as me that you, these ladies, or me ain't about to stop him from doin' what he's sworn to do. He's one helluva man. I'm right glad he's on our side. An' you know what? I figger he's maybe the only man in this country can carry out what he's tryin' to git done."

Burston sighed, then nodded. "Reckon you're right. I just wish they wuz somethin' we could do to help."

"They is somethin' we can do, but I'm gonna ask for you an' Singleton to help me git it done. We gonna quietly, one by one, put as many of that gang outta circulation as we can round up. Y'all gonna help."

Megan had been watching them closely. At Provo's words, Burston seemed to gain new life. His eyes took on a hard, granite-like look, his mouth slitted to a straight line, his jaw muscles knotted. He nodded.

During the ride back to Laredo only the soft sound of the hooves, and an occasional blow from the horses, broke the silence.

When they reached town, the marshal and the rancher escorted the women to the cabins they had forcibly vacated a few weeks before. With all that had happened since that fearful day, it seemed like years to Megan.

When the men left, the women kept their Winchesters. Many of them clung to them as to an old friend. Singleton looked at each of them, winked, and gave them all what passed for a smile on his wrinkled old face, then followed Provo and Burston.

Megan waited until they disappeared around the side of the saloon, then motioned the girls around her. "Girls, we're not going to sit here waiting for the men to protect us." She swept them with a hard gaze. "Some of you, I can name at least three, have found men out here you might be thinking of as more than just friends. We might as well get used to helping in any kind of fight that's brought to us."

Jeannie, a pretty little blonde, giggled. "Miss Megan, I could name four women in this bunch what's found her man out here in this country." At her words, all the girls laughed. Megan felt her face turn hot, and knew the flaming red of her face told them who the fourth woman was.

She pulled her Winchester from its scabbard and looked at them. "Never mind how many of us have found more than we bargained for out here." She patted the stock of her rifle. "Every one of us is going to tote her rifle to bed, and anywhere else she has to go." She nodded. "You're even gonna carry them to the outhouse, and when we go anywhere, we'll always have two or three of us together." She turned blue eyes, now more steel gray, on each of them. "Any of you disagree with what I'm saying?"

Charlotte—everyone called her Charley—cut in: "Ma'am, I'd surely like to get back to work. You think maybe we could go back to our jobs?"

Megan nodded. "That's exactly what I think. We're not going to be pushed out of our normal life, and if anyone tries it, I think he or them will face a whole lot of Winchesters." She pulled her bedroll from her horse. "Now, I want you to go to your cabins, store your belongings, and join me here. We're going back to the Buckle. And remember, regardless of what you're doing—dancing, serving drinks, or helping behind the bar—keep your rifles with you."

Less than a half-hour later, she and the girls marched, almost in military formation, into the Buckle. For the time of day, early afternoon, the place was crowded, and when Megan escorted her little flock through the batwings, a cheer sounded to the rafters.

Before turning the girls loose, Megan pulled them around her again, then motioned the two bouncers to her. "Here's the way we're gonna do it, ladies and gentlemen; I want at least three of you upstairs by the railing where you can see everything on the floor below. Keep your weapons fully loaded and cocked. We'll rotate that job every hour." She made a sweeping motion with her left hand. "All right, let's do our jobs."

As soon as the bouncers and girls took their places, Megan motioned the piano player for silence. Then, so everyone in the place could hear, she said, "Folks, the girls and I have had a pretty rough time of it since we last saw you. We're back, and we're not the same bunch of timid women you might expect us to be. If any of the rough bunch comes in here, we're gonna see that they leave posthaste—or we're gonna shoot them where they stand." She carefully swept the crowd with a hard gaze. "Now I see three here who will be leaving suddenlike, or we'll be carrying you out." She pointed to a ranny wearing tied-down guns. He stood against the back wall. "You're the first to go. Now get!"

The gunny made as if to protest, but found himself facing about forty six-shooters in the hands of patrons. Megan pointed to two others. "Join him. Don't ever come back in this establishment." As soon as they left, Megan signaled the piano player to commence playing, and then wandered about the floor, greeting people she'd come to know as ranchers or cowboys before she and the girls were abducted.

She wondered at herself. She was not the same reserved, icy cold gambling lady of the riverboats. Since coming west of the river she'd undergone subtle changes in her thinking, in her demeanor, in her values; and, in her mind, she gave credit to The Gunfighter, who had so selflessly protected them all. She admired his toughness; in fact, she admired the rough, tough, everyday people she met—hard-working people who gave no thought to fine dress and smooth manners. The people out here were real; what you saw was what you got.

She stopped to ask a young cowboy about his wife, who, before Megan's time in the Buckle, had worked there. She was told his missus was expecting in a couple of months. And so it went.

About sundown, Provo and Burston came through the batwings. Burston came directly to Megan, who had taken a chair to the end of the bar and sat watching the goings-on. Provo had a smile that threatened to stretch to his ears. "Them three you ran outta here? Well, I sent 'em packin'."

Megan's stomach tightened; her throat muscles closed up, limiting her ability to swallow. "Y—you turned them loose? Won't they go on to San Antonio, and just be that many more The Gunfighter will have to face?"

The marshal stared at her a moment. "Ma'am, I seen a long time ago how much you care about that man, an' no, ma'am, I ain't gonna do nothin' to make his job harder. I stripped them three of all their hardware, give 'em each a canteen o' water, an' set 'em across the desert without no horses." He shook his head. "Ma'am, I don't figger they gonna be no threat to The Gunfighter." He grinned. " 'Sides that, I told 'em I'd personally hang 'em if I ever seen 'em back in Laredo. No, ma'am, I don't reckon they gonna be no trouble to no one no more. They ain't gonna be in no shape to fight when they git where they're goin'."

She looked him in the eye for a moment, then envisioned the long stretch of waterless, cactus-covered, hell's own acres and miles the three men would have to cross on foot. She nodded, then smiled. "Behind that star you wear is a man who's half devil, but he's overshadowed by a real gentleman. Thank you, Marshal Provo."

The batwings flapped, and two more of the rough bunch walked in. They looked around and apparently saw Provo, then headed directly toward him. The marshal glanced at Megan. "You better move away, ma'am. Them two're lookin' for trouble." He sighed. "Yes'm, they come lookin' fer it, an' I reckon they done found it." He flicked the thong off the hammer of his Colt .44.

Turnbull showed Malloy the telegrams, told him what he suspected, then sat back in his chair, spread his hands palms up, and shrugged. "You figger it out, Gunfighter. I ain't got no idea who's gittin' these messages in the end. They're being sent to Shug Bentley, but I cain't make myself believe he's got the brains to be runnin' a gang like we done run into."

Malloy stared at the stack of messages. After a few moments he stood, poured them each a cup of coffee, and again took his chair. "You been watchin' where he goes, who he sees after gittin' one o' these?"

Bull shook his head. "I ain't been able to watch the depot an' the town marshal at the same time." He grimaced. " 'Sides that, I'm tryin' to keep headquarters off'n my rear end. That damned Clausen's been fillin' the telegraph wires 'bout how I'm mistreatin' the good, upright citizens of this town." He shrugged. "I figger the boss is gonna strip my Ranger's badge off'n me the next telegram I git."

"You'll get it back. Don't worry 'bout it." Malloy sat forward, then grinned. "Remember, you got another badge in your pocket." His grin widened. "And that badge is one powerful piece o' metal. Fact is, if you lose your Texas

Ranger badge, I want you to pin your deputy U.S. marshal badge on right then. I'm gonna keep mine under my shirt for awhile."

Turnbull frowned. "For sure you ain't done nothin' to make yoreself loved by none o' that bunch. Fact is, they hate you more'n they do the law. What you gonna do when you have to let 'em know you *are* the law? You ain't never let nobody know you carried that badge before."

Malloy shook his head. "Don't know, Bull. I been thinkin' 'bout turnin' it in, maybe settlin' down. Hell, I been pushin' myself into situations beggin' to get me killed for a number of years now. Yeah, I'm thinkin' when I get this assignment wrapped up, I'm gonna go courtin'. I've found the woman I want, now what I gotta do is convince her she wants me. Don't know how that's gonna work out."

Bull reached into the bottom drawer of his desk and pulled out an unopened bottle. He smiled. "Reckon that calls for a drink. She know you're a lawman?"

Malloy took the glass of whisky Bull held out to him, then shook his head. "Bull, she's used to bein' around well-dressed, mannerly gentlemen. I could fit into that bunch pretty well, but I don't want that kind o' life. I like life west o' the river. Hell, when I cross the Mississippi comin' west, I feel like a different man—I *am* a different man. Don't know how she's gonna feel 'bout becomin' a western woman, a cattleman's woman." He shrugged. "Reckon that's somethin' I gotta find out." He knocked back his drink, stood, and squinted toward the glare of the front window. "Reckon right now I'm gonna see can I find who's gettin' them telegrams. Whoever he is, he's covered his tracks better'n an idiot like Bentley could ever figure out how to do it."

Malloy pulled the door shut on Bull's "Be careful," and ducked at the whine of a bullet close to his ear. He hit the boardwalk, rolled, and fell off the edge bordering the alley. That fall saved his life. Another bullet gouged a furrow in the rough boards right where he'd been only a moment before.

While falling, his Colt slipped into his hand. He snaked his way back into the alley a few feet, then peered above the edge of the walk. He could see no one, but a wispy tendril of smoke drifted from the corner of the building across the street. He drew a bead on the edge of the board where he figured the shooter's head might appear if he tried to see what damage his shot had done. The brim of a hat slowly inched into sight. Malloy thumbed back the hammer and waited. Another inch or more of the hat brim appeared. Malloy took the grip of his revolver in both hands. Angry blood pushed into his head, drowning the fear that only moments ago had caused his gut to churn sour bile into his throat.

A little more of the hat brim, and a shot broke the stillness. A man staggered from the corner of the building, took a couple of limp-legged steps toward the street, and fell facedown into the dust.

Turnbull pushed through the doorway of his office, looked toward the alley Malloy had disappeared into, and said, "Stay where you are, Gunfighter; there may be more of 'em."

Malloy stood. "To hell with that, Bull. If they's more, then you an' me's gonna get 'em together." He walked to Bull's side. "Let's see if we know that dry-gulchin' jasper."

While crossing the street, Malloy swept the rooflines and storefronts for any sign there might be more than one after his hide. The only persons who bolted into the street after the shots were Bentley, who ran from his office down the street, and Clausen, who stepped gingerly from the boardwalk in front of his store. He was the first to reach the still body. "Well, Ranger, who of our citizens have you shot now?"

Turnbull ignored the storekeeper, then bent to flip the body to his back. He looked up at Malloy. "You know this piece of garbage, Gunfighter?"

Malloy shook his head. "That don't mean nothin'. Seems like most o' them what shoot at me nowadays I ain't never seen before."

Clausen butted in. "I'll tell you who he is. He's a rider from the Bar-C-Bar, a good cowboy who minds his own business. Wait'll I send word to your boss about this killin'."

Turnbull straightened from examining the body, his face hard as granite, his eyes pinpoints of blue fire. "Gonna tell you somethin', you spineless, sanctimonious bastard: you, an' that sorry excuse for a lawman standin' beside you, have cost me some time wasted on hatin' you." He shook his head. "Maybe it wasn't wasted, 'cause it's built a head o' steam that's gonna help me beat the livin' hell outta you—both o' you at the same time. Now git the hell outta my way while I try to figure who this trash wuz workin' for."

Clausen stood still for a moment, stared at Turnbull, looked toward Bentley, and nodded. "All right, marshal. I want you to go with me to the telegraph office and cosign the telegram to Texas Rangers headquarters." He turned his look again toward Bull. "Be ready to turn that badge you wear over to a better man."

Malloy waited until the two were out of hearing, then looked at Bull. "Know what? Seems to me that oily slime's awful anxious to get you out from behind that star." He pushed his hat to the back of his head and pulled on his ear lobe. "Wonder why?"

Bull stared after the two and shook his head. "Hell,

Gunfighter, he an' me ain't never seen eye to eye, but don't seem like our differences are enough to cause him to carry such a grudge."

Malloy nodded. "Yeah, Bull, some men hide cowardice behind bluster, an' if it's not cowardice, then he must have somethin' else he's hidin'. We gonna watch him mighty close."

19

As soon as Megan saw Provo flick the thong from the hammer of his six-shooter, she glanced at her girls, and motioned toward the two hard cases who were approaching the marshal. The one in the lead, hawk-faced, hard-eyed, and dirty enough to have come off the trail only a short while before, stopped in front of Provo. "Hear tell you sent some friends 'o ours packin'. Didn't even let 'em take horses or weapons with 'em. That true?"

Provo nodded. "Reckon you got pretty good ears. I sent 'em off; told 'em to not never come to this town again. That's what I'm gonna do with the two o' you."

The gunny standing only a couple of feet behind and to the side of the hawk-faced one flicked his hand toward his gun. A shot sounded from the balcony. The gunny's hand turned to a bloody pulp at the same time hawk face made a pass for his handgun.

Provo started his draw at the sound of the balcony shot. He never fired it. Instead, in one smooth motion his handgun cleared his holster and continued upward to hawk face's mouth. The marshal slammed the barrel into lips, teeth, and gums. With his left hand, he grabbed the hand reaching for the six-shooter, and twisted the weapon out of the gunny's grip. Both of the would-be bad men stood there—staring. Hawk face spit a couple of teeth to the puncheon floor, gagged, and tried to clear his mouth of Provo's gun barrel.

The marshal grinned, stared straight into hawk face's eyes. "Now you gonna see what a nice man I am. I ain't gonna set you afoot for a couple o' days. *But* I'm gonna send you on yore way. Only difference 'tween the way I'm gonna treat you an' yore friends is, you ain't gonna be wearin' no clothes." He chuckled. "That there desert sun's gonna cook the hide off'n you. It's gonna cook you real tender fer them coyotes to chew on when you cain't walk no farther. Now turn around and head outta here fer my calaboose."

The gunny who tried for his gun first whimpered. "Ain't you gonna git us a doctor? I might bleed to death."

"You better hope you do. It'll be one helluva lot easier than what I'm gonna do to you. Now git. You goin' to jail, but only fer a couple o' days." He took a step toward the batwings, then glanced toward the balcony. "Nice shootin', young lady." He left with those words.

Megan had separated herself from the action by only a few feet. During the entire scene, she wondered that the life she led could be so different, so changed, so hard. She'd stood here and watched two men horribly maimed—and promised much worse—yet she'd felt no sympathy for them. In fact, when one of her girls fired into the man's hand, she'd wished she'd been the one who fired the shot; and when Provo brutally smashed his revolver through the other gunny's teeth, she'd wanted to cheer. She mentally shook her head in wonder.

She scanned the room, then signaled the bartender. "Set

up a round for the house in celebration of Marshal Provo's efforts to clean up this town."

Ranchers and cowboys crowded to the bar, all talking of Provo and the guts Megan's girls showed. Pride swelled the Ice Lady's chest. These girls were not the giggly, immature bunch she'd ridden from New Orleans with; they were women, and from where she sat, she'd say they were ready to marry one of these hard-bitten men—ready and willing to suffer any hardships the world could throw at them. Each of them would make a man a home, even if it was no more than a soddy, and they'd make the man feel as though he lived in a castle.

Her thoughts turned to The Gunfighter: What was he doing? Was he safe? Why did trouble always follow him, and why did he so stubbornly meet it head-on? She walked to look into the mirror behind the bar, studying the woman who looked back at her. She admitted to herself that she was what most would call a beautiful woman, a woman most men would pursue if she'd let down the barrier she had long ago raised between herself and men— but she'd gotten so accustomed to its shield of safety that she kept it in place. She frowned. Had she kept it between her and The Gunfighter? She wanted him to look at her, wanted to see a glint of longing in his eyes, wanted to see his appreciation for her as a woman any man would want. If she could see any of those things, she'd make certain she destroyed the shield between them.

Abruptly, she became aware that she still stared into the mirror, although not seeing what it reflected. She turned to look at the room filled with men. The one man she wanted to see in that room was somewhere in San Antonio. A slight smile creased the corners of her lips. If he wanted to be in San Antonio, that's where she'd go.

• • •

Malloy looked at Turnbull. "Let's go back to your office. We need to give these telegrams some thought."

"Hell, Gunfighter, I done spent days givin' 'em some thought. I ain't no further toward figgerin' this out than 'fore I found the first one over yonder in New Orleans."

Malloy shook his head. "You're wrong, Bull. I figure we're missin' only one small piece of this puzzle. If we can find it, we can wrap this assignment up."

In Bull's office, Malloy poured each of them a cup of coffee, then sat across from his old friend. "Your checks comin' in from the Federal Marshal's headquarters?"

At Bull's nod, Malloy smiled. "Good. Now, if the Rangers want your badge, you have a better one."

"Ain't none of 'em better'n that Texas Ranger star."

Malloy studied his coffee cup a moment. "Didn't mean it that way, Bull. What I meant was there ain't a damned soul gonna take that deputy marshal badge from you 'less I say so." He took a swallow of coffee. He glanced at the door, then back to Turnbull. "There's not many who'd take a shot at a Texas Ranger here in the middle of town—or a deputy U.S. marshal. I figure you're relatively safe, 'less someone takes a shot at you from an alley or rooftop." He stood and took a turn around the room, then sat again. "I'm tempted to wear my badge, but there might be something I can uncover as a plain citizen that I might not have a chance to look at otherwise."

Bull smiled. "Plain citizen? Hell, Malloy, I doubt there's anybody in Texas would call you a plain citizen." He nodded. "But you might be right, 'cept you done made enemies o' that whole bunch we're chasin'. I guar-an-damn-tee you, ain't none o' them gonna tell you nothin'."

"Didn't figure they would, but there might be a chance to find what I want by usin' illegal means." He grinned. "Wouldn't want an upright, God-fearin' man like citizen

Clausen to see the law bent a little by a U.S. marshal. Why, hell, he might even write the president to get my badge stripped from me." He shook his head and, still grinning, said, "Don't figure I could stand that." He stood. "Got an idea. I'm goin' over to the saloon across the street. Don't want you with me. I'm gonna try to milk some information outta that weasel Bentley." He shrugged. "If I can't, then I'll see can I beat it outta him."

Bull stared at Malloy a moment. "You're a damned fool. Don't you know ever' stinkin' bit o' border slime in this area's got a bullet in his gun with your name on it?"

Malloy put on his most innocent look. "A shame, that's what it is, a terrible shame."

Turnbull stared at his friend, a deep furrow between his brows. "What's a shame?"

Malloy grinned. "A shame to waste all them bullets when it'd take only one to get rid o' me."

Bull grimaced. "Okay, go ahead, get yoreself killed. I'll be along later to clean up the mess."

Malloy nodded, pushed through the door, and left Turnbull staring at his desk, a deep frown cutting furrows across his forehead.

Out on the boardwalk, Malloy stood in the deeper shadows until he could sweep the rooftops, alley entrances, doorways, and windows with a searching glance. After a full five minutes, satisfied that no one waited to dry-gulch him, he stepped from the boardwalk onto the dusty street.

The harsh light of day had softened to a set of purples, blues, and blacks in the dusk that pushed shadows into every broken surface: road ruts, storefronts, tree trunks, and walkways. Malloy stepped back onto the boardwalk, opened the gate of his revolver, and shoved a cartridge into the empty chamber, which as a safety precaution he always let the hammer ride on. When he eased his Colt back into the holster, he did it gently—and left the thong off the hammer. Then he walked boldly to the batwings and pushed through.

Malloy stayed close to the wall while walking toward the bar. His fingers never strayed more than an inch or two from the walnut grip of his Colt. By the time he reached the bar, he knew where every man sat who he'd classify as belonging to the gang he wanted broken up.

When still several feet from where the bar joined the wall, he spotted Shug Bentley, the man he intended to pick a fight with. As it turned out, he didn't have to start trouble. One of the men he tagged as belonging to the gang pushed his way between a couple of men about five feet down the bar, looked at Malloy, and said, "You ain't drinkin' in this waterin' hole. Most in here are my friends. Don't none o' us cotton to drinkin' in air stunk up by a man what always sides with the law. Git out!"

Between Malloy and the gunman who challenged him, every man had moved away to leave that space empty—but Malloy figured there were already a number of guns drawn and pointed at him. He recognized the man. The name he'd used when Malloy saw him last was Dikes. Maybe he could bluff his way out of this.

Abruptly he smiled. "Hell, Dikes, you an' me ain't never been what a man could call friends, but I never pushed you any." While talking, he took a step toward the gunman, then another, until he stood within inches of him. " 'Sides that, I never shot nobody what didn't have a gun pointed at me."

Dikes frowned, obviously puzzled. He glanced behind Malloy, then brought his eyes back to The Gunfighter. When he glanced to Malloy's rear, The Gunfighter took that as his chance, maybe his only chance to get out of this. He drew his Colt, thumbed back the hammer and pushed it into Dikes's gut. "Now, you cheap, no-'count border trash, tell them friends o' yores to drop their side guns back in their holsters. You don't, an' there ain't no way I can keep from bustin' yore spine slam in two when my bullet goes through you."

A sigh, then low growls came from the crowd—but also the muted sound of iron sliding into leather. His nerves tied in knots, Malloy knew he'd only gotten in the first punch. This bunch wouldn't give a damn if he shot Dikes, or two more like him. They all hated the man called Gunfighter.

Without warning, Malloy grabbed Dikes by the shoulder and spun him so that his back was to the gun Malloy held. Then he prodded the gunman toward Shug Bentley. Before he reached the town marshal, Bentley stepped in front of Dikes.

"Gunfighter, drop that gun and walk to the hoosegow with me. You're under arrest."

Malloy grabbed Dikes by the back of his belt and, with as little effort as tossing a bag of garbage, threw him into the crowd. Then, before Bentley could react, he pushed his Colt into the marshal's gut. "Bentley, I don't like you. One more word outta you, an' I'll scatter yore guts all over this room. Now tell yore friends to back off and get the hell outta here, or it ain't gonna take any more talk to let my finger slip off the hammer o' this .44." He jabbed the barrel of his gun deep into Bentley's gut, bringing a gasp. Malloy took that opportunity to take the town marshal's handgun.

Bentley, bent at the waist, looked at Malloy through pain-filled eyes. "You're buckin' the law, Gunfighter. I'll have every lawman in Texas huntin' you. You cain't git away with this."

Malloy glanced behind, saw there was no one between him and the wall, then took a handful of Bentley's shirt and swung him around to get him next to the wall. "You better pray they ain't one o' yore friends dumb enough to take a shot at me. They do—you die right along with me." One slow step at a time, he pushed the town marshal toward the batwings.

Before pushing through the swinging gates, Malloy's back muscles stretched so tight he thought they'd tear his ribs from his backbone. His head throbbed. A bullet could tear into him from behind, or when he pushed through the batwings, there could be guns on either side unleashed at him. He sucked in a deep breath, and shoved Bentley out ahead of him.

Only three or four feet from the saloon doors stood Turnbull. He held a double-barreled Greener in each hand, pointed directly at a crowd of the ruffians Malloy had run out of the saloon. "You men break it up. Break it up now, 'fore I git mad and cut a whole bunch o' you down." Over his shoulder, he said to Malloy, "You an' that garbage you got under yore gun head for my office. I'm gonna find out from each o' you what the hell this is all about."

Malloy pushed Bentley ahead of him, past Turnbull, and on across the street to the Ranger's office.

Inside, he shoved Bentley into the chair across the desk from the one the Ranger usually sat in. Turnbull came through the door while Bentley settled himself into the chair. Then, while seating himself, Bull placed the two Greeners on his desk, muzzles facing the door. He glanced at Malloy. "All right, you got 'im here, what you gonna do with 'im?"

Malloy grinned. "Figure to have 'im tell us who's runnin' the gang. Know he isn't, he's too dumb."

"How you figger to do that?"

Before Malloy could answer, a loud pounding shook the heavy door. Malloy walked to the side of it. "Yeah? What you want?"

"Telegram for the *ex-Ranger*. He ain't got no more right to take our town marshal in there with you."

Malloy crossed to the door, lifted the bar from across it, and twisted the white, porcelain knob. "Come in—alone."

Barge, the telegraph operator, slipped through the small opening Malloy had allowed. He glanced at the three men, his eyes wide, jaws tight, face white. He waved a yellow sheet of paper in front of him. "Telegram from Ranger Headquarters." He held the telegram close to his face and read: "Texas Ranger Turnbull. You're relieved of all duties. Stop. Await the coming of your relief. Stop. Brief him, and proceed to Headquarters. Stop. Signed, Commanding Officer."

The telegrapher, although obviously scared spitless, grinned a sickly grin. He looked from Turnbull to Malloy. "Your friend, Mr. Turnbull, here, ain't got no authority. Fact is, you're both breakin' the law by holdin' a gun on 'im."

Turnbull reached for his shirt pocket, unpinned the Ranger badge, placed it on the desk in front of him, then reached back to his pocket. "Reckon it's 'bout time I showed the town—an' yore boss, whoever he is—that I still carry a pretty good-sized stick." He pulled the deputy U.S. marshal badge from his pocket and meticulously pinned it in the same place the badge he loved had been. "Now sit down—on the floor there between me an' Mr. Gunfighter. We might as well get as much information as you two will give us."

Malloy shook his head. "We ain't gonna question neither one o' these rats where the other can hear what's said. Take Bentley back to a cell an' lock 'im in 'til we get through with this worm."

Bentley stared at Turnbull a moment with a puzzled, frowning look. "Why for you takin' orders from a gunfighter who ain't no better'n them he faced up to in the saloon?"

The former Ranger shrugged. "Don't know why I

should answer that question, but I'll just say this: The Gunfighter, to my knowledge, ain't never turned his gun on the law, an' he's been a great help to me." His voice hardened, "Now git off yore butt an' head for the back 'fore I drag you."

In only a moment, Bull came back into the office. He glanced at Malloy. "He kept staring at this badge. Reckon it's beginnin' to sink in that the influential citizens of this town ain't got any pull with the U.S. marshal's office."

While he talked, Malloy picked Barge up by his shirt front and slammed him into the chair vacated by Bentley. "Now, little man, you been deliverin' telegrams to Bentley." He nodded. "Yeah, I know they all been addressed to him, but I reckon you gonna tell us who he relays them messages to."

All signs of Barge's gloating had disappeared when Turnbull pinned on the deputy U.S. marshal's badge. Now he slumped in his chair, obviously scared by the turn of events. He clamped his jaws tight. "Ain't my job to know what none o' them who get messages do with 'em." Then, from somewhere deep inside of him, he found a trace of guts. " 'Sides that, even if I knowed, I wouldn't tell the likes of you."

Malloy forced a cold smile that only broke the corners of his lips. "Gonna tell you somethin' I reckon you ain't figured out yet. First off, I ain't bound by all the rules an' regulations my friend here is, what with him carryin' a deputy U.S. marshal's badge. So you can just figure the things I can do to you that no lawman would even think o' doin'."

Barge straightened and looked at Turnbull. "You ain't gonna let 'im do nothin' outside the law, are you?"

Bull shook his head and assumed a woeful look, his brow puckered, his cheeks sucked tight against his teeth, and his eyes wide. "Naw, I ain't gonna set here an' let 'im do nothin' like that—but then you gotta think: I ain't gonna be here with you all the time. Hell, I might be out trackin' down one o' them who're takin' all them women. Don't know what he might do to you while I'm gone." He shrugged. "I hear tell The Gunfighter can think up things to make you yell out the answers he wants. The word's been goin' around that the Apaches tracked 'im down a few years back just so's he could teach them some o' them things we hear they do to men fer fun." He shook his head. "They been gettin' credit for inventin' them torture things, but most o' them come right from The Gunfighter."

While Bull talked, Barge's face faded from an alkali hue to the pristine white of new snow. He looked from Turnbull to Malloy, and back again. "You ain't never gonna leave me here alone with him—are you?"

"Don't know what my job's gonna demand of me, but I won't unless I have to."

A slight look of hope crossed Barge's face.

Turnbull poured them each, including Barge, a cup of coffee. "Tell you what, the best way to make sure The Gunfighter don't work on you is to tell 'im what he wants to know." He grimaced. "Might save a lot o' broken fingers, burns on all parts o' yore body, even gettin' yore hair peeled off'n yore head a inch at a time, real slowlike."

Barge groaned, then said, "Oh my Gawd." He looked at Malloy. "You wouldn't do that to a man, would you?"

Malloy, his face a frozen mask to keep from laughing at the picture Bull painted of him, stared into Barge's scared eyes. "Try me."

Barge's face, unbelievably, paled even more. A pounding shook the door; then, without waiting for an answer, a bevy of the town's finest citizens, led by the mayor and Clausen, pushed their way into the room.

• • •

Megan pondered her decision to go to San Antonio. Would she help or hinder The Gunfighter? What could she, one lone woman, do to help him? Would he be angry with her for taking a chance on undoing all he'd done to ensure her safety? She shrugged mentally. The only way to answer those questions was to go where he was and see what happened.

That night, after they'd closed the Buckle, Megan gathered her girls about her, then motioned the bartender to join them. "Tell you folks what I've decided. I'm going to San Antonio to see if there is anything I can do to help The Gunfighter. He's done so much for us, and I think it's time to pay back some of the debt we owe him. If any of you will go with me, I'll welcome you." She turned to her bartender. "You'll run the Buckle while I'm gone." She swept the girls with a penetrating look. "Any of you going with me?"

Every one of them nodded. One sighed, and said, "Reckon Jimmy an' me's gonna have to put what we got goin' on the back of the stove. I'm sure as h—, uh, I'm goin' with you."

Megan shook her head. "Wait a minute. I want all of you to sleep on what I'm asking you to do. You've got to question whether you can shoot a man. It won't be easy, and I think if we do have to put a bullet in a man, we'll all have nightmares about it later."

Jenny giggled. "Miss Megan, we all love that big man." She giggled again. "Course, don't none of us love him the same way we all know you do."

Flustered, and knowing her face must be red as a garden-ripe tomato, Megan lost all composure. "Wh-why, I can't imagine what you mean. He's a friend, a friend who's put his life in danger for us." Primly, she added, "I think it's the least we can do for him."

At those words, every one of the girls burst into gales of

laughter. Then Jenny looked at them and turned her eyes on Megan. "Ma'am, you might not have admitted it to yourself yet, but there ain't a one of us can't see the real woman-like feelin's you have for that man. We've asked ourselves how a woman with all the fine things you must have back in New Orleans could fall in love with a man who probably knows nothin' 'bout fine things." She shrugged. "We all come to the same answer: when a woman meets the right man, the only fine thing in the world is him." She frowned. "To answer your doubts, I figure I can shoot any man who threatens one I think a whole lot of. I'm goin' with you."

Megan studied the face of each girl who had become a woman. She saw only determination on each. "All right. We'll go to our cabins and pack those things we'll need to stay clean while we're gone. And pack one nice dress to wear if we find a place to wear it once we're there."

"Uh, ma'am," the bartender cut in, "you're forgettin' one thing. What about Mr. Burston an' Marshal Provo? I'm thinkin' they ain't gonna stand still for y'all goin' off to git shot maybe."

Megan smiled. "If I have it figured right, Marshal Provo has to stay here because of his duties. Mr. Burston and Rance Singleton will go with us because they won't be able to think of any other way to take care of us." She laughed. "Mr. Burston'll be mad at Rance for creating us as a monster, but he'll go just so he can fire Rance when it's all over. Then, of course, he'll hire him back."

Jeannie hesitated a moment, then said, "Reckon y'all know to pack plenty of loads for those Winchesters." She stepped toward the door. "Well, let's get on with it. We got packin' to do."

The next morning Megan, having a last cup of coffee at the café, heard footsteps on the boardwalk; then the door opened and Provo and Burston entered. Despite her brave words to the girls, Megan had dreaded this moment, fearful of telling those two men what she and the girls were going to do. She looked at them and smiled. "My, we didn't expect to see you in here. Thought perhaps you'd both eaten much earlier."

Burston gave her a sour look. "What you mean, earlier? Hell, it ain't even daylight yet." He swept the group of pretty women with a questioning look, then centered his attention on Megan. "Y'all spend half the night workin', then show up for breakfast 'fore daylight makes me ask what you got up yore sleeve besides a pretty arm."

Megan's face turned warm. She should have known not to try to fool either of the two men. She turned her look directly on Burston. "Well, here's how it is, sir. We've decided, since we're all pretty good shots, that The Gunfighter can use our help in San Antonio. We're all packed and ready to go."

Before she finished speaking, she thought Burston would burst a blood vessel. His face turned pink, then red, then purple. "You—you're gonna do what?" He slammed a fist into his palm. "Now, young lady, I've heard all of the nonsense outta you I'm gonna put up with. Y'all git yoreselves back to yore cabins, unpack, crawl back into yore beds, and rest up for work tonight."

"Clint, I don't want to hear any more out of you. We've made up our minds. We can all shoot with the best around here. Roan will need all the help he can get, and we—every one of us—owe him—including you. We're goin' whether anyone comes with us or not."

Obviously wanting to vent his anger on something, or someone, Burston decided on his foreman. "Damn Rance Singleton! He done this. He made all o' you figger you could fight good as a man. Why—why I'll fire 'im soon's I see 'im."

The door swung open and Singleton walked in, just in time to hear the last few words. "Reckon you're firin' me agin." He looked at Megan. "Told you I'd git fired. Now all I gotta do is find somebody who'll hire a stove-up old cowboy 'fore winter sets in."

"Y—you'll damned well stay hired 'til I tell you you're fired. First, since you made this mess, you gonna go to SanTone with us."

Megan knew then that she'd won, but didn't push it. She waited to see what Burston would say next.

Still standing by the girls' table, Burston shuffled his feet a couple of times. He turned his wrath on Singleton. "Well, what the hell you waitin' for? Git packed. We gonna leave in one hour.

20

THE SECOND MORNING Burston led them toward San Antonio, a hard knot pulled at his back muscles. He hadn't had this feeling for a long time, not since the Comanche were on the rampage. He knew the feeling for what it was: someone followed them, and the only reason he could figure for that was to do them harm. He looked across his shoulder at Singleton. "We got trouble. See kin you find a place to git the girls a little cover."

Singleton chomped down on his ever-present cud of tobacco. "Knowed they wuz back there a hour ago. That's why I been leadin' us off the trail a little." He chomped again, and spit a stream of brown juice onto a ripening cactus pear. "Up ahead, 'bout a hour, they's a ol' 'dobe shack we can hole up in. Walls're 'bout two foot thick. We should oughtta be pretty safe in there 'cept for ricochets." He spit again. "I'll git y'all to the shack, then I'm gonna take a look behind us: see who we're facin'."

"You are, like hell. I'll go back an' see who's followin' us."

"Boss, dadburn it, jest 'cause I'm old don't mean I done forgot what I learned 'bout slippin' up on varmints."

Burston shook his head. "I'll go. You so damned stove-up you'd prob'ly break ever' bone in yore body if you had to take a fall to git away from 'em."

Rance sputtered, then pinned Burston with a no-nonsense stare. "G-g-gonna tell you somethin', boss, I can still outshoot, outtrack, an' outride you seven ways from Sunday." They rounded a huge clump of prickly pear cactus at the end of his tirade. The old adobe shack stood only a few yards in front of them. Singleton pointed. "That there's the place I wuz tellin' you 'bout. Now you git them women in there. Get 'em set up fer a fight." He climbed from the saddle, stood a moment, kicked each leg out in front of him a couple of times obviously to rid them of stiffness, then handed the reins of his horse to Burston. "Be back in 'bout a hour." He didn't wait for Burston to argue with him.

Burston watched his old friend head back the way they'd come. He had trouble swallowing. Suppose Rance caught a bullet out there? He tried swallowing again. Fire him? He'd rather cut off his right arm than fire the old man—but he also knew that Singleton was one of the best danged scouts the army ever had. He took a deep breath and looked at the women. "All right, that there jacal is home 'til Singleton gits back here; an' then 'til we take care of whoever's on our trail. Git inside. Take the horses in with you and stay down low, below the ledge on them openings them Mexicans use for windows."

He climbed from his horse, handed the reins to Megan, shucked his rifle from the scabbard, and nodded toward the chaparral. "I'm gonna be out yonder where that big mesquite looks down on that prickly pear. Don't shoot me. Fact is, don't shoot at nothin' you cain't see."

Megan watched him walk away, a tall, handsome man she might have loved had there not been Roan. As it was, she did care for Burston, but it was the kind of caring she would have shown a big brother, a brother she'd never had.

She turned her look on the girls. "All right. You heard Mr. Burston. Get inside that shack and make yourselves as small as you can. I couldn't stand it if any of you got hurt."

Charlotte cut in, "How you think we'll feel if you get hurt, Miss Megan?" Her voice broke. "We love you, too."

Megan pulled Charley to her breast. "I know. I know how all of you feel, but I'm responsible for you being out here with me. If I hadn't had this dumb sense of honor toward The Gunfighter, you'd all be safe back there in Laredo."

Jeannie chuckled deep in her throat. "Ma'am, I ain't much used to cussin', but I'm gonna say you'd of played hell makin' even one of us stay back there."

More overcome than she would ever admit, Megan blinked her eyes, hard, to clear them of the tears that had welled to the surface. "All right, girls. Let's do like Mr. Burston said. Come on."

The inside of the shack pushed heat in on them as though from an oven. Before stretching out on the earthen floor, Megan had each girl check the area for scorpions. They found five, and stomped them into the dirt; then she pushed the scorpions onto a piece of broken pottery and dumped them out the window. After cleaning house to that extent, they stretched out below the opening each had chosen to defend.

Megan lay at her station, sweated, sniffled fine dust from her nostrils, and worried about the girls, Burston, and Rance Singleton. She blamed herself for all of them being here, but knew there was nothing she could have done or said to keep them from coming with her. And she was scared. Each nerve at the back of her neck pained, burned, and pulled tight on her scalp until she had to clamp her teeth to keep from moaning. Then Charley broke the silence. "Anybody in here scared as I am?"

A chorus of "darned right" echoed through the shanty. Megan gave a loud "shhh" to silence them. "If those men are close, we don't want to give them warning that we expect them." Silence again reigned. Then she said, "Better pull the horses down. Hold their reins up close to the bit so they don't try to get up."

Time dragged. Small green flies discovered them, and made life even more miserable. By Megan's reckoning, a half-hour passed, then another. Each girl had her Winchester in front of her, pointed out her particular window. Megan wiped sweat from her brow, saw a movement out by a tall yucca, moved her sights an inch or so, tightened her finger on the trigger—then Singleton stepped from the brush into view.

Megan relaxed, but in that moment knew she could pull the trigger on a human being. Singleton said, only loud enough for someone nearby to hear, "You out there, boss?" He waved a hand toward the jacal. "Come on in. I'll tell y'all what I found."

In the shack, they gathered around the old man. He swept them with a look. "Gonna tell y'all right now, we got trouble." He dumped his chaw into his hand, tossed it out the window, bit off another chew, settled it in his cheek, and nodded. "Yep, we got trouble. Three o' them varmints Provo sent out into the desert to die must of run across a family on the move. Prob'ly killed 'em. They wuz ridin' hosses what looked like work animals. They don't none o' 'em have a saddle—but they all have long guns. The clothes two of 'em's wearin' don't fit too good, so I figger them wuz ones the marshal cut loose without nothin' on."

"How long 'fore they get here?" Burston had started to roll a quirly, but stopped when he asked the question.

"I figger maybe a half-hour." Singleton nodded toward Burston's hands. "You got time fer a smoke, then I reckon you an' me better git out in the brush. Don't want all o' us in one spot." He glanced at the girls. "How y'all makin' it, ladies?"

Megan answered for them. "Well, Rance, if you'd asked me that question before you walked from the brush, I don't know how I might have answered it, but when you stepped into sight, I was ready with the trigger. I figure we're ready."

He looked at her, a grim humor showing around his wrinkled, creased eyes. "Found out you could pull the trigger, huh?"

Megan swallowed hard, then nodded. "Yes. Nothing to be proud of, but I figure these girls are made of the same stuff as I am." She nodded. "Yes, sir, I believe there's not a one of us who will shy off from doing what she must to rid us of that vermin."

Singleton's face broke into hundreds of wrinkles in what passed for a smile. "Knowed dang well y'all had what it takes. You about to find out they ain't a thing these western women kin do that you cain't." He shook his head. "Don't figger they's a one o' you what will ever go back east o' the river."

"Not as long as our men are out here. We didn't come here to tuck our tails and head back when the goin' got rough." Charley smiled at the old man. "Are you taken, Mr. Singleton? I ain't got me a man yet, but I'm lookin' for one just like you."

Rance chuckled. "Aw, pshaw, now you're teasin' an ol'

man. You should oughtta be ashamed o' yoreself. But if
you ain't found a young man by Christmastime, danged if
I don't b'lieve I'll saddle up an' come git you."

The joshing back and forth had done much to settle the
nerves of the girls—as well as of the two men. Burston
threw his burned-out cigarette to the ground, stepped on it,
and nodded. "All right, let's get set to take care of them
renegades what Provo thought we wouldn't be bothered
with no more."

Before Singleton stepped through the doorway, he
looked at Burston. "If you kin, use yore Bowie; if not, then
blow 'em to hell."

Burston nodded, and followed Singleton into the open.
The sharp crack of a rifle broke the stillness. Burston fell
backward.

Before Burston hit the ground, Singleton hovered over
him. "Where they hit you, boss? Danged coyotes, dang
'em anyway."

Burston rolled to his side. "Didn't hit me, just scared
hell outta me." He sat, frowned, and said, "Wuz hopin' we
didn't have to all be in one place for this fight."

"We ain't gonna be, boss. I'm gonna git out the back—
less, o' course, they already got it covered."

"Don't be a fool, old friend. Stay here with us."

Singleton chewed hard on his cud, then shook his head.
"Naw. A couple o' you rake them bushes with lead out the
back way. Time y'all git off 'bout three shots apiece, I'll be
behind one o' them cactuses out yonder."

Before anyone could protest, Singleton ducked through
the door and sprinted toward the chaparral. All of the girls
turned their rifles toward the brush and fired fast as they
could pull trigger. Burston covered the front of the hovel.

Singleton had covered only about fifteen yards when
Megan saw him stagger and fall. Without thinking, she

ducked through the opening and ran toward the old man, only slightly aware that someone ran with her.

She reached Singleton's side, stooped, and caught an arm. Across the old man's chest, Jeannie had caught the other arm. Bullets peppered the ground around them. The outlaws obviously were attempting to hit the old man again. As much as possible, Megan turned to get herself between the bandits and Singleton. She and Jeannie dragged him sideways toward the shanty. Muscles braced for the tearing, burning, agonizing feel of a bullet puncturing her, Megan looked across the old man's chest. Jeannie, eyes wide with fear, pulled desperately at Singleton's arm.

Months, years, a lifetime later, it seemed, they pulled and pushed the old man into the shack. Megan knelt at his side. "Where you hit, Rance? Damn you, you better not be hit bad. You have too much to teach me about cows. Say you're not hit bad."

Rance looked into her eyes. "Hit two places: in the leg, an' high in my shoulder. Don't think they're bad. Git back to yore window. I ain't gonna bleed to death while y'all take care o' them skunks."

Megan tore her blouse loose from her body, unmindful of any sense of modesty, and shredded it into rags, folded them, and then stuffed them inside his clothing. When certain the bleeding had slowed to a trickle, the steady crack of rifles pushed through her concern, then Burston's words, "Ladies, don't burn all yore bullets at once. Make sure you see something to fire at." There was only a barely discernible slackening of sound. Then all firing stopped.

"Don't none o' ye show yoreselves at them openin's," the old man said. His voice sounded strong to Megan.

Through the long afternoon they lay there and sweated, occasionally brushing flies from their arms and faces. Megan noticed Burston sitting against the wall, searching the inside of the hovel. "What're you looking for, Clint?"

"Wuz sorta checkin' to see if they wuz anythin' to catch fire in here. Don't see nothin' we gotta worry 'bout. The roof's been burned for firewood long ago by passersby." He shrugged. "Ain't nothin' else in here that'll burn."

"Why're you worried about that?"

Burston wiped his forehead. "Well, gonna tell you, miss, it's gonna be dark soon. I figger them jaspers out yonder gonna make a move to come in on us soon's they figger we cain't see 'em."

Despite the heat, a chill ran up Megan's spine. She frowned, then forced a smile. "Mr. Burston, as you and The Gunfighter would say, 'I figger that'll be better than sittin' here waitin'.' " She jacked another shell into the magazine. "How do you think to handle their rush?"

Burston scratched the beard stubble on his jaw. "Been givin' that some thought. They gonna be firin' a steady stream when they come. We don't wantta be in the middle o' the shack shootin' at them windows an' doors, an' we don't wantta be firin' so as to hit one o' our own. Gonna be a whole lot o' chances they gonna hit one o' us."

Megan's nerves screwed down tighter—enough to give her an instant headache. "How do you plan to fight them, then?"

Burston's brow wrinkled. "I finally come up with the idea that our eyes gonna get used to the darkness better'n theirs 'cause it's gonna be darker in here than it's gonna be on the outside. So I reckon if we lie down, stay as close to the ground as we can underneath them windows, an' shoot straight up when we see anythin' block out the light, I figger we gonna have a good chance."

Megan swept the room with a look. "All right, girls, you heard him. Make ready to defend this palace we've occupied the last few hours."

Each of the young women checked her rifle to ensure it was fully loaded, then went to the window she was defending and lay on her back.

Through the deepening dark, Burston said, "Hold your shots a wee mite high. We don't want to hit none o' us." Those were the last words to break the silence for over a half-hour. Darkness settled in. Then, from the chaparral on each side of the jacal, rifles opened up. The ricochet of bullets whined about the stifling room. Megan drew herself into as small a knot as she could, legs tight to her stomach, holding her elbows against her sides, but leaving room to work the lever of her rifle.

She kept her eyes on the slightly lighter oval where the window would be. A shape blotted out the light. She fired up into it. Simultaneously, there was a sound like a palm slapping a side of beef, followed by a loud groan accompanied by a loud gasp, then the fall of a body close to her. She twisted, put another shot into the body, then turned her attention to the window again. Twice more while lying there, she heard similar sounds and grunts from other parts of the room—then the whine and buzz of insects, the rustle of leaves from the mesquite, even the nervous breathing of those in the room ceased.

Megan lay there, her eyes straining toward the window. Gradually the sounds of insects began; sounds of breathing, some nervous, some labored, pushed in to break the stillness. Then Singleton's voice, "B'lieve we done got 'em all." His voice turned harsh with worry: "Each o' you young'uns say yore name, then you, boss."

Each girl spoke her name into the darkness, and Burston followed. When the last name sounded, the flare of a lucifer lit the room. Before it burned down to Burston's fingertips, a time Megan identified by his curse and his throwing the glowing match to the floor, she saw each girl, along with the bodies of the bandits. The outlaws sprawled in grotesque shapes. "Any of you girls hurt?"

None responded. Then, after a moment's silence, Charley said, "All I got is a bruise where this trash fell across me."

Burston's voice cut into the gloom. "All right, let's build a fire, drag these varmints outta here, an' make some coffee an' supper. We gonna go to that there settlement settin' alongside the SanTone-to-Laredo trail soon's we get some light in the mornin'. I know a horse doctor there who can fix up Singleton's scratches."

While Burston talked, Megan took a couple of matches from Singleton, struck then, and inspected the bandits. All dead.

A half-hour later, with a small fire burning in the middle of the room, the girls sat around the glow of it and laughed louder than usual, talked louder, and cried a little when their eyes rested on each other. Megan had seen this reaction during the war. It was a way some, most, had of relieving the tension built up during the fight. While they waited for the coffee to boil, Burston dragged the bandits' bodies out into the brush after stripping them of weapons and cash.

Malloy looked from Clausen to the rest of the town's leading citizens. He waited for them to notice the badge on Turnbull's shirt. They didn't.

Clausen stared at Bull. "We're relieving you of your duties. You've bullied the last citizen you ever will in this town." He glanced at The Gunfighter. "And you, Mr. Gunfighter, we intend to try you and hang you before mornin'. You've been ridin' high, wide, an' handsome since gettin' back to town. We've had enough of you and your kind."

"You're mighty fast with yore tongue, Clausen. You ain't hangin' me, an' you damn shore ain't gonna hang a deputy U.S. marshal." Malloy grinned, anticipating the look on Clausen's face with his next words. "You, an' nobody else in this room, got the authority to relieve Deputy Turnbull of his duties. Only the marshal who appointed him, or the President of the United States, can do that."

All eyes swung to Turnbull, then dropped to his chest. Malloy studied each face. Most showed only mild surprise, but Clausen's complexion paled, then an angry red moved up from his collar. "What kind of deal you ringin' in on us, Turnbull? Where'd you get that badge? There hasn't been a U.S. marshal in this town in months."

Bull's face hardened. "Ain't none o' yore damned business, mister, but I been carryin' this badge in my pocket for quite a while." He stepped around his desk. Every man, including the mayor, backed up a step. Clausen stood firm.

"Where you got Bentley? You got no right to hold him for anything."

Malloy moved to stand beside his friend. "Legally, we can hold 'im for twenty-four hours." He pushed a cold smile to his lips and nodded. "That there should be enough time for us to do what we need to do."

Clausen's lips curled into a sneer. "Well, well, we got a gunfighter tellin' us what the law is." His face pulled tight. His eyelids closed to slits. "Gunfighter, you better be outta this town come daylight; you ain't, an' we gonna have us that hangin' I wuz talkin' about earlier."

Cold anger pushed into Malloy's brain. He slipped into the language he'd use on the other side of the river. "Clausen, you'd best think real hard on that threat. To get a rope around my neck, you and your cronies will have to wade through lead slugs, and hereafter I'll be wearing two

.44's. You can bet I'll take twelve of you to hell along with me." He grinned. "You'll be the first to take a bullet—right in the gut. Somehow, I don't think you're the kind who does his own fighting—not as long as you can hire some trash to do it for you."

The general store owner looked at Turnbull. "Well, you're carryin' that badge we cain't strip you of. Is it your policy to let border riffraff threaten the good citizens of a town?"

Bull shook his head, his expression a studied serious one. "No, suh, it shore ain't. So reckon soon's y'all clear outta here, I'm gonna check around an' see if they's any o' that happenin'." He frowned. "First, I reckon I gotta find who the good citizens are, then I'm gonna have to question 'em as to whether they been bothered by any o' that border riffraff you talkin' 'bout." He again shook his head. "Uhh-uh, shore would be bad to find anythin' like that happenin' around here."

Clausen apparently knew he'd lost this confrontation. He glanced at those who came with him, said "Let's go," and before leading the way from Turnbull's office, he said, "This ain't near 'bout over."

As soon as the door closed behind them, Malloy poured a cup of coffee, then pinned Bull with a hard, penetrating look. "Bull, I'm beginning to get a mighty strong feelin' I know who Bentley's been deliverin' them telegrams to."

Bull nodded. "I got the same feelin'." He walked around his desk and sat. "We might suspect it, but provin' it ain't gonna be easy. So far he's been right cagey about coverin' his tracks."

His face feeling like he'd let soap dry on it, Malloy pushed a hard smile to his lips. "Bull, I don't figure to let a small-time crook outsmart me. I ain't gonna go to him for answers. We got the one locked in that cell back yonder who's gonna give me the answers. An' despite us both knowin' it ain't gonna stand up in front of the law, I'm gonna get them answers from 'im if I gotta break every bone in his arms, hands, legs, and feet."

Bull stared at his friend. "Malloy, you cain't do that. Hell, you're too good a lawman to turn to torture."

Malloy gave a jerky nod. "*Was* too good a lawman, Bull. I figure anybody who'd let innocent women be kidnapped and sent into a life of pure hell ain't deservin' of humane treatment."

"Naw, don't reckon he's deservin' of it, but I don't believe you gonna do it. You're too decent a man to let someone like him make you do what would tear yore guts out for the rest of yore life. 'Sides, we got the good folks in this town agin us, as well as all that border trash what's been hangin' 'round, an' more of 'em driftin' in all the time."

Malloy sagged into the chair across the desk from Bull. He took out his tobacco, held it to his nose, and inhaled. The rich aroma of black cavendish tobacco caused him to pack his pipe and light it. Through a great cloud of smoke, he looked at his old friend. "Didn't mean to get you into this kind of a mess when I give you that badge, Bull. Slide it 'cross the desk to me, an' clear outta town 'til this is over."

The former Texas Ranger's face turned red, then purple. "You know danged good an' well you couldn't run me outta town with one o' them twelve-gauge Greeners, Malloy. Now cut out that kind o' talk." He glanced at the rack of shotguns. "Talkin' 'bout them Greeners, reckon it might cause that bunch to hesitate a mite if we went to carryin' one o' them." He stood, pulled a twelve-gauge from the rack, and tossed it to Malloy, then took one for himself.

Malloy grinned. "You ever look into the bore of one of these from the wrong end?"

"Once. Never want to do it agin. Fact is, lookin' down the wrong end of a shotgun shore makes a man think about changin' the way he lives, if he's got any more livin' to do." He opened the top drawer of his desk and pulled out a box of shells, stuffed several into his pocket, then passed the box to Malloy. "Before we question Bentley, let's take a turn about town, see can we figger how many o' that bunch we might have to face."

Malloy shook his head. "Don't reckon that'd be very smart. Better one o' us stay here an' make sure Bentley stays locked up. Both of us leave, an' they'd break 'im outta here in a minute."

Malloy went to the side of the window and peered out. "Don't reckon we gonna worry 'bout leavin' here. That bunch has split up. Clausen's tryin' to stir up the trash, an' looks like the mayor's tryin' to quiet down the respectable folks of the town."

Turnbull came to stand at his side. A frown creased his forehead. "Malloy, that bunch Clausen's haranguin' out yonder'll go to the saloons, drink 'til them waterin' holes close to git their guts pumped up—then I figger they'll try to take Bentley outta here."

Malloy slanted his friend a look. "Bull," he said, keeping his voice soft, "I believe you said they'd *try*. Well, we got plenty o' time. Let's get ready for 'em. Stand a Greener against the wall at each window, along with plenty o' shells. Then I'm gonna go back there an' see can I get anything outta Bentley."

Turnbull nodded stiffly and went to the gun rack.

The morning after the fight with the bandits, Burston led his group of lady warriors into the small settlement alongside the San Antonio-to-Laredo trail. Two of the women rode, one on each side of Singleton, to make sure he stayed in the

saddle, despite his growling that he didn't need to be mol-
lycoddled. "Why, gol-ding it, I done got slivers from
choppin' stove wood that hurt worse'n these here scratches. We gotta git on to SanTone right sudden, or them outlaws're gonna maybe give The Gunfighter more'n he kin
handle."

Burston pulled his horse in in front of the livery stable.
After dismounting, he held his hand up to help the old man
from the saddle, and promptly got what he knew Singleton
considered a good cursing. "Gol-ding it, I ain't no baby.
Git the dang blasted hell outta here an' go find that there
hoss doctor." The old man swung stiffly from the saddle,
held on to the saddle horn a moment, then headed into the
maw of the stable. He looked back over his shoulder.
"Soon's he doctors me, we gotta git on the trail."

Burston stared at his foreman, and knew that no kind of
argument would deter the old man. He walked past
Singleton and yelled for the liveryman, who also did the
doctoring on animals brought in for screwworms, fence
cuts, and other ailments.

The liveryman went by the name of Buck. No one had
ever heard him called by any other name. While Buck
cleaned and put an ill-smelling ointment on, and in,
Singleton's wounds, he looked over his shoulder at the
heavily armed group of young women, then turned his
look on Burston. "Where y'all headed?"

"SanTone. Why?"

Buck tied a knot in the bandage circling Singleton's
shoulder, then shook his head. "Don't know as how I'd do
that right at this time, suh." He straightened, wiped his
hands on a piece of gunnysack, and pushed his hat to the
back of his head. "They's been a mighty lot o' hard cases
tricklin' through here the last few days—all headed for
SanTone." He shook his head. "Seems to me that there

town ain't gonna be safe fer nobody, let alone a bunch o' pretty young ladies."

Singleton laughed. "Hell, man, you notice anythin' different 'bout these here women?" Then, not waiting for an answer, he said, "These here women done all got blooded last night, an' I'm here to tell you they kin fight with the best of any men. We left some o' that bunch you're talkin' 'bout out yonder in chaparral fer the coyotes an' javalinas." He stood, looked Burston in the eye, and, in a voice that brooked no argument, said, "Let's ride. I'm good as new."

Burston stared at him a moment, shook his head, and set his jaw. "Figured to leave you here 'til we got back."

"Boss, ain't no way you kin make that stick. You done fired me so many times I done lost count." He shrugged. "Don't know as they's anythin' worse you kin do to me." He chomped down on his chaw. "I'm goin'. Nuff said." He headed for his horse, gathered the reins into his hand, and swung aboard.

About four o'clock that afternoon, tired, hungry, and looking for a place to make camp, they rounded a bend in the trail. A group of five riders rode a couple of hundred yards ahead. Megan pulled her Winchester from its scabbard, looked at the girls, and said, "Do the same, and jack a shell into the chamber. We might save The Gunfighter some trouble."

Despite obviously trying to hide a smile, Singleton glanced at the riders ahead of them, then at Megan. "Good idee to keep yore rifles ready, but don't jump the gun. Them jaspers might be friendly." He grinned and looked at Burston. "Boss, these here women done got the taste o' gunpowder, an' now they don't seem to be able to get enough o' it."

Megan swept her girls with a hard look. "All right, do what Rance says, but I'm saying pull those hammers back and keep your rifles pointed at those riders until we know what their business is."

The group ahead looked back, and pulled their horses down to a walk. They waited for Megan and her group to catch up.

Burston rode to the front of his charges. "Stay bunched. Don't none o' you separate yoreselves so's to make it easy for one o' them to grab you."

As they drew closer to the riders, Megan studied each of them. She had no doubt they were of the same ilk as those who had taken her and the girls across the border. When they drew rein in front of the five, Burston, holding his .44 in his right hand, swept them with a glance. "You men got some claim to this here trail, or you gonna let us pass?"

A burly, dirty, unshaven man of about forty years pulled ahead of the others. "Seems like you folks got a burr under your saddles. We're peaceable. We waited, figgering maybe y'all could use some company along the trail."

Without exception, the strangers got that oily look to their eyes Megan had seen in the eyes of too many men. They looked at her and her girls as though they couldn't wait to get their hands on them. "Mister, we have all the company we need. We don't associate with the likes of you." Abruptly she jabbed her rifle muzzle toward him. "We don't dare ride ahead of you—I sure as Satan don't want you behind us." She paused a moment, to let her words sink in. "Now each of you, real careful-like, unbuckle your gun belts and let them drop. You make a move that distresses me, and I'll empty your saddle." She waited a moment to see her order carried out, then, from the side of her mouth, said "Girls, keep your rifles on them now. I want you to watch their hands." Then, to the hard cases in front of her, "All right. Now I want you to lift your saddle guns from their scabbards with your fingers touching only the stock and let them drop to the ground along with your handguns. You make a move toward the trigger guards, and you won't be accompanying us to town."

Burston and Singleton followed Megan's lead. When handguns and rifles lay in the thick dust, Burston motioned their prisoners to back their horses clear of the weapons, then he walked the few feet to pick them up. He looked at Megan. "Why'd you jump the gun so quick? We don't know these men figured to harm us."

Without taking her eyes from the prisoners, Megan said in a hard voice, "Mr. Burston, I've seen the same oily look in the eyes of more men than you can count." She nodded. "Oh, yes, they meant the girls and me harm—and you and Rance, death. Now we have to worry about getting to San Antonio along with them, and staying free of their clutches."

Singleton, his voice weak, clutched the saddle horn. "Ma'am, I don't figger to take a chance. We'll tie 'em to their saddles, an' then we ain't gonna stop 'til I get y'all safe and sound into that there Minger Hotel."

"You ain't in no shape to ride, old friend. We'll camp. I'll watch 'em 'til we get back on the trail in the mornin'," Burston said.

"Ain't doin' no such, boss. Tie 'em an' let's git ridin'. Figger we'll git to SanTone by daylight."

Burston looked at the bandits. "You heard 'im. Now I'm gonna tell you: stay bunched. Any o' you even look like you're ready to bolt, an' I guar-an-damn-tee you, you ain't never gonna git to SanTone or nowhere else. Let's go."

True to Singleton's reckoning, the eastern sky showed the first promise of dawn when they pulled rein in front of the Minger. Burston took them in, got them registered, told them to get a little sleep while he tested the town's feeling, and then he'd roust them out for breakfast. Whatever they did, or wherever they did it, they were to keep their rifles with them and not open the doors to their rooms until the person had identified himself. Before leaving them, he sighed. "Reckon Singleton's got them we took prisoner safely locked in the calaboose by now." He left.

He went out on the street, and the first person he came face to face with was one of those who'd taken the girls to Mexico.

The bandit stared a moment, jaw hanging slack, then went for his gun. Burston's hand dipped and came up spewing flame. He'd not had time for nerves to take over; he'd reacted to unexpected danger the way he had years before, when he'd visited the wild trail towns. The outlaw, his jaw now even more slack, his eyes bulging, grabbed his gut and bent at the waist. He dropped his handgun and followed it to the ground.

Burston swept the deserted street with a glance. He'd not expected to run into any of the bandit bunch this early. The man he'd shot only moments ago must have sat in on an all-night poker game. He stooped, picked up the fallen man's gun, grabbed him by the collar, and dragged his dead weight down the street to the office he remembered as the Ranger's.

He pounded on the door, again looked down the street and across the square. Not a soul stirred. The gunshot had not caused concern, which was not so odd; gunshots were part of everyday life here. He pounded the door again.

A guarded voice answered his knock. "Yeah, what you want?"

He thought he recognized The Gunfighter's voice. "Roan, let me in. I got a body here you might want to look at 'fore I dump 'im back on the street."

"That you, Burston?"

"Hell, yes, it's me. Let me in 'fore somebody decides to take a shot at me."

Wood scraped against wood when Malloy removed the bar from across the door. He opened it a crack, peered out, and swung the door open. By the time Burston dragged the bandit inside, Turnbull had a fresh pot of coffee on the stove.

Malloy, his greeting anything but friendly, stared at Burston. "Thought I left you back yonder to watch out for the womenfolk."

Burston nodded. "Yep, you did." He pushed his hat to the back of his head, obviously too tired to argue. "Let's sit. Gonna tell you what's happened."

An hour later, having finished the pot of coffee, Malloy and Burston had caught up on what had happened since The Gunfighter left Laredo. Malloy shook his head. "You gotta keep them women outta any shootin' we might have."

"Ain't no way, Roan. They come here to fight, an' I reckon all hell an' half o' Georgia ain't gonna keep 'em outta it." Burston tilted his cup, drained it, and put it back on the desk. "You say you figger them bandits're gonna try to take Bentley outta here tonight?"

Malloy nodded. "Figured they'd try it last night, but they must not have got liquored-up enough." He nodded again. "Yeah, they gonna try it tonight."

Burston closed his eyelids to slits and frowned. "Tell you what I'm gonna do: I'm gonna make sure them women are in as safe a place as I can make 'em stay in—but one where they can fire when needed.

"I'm gonna pin this here U.S. marshal's badge on you give me a while back, then I'm gonna visit every businessman in the stores around the square. Gonna tell 'em how the cow ate the cabbage. Gonna ask 'em to help if they can. If they balk at that, I'll tell 'em to stay outta the fight, or they gonna be facin' federal charges of con-con. . . ."

"Conspiracy?"

Burston nodded. "That's the word." He glanced out the window. "Full daylight now. Reckon some o' them stores're open by now. Might as well git busy an' line up all the support I can." He stood.

"Burston, they'll be stirrin' around soon. Ain't but few in this town your friend—watch yore back." Malloy looked at Turnbull. "Think I'll go out with Burston an' see can I find a store open besides Clausen's. Wantta get somethin' in here to eat. I don't, we gonna have a long, hungry time."

Malloy left with Burston, noticed several of the store-keepers sweeping the boardwalk in front of their stores, but saw none of those he'd figure were of the bandits' bunch. He went to a store a few doors off the square and loaded up on jerky, coffee, hard biscuits, and a few cans of peach-es. About to pay the man, he added four cans of beans to his order. Tempted to go to the hotel and see Megan, he decided against it: she'd be tired, and needed what sleep she could get. And in the event one of the gunnies saw him, he didn't want to alert any of the bandits to her where-abouts. He returned to Turnbull's office.

When he walked in, the day's heat had already taken hold. It would be stifling in the close quarters by noon. Bull inspected the items Malloy dumped on his desk. "Good. I hoped you'd get jerky. We prob'ly ain't gonna have time to cook nothin'. Them biscuits an' jerky'll set right well on an empty stomach."

Malloy sat, looked at his friend, and shook his head. "Might's well get comfortable. Don't figure anythin' much is gonna happen 'til they have a chance to get liquored up tonight, but I don't believe Clausen's gonna wait any longer'n that."

Turnbull stared at the wall for a moment, then pinned Malloy with a look. "Reckon you done made up your mind Clausen's the leader of that bunch."

"Tell you for a fact, Bull, I'm not absolutely sure, but he's sure givin' all the signs of bein' heavily involved." He packed his pipe, lit it, and peered through a cloud of smoke at the former Ranger. "The thing that bothers me is why would he do such. He's obviously got more money than he'll ever spend. He's the most influential man in town. People look up to him." He shook his head. "What's he got to gain?"

"More money, an' money's power. He's the kind who likes to control people. But"—Bull sat forward—"we still got no proof he's our man."

Malloy stood. "Reckon it's time I worked on Bentley's brain a little. I don't figure the telegraph operator knows— he might suspect, but I don't think he knows. We'll leave him alone." He walked into the cell block.

21

MALLOY UNLOCKED THE cell door, walked to the bunk where Bentley lay, and stared at him a moment. "Well, Mister Town Marshal, your boss finally come out in the open. He's taken charge of all the trash in this town, and he's buckin' the federal government. He's a loser, and he's gonna drag you down with him."

Bentley turned from his side to his back and stared up at Malloy. "Why're you takin' a hand in this, Gunfighter? You got no authority, an' even if you got a confession outta my boss, as you call him, you got no way to use it."

Malloy smiled. "Bentley, I'm gonna tell you a little secret. The very fact that I have no authority is in my favor. Once we kill the riffraff, he's gonna be standin' alone. I figure to force him into a gunfight and do what I do best—draw an' fire my Colt. He's got no chance, and right along with him I figure to take you down." His smile widened into a grin. "You see, you have no more chance than a twig in a prairie fire."

"I ain't drawin' agin you, Gunfighter. Ain't nobody around here fast enough to beat you."

Malloy shook his head. "You're wrong. There're probably some in this town could beat me, but they don't have the guts to try. I figure you fit that category, at least where lack of guts is concerned." He walked to the bunk and sat on its edge. "Of course, I could forget about killin' you, *and* your boss, if you'd cooperate with that deputy U.S. marshal out yonder. Soon's he had you testify, an' before we hang Clausen, I could let you climb on your horse and ride like hell outta here."

Hope glinted in Bentley's eyes. "I ain't got nothin' but yore word you'd let me go. 'Sides, you cain't tell Turnbull what to do, he's the one wearin' the badge."

Malloy shrugged. "Figure it any way you like, Bentley, it's your rear end." He pulled the cell door open, walked out, and locked it. "Call me if you have something to tell me."

Malloy walked into the office and closed the door. He looked at Bull. "He'll talk before the day ends. Then we can carry the fight to Clausen within the law, and with a clear conscience."

"You didn't have to hurt him. I didn't hear no yells."

"Sometimes, Bull, words can throw more fear into a man than all the brutality in the world."

Burston, so weary his legs felt like wet rags, looked toward the Minger, longing for the feel of a bed under his tired body.

He went to every store bordering the square, and in each told the proprietor what he knew of the happenings, and why The Gunfighter and Turnbull were opposed to the border trash. He told them about the stealing of women, the tie-in with New Orleans, the tie-in with someone in San

Antonio, and that the leader of the whole thing was located in their town. He also told them that he had no idea who the leader of the gang was, but that he knew those wearing their guns tied down were of the kind who'd kidnapped Megan and her girls. He closed his argument with the words "I ain't askin' none o' you to help us stop these outlaws, but I am askin' you to stay outta it an' let The Gunfighter, the marshal, and the girls an' me do what we can to stop the lawlessness. Them women I brung into town with me can tell you I'm tellin' it straight. They wuz took below the border to live a life of hell, but The Gunfighter rescued 'em."

When he walked from the last store without having gotten a commitment from any of the citizens, he looked at the Alamo, standing shabbily but proudly next to the Minger. He looked from the old mission to the front of Turnbull's office. The Alamo stood well within rifle range of any place on the square. He thought about that, and the safety the thick adobe walls offered, then nodded. He knew where he'd station some of the best riflemen he's seen in many a day—in this case he'd station riflewomen—Megan's girls. He turned his footsteps toward the hotel.

Burston pulled his heavy gold watch from his vest and glanced at it. Three o'clock—a couple of hours and it would be time for supper. He had time to wake the girls, get them fed, and into the Alamo.

After they'd eaten, cleaned their rifles, filled the magazines, and changed from their Sunday-go-to-meeting clothes to trail clothing, the girls, led by Megan and Burston, went to the Alamo.

Burston placed each woman where she had a good field of fire but was in as safe a place as he could find behind the thick, crumbling old walls.

He looked out on the square. The riffraff were already

out in force, most of them with a bottle in hand. They staggered from one watering hole to another.

Clausen, too, went from one saloon to another. He'd stay a few minutes in each, then go to the next. With all the trash getting liquored up, Burston would have bet his ranch and all his cattle that Clausen was paying for most of the drinks in each saloon. Burston allowed himself a thin smile; he hadn't seen one respectable citizen mingling with the trash.

Then the tall, handsome figure of the mayor appeared. He went to each place of business, stayed a few moments, then went to another. Burston hoped he knew what the mayor was about.

Twilight, then darkness, descended on the town. Things would get rough from now until the drunks had enough whisky to give them courage to attack the Ranger office.

At ten o'clock by Burston's watch, Clausen came to the front of his general store. He waved a torch above his head. His voice sounded above the steady noise of the crowd. "Men, our town marshal's been took prisoner, as all o' you know. He was took by two men who ain't never showed any of you a kindness. One o' them's wearin' a badge: where he got it, Lord only knows. The other is the man you know as The Gunfighter. He ain't got any reason to be where he is other than to git the favor of the law. An' I'm gonna remind all of you, to my knowledge he's killed several of your friends in fights he had no business gettin' into. I'm sayin' we gonna take Marshal Bentley outta that jail. If we have to kill both of them who's got 'im locked up—then that's what we gotta do."

By the end of his speech, Burston counted twenty-three torches. He would have bet Clausen had them ready to be handed out while he made his talk. In addition to the torches, they all had rifles. They drew into a close body, then, as if on signal, walked toward the Ranger office.

The soft pad of horses' hooves drew Burston's attention from the mob. Six riders—and the light from the torches showed them to be a hard-bitten lot. All were armed with side guns and saddle guns. Burston saw Bowie knives at their belts, and their chests were crossed with bandoliers. Burston's shoulders sagged. All they needed now was for the bandits to get reinforcements.

The riders pushed their horses through the mob and on to the front of the Ranger office. They dismounted, pulled rifles from saddle scabbards, and went to the door. One of them pounded on the door with the butt of his rifle. After identifying who the callers were, someone opened the door a crack, then widened to let them enter. Burston frowned. That was a helluva note: letting characters of that stripe come into the only secure place for holding the prisoner.

When Turnbull saw the man who had knocked, he swung the door wide, grinned, and grabbed him by the hand. "Damn, Captain Story, you cain't have any idea how glad I am to see y'all. Come on in."

Story frowned. "Glad to see us? What the hell you mean? Didn't you get the message that you're relieved of duty?" Then his gaze went to Turnbull's chest. "Where'd you get the deputy U.S. marshal's badge?"

"Reckon I gave it to 'im, captain." Malloy stuck out his hand. "I'm Roan Malloy, U.S. marshal, down here on assignment." They shook hands, and before sitting where Turnbull indicated, Malloy looked at the rest of the men. "Looks like you men came ready to do war. Who're you after?"

"We came down from Austin to relieve Turnbull, and take up where he left off in his duties." Story nodded toward the door. "What's that bunch outside doin'? Looks like they're ready to do battle—mostly against you two."

Malloy nodded. "Reckon you roped that bull right neat. Sit, an' we'll bring you up to date on all that's happened."

In short, clipped sentences, Malloy told them the story, and who they suspected of being the leader, and why. "Hell, Captain, the man we suspect is the one leading that bunch out there, and in that gang there isn't one single citizen of this town. They're all, right down to the last man, trash who've collected up here from the border towns." He forced a hard smile. "Reckon I'm the reason they've come up here. Don't any of them know me for a federal marshal. I've kept that between Bull, me, an' a couple of others. I find it easier to get information that way."

Malloy poured water for a fresh pot of coffee, then turned back. "That man stirrin' the pot out there is the one who's been sendin' the telegrams to your headquarters to get Turnbull relieved of duty."

Captain Story, apparently a man who made instant decisions, told Turnbull to pin his Ranger badge back on, then walked to the window. "They're 'bout ready to charge this building, Bull. This is your station, so what you gonna do?"

Turnbull picked up his Greener, glanced at Malloy, and nodded. They stepped toward the door. "Cover us, Captain."

Malloy pinned his badge to his shirt pocket and eased out the door ahead of Turnbull. He held a Greener in each hand, hammers eared back, fingers riding lightly on the twin triggers.

"Gonna tell you trash somethin', these shotguns're loaded with double zero buckshot. You'll notice Ranger Turnbull's holdin' two just like mine, an' inside there's six Texas Rangers got rifles trained on you. . . ."

From the bandits' rear, another voice cut in, "An' back here, we got seven Winchesters pointed at yore backs. I figger we can cut you down to the last man 'fore any o' you git off a shot. Now, hang onto them torches, an' with yore right hand unbuckle yore gun belts an' let 'em drop in the dust."

While the bandits reached for their belt buckles, another voice sounded, that of the mayor. "And I'm here to tell you, every man with a business in this town has a rifle in hand, and all are pointed at your backs." Then another voice. "An' if them lawmen need any more help, me an' my sister can shoot. Our rifles're pointed at you, too."

Clausen, standing on the boardwalk in front of his store, yelled, "Don't listen to them, men. Git to the jail, an' take our town marshal from it."

A burly, dirty, unshaven bandit at the front of the group dropped his gun belt to the ground, looked at Clausen, and shrugged. "You gotta know when to hold 'em, an' know when to fold 'em, boss. You notice I done folded my hand."

The soft thud of weapons hitting the dirt sounded, and as a body the bandits turned toward the nearest watering hole. "Hold it! You men ain't goin' nowhere." Turnbull's yell brought them up short. "Rangers, come out here an' take these men into custody. We gonna have to use the town jail, an' mine, to hold 'em all. We'll figger somethin' to hold 'em on later. Take all their cash an' put it in a pile on my desk; I got a need fer it."

"Why, you lily-livered bunch o' garbage! I'll kill them two if you ain't got the guts!"

At the words, Malloy turned and saw Clausen dragging a handgun from under his coat. Without thinking, Malloy, holding the barrels of the Greeners low, swung both toward the store owner and pulled both triggers on the one in his right hand. The buckshot cut Clausen's legs from under him as though with a scythe. He dropped to both knees, then, still intent on putting lead into Malloy, brought his handgun to bear on the U.S. marshal.

Malloy rushed him. Just as he squeezed the trigger, Malloy swung the barrel of his right-hand Greener, hit the handgun, knocked it to the side, and felt the burn of the bullet as it cut through his shirt, creased his side. Then he swung the butt of the shotgun against Clausen's head. He looked over his shoulder and yelled for someone to get the sawbones. He wanted Clausen to live to stand trial.

Inside the Ranger office, Turnbull stripped each prisoner of cash and piled it neatly on his desk. Then, when all had been collected, he put it in a half-gallon Mason jar. He looked at his captain. "You reckon you could have one o' yore men go outside and bring them two kids, Maggie' an' Sam Cahill, in here?"

Story glanced at the Mason jar and, stone-faced, directed one of the Rangers to get the kids.

In only a few moments the Ranger reappeared with the two youngsters. Turnbull picked up the jar, almost full of cash, and held it toward Sam. "Reckon you an' Maggie there could use a good bit o' money if you gonna buy any cows to stock that spread o' your'n. Don't know how much is in this here jar—but it's a bunch."

Sam looked at the Rangers, then back to Turnbull. "You gonna git yoreself in a passel o' trouble doin' this. You ain't got no right to give away what them outlaws wuz carryin'."

Captain Story, his face devoid of all expression, said, "Son, there's nary a man here ever saw that Mason jar, or even if we had, there isn't a one of us who saw what Ranger Turnbull did with it. Go on, take it, and get outta here. An' good luck."

Sam and Maggie, along with the Mason jar, disappeared out the door into the dark.

Malloy stayed in front of the Ranger office long enough to see that all prisoners were locked securely in the two jails, and to hear the doctor's pronouncement that Clausen would live to stand trial, but he'd never walk again. He had no doubt that among those taken prisoner there would be several who would tell enough to keep Clausen and Bentley behind bars for the rest of their lives—if they escaped hanging. And he'd bet his best Colt .44 that they'd hang—Westerners didn't take kindly to anyone messing with their women. He turned his steps toward the Minger. He wanted a bath, clean clothes, and, above all, he wanted to rid himself of his beard.

An hour later, dressed in the gray swallowtail suit he'd worn the last time he played poker with Megan and Burston on the riverboat, Malloy walked into the hotel dining room. He heard Megan say that all it would take to make this a perfect gathering would be for The Gunfighter to join them, and Burston's reply that he'd probably show up soon.

Megan looked up from talking to Burston and the girls. Her eyes widened. "Why, Mr. Malloy, what are you doing out here west of the river?"

"Well, Miss Dolan, I had a bit of business to take care of, and now that I've done so, I think I might stay out here, go into the cattle business. And if not, I'm sure there's something here to interest me. How's the saloon coming?"

Megan ignored his question. "Mr. Malloy, I can't imagine you taking to this unpolished, rough life out here. It's hard to separate you in my mind from the clubs and gambling houses in New Orleans, or the riverboats."

Malloy smiled. "I might say the same about you. I never thought, when you left the river, you'd stay."

Singleton coughed, and when all looked at him, he nodded. "Gotta tell you, this here lady an' her girls are Texans to the bone. Why, you oughtta seen 'em down the trail a ways: in a real firefight they wuz, an' they done their fightin' as good as any man. An' then, here in town, they had their rifles ready to keep The Gunfighter from gittin' hisself filled full o' lead." He nodded. "Yes, sir, they wuz set up in the Alamo, an' ever' danged one o' 'em wuz itchin' fer a fight."

The girls laughed; Burston and Malloy frowned. Malloy looked at Singleton. "You mean when The Gunfighter went out there to face that bunch, these women were also in danger?"

Singleton gave him a jerky nod. "You danged tootin' that's what I mean. These here women got sand in their craw, an' Miss Megan would a done it alone if she had to." He gave her a knowing look. "I reckon she thinks a awful lot o' that there Gunfighter."

Before he could go further, Megan cut in, her face a deep shade of delicate pink. "Why, of course I think a lot of that man. He saved all of our lives on numerous occasions. There's not a one of us who doesn't owe him her life."

Malloy cleared his throat and, not wanting anything said that might embarrass Megan or the girls, said, "Of course the man did what needed to be done, but I doubt he'd think of whatever he did as heroic, or that he'd consider that he'd saved anyone's life."

Megan bristled. "Mr. Malloy, I'll have you know Mr. Gunfighter, as we all know him, is a hero, and would be considered such by anyone who has seen the things and situations he puts himself into for others."

Malloy couldn't let this go further. He stood and walked around the table to stand at Megan's side. "Ma'am, if you'll take a good look at me, imagine me with a full beard, in range clothes, a hawg leg strapped to my side, and—although not lacking in manners, consider me a crude, uncultured man—do you think I'd look like a hero?" He smiled. "Why, ma'am, I reckon they ain't no woman nowhere who'd figure me for a hero—or even give me a second look."

When he slipped back into talking Texan, Megan frowned, then the frown disappeared and her eyes widened. "Roan?" her voice softened. "Roan, is that you, really you?" Then her face glowed. "Why, of course. Why couldn't I see it before? Why didn't the girls or Clint see it?"

Jeannie and Charley spoke almost as one. "Miss Megan, we never knew Mr. Malloy before, but maybe Mr. Burston should have recognized him."

Still standing, Malloy swept the table with a glance. "I reckon you folks have a right to know." He pulled his badge from his pocket. "I came here on assignment." His face turned hot. "I'll admit, when I saw y'all climb on that stagecoach in New Orleans, I sorta altered the assignment, mostly to keep Miss Megan safe, an' of course I wanted you girls safe, too. Now, I'll offer to escort you back to the river city, an' see you safely in your old jobs."

"Mr. Gunfighter," Jeannie piped up, "you ain't takin' me back to that sweatshop. Some of us has found ourselves a man, an' them what ain't, still figure to do so." She shook her head. "No, sir, you ain't gettin' me back the other side of the river."

All of the girls started talking at once, then Charley quieted them. "I reckon you get the idea, Mr. Gunfighter. Ain't a one of us would think of leavin' this country. We like it an' the people. We're gonna stay."

He looked at Megan. "I'll escort you back, Megan, if you want to go. I'll have to be fair about it, though. You see, you really don't own the Silver Buckle. Mr. Burston did the only dishonest thing I've ever seen him do at a poker table. He folded the winning hand in order for you to win his saloon. He did it to get you out here, where he figured to court you."

Burston stood. "Gonna tell you somethin', Roan." He dropped his gaze to the table, then lifted his eyes to stare at Megan. "Ma'am, I soon reckoned that I didn't stand a chance when I seen how you felt 'bout The Gunfighter. If you don't know it already, I'm here to tell you that you love the man, an' if you don't admit it, you ain't got the sand in yore craw I figger you got."

Megan, her face now flaming, looked into Malloy's eyes. "It wouldn't be ladylike to admit to loving a man who has never showed he cared one whit for her."

Malloy took her hand, pulled her gently to her feet, and folded her in his arms. "Reckon I was scared you'd say you wouldn't stay out here with me. I don't just reckon—I know—I loved you since I sat across the table from you on my first trip up the river." He pulled her closer. He stared into her eyes, which for some reason were misty, then he kissed her—soundly.

When she stepped back from his arms, she said, "I'll have to go back to New Orleans to shed myself of some property. Will you come with me?"

"Only if you'll marry me before we leave here. I, too, have property there. I want my old friend Josh to have it, and I want to settle a bit of money on him." He grinned. "But I gotta tell you, ma'am, I figure he's gonna pack up an' come on out here with me."

Megan smiled. "Sounds fine to me." She took his hand and led him around the table. "Slide around, girls. We'll dine, then I'll see the man at the desk about where to find a preacher."

Charley giggled. "Miss Megan, don't look like you're gonna give The Gunfighter a chance to get away."

Megan looked Malloy in the eye. "Not a chance in the world. Mr. Gunfighter, you're mine." She kissed him again, a kiss that showed smoldering coals had been flamed into a full-blown fire. She might call him The Gunfighter on occasion, but he'd never again be able to think of her as the Ice Lady.

No one knows the American West better.

JACK BALLAS

❑ *THE HARD LAND*

0-425-15519-6/$5.99

❑ *BANDIDO CABALLERO*

0-425-15956-6/$5.99

❑ *GRANGER'S CLAIM*

0-425-16453-5/$5.99

The Old West in all its raw glory

PETER BRANDVOLD

□ **ONCE A MARSHAL**   0-425-16622-8/$5.99

The best of life seemed to be in the past for ex-lawman Ben Stillman. Then the past came looking for him...

    Up on the Hi-Line, ranchers are being rustled out of their livelihoods...and their lives. The son of an old friend suspects that these rustlers have murdered his father, and the law is too crooked to get any straight answers. But can the worn-out old marshall live up to the legendary lawman the boy has grown to admire?

□ **BLOOD MOUNTAIN**   0-425-16976-6/$5.99

Stranded in the rugged northern Rockies, a wagon train of settlers is viciously savaged by a group of merciless outlaws rampaging through the mountains. But when the villains cross the wrong man, nothing on earth will stop him from paying every one of them back—in blood.

> "Make room on your shelf of favorites:
> Peter Brandvold will be staking out a claim
> there." —Frank Roderus